THE
SAMURAI
INHERITANCE

James Douglas

D0892870

CORGI BOOKS

TRANSWORLD PUBLISHERS
61–63 Uxbridge Road, London W5 5SA
A Random House Group Company
www.transworldbooks.co.uk

THE SAMURAI INHERITANCE
A CORGI BOOK: 9780552167932

First published in Great Britain
in 2014 by Corgi Books
an imprint of Transworld Publishers

Copyright © James Douglas 2014

James Douglas has asserted his right under the Copyright, Designs and
Patents Act 1988 to be identified as the author of this work.

This book is a work of fiction. Where true life figures appear,
their actions and conversations are entirely fictitious. All other
characters, and all names of places and descriptions of events,
are the products of the author's imagination and any resemblance
to actual persons or places is entirely coincidental.

A CIP catalogue record for this book
is available from the British Library.

This book is sold subject to the condition that it shall not,
by way of trade or otherwise, be lent, resold, hired out,
or otherwise circulated without the publisher's prior
consent in any form of binding or cover other than that
in which it is published and without a similar condition,
including this condition, being imposed on the
subsequent purchaser.

Addresses for Random House Group Ltd companies outside the UK
can be found at: www.randomhouse.co.uk
The Random House Group Ltd Reg. No. 954009

The Random House Group Limited supports the Forest Stewardship
Council® (FSC®), the leading international forest-certification
organisation. Our books carrying the FSC label are printed on
FSC®-certified paper. FSC is the only forest-certification scheme
supported by the leading environmental organisations, including
Greenpeace. Our paper procurement policy can be found at
www.randomhouse.co.uk/environment

Typeset in 11/14pt Sabon by
Kestrel Data, Exeter, Devon.
Printed and bound by
CPI Group (UK) Ltd, Croydon, CR0 4YY.

2 4 6 8 10 9 7 5 3 1

To Jimmy and Helen, proofreading has
never been such a pleasure.

WEST DUNBARTONSHIRE LIBRARIES	
C 03 0252690	
Askews & Holts	04-Dec-2014
AF	£6.99
CL	

PROLOGUE

Bougainville, 18 April 1943

The plane had been in the air for almost two hours and would begin its descent to Buin airbase in a few minutes. Long experience had taught the man in the immaculate green uniform that he could allow himself to doze despite the all-pervasive drone of the twin engines and the constant vibrations running through the aluminium fuselage. He tried to relax. If the relentless metallic clamour meant nothing useful could be achieved, forty years of naval discipline and his Samurai blood dictated he should rest body and mind. But how could a man, even a man as inured to discomfort as he, ever become accustomed to this cramped steel bucket seat? The damned thing seemed to sink its claws into every piece of flesh it touched. He allowed himself an inner smile, though his lips didn't twitch. Not even an admiral had the privilege of a cushioned seat in a converted Mitsubishi G4M, but that was no one's fault but his own. After all, he'd personally approved the design of the swift and agile light bomber the crews called the Flying Cigar.

It occurred to him that the American enemy, five hundred miles south at Guadalcanal, called the plane a different name. For reasons that escaped him despite his familiarity with their ways, they'd nicknamed the G4M 'the Betty'. He turned to stare out through the perspex blister over his right shoulder. A second, identical transport flew in formation five hundred feet away carrying the remainder of his staff for the long-delayed inspection tour of the Solomon Islands defences. He'd witnessed the scene a hundred times, but he was always oddly moved by the sight. The jungle green of the plane's upper surfaces contrasted starkly with the hazy eggshell blue of the South Pacific sky, and the scarlet disc of the Rising Sun shone like a drop of fresh blood on its flank. A few thousand feet above, out of sight but a comforting presence, six Zero fighters supplied top cover in the unlikely event of a stray Allied pilot happening on the formation.

Admiral Isoroku Yamamoto of the Imperial Japanese Navy grunted as he attempted to manoeuvre himself into a more comfortable position. The weight on his right arm came almost as a surprise. Nothing useful could be achieved? What was he thinking? He reached down to grasp the handle of the heavy buffalo-hide briefcase chained to his wrist and lifted it on to his lap. As he remembered the contents, Yamamoto's eyes glowed with suppressed rage at his compatriots' stupidity. How could they have kept it from him for so long? The information had only reached the fleet headquarters in Rabaul on New Britain the night before; a report from a well-connected agent in one of the Allied capitals. For the last twelve months specialist officers at the military intelligence HQ in Tokyo had been evaluating it. *Evaluating*. He knew exactly what that meant. Shunted on a conveyor belt of bureaucracy from one office to the next, and back again, and everyone with a different opinion. *I think it is authentic. I'm not so sure. It's a fake. Our man's been turned, we know he was under suspicion. He has never let us down.* Analysed, re-analysed and analysed again, until the actual significance of the message was lost. Only *now* they sent him one of the two existing copies.

Yamamoto had been presented with the briefcase by his American friends at the end of his second posting as naval attaché to Washington. He stroked the thick leather with a fondness alien to his martial nature. Unhampered by the two fingers missing from his right hand, he opened the straps and withdrew the file. A few paltry sheets, and of those only one truly mattered. A year ago this would have been a weapon as potent as the terror bombs the scientists of the Nishina programme claimed the enemy was incapable of producing. His eyes ran down the long columns of script, and he gritted his teeth against the frustration that was almost a physical pain. In the summer of 1942, at the high watermark of Japan's victories, he could have used the information to tear the western Allies apart: bankrupted the one and isolated the other. The war would have ended with honour and Japan dominant in the Pacific. The destructive battle at Midway would never have been fought and his beloved Nippon would have been spared years of war and countless lost sons. But now? He studied the document intently, dark eyes roaming the script for inspiration, pausing only to flick an annoyed glance when he sensed the curious gaze of Fukusaki in the seat opposite. The young naval commander, a trusted aide for two years, looked away sharply. Ha! Yamamoto was disproportionately pleased his reputation as a disciplinarian still had the power to awe.

He returned to the typed sheet. It had a shiny surface caused by the new compound he'd been told made it impervious to damp, but would, conversely, incinerate at the touch of a naked flame.

Yamamoto's studies at Harvard had inspired an affection and a respect for the Americans not shared by most of his countrymen. Likewise, familiarity ensured he understood and feared the strength of United States manufacturing. He'd argued against making war almost to a point that invited death at the hands of Prime Minister Tojo's assassins. Only Imperial connections and the fact he could count on the loyalty of the navy saved him. But when the Emperor decided the only way to break America's economic stranglehold on Japan was to fight, his duty was clear. Isoroku Yamamoto would become his nation's shield and lead the battle line with knife, bullet and bomb; he would do whatever it took to bring eventual victory.

It had been he who planned the surprise attack on Pearl Harbor, destroying or damaging eight of the enemy's battleships and killing thousands of American sailors. Yet he felt a dull ache of disappointment at the memory. The action had been a stunning tactical victory, but not the overwhelming blow he'd intended because the enemy's aircraft carriers had been at sea and escaped the bombs.

In the euphoria after the attack he'd warned that true victory would only be achieved when the first Japanese soldier marched into Washington. The message had been intended as a reminder to his people of the great sacrifices that would be required, but the Americans had interpreted it as a boast and a threat. In his heart of hearts he'd known then that little Japan could never destroy the mighty American industrial machine. Their only hope was to inflict casualties so terrible as to ensure the American public became sick of war. His face hardened and his thoughts turned to his children back in Tokyo. How many sacrifices would they have to make before the end? This document, which he believed was genuine, contained a single provable and undeniable fact. As the true implications of that fact dawned, his heart soared at the possibilities it created. He nodded slowly to himself. There was still time. He lay back against the angled metal and closed his eyes. Before he had the opportunity to expand on the thought a cry of alarm rang out from the rear of the plane.

'*Sentoki!* Enemy fighter! On our tail.'

The tail gunner's shout was followed instantly by the staccato rattle of his 20mm cannon and within seconds the acrid stench of burning cordite filled the aircraft. Yamamoto's mind raced, calculating the odds against them. If it was only a single plane all they had to do was survive until the escorting fighters could intervene. As well as the tail cannon, the G4M also carried four light machine guns, but only the nose and top turrets were permanently manned. Whoever was attacking them would have vastly superior firepower. Everything depended on the skill of the pilots and the accuracy of the defence. Fukusaki had already snatched up the port blister weapon, while Commander Toibana, the admiral's second aide, was firing at some unseen opponent with the starboard machine gun. Yamamoto's stomach lurched as the pilot put the plane into an emergency dive for the cover of the trees below. In his seat behind the cockpit the radio operator screamed a panicked plea for help into his microphone.

'This is impossible,' Fukusaki shouted over the buzz-saw rasp of the machine guns. 'Where have they come from?'

Yamamoto ignored the frantic cry and calmly replaced the papers in the briefcase. With only the slightest change of expression he strapped himself into his seat, closed his fingers over his ceremonial sword and shut his eyes.

Though he couldn't know it, sixteen P-38 Lightnings of the 339th fighter squadron based on Guadalcanal made up the force that shouldn't have been within a hundred miles of Admiral Yamamoto's plane. They'd flown north to Bougainville using long-range drop tanks designed to allow them to make the two-hour flight with just enough fuel remaining to get home. The pilots of the ambush planes knew only that a high-ranking

Japanese officer had been seen boarding a plane by a Coastwatcher on New Britain. The reality was that the Japanese naval code had been broken long ago. Yamamoto's route and itinerary were known down to the minute.

By some miracle combination of expert navigation and downright luck, the P-38s had arrived at the interception point four minutes early, after a complicated dogleg journey of almost five hundred miles. The attacking Lightnings split into four flights. Three roared upwards to take on the escorting Zeros and one, led by Captain Tom Lanphier, closed in on the two Bettys. The flight's second pair were forced to turn away because of problems with their drop tanks, but Lanphier and his wingman Lieutenant Rex Barber pressed on despite the drastic change in odds. Unique in the Second World War, the Lockheed P-38 Lightning was designed with twin booms and a central nacelle where the single pilot sat flanked by two Allison V12 engines. It had a speed advantage of almost 180 miles an hour over the fragile Japanese bomber.

'Zeros at twelve o'clock.' Barber heard Lanphier's laconic voice in his headphones. 'I'll take them. You go after the bombers.'

The wingman was vaguely aware of his commander's fighter peeling away, but he only had eyes for the green-painted plane ahead and a thousand feet below. Barber, a twenty-six-year-old engineer from Oregon, curved in, always turning right, so he was a little to the left of his target. He flinched at the familiar twinkle of gunfire from the Betty's tail and the flash of tracer rounds, but he held the big twin-engined fighter steady and waited. When the plane's airframe filled his reflector sight his fingers crept towards the firing buttons. He was hardly aware of touching them until the three Browning machine guns and single 20mm cannon in the nose opened up, making the whole plane judder. Rex Barber liked the P-38 because it had two engines. That was important when you were flying over impenetrable jungle and shark-infested seas, fighting an enemy more inclined to chop off your head than rescue you. But he also liked it because the guns were concentrated all together in a bunch. No need to wait for the bullet streams to converge like on the Thunderbolts he'd flown in training. You just hit the buttons and poured it on.

Tiny firefly sparks flickered on top of the enemy plane's fuselage just in front of the tailplane. He allowed the big Lightning's nose to drift slightly to the right so his cannon shells hammered into the wing roots and the starboard engine. A split second later the big bomber seemed to stop in mid-air and fell away to be lost in a pyre of smoke in the dense jungle below.

Without another thought Barber turned his attention to the second Betty.

I

New South Wales, Australia, 2010

The lunchtime view across the bay to Sydney Opera House justified all the ludicrous superlatives heaped on it during the flight over, but Jamie Saintclair seemed to be the only person at the table interested. Certainly Lizzie, the six-year-old daughter of his partner Fiona Carter, appeared entirely absorbed by the multicoloured mountain of ice cream in front of her. He felt a surge of what he disconcertingly realized might be paternal affection as she wiped a smear of melted pink across the front of her specially bought, pale yellow cotton dress. Fiona, being Australian, albeit of the exiled variety, had seen the view from the Rocks often enough not to be awed by its glory. In any case, she was absorbed in conversation with Nico, the young lawyer with swarthy, handsome features, who probably dined at the Rockpool at least three times a week.

Their host, Leopold Ungar, just the right side of eighty, but as sharp eyed as a teenager, noticed Jamie's look and smiled. 'This city is like every other, Mr Saintclair; sadly, no matter how iconic the building, when you've lived here for a while it begins to blend in with the background, don't you agree?'

Jamie wondered how many times he'd have to ask Leopold to call him by his first name before the Jewish haulage company owner remembered. Ungar was short, broad in the chest, with a bald head scattered with the liver spots of age. His choice of clothes reflected his age and affluence: razor-creased tan slacks and a navy blazer with a yacht club badge on the breast pocket, over an open-necked shirt.

'I'm just glad to have the chance to see it, sir.' Jamie opted for equal formality. 'We have to thank you again for bringing us out here and giving us the opportunity to spend some time in this wonderful country.'

The older man nodded gravely, acknowledging that the thanks were nothing but his due. Leopold Ungar was not the kind of person who splashed out on business-class return flights for just anyone. Born in Bratislava, he'd spent two of the first eight years of his life with his twin brother, Felix, in the Auschwitz death camp, a painfully memorable part of them under the tender ministrations of Dr Josef Mengele. In the diabolical lottery of Mengele's clinic it had been Leopold's fate to survive and subsequently emigrate to Australia.

For thirty years it had been enough that he lived, even if he couldn't have children of his own, but with the success of his business, came a certain amount of wealth. Wealth brought both responsibility and guilt.

Over the past decade he'd expended much energy and money trying to recover a painting that had hung above the mantel of the family home. It was a portrait of a young girl at a window, perhaps by Vermeer, but probably by an apprentice, and possibly even by the artist's daughter Maria. It was not artistically important or even particularly valuable, but the Ungar brothers had formed a childhood attachment to the girl in the picture.

Leopold had convinced himself that Felix would never be at peace until it was back in the family's hands. After several disappointments, his lawyer Nico had contacted Jamie Saintclair. It took a year of searching, but Jamie finally tracked down the painting to a private gallery close to the Ponte Fabricio in Rome, where it had arrived by some tortuous route. Eighteen months, and much legal wrangling, later Leopold was confirmed as the rightful owner. When the transaction was complete he invited Jamie and his partner to escort the painting to Australia as a bonus for the successful recovery.

'It was the least I could do,' Ungar said appreciatively. 'You succeeded in a year to do what others – well-paid others, I should add – have failed to do in a decade. It gives me a sense of peace to have the portrait hanging where it belongs, in an Ungar household, and, to me at least, it is priceless.' A diffident smile transformed his wrinkled features. 'An old man's foolish fantasy, you may say, but we must find happiness and contentment where we can. You would be surprised where it can be found,' he shook his head at some painful memory, 'even in the very heart of evil a child can find something to be cheerful about.'

Jamie Saintclair took genuine pleasure from the hard-won praise. He knew Leopold Ungar had been initially sceptical about his ability to do the job, believing he was too young at just past thirty, too inexperienced, and that his methods were, frankly, too unorthodox. All that changed when the Princess Czartoryski Foundation in Cracow announced that the Raphael Jamie had discovered in a secret bunker in the Harz Mountains two years earlier was, indeed, the real thing. The foundation's decision also brought with it a substantial finder's fee. It meant that for the first time since opening for business in the tiny shoebox of an office in London's Old Bond Street, Saintclair Fine Arts was in funds. Jamie was still puzzling over the unlikely combination of good fortune when the old man excused himself and disappeared in the direction of the men's room. He felt Fiona's eyes on him, that curious way she had of making his skin feel as if it had been stroked by soft fingers, and turned to meet her gaze.

'You look like the cat that got the cream, Saintclair.'

He grinned back. 'What could be better than good food and good company in one of the most beautiful places on the planet?'

Fiona smiled at the compliment to her home city. Her pleasure was reflected in dark eyes that glittered in the kind of narrow face you sometimes see on a cat-walk. She had shoulder-length blond hair styled in a tight plait and strong features that made her striking rather than conventionally pretty. Her swimmer's build

– wide shoulders, a narrow waist and long legs – allied to something indefinable, had attracted him at a gallery opening in London. Somehow, she'd worked her way under his skin before he'd even realized it.

'Good wine, too.' She raised her glass of what a surreptitious glance at the wine list proved to be a mind-blowingly expensive grand cru Burgundy. 'But I notice that you're being very sparing, which, dare I say it, is suspiciously out of character.'

'That's because I'm savouring it.' He picked up his own glass and put it to his lips. 'This is a wine to be sipped.' That wasn't quite true. He exchanged smiles with Nico, who'd also barely touched his wine. Jamie had noticed the Australian studying him in a shrewd and quite unashamedly calculating manner that he found intriguing.

Leopold returned, apologizing for having to leave them. 'My afternoon nap,' he claimed, but Jamie suspected that even at his age he still liked to keep an iron grip on his company. 'The bill is dealt with; but feel free to stay and have another bottle of wine and they'll charge it to my account.' They all stood up to say goodbye. Jamie shook hands and Fiona presented her tanned cheek to kiss. Lizzie ran round the table and gave the portly figure an enormous hug that made everyone laugh. Nico stood a little apart making his own farewell with a polite, businesslike nod.

Jamie sensed he was waiting for something.

'Why don't I walk you folks back to your hotel?' the lawyer said, confirming Jamie's suspicion. 'It's on my way.'

They strolled back up George Street in the relentlessly bright, almost too perfect afternoon sunlight. Nico held back to allow Fiona and Lizzie to walk ahead, and Jamie kept pace with him. Jamie smiled as he watched the slight golden-haired figure dance around her mother, interested in everything. Fiona was forced to walk with a slight stoop while she explained the use of each building and the history of each statue.

'You have a lovely family, Jamie,' Nico complimented him.

Jamie tried to disguise the inner turmoil the word created. *Family?* The concept conjured up an odd and disturbing mix of feelings and emotions. A missed heartbeat. A sudden loss of breath. A moment of needless panic. It had taken him a year after Abbie Trelawney's death in a London terrorist attack to find the faltering courage to enter into a serious relationship. Fiona was his friend and lover and that was enough for now. They saw each other most evenings, but were content to live separate lives. Lizzie came as part of the package. He took her to the park, enjoyed the innocence of her smile, the pleasure she took from simple play and the way everything was shiny and new. But family? He knew the reaction was partly a psychological flaw caused by his own past. Jamie Saintclair had never known his father. Before she passed away, his mother had given up any chance of a life of her own so that her son could go to university. It was two years now since his grandfather, his last living relative, had died. Maybe that was the problem. How could someone who'd never experienced being in a family know if he was part of one? He realized Nico was staring at him and that the lawyer must have continued the conversation without him.

'Sorry,' he apologized, 'I was in a bit of a dream. Must have been the wine.'

'Of course.' The Australian gave a tight nod of understanding. He paused and Jamie realized he was mentally preparing himself for something. 'I wondered if you'd care to meet a friend of mine – a former client. He has a problem he believes you might be able to help him solve. A commission, if things work out. Possibly a very lucrative one.'

Jamie's eyes wandered to where Lizzie was trying to catch water droplets from the fountain in Herald Square. The only work he'd planned for this trip had been delivering the painting to Leopold Ungar. It was supposed to be a two-week holiday for the three of them, and a chance for Fiona to visit her extended family. Thanks to the money from the Raphael he found himself in the unusual position of being able to pick and choose his commissions, and was in no hurry for the next.

'I'm not sure . . .'

Nico wasn't to be put off so easily. 'I'd consider it a favour,' he said.

Jamie suppressed a surge of irritation at the man's persistence. He'd as good as said no. Why would the lawyer keep pushing when his reluctance was so obvious? He was about to confirm his refusal when he recognized something in Nico's eyes that might have been an appeal; desperation even. He sighed, cursing the gene that had made him so bloody accommodating. What harm could it do? 'Sure, Nico,' he conceded with a sigh, 'why not? I can give him fifteen minutes. Let me talk to Fiona.'

The lawyer visibly relaxed and reached into his pocket for his mobile phone. 'Thanks, mate. Take your time. I'll set it up for three.'

II

The private elevator rose with the seamless ease of a flying carpet towards the upper floors of the enormous glass, steel and concrete tower that was such a surreal contrast with the vivid greenery just across the way. Fiona had met Jamie's announcement that he had some business to attend to with raised eyebrows, but she'd seemed cheerful enough as she lured Lizzie towards the nearby botanical gardens with the promise of an encounter with a possum.

Outdoors had been balmy and breeze kissed, but the atmosphere was decidedly chillier in the brushed-aluminium confines of the elevator. Jamie's normal easy-going demeanour had been knocked out of kilter by Nico's insistence that he meet his mysterious *former client*. He'd have been much happier scratching around in the bushes for an elusive and likely non-existent possum. Then again that would have raised the possibility of an encounter with one of the nasty eastern brown snakes he'd been warned about. In the past couple of years he'd been shot at, blown up and survived a plane crash, but he'd cheerfully go through it all again rather than come face to fangs with a venomous reptile.

Nico shuffled uncomfortably at his side and he sensed the lawyer was just as unhappy about the position he'd been placed in. Or at least as uncomfortable as a lawyer was likely to get about anything. Even when pushed, Nico had refused to divulge the identity of the man Jamie was about to meet. 'He'll tell you all about himself,' he insisted. 'All I can say is that it will be worth your while to talk to him.'

The lift doors opened as a detached female voice announced their arrival at the forty-fifth floor. Nico led the way out into a broad, carpeted hallway which had walls lined with golden silk and a receptionist's desk at the far end. Framed paintings of brightly coloured exotic birds dotted the silk in clusters of four. They reminded Jamie of Audubon's American works, but with a rougher, less realistic edge.

'John William Lewin. They're worth next to bugger all, but I like 'em.'

The throaty growl challenged anybody to disagree with the speaker – a tall, heavy-set figure who appeared without warning through the double oak doors behind the reception desk. Jamie took in a weathered face, a nose like a Roman galley's ram and thick grey hair swept back from a broad forehead. He found himself the focus of shrewd, pale blue eyes that had you measured, suited and booted before you could say hello. Commanding was the word he'd use to describe a man who would dominate any room he entered. The

Australian wore cream slacks and a striped shirt with the sleeves rolled up to the elbows; the gold watch on his left wrist would have bought a Ferrari. Nico hesitated, uncharacteristically uncertain whether to usher Jamie forward or wait for some command. Their host's features broke into a grin and he strode the length of the hall to greet them. Jamie stood six foot tall, but he was forced to look up as his hand was engulfed in a callused, meaty fist.

'You must be Mr Jamie Saintclair.' The stranger nodded approvingly. 'Good to meet you at last. Thanks, Nico.'

The casual dismissal verged on the contemptuous, but if Nico took any offence he gave no sign of it. 'I'll call you later,' he said to Jamie and walked back towards the lift.

In the seconds that followed, Jamie and his host studied each other like prizefighters limbering up for a bout. Finally the big Australian broke the silence. 'Keith Devlin, but just call me Keith, and we'll get along just fine.' The big hand released Jamie's fingers and moved to his shoulder, easing him in the direction of the doors in a gesture that was both casual and possessive, as if, now he was here, he wasn't going to be allowed to escape.

'Lewin was Australia's first painter that anybody'd heard of, and we're proud of our heritage, what little there is,' Devlin explained conversationally. 'But I'm sure a man of your taste finds him a little crude.'

Jamie wondered just how much the Australian knew about his taste, in paintings or anything else.

The name Keith Devlin meant nothing to him, but the surroundings and the manner of his welcome suggested he was in the presence of business royalty. That made the summons all the more puzzling. Still, all he could do was humour Devlin until he found out enough to politely decline whatever it was he had in mind. In the meantime, he turned back to the paintings. 'They're a little raw,' he agreed. 'But isn't that what art is all about, personal preference? I have paintings at home I'd never have bought for profit. The reason I did was because I liked them.'

'They tell me you have a reputation as a linguist.'

Jamie blinked at the sudden change of subject. It took a second to sink in that the words were in fluent Russian.

'It's no secret,' he replied in equally perfect German. 'It says so on my CV.'

'It's just that it could come in handy for what I have in mind.' Devlin had switched seamlessly into Spanish, followed by a burst of an Oriental language that left Jamie staring in incomprehension. The businessman laughed. 'Japanese.' He grinned. 'Now I'm just showing off.'

'We all have our talents, Mr Devlin.'

Devlin gave a bark of a laugh. 'A diplomat's answer.' He swept through the oak doors into a room – an office? – that took up most of an entire floor of the building, with wall-to-ceiling windows on two sides overlooking Sydney Harbour and the Opera House. Jamie took in his surroundings. A desk the size of an aircraft carrier dominated a third wall. Behind it hung an enormous framed map of the world that included a large insert showing Australia and the South Pacific. A series of waist-high marble plinths were scattered artistically across the carpeted floor, each supporting a glass case containing a chunk of rock or a jagged piece of metal. At least one of them had a gleam Jamie thought he recognized. The fourth wall, where they'd just entered, held a surprisingly eclectic range of paintings and prints that included a Picasso nude and a Bruegel hunting scene; impressive enough, but not a collection, more of an accumulation. Devlin confirmed that view with his next word.

'Investments.' He shrugged, as if that was explanation enough. 'The shirtlifter who designed this place had half a dozen bits of abstract rubbish hanging there, but I replaced it with stuff I liked.' He saw Jamie blink at the casual homophobia and laughed. 'You're not offended, are you? Christ, I reckon I've been around long enough to earn the right to call a spade a bloody shovel when I feel like it. The old bugger was as bent as a nine-bob note and cost a bloody fortune.'

He led the way towards two leather couches positioned to allow the occupants to face each other while they looked out on to the most spectacular views in Sydney. Jamie realized that everything in this room was designed to impress, either by its scale or by its expense. Everything except the rocks and the map behind Keith Devlin's desk.

'You'll be wondering why I brought you here?' The Australian took the couch facing out to the botanical gardens and the Opera House and waved Jamie to the seat opposite. His expression was suddenly all business and he sat with his upper torso angled forward and his hands clasped between his knees.

'Did you bring me here, Mr Devlin?' Jamie's gaze wandered out over the grass and trees forty-five floors below where Fiona and Lizzie would be among the ant-like figures in the park. 'I was under the impression that I'd consented to a fifteen-minute chat to keep Nico happy.' He looked at his watch. 'I've seen your art collection. You've impressed me with your linguistic skills. By my reckoning we have about ten minutes left.'

Rude, if you like, but he owed his host nothing and he'd felt a sudden urge to take the wind out of Keith Devlin's sails. He might have saved his breath. The peasant face split into a broad grin of appreciation. 'So I'm not the only one who's prepared to call a spade a bloody shovel. Good. That'll save us some time. Let's get right down to the nitty-gritty. The bottom line is that you specialize in finding things and I've lost something.'

'I specialize in finding artworks,' Jamie corrected. 'Specifically those stolen during the Second World War. So unless that's what you've lost I probably won't be able to help you.'

'Just hear me out, Jamie.' The other man raised a hand like a cop stopping traffic. 'If you're not intrigued enough to take the job on by the time I've finished, we'll part with no hard feelings on either side. Agreed?'

Jamie shrugged. He wasn't due to meet the girls for another hour.

'Good.' Devlin nodded. 'First a little bit of history.

All this,' he waved a hand expansively around the enormous office, 'started with a little scrape in the rocks beside the Cudgegong River.' He got up, went to one of the stands and picked up the glass box sitting on it. 'That was where my old granddad made his first strike before the war.' He handed over the case and Jamie found he was holding a gold nugget about the size of his fist. 'That's not the original,' the Australian explained. 'He drank away what he got paid for it, but it's about the same size and he reckoned it was proof positive he could smell the bloody stuff. He was more careful with the next one, and bought another couple of claims and hired a few pick and shovel merchants. By the time my dad took over it was a good going business and he'd moved over to Kalgoorlie. It was Digger Devlin – that's what they called the old man – who realized that gold wasn't the only precious metal in the mines. He invested in copper extraction and with the profits he made he was able to expand and make Devlin Metal Resources an international company. Course,' the weathered face split in a self-deprecating grin, 'we were pretty small beer then, and it was up to the next generation to turn it into the third biggest mining conglomerate in the world.' Devlin waved Jamie across to the map behind the big desk. Glass shelves on either side held sporting medals and framed portraits of the host smiling with a selection of instantly recognizable world leaders, but the tycoon ignored them. 'The red dots are the sites of Devlin mines in Oz, South America and Asia.' He pointed out what looked like a bad case of measles in each region. 'But what could be the biggest prize of all is out there waiting for us and that's where you come in, Jamie.'

'This is all very interesting, Mr Devlin, but I recover stolen art. I'm not a geologist or an explorer or a negotiator or whatever it is this job requires. I'm also on holiday with my . . . family.'

Devlin waved away the protest and marched to the window overlooking the botanical gardens. 'As to the first, that's *exactly* why I want to hire you. Second, if you take the job, Devlin Metal Resources will lay on the works for Fiona and the wee one while you're gone. Nico tells me they have relatives in Perth and up on the Gold Coast? Well, there you are. Luxury travel to wherever they want to go, staying in the best hotels. All the possums, roos and koalas a girl could want.' He smiled. 'When the job's done you can join them for as long as you like at a little private island I happen to own up near Cairns.'

Jamie saw the seductive bait for what it was, but he was still drawn towards the hook. He knew this was exactly the type of trip Fiona had always craved and the college where she lectured didn't reopen for another month. 'How long would it take?'

Keith Devlin's face split in a wolfish grin. 'If a man like you can't track it down in a couple of weeks, you probably never will. The usual deal. A daily stipend and a finder's fee. First Class all the way. Just name a figure and I'll sign a cheque for half up front.'

The man's relentless enthusiasm was overwhelming and the seemingly bottomless resources tempting, but Jamie was still cautious. First-class travel always sounded good, but experience told him all it meant was you ended up in the deep stuff with a champagne glass in your hand. 'I'm listening, but I'll have to speak to Fiona first before I agree to anything,' he said warily.

'Of course,' Devlin said as if he had no doubts about the outcome.

'Then I suppose it comes down to what *it* is.'

The tycoon's grin widened if that were possible, and he reached into one of the desk drawers to withdraw a brown envelope.

When he saw the package Jamie felt a shiver of expectation. It was one of those moments. The instant his fingers opened the ancient journal from his grandfather's wardrobe. The first time he heard the words 'Crown of Isis'. Or when Adam Steele read the name Excalibur from the codex to a former Nazi soldier's last will and testament. Each of them had radically changed his life and he had a sudden breathless feeling this would be no different.

Keith Devlin handed him the envelope and his fingers fumbled at the flap. The contents turned out to be a single blurred sepia image on photographic paper. His eyes struggled to make sense of an ugly little shrivelled object the size of a pomegranate hanging from what looked like a thick dark rope. Was this some kind of sick joke? 'What is it?'

'That, Mr Saintclair, is a shrunken human head.'

III

Jamie stared at the photograph for a disbelieving moment before he dropped it on the desk. 'You've got the wrong man, Mr Devlin.' He turned, ready to walk out of the room, but Devlin laid a hand on his arm and the charming smile, so difficult to refuse, was back.

'Just hear me out, son. I promise you won't regret it.'

The mining boss picked up the print and walked over to the map. He traced his finger north-east from Sydney to a series of tiny fly specks that trailed like the wake of a ship from the land mass of Papua New Guinea. The digit finally came to rest on a green streak at the top of the string of islands. 'Bougainville.' His voice took on an almost mystic quality as he said the word. 'Does the name mean anything to you?'

Jamie shook his head.

'I'm not surprised. Four thousand square miles of jungle, rock and mountain, with a couple of active volcanoes thrown in to keep life interesting. Some of the people are still living in the Stone Age despite everything we've done to help them. Until a few years ago the economy was entirely based on *copra* – that's dried coconut shipped from the islands to be turned into oil. Not much to attract a bloke like me, you'd say?' Jamie shrugged. 'And you'd be right, unless it's also home to the world's largest copper mine.'

Jamie looked at the map with slightly renewed interest. 'I don't see any red dots?'

'Naturally, because Devlin Metal doesn't own it . . . yet. The mine is shut down because of a few labour problems and some local difficulties with community leaders. Helluva place. My old man sent me there to get a bit of experience when I was just starting out and, believe me, some of the natives can be a bolshie lot. The current owners are fed up of working in that kind of environment. They're talking about offloading all or part of it, but Bougainville politics will effectively decide when, or if, the mine ever reopens, and who runs it.'

'What has this got to do with a shrunken head?' Jamie was puzzled. 'Surely to God there's no such thing as headhunting any more, even out there?'

'Of course not.' Devlin smiled again. 'At least as far as we know. But the natives on Bougainville still revere the heads taken by their ancestors. Or, in this case, taken *from* their ancestor. If we can get agreement to buy the company, we still need the consent of the big chief from the area around the Panguna Mine to restart work and provide us with local labour. My fellas have been talking to him for a while, but during our negotiations a briefcase containing some very important documents went missing – some of the natives on Bougainville would steal the sugar from your tea – and we've asked for them back. The price the crazy old bastard is demanding is the return of *that* – his ancestor's head. Would you believe it?'

'What I don't understand is how you expect me to find the bloody thing.' Jamie didn't hide his exasperation. 'It could be anywhere on the island. Jungle, rocks and volcanoes? You don't need Jamie Saintclair, Mr Devlin, you need Indiana bloody Jones.'

'If the head was on the island maybe you're right,' the big Australian admitted, 'but it hasn't been on the island for the best part of a hundred and fifty years. Bougainville is part of Papua New Guinea these days, but before the First World War it was a German colony. German merchant adventurers exchanged trade goods worth a few *pfennigs* for boatloads of coconuts to turn into *copra* and oil. They were followed by geologists, scientists . . . and anthropologists. Our chief's tribe had recovered the head of their ancestor from the group who'd killed and probably eaten the rest of him.' He laughed at the change in Jamie's expression. 'Don't knock it till you've tried it. They believed eating the flesh of their rivals passed on their strength and courage. The story that's come down over the years is that it was stolen by a German who visited the islands around that time. More likely one of their own fellows traded it to him. There's a fairly extensive record of who visited the islands. We think the original of this,' he waved the picture, 'was taken by the anthropologist who took the head and was part of the price he paid for it. My people have pinned it down to a bloke called Adolfus Ribbe,

34

a Hamburg collector who spent five years touring the islands in the eighteen nineties. Apparently, he sent back bits and pieces to Berlin museums. So now you know why I was so keen to have you on board.'

'That's it? A German collector might have taken the head. He might have presented it to a museum in Berlin. Have you any idea how many museums there are in Berlin?'

'No,' Devlin said evenly. 'But I'm sure you do.'

A few moments earlier Jamie had been on the verge of walking out, but his belligerence faded under the steady blue eyes. It was the craziest thing he'd ever been asked to do, but Keith Devlin was a difficult man to turn down. And in a twisted way it appealed to him. Take it back to the basics and it was simply tracing an artefact through the museum system. And that was a damn sight easier than chasing all over Germany looking for the sun stone with neo-Nazis dogging his every footstep or literally crossing swords with a power-crazed maniac who wanted to get his hands on Excalibur. It would be safe and whether he found the head or not he'd have two weeks with Fiona and Lizzie at a luxury resort to look forward to. He had plenty of contacts in Berlin and he worked his way through the list of museums in his head. Not the newer ones, for the simple reason that they wouldn't have been around then. By the time they opened their doors a reputable German museum wouldn't have touched a human head with a barge pole, not after what their compatriots had done at Dachau and Auschwitz. Likewise the specialist museums, the Bode and the Pergamon, with their massive collections from antiquity. But there were other possibilities . . .

He felt Devlin's eyes on him. 'You understand that hundreds of thousands of artefacts were destroyed in Berlin by British and American bombs, and that hundreds of thousands more either disappeared or were stolen for Stalin by the Red Army? This is very likely to be a complete waste of your time and your money.'

Devlin clapped him on the shoulder. 'I think the time is worth spending and money is no object, son. All I ask is that you follow your nose, like my old man did with his gold, and if you pick up a scent stay with it.' He reached below the desk and came up with another map, this time a large-scale version of a long, slim island. 'Bougainville,' he said. 'The people are a hotchpotch of tribes, clans and extended families who between them speak nineteen or twenty different languages. Here's the Panguna Mine.' He pointed to a conglomeration of narrow contours in the south of the island. 'Our chief is the leader of a Naasioi-speaking tribe who inhabit the area to the south. The one thing that makes the head distinctive and recognizable is that the natives are very black-skinned compared to the other groups in the Solomons or Papua New Guinea. Aaach,' he threw the map aside, 'we'll put together a pack with all this stuff in it, Jamie. For the moment, just tell me you're on board.'

Jamie met his grin, with a shrug of surrender. 'Fiona has to have the final word, but I think I can persuade her. If I'm in it will cost you.' He named a price at least double what he had been paid for any past commission.

Devlin didn't even blink as he reached for his cheque-book.

Before he left to break the news, Jamie glanced again at the green and brown contours of the map. Even on paper Bougainville sent a shiver through him. *Mountains and jungles and active volcanoes*. He still wasn't certain he would find the shrunken head, but if he ever did, he pitied the poor bugger who had the job of repatriating it.

Keith Devlin watched the elevator door close as a second man appeared from the far end of the corridor. Wiry and alert, the newcomer walked with a soldier's economy of movement and his suspicious blue eyes swept the ground ahead like an IED detector. He had tanned, gaunt features and wore his silver hair swept back from his forehead in an old-fashioned style that made people he met think of a Fifties matinée idol. All it would take to complete the effect was a thin moustache, but he'd never worn one, not even in the field, and he never would.

'What did you think, Doug, is he up to it?'

'He's capable enough, I grant you,' Devlin's head of security said thoughtfully. 'That poncy English-gent stuff is just an act and there are a few unexplained bodies in his file I'd like to know a bit more about. But . . .'

'But what?'

'The psychological profile says he's an idealist who sometimes makes decisions based on instinct, not logic. When he finds out what's really happening on

Bougainville he may decide he has to take sides. What if he chooses the wrong one?'

Devlin's face twisted in a grimace of distaste. 'That would be too bad.'

'The woman and the girl . . .'

'Yes.' Devlin saw the possibilities immediately. That was what he liked about Doug Stewart: the combination of practicality and ruthlessness he brought to the corporate decision-making process. The same practicality and ruthlessness that had seen him through Australia's short and comparatively glorious involvement in America's Vietnam fiasco. He nodded. 'Keep them close, they might come in handy somewhere down the line. And Doug?'

'Yes, chief?'

'No mistakes this time. I want him watched every step of the way. There's too much riding on this to take any chances.'

IV

'It will be for two weeks at most.' Jamie tried to sound upbeat, but Fiona's narrowed eyes informed him he wasn't succeeding. Lizzie mirrored her mother's disapproving frown. 'You'll be able to spend a bit of quality time with your aunts and uncles, and we'll still have a fortnight together as a . . . a family at the end of it.' Fiona sucked in a breath and he knew he'd made one of those male mistakes that are only perceptible to women. Sweat prickled in his thick dark hair as they sat on the grass beneath a big palm tree in the botanical gardens. 'It'll be great.' He hurried on, hoping to bypass the storm. 'No expense spared on my client's private island up by Cairns. Koalas, possums and platypuses, er, platypii, and whatever. We can explore the Barrier Reef and scuba dive, swim with dolphins and turtles . . .' He ended with a winning smile at the little girl, which didn't change her expression one bit.

'In a real family the hu— . . . head of the family doesn't just up sticks and abandon the rest without so much as a discussion.' Fiona's tight smile was as dangerous

39

as the fire that flickered in the depths of her dark eyes and Jamie decided he'd much rather be facing gun-toting Al-Qaida assassins than this woman he . . . No, it was too soon after Abbie for that kind of emotional commitment, but he liked and respected Fiona too much to hurt her and he was already regretting accepting Keith Devlin's offer. All he'd said was that someone had commissioned him to track down something and the client was in a hurry. She hadn't asked what the something was or the client's name. He saw another change in her expression as she read his mind and didn't like what she found there. 'Maybe you don't realize what I – what we – invested in this trip. It's not about a free holiday and a chance to see the old country again, Jamie, it's about *us*. We do things together. We enjoy each other's company. And that's about it. When I lie next to you I can hear you breathe and I can feel your heart beating, but I don't know what you're thinking or feeling. You're a lovely person and you have great qualities, but showing your emotions isn't one of them. I thought spending two weeks together would give me a chance to get to know the real Jamie Saintclair.' She noticed the concern on Lizzie's face as she contemplated the two adults and the smile reappeared. 'Lizzie, honey, why don't you go and play with the ducks for a second?'

Jamie put a hand on her arm. 'No. Let's go and get some more ice cream instead.' The little girl's eyes lit up and she skipped away a few metres towards a vendor dispensing his wares from under a brightly coloured umbrella. Jamie got to his feet, brushing grass from his trousers and offered Fiona his hand to help her up.

'I'm sorry,' he said, taking her by the waist and leaning over to kiss her cheek. 'You're right. I've behaved like a selfish idiot. I'm too used to just thinking about yours truly.' He slipped his hand into the inside pocket of the cotton jacket and pulled out his mobile phone. 'I'll call Devlin now and tell him the deal's off. Family comes first.'

'Devlin?' She stopped and looked at him.

'Yes, Keith Devlin, have you heard of him?'

'Of course I've heard of him; he's one of the most famous men in Australia. He turned the family firm into an international conglomerate and is probably the country's biggest philanthropist. It was the Devlin Foundation who originally paid me to come to Britain to study. He set it up as a charitable trust to promote the arts and sciences. His big interest is creating a more environmentally sustainable mining industry. Keith Devlin is inviting us to his private island?'

'That was the plan.' Jamie continued to tap Devlin's number into the mobile. 'For the two weeks I was away you'd have been ferried round the country by private jet. After that we'd meet up in Queensland, do the national park thing and then head out to the island, sit in a hot tub, drink beer and . . . whatever.' He put the phone to his ear. 'But I'll tell him it's a no-go.'

She reached across and gently removed the machine from his fingers and hit cancel. 'Let's not be too hasty. Two weeks isn't that long and I like the sound of "whatever".'

'But what about finding the real me?' He gave her a sideways glance.

41

'Bastard,' she said lightly, punching him on the shoulder. 'You set this up. Waited until I'd got all my girly emotion out of the way and then dangled Keith Devlin in front of me like a juicy piece of mackerel in front of a hungry barracuda. And I swallowed it hook, line and sinker.'

'That's much too devious for me. You must be thinking of a different real Jamie Saintclair, the one who went to the Machiavelli School of Social Engineering. A lovely man with nice qualities would never consider such a thing.'

'When do you leave?'

'I'm booked on the afternoon flight to Berlin tomorrow.'

'Good,' she said, all businesslike now. 'The sooner you're gone, the sooner you're back. I'm looking forward to spending two weeks in our hot tub finding the real Jamie Saintclair.'

'I think he might be a bit wrinkly.' He grinned. He looked over to where Lizzie was squatting next to a sleeping duck. 'How will you square it with her?'

'Oh, Lizzie takes after her mum,' Fiona laughed. 'The promise of another ice cream and a cuddle from a koala and she'll be wriggling in the net in no time. Come on,' she pulled him by the hand, 'we have some heavy-duty sightseeing to do. That little lady has been staying up too late. It's bed by eight tonight.'

'Now who's being devious?'

'Mmmmh.' She turned to him, stepping up close. 'But I think you'll find this is much more worthwhile.' As she said it she ran a finger nail down the V of his shirt through the hairs on his chest. There was a promise in her eyes that made his blood fizz like champagne.

'Two weeks,' he promised. 'Quicker if I can make it so.'

'Just see that you do, lover boy.'

Jamie flew into Tegel airport three days later, refreshed and full of enthusiasm thanks to the unfamiliar experience of Devlin's promised First Class all the way. The ten-thousand-mile journey had been broken by a day's lay-over in Abu Dhabi where his clothes had been ironed by a smiling Pakistani girl while he showered and he'd even been able to catch up on a bit of sleep in a proper bed. No queues for the First Class traveller. By the time he cleared customs his baggage had already been collected and placed in a waiting limousine. Outside the terminal he stood for a moment taking in the peculiarly distinctive scent of a central European autumn; the promise of rain despite the eggshell-blue sky, and the lingering warmth that paradoxically contained a warning that it wouldn't last. The driver was a big man in a too-tight suit who wore an expression that said he'd seen it all before. Jamie gave him the name of his hotel and relaxed in the rear of the big Mercedes.

'Can we take the scenic route, please?' he suggested in German.

'Sure.' The driver nodded and took the first exit off the autobahn. 'My name is Max and I am at your service for the duration of your stay. We will go through Charlottenburg and then head for Tiergarten, yes?'

Jamie had mixed memories of Berlin, but there

was something about entering a great city that made him feel like an explorer starting a journey of infinite possibility. He found himself grinning. Out there, beyond the apartment blocks and the factories, were some of the world's most wonderful art collections: hundreds, maybe thousands of years of potential and endeavour. The greatest heroes and villains in history had lived here, experiencing triumph and tragedy in equal measure.

Their route took them down the east bank of the River Spree, with the Schlosspark an island of green on the far side. That was what Jamie liked best about Berlin, the open spaces and broad avenues and the way it could always surprise you. As they drove, he kept up a stream of small talk with the driver, testing his German and re-attuning himself to the rhythm and cadence of the language. By the time they reached the Tiergarten, Berlin's sprawling central park, he didn't even have to think about his replies. They talked about the weather and whatever they were passing at the time. This arrow-straight avenue had not long ago been at the heart of a tiny effervescent bubble of capitalism in the turgid Communist sea of eastern Europe. At the far end, beyond the column of victory, the road had come to an abrupt end at a twelve-foot concrete wall, a sanitized, mined death zone, and towers manned by guards who would shoot first and not bother asking questions after.

They passed the familiar silhouette of the Brandenburg Gate and drove down the Unter den Linden. He'd had his pick of the city's hotels, but Jamie had opted for a modern hotel on Karl-Liebknecht Strasse, within a grenade throw of the city's museum district. His gaze swept over the brightly lit upmarket shops thronged with late-afternoon crowds. He remembered walking along this same street with Detective Danny Fisher. It occurred to him that an hour later he'd been chest to chest with a knife-wielding maniac surrounded by men with guns. Perhaps he'd give the sightseeing a miss this time round.

Seconds later Max drew up in front of what looked like a futuristic shopping complex and jumped out to open Jamie's door before darting to the boot to retrieve the Englishman's luggage. Jamie put out a hand for his backpack, but the driver was already on his way to the hotel entrance with it.

Inside was an enormous glass-roofed entrance hall. Max handed the luggage to a porter with a whispered order and slipped him a sheaf of folded notes. Jamie stared at the great shimmering blue bowl that dominated the entire area twenty feet above.

'I suppose there's no argument about what I'm having for dinner?'

The limo driver glanced upwards. 'The AquaDom. Biggest fish bowl in the world, they say. Reception is over there, sir.' He pointed to a curving row of desks. He reached into his inside pocket and withdrew an embossed pasteboard card. 'Call this number any time, day or night, and either I or one of my colleagues will come and pick you up. There's an emergency number if you should have an accident or get in trouble with the authorities.'

'If I end up in a cell,' Jamie grinned, 'I'll be too embarrassed to call anybody.'

Max's lips didn't even twitch. 'It's there for your convenience, sir.' He nodded. 'Enjoy your stay in Berlin.'

When Max returned to the Mercedes, Doug Stewart emerged from the hotel entrance and slipped in beside the driver. He'd watched from the bar as Saintclair had completed the formalities and been directed to the lifts, as certain as he could be that no one was tailing the art dealer.

'Remember, I want to know where he goes, who he meets and what he eats for breakfast,' he told the German. In Stewart's view it was a long way to come just to make sure Jamie Saintclair had his mind fully on the mission, but he'd been with Keith Devlin long enough to understand that he liked to cover all the bases. Then again, if any other party realized the true significance of the Bougainville head, this was where they would pick up Saintclair and the best place to spot them. 'If you see anything suspicious let me know and we'll put a full team on him.' Max nodded and pulled out into the traffic.

As the Mercedes drove off a young Oriental man stepped from a shop doorway on the other side of the street. His eyes followed the car until it was out of sight and his lips barely moved as he spoke into a hands-free mobile phone.

At the same moment Jamie stood at the floor-to-ceiling window of a fifth-floor suite big enough to host a Premiership football match. He took a contented sip of weiss beer and stared out over the glittering waters of the Spree to Museum Island and the distinctive green domes of Berlin Cathedral. Behind it he could just make out the outlines of the museums complex, where tomorrow he would begin his strangest quest yet.

There were worse places to be, he reckoned. If Keith Devlin's shrunken head was out there, he would find it. If not, the philanthropical tycoon could whistle for his next copper mine and Jamie would go back to Fiona where he belonged.

V

Bougainville Island, 1943

Signals Lieutenant Tomoyuki Hamasuna of the Imperial Japanese Army carefully plucked the hooked thorn from his faded green uniform shirt and pushed through the almost impenetrable wall of bushes and vegetation. To his left and right he could hear the other members of his twelve-man patrol cursing softly as they struggled to keep station in the thick jungle. Sweat soaked his peaked cloth cap and streamed down his face, the coarse material of the shirt stuck to his flesh and the pack over his shoulder chafed everywhere it touched. He would never have admitted it to anyone for fear of ridicule, but Hamasuna found the jungle an oppressive assault on the senses. The relentless buzz of clouds of black flies and countless stinging insects filled his ears, the air around him stank of decay and damp and the foliage was like a green curtain that wrapped itself around him to the point of suffocation. He tightened his grip on his pistol. The atmosphere wasn't the only intimidating thing about the jungle. It wouldn't be the first time a small patrol like this had been attacked by the filthy blacks who inhabited these islands at the instigation of their white masters.

Hamasuna had been searching for three torturous hours since he'd been alerted to the smoke the sentries had spotted from his little outpost at Aku, east of the former Catholic mission station at Buin. They reported a crashed plane south of the Buin road down towards Moila Point. Whether Japanese or American it was vital that it be checked for survivors and possible intelligence.

An hour later he was almost ready to give up when his nostrils detected a different combination of scents: aviation fuel and the distant, but still acrid smell of burning.

'*Chūi, sā! Kono hōhōdesu.*'

The warning cry came from his left side and made Hamasuna's heart hammer in his chest. He stumbled blindly through the bushes towards its source, shouting to the men on his right flank to follow and form a perimeter.

It wasn't a clearing as such, more a scar in the jungle canopy and it took time to work out what he was seeing. He'd half expected an American plane from one of the formations that pounded Rabaul every day, but the little he could see was clearly Japanese. Some kind of bomber? One part of the jungle revealed the camouflage green and silver bar of a wing propped against the bole of a large tree, as if carefully laid aside by a giant hand, the blood-red roundel of the *Hinomaru* almost

49

obscured by leaves. A few metres further and the bitter smell of petroleum filled his nostrils to the exclusion of all else. Amongst blackened grass and torn branches, the dark eye of a Type 99 cannon glared out from the wreckage of the plane's tail assembly. He noted that the inside of the perspex turret almost identically matched the hue of the *Hinomaru*, evidence of the certain fate of its occupant. Beyond the tail, scattered across a scorched patch of earth and surrounded by splintered branches, lay three more bodies, crushed and broken. One of them was headless and their limp, boneless poses were indicative of a condition only permitted the recently dead.

Lieutenant Hamasuna approached them. Something wasn't right here. His mind registered the main fuselage and one engine on a truncated, still attached, second wing, but his unease grew as he studied the uniforms of the dead men. Not air force uniforms, but navy. Tailored uniforms, with the insignia of high-ranking officers. This wasn't a bomber, but a transport: a transport carrying important people. His breath caught in his chest. It must be reported. Hamasuna fought off panic as he tried to come to a decision. He knew he should secure the crash site, but logic told him not to split his patrol. He had few enough as it was to fight off an ambush and if he left two or three behind the likelihood was he'd return to find them with their throats slit. No. He must leave everything exactly as it was and return to Aku to call for help. But first he had to search the entire area for possible survivors.

He was drawn to the fuselage. What other secrets

did it contain? Not the pilots who would have fought to bring the plane down safely even in this impossible terrain. They would still be in the crushed and shattered nose on the far side of the clearing. Despite the smoke he judged it safe to move closer. Whatever fires had been caused by the crash had long since burned out. He walked down the side of the plane, taking in the shattered windows, the bright silver splashes where cannon shells had torn through the metal. Then, from the very corner of his eye, he saw him.

Tomoyuki Hamasuna had served in Manchuria. He had seen death in every form and on countless occasions, but no individual death had affected him as this one did. His whole body started to shake. The man still strapped upright in his aircraft seat was instantly recognizable. Admiral Isoroku Yamamoto sat with his head slumped forward as if deep in thought. His gloved left hand rested on the hilt of his ceremonial sword, the index and middle fingers empty of the digits he had lost at the battle of Tsushima. Hamasuna took a few hesitant steps until he stood over the still figure. The right hand dangled by the side of the seat, a broken length of thin chain hanging from the wrist. A bloodstained exit wound in the front of the admiral's dress jacket indicated he'd been hit in the back. Dried blood streaked the right side of his face from a second wound above the eye. Belatedly, Hamasuna realized he hadn't breathed for more than a minute and he gulped in a mouthful of fetid, fuel-heavy air. His hand reached out slowly to touch the pale neck above the collar, and he flinched as he felt the chill flesh. No sign of a pulse.

Admiral Isoroku Yamamoto, father of the Japanese navy and victor of Pearl Harbor, was dead.

Hamasuna stepped back and bowed from the waist, pausing for a moment to say a silent prayer. When he finished paying his respects he collected his thoughts, consulted his compass and called his men together.

'Sugino? Check the cockpit for signs of life,' he ordered. 'Murayama? Take the point. This way. Back to the road. We will blaze a trail so that we can find our way directly back to the crash site.'

'Is that—'

'Obey orders,' Hamasuna snarled. 'You saw a crashed plane. Nothing more. If I hear a single word before the official announcement I will have every one of you transferred to the tiniest fly speck in the Pacific. Understand?'

'*Hai!*'

As they prepared to leave the clearing he noticed a leather briefcase lying in the thick grass ten feet from Yamamoto's body. It was old and battered, made of unusual heavy hide, and blackened by fire. He moved to pick it up, but thought better of it. He imagined the wrath of his superiors if he tampered with the scene. More sensible to leave it exactly as he found it. The soldiers filed out of the crash site, hacking a way through the thick jungle.

Hamasuna waited until they were out of sight, struggling against the instinct that drew him back to the briefcase that had been attached to the admiral's wrist. Surely one look would not matter? He bent over the scorched leather and reached for the straps.

A few minutes later he cast a last dejected glance at Yamamoto's body and followed his men down the track.

The Japanese had been gone for only a few minutes when a shadow moved in the bush to the south of the clearing.

It took another hour for the patrol to return to the main track and they doubled along it until they reached the camouflaged tents and grass huts at Aku. Hamasuna shrugged off his fatigue and ran to the radio hut where he breathlessly ordered the operator to call head-quarters at Rabaul. Taking a pencil between shaking fingers he put together a coded message: 'Found crashed G4M tail no 323 south-west Aku stop No survivors stop Await instructions stop'.

'Send it,' he snapped. The operator tapped out the unit's call sign and then the message. He darted apprehensive glances over his shoulder as Hamasuna paced the little hut for twenty minutes waiting for the answer. Without warning the distinctive Morse signal echoed tinnily through the headphones. Hamasuna froze as the operator began writing.

'Well?'

'I must decode it, sir.'

'Then be quick about it.'

He looked over the man's shoulder as the words began to form. 'Secure . . . crash . . . site . . . await . . . senior . . . naval . . . presence . . .' There was a pause, as if the sender was awaiting instructions, then: 'ensure . . . nothing . . . moved . . . stop'.

'Acknowledge.' Hamasuna threw the order over his shoulder as he darted out of the door already shouting for his men to reform with enough rations for three days. He left one man as guide for the 'senior naval presence' and hurried the rest back to the crashed plane.

As he made his way through the jungle for the third time that day, Lieutenant Hamasuna felt a griping in his guts that had nothing to do with the fact that all he'd eaten since breakfast was a handful of rice. Should he have secured the site with ten men and sent two back with the message? No, he was certain he'd done the right thing. He knew he was a man of little imagination, that was why he was still only a junior lieutenant at thirty, but he was methodical. The priority had been to inform headquarters about Yamamoto. Everything else was secondary to that fact. In any case, what was worth stealing? His heart stopped as he remembered the white-gloved hand resting on the sword hilt. Yamamoto's sword. What if . . . ?

'Faster,' he barked, breaking into a trot. 'Get your lazy arses moving.'

They reached the crash almost before Hamasuna realized it and the first thing he did was rush to the admiral's corpse. With a surge of relief he saw the sword was still in place. He closed his eyes and let out a long breath. When he opened them again they strayed towards the patch of scorched grass where the briefcase had lain.

It was gone.

VI

Central Berlin, Jamie reflected, was like the centre of many German cities: an illusion. The beautiful old buildings that looked as if they'd been built when it was the capital of Prussia were modern replicas, a legacy of April and May 1945 when Allied bombers and the Red Army turned the city into a gigantic rubble field. No matter what you thought of Germans, you had to admire their resilience. When the dust settled they'd gone to work with their celebrated efficiency to disguise the scars of war. Whether it was with a great, rust-stained block of workers' flats as favoured by Walter Ulbricht or the initial restoration of the Reichstag by Paul Baumgarten, most of the ruins were replaced within a couple of decades.

It took less than five minutes to walk from the hotel, over the Liebknecht brücke to Museum Island, and across the grass of the Lustgarten into the shadow of the Altes Museum. As the name suggested, it was the oldest of the museums on the island. It held some of the ancient world's greatest works of art and Jamie would have liked nothing better than to spend a couple of hours among the Greek statuary, but his destination was the nearby Neues Museum.

Museum Island had been east of the wall, in the care of the *Deutsche Demokratische Republik*. Fortunately, Jamie decided, if the leaders of the DDR were keen on one thing it was museums. It took a few years for their masters in Moscow to acknowledge that most of the contents of Berlin's museums had ended up in the Hermitage or the basement of the Kremlin, but by the late Fifties they'd recovered most of their important exhibits. A few bits and pieces were still missing. Priam's Treasure, the hoard of gold and silver Heinrich Schliemann dug up from what might have been Troy, was one. It eventually turned up in the Pushkin Museum, but the Russians decided they'd keep it as war reparations. Jamie thought this had a certain ironic symmetry considering Schliemann more or less stole it from the Turks in the first place. That was the thing about the early German archaeologists and anthropologists, many of them were little better than looters. Not far away, the Pergamon Museum owed its existence to an engineer called Carl Humann who had excavated a site in Izmir, Turkey. In 1880, Humann did a deal with the Turks to keep fragments of friezes he discovered, and ended up taking an entire Greek temple back to Germany, an act of cultural vandalism that made Lord Elgin look like a high-street hustler. Naturally, the Turks asked for it back, but the German authorities ignored the request, as they did Iraq's for the return of the museum's Ishtar Gate, a thirty-foot masterpiece of glazed blue brick that was once one of the Seven Wonders of the World.

Priam's Treasure had been the centrepiece of the New Museum collection. The original Neues had been built in the 1850s and, unsurprisingly, got its name from being slightly less old than the Altes. The Egyptian collection was probably the finest outside Cairo, but today Jamie had no time to spare with the star exhibit, an iconic limestone bust of Queen Nefertiti. He had other things on his mind as he followed his escort through the exquisitely painted rooms and past the glass cases to the Herr Direktor's modest office on the fourth floor. When the Neues opened, it had been the repository for anything that couldn't be displayed properly in the Altes, which meant just about everything not Greek or Roman. If the Bougainville head had been deemed of sufficient importance it could be here.

A secretary ushered him through a door and a tall, lean figure in a dark suit welcomed him with a grave smile and a formal handshake. 'You would like some coffee, Herr Saintclair?'

'That would be lovely, sir,' Jamie greeted Museum Direktor Muller. 'Milk, no sugar.'

It was two years since Jamie had last been here, just after the museum reopened, but the man opposite him appeared about a decade younger. Then, the Herr Direktor had exhibited all the signs of a man under overwhelming stress: all twitching moustache and eyes darting nervously from a bony, pallid face. Now he exhibited the urbane air of a man in charge of his destiny. A man who knew the position of every bust and every mummy in his diverse collections. They waited until the coffee arrived and Muller took a delicate sip before opening the conversation.

'First I must thank you for the generous donation to our funds,' he said with a smile. 'The state, of course, is bountiful, but conservation and research is expensive.'

Jamie returned the smile. 'It was the least I could do after the help you provided on my previous commission,' he acknowledged. 'My client was most grateful for the return of the crown.' In truth, the recovery of the Crown of Isis had brought him a modest cheque from the New York Police Department. The donation had come from the Princess Czartoryski Foundation finder's fee for the Raphael. Nonetheless, contacts like Herr Direktor Muller were like plants: they required nurturing. A few thousand euros was money well spent now he could afford it, as his host's genial cooperation confirmed.

'And now you are here on another mysterious quest. I am intrigued. How can we be of assistance to you?'

Jamie hesitated. He'd been turning this conversation over in his mind since he'd landed at Tegel. It was all very well asking about Italian renaissance masterpieces and Egyptian crowns, but how did one broach the subject of a severed human head? There really was only one way. He took a deep breath and twisted his features into the apologetic grin that had seen him through a hundred dodgy negotiations.

'The object I'm attempting to locate is a shrunken head that originated on the island of Bougainville.' He saw the smile freeze on Herr Direktor Muller's face but carried on without pausing for breath. 'It would have been donated to the museum by an anthropologist named Adolfus Ribbe at some point between the years eighteen ninety-five and nineteen hundred. I'm aware it won't be in any of your main collections, but I wondered if it might be hidden away somewhere in your basement?' he ended lamely.

Muller stared at him, lips twisted in an expression that might have been puzzlement, disapproval or the precursor to a burst of hysterical laughter. The manicured hands rubbed at each other as though he were trying to rid them of some unwanted substance. Now Jamie thought of it, the idea seemed so outlandish he felt like running from the room. Before he could decide, the Herr Direktor remembered the cheque, composed himself and gave a sorrowful shake of his head.

'I'm afraid that anything *hidden away* in my basement would have been consumed by American incendiary bombs in February nineteen forty-five, Herr Saintclair. To my certain knowledge we do not have an artefact of that nature within these walls . . .'

The news felt like a kick in the teeth, but why should he be surprised? It had always been a long shot. Still, something in Muller's voice gave Jamie hope that it wasn't a complete dead end.

'But . . . ?'

'But there is another possibility. First . . .' The Herr Direktor pushed a buzzer on his desk. He picked up a fountain pen to dash off a note on the pad by his right hand, the metal nib darting back and forth in neat, regimented lines across the pristine white paper. 'Ribbe, you say? Have you any other details?'

Jamie mentioned that the anthropologist may have been based in Hamburg and the German added the information just as his secretary appeared in the doorway.

'First we must discover if the artefact was ever donated to this museum. Fortunately, the archives for early contributions had been moved out of the building to the Zoo flak tower before the bombing and survived the war.' Jamie knew the Zoo tower had been an enormous anti-aircraft bunker and bomb shelter out beyond Tiergarten. In addition to its more warlike function, it had accommodated the treasures of Berlin's museums. When the Russians had captured it they'd been dissuaded from their usual wanton destruction by intelligence officers seeking information about Germany's nuclear programme. 'We have the originals in storage,' the German continued. 'For convenience the records have also been computerized so it should not take too long. In the meantime, perhaps I can explain why I am so certain there is no shrunken head in this museum?'

'Of course.' Jamie smiled, knowing this was his penance for wasting the Herr Direktor's time with his foolishness.

'Much has changed since your fellow Ribbe made his donation – if indeed he did. In those days studying the differences between various ethnic groups by examining their remains was a perfectly legitimate scientific pursuit.' He paused and stroked his bottom lip with his index finger as if that would somehow provoke the correct words. 'At one time most museums

– including this one – would have had quite a collection of skulls, mainly for research purposes. These days they would never accept something of that nature, unless it had a specific value, such as giving an insight into ritual practices. In fact, we in the German Museums Association are already working on the details of a repatriation policy for the bulk of our human remains. The Museum of Medical History, for instance, has an extensive collection of skulls of the aboriginal peoples of Australia and Papua New Guinea, many of which will soon be returned.'

'Then perhaps that's where I should be looking?' Jamie suggested.

'Perhaps,' the Herr Direktor took another sip of his coffee, 'but we must ask ourselves what medical value a shrunken head would have? It would have gone through an extensive preservation process, which would leave it with little resemblance anatomically to its former self. For a scientist it would be like studying the badly stuffed remains of an animal. I doubt whether the medical museum would have accepted such a donation, unless it was for novelty value alone.'

'Does this mean you'll be repatriating all the Egyptian mummies I saw on the way up here?'

A thin smile creased Muller's face. 'You are joking, of course, but it is a legitimate question and one that requires addressing. In future we must recognize that these wonderful artefacts are human remains and can no longer be treated merely as objects. When we can, we must show the face behind the bandages, and tell the story of the person within.'

'Is that something you can do?' Jamie's professional interest was piqued.

'Of course.' Muller spread his hands like a messiah spreading his message. 'With the developing technologies at our disposal anything is possible—'

A knock at the door interrupted the conversation and the secretary entered to hand the direktor a computer printout. He scanned the contents and lifted his head to fix Jamie with an amused look that made the Englishman's heart beat a little faster. 'It seems your instincts were correct, Herr Saintclair, though you were fortunate Greta decided to search several years either side of our potential dates. In November of the year eighteen eighty-five, the museum purchased from Herr Adolfus Ribbe, lately returned from German New Guinea, "one canoe god – to be placed on the prow or stem of said vessel – seven fish spears in a variety of patterns, a model canoe – five feet in length, with foliage sail – various frond bowls, two clubs, four skulls of varying antiquity and . . . one shrunken head of a warrior chieftain". You appear surprised.'

'Frankly, Herr Direktor, I'm bloody astonished.' Jamie grinned as Muller blinked at the bluntness of his reply. 'When I first heard the words "shrunken head" I thought I had as much chance of finding it as winning the lottery.'

'Of course, this does not mean it is here now,' the museum boss cautioned. 'The head would have remained in the Neues for just two years until the new Ethnological Museum in Stresemannstrasse opened its doors. Our entire collection moved there. It is now housed in a rather depressing modern building out at Dahlem, but I must warn you that the Stresemannstrasse site suffered even more gravely than this museum in the latter years of the war. Much of their collection was lost.'

But Jamie was barely listening.

Every hunt began with a first step. Against all the odds, the Bougainville head was more than just a fuzzy photograph taken more than a century earlier. It was a reality.

VII

The suburb of Dahlem is in the west of Berlin and one of the most affluent areas of the city. It lies near the Grunewald, the great playground of forests and lakes that draws Berliners in their tens of thousands each summer to swim and picnic. According to Herr Direktor Muller, the Ethnological Museum was in the centre of town close to the Free University of Berlin.

It took Max half an hour to reach the museum and he dropped Jamie off outside the gates of a modernist cube of a building set back from the road. The first thing that struck the Englishman was the enormous banners draped across the upper storey above the entrance. In turn they represented Africa, America, Oceania, Asia and Europe, and each continent was identified by the staring eyes, prominent nose and grinning mouth of a stylized head. For a moment he stood transfixed. Was this an omen? Could it really be that easy?

He carried the mood of optimism with him as he walked up the concrete stairs to the hallway where he'd arranged to meet the museum's curator.

'Herr Saintclair?'

'Yes.' He turned, pleasantly surprised to discover he was being addressed by a tall, slim figure wearing a powder-blue sweater and tight-fitting designer jeans that showed off her long legs to advantage. He guessed she was around his age – perhaps in her mid-thirties – and she had hair the colour and sheen of a raven's plumage cut in a short bob. Chestnut eyes studied him appraisingly and there was an amused half-smile on her fine-boned features. The moment he set eyes on her he knew the first thing he said would make him sound like an idiot. Naturally, he obliged. 'I'm here to see the curator, Herr Fischer.'

'Perhaps you'll put up with me instead?' She offered her right hand and when he took it her grip was firm and dry. 'I'm Herr Fischer's deputy, Magda Ross. Dr Magda Ross.' She spoke in a flat, precise English that in Jamie's experience was peculiar to people who travelled widely, but with a slight accent that told him it was her native tongue. For some reason the perfume she wore took him back to a beach on the Norfolk coast and a night he'd long forgotten. The emphasis she placed on the word doctor made it a challenge, or possibly a warning, and he smiled.

'You find something amusing?' she asked.

'Not at all,' he lied. 'I'm just surprised and pleased to find a fellow Brit here. My German is good, but it's always easier to talk about a complex subject in one's own language, don't you think?'

She didn't answer directly, but set off briskly in the direction of a door on the far side of the hall. 'The Herr

Direktor said you are interested in information about our Melanesian collection?'

'If the island of Bougainville is in Melanesia, that is correct.'

She looked at him over her shoulder. 'I don't believe it's moved recently.'

Jamie reflected that a conversation with Dr Magda Ross was like being a knife-thrower's assistant: you felt relatively safe until the next missile was launched.

They walked in silence through a series of long, wooden-floored corridors and wide rooms filled with glass cases. Eventually, a lift carried them to a larger chamber on the first floor, which was dominated by a series of full-size huts or houses with walls and roofs made of woven grass or leaves. At the far end a big outrigger canoe was displayed on a stand and glass cases around the walls held fearsome masks, tools and weapons.

Jamie studied the exhibits but could see no sign of his target. 'The artefacts I'm interested in would have come to the museum from the Neues around a hundred and thirty years ago. Is it possible some of them would still be here, either on display or in storage?'

Magda Ross reached out to stroke an intricately carved hollowed log that appeared to be some kind of drum. 'You have to understand that we lost a high percentage of our early collections during the war. It would depend on what the artefacts were and their con-stituent materials.'

Jamie reeled off the list Direktor Muller had given

him: 'Four skulls of varying antiquity and one shrunken head of a warrior chieftain.'

She frowned and walked to one of the cases. 'This has been in our collection for over a hundred years.' She pointed to what looked like an axe, with a stone blade and a polished wood handle. 'It is originally from the Mount Takuan region of Bougainville Island.' Some memory made her smile for the first time and the thought occurred to Jamie that she'd been nervous about meeting him. 'I visited Bougainville about ten years ago when I was studying for my doctorate. It's one of the most fascinating places in the world for an anthropologist, I . . .' She stopped and shook her head. 'Forgive me, I'm getting carried away. I'm not here to give you a lecture . . .'

'Not at all.' Jamie smiled back. 'I'm interested in anything about the area. As you've probably noticed, my knowledge is a bit thin.'

'When it comes to Melanesia, I'm what they call a geek,' she confessed with a grin. 'Anyway, to get back to the subject, the spears may still be on show, but I doubt the pots would have survived. These days, for reasons of sensitivity, we would never display objects like the skulls or the head. If you'll come with me, I'll see if we have any record of them.'

They walked side by side to a small open-plan office with views over the museum entrance. Magda waved Jamie to a chair and sat at a computer on what was obviously her personal desk. 'If you'll bear with me for a few moments . . .'

Jamie watched as her long fingers fluttered expertly over the keyboard. 'I'm surprised your records survived if the bombing did so much damage to the museum,' he said.

'Fortunately they were stored somewhere they had a chance of surviving.' She looked up and their eyes met almost by accident. Jamie had to fight off the sensation of being sucked into the centre of a whirlpool. A little voice in his head shouted a warning and he concentrated so hard on Fiona's face he almost missed Magda Ross's next words. She frowned at the incomprehension on his face. 'I said that in those days we would have had to go to the other side of the city to access them. Now I just type a few letters and wait.' A printer at the rear of the office began to chatter and she rose to collect the sheets as they emerged from the machine. She split them into two bundles and Jamie accepted one.

As he scanned the contents, he realised it was a list of annual audits mentioning the objects sold by Adolfus Ribbe to the Neues Museum in 1885. Each was identified by a catalogue number and marked with a (d) for display, (s) for storage or (l), which meant out on loan. His eyes automatically went to the year 1946 and disappointment hit him like a sucker punch when he saw that though the four skulls were listed, the shrunken head had disappeared along with the fish spears, the bowls and the model canoe.

'It looks as if it went up in smoke at the end of the war.' He shook his head. 'I'm sorry, it seems I've been wasting your time.'

'You were seeking something specific?' Did her eyes betray something more than casual interest?

'My client is keen to see the shrunken head repatriated if it still exists, but . . .' He tailed off with a shrug. 'I have a photograph if that helps?' From his inside pocket he produced a brown envelope with the picture Keith Devlin had supplied him.

She took it and removed the picture. 'Yes,' she squinted as if she.was trying to extract every pixel of information from the sepia print, 'I recognize the technique and the style. Typical of similar artefacts from the island from around the mid-nineteenth century. The skull has been removed and the features preserved and padded out with organic material.'

She handed back the print and looked over the printout again, lips pursed in concentration. Eventually, she gave a nod of understanding. 'Yes, it disappears, but I think you've reached the wrong conclusion. See . . .' She twisted so he could read the sheet and drew her finger across a series of dates. 'The head was never in the museum during the war. The last time it appears is in November nineteen thirty-six, but by the time of the next audit,' she gave a shrug, 'it's gone.'

Jamie's heart took a lurch and he studied his own sheet more closely. 'So it could have disappeared any time over the next year?'

'No.' Magda shook her head. 'Two or three months. The next audit is in January of the following year.'

'Isn't that unusual? After all, an audit of a museum is a massive undertaking.'

She gave him a look that hinted he was straying into

dangerous territory. 'Not so unusual if you consider the times, Mr Saintclair.'

'You mean the Nazis, of course.'

She nodded. 'Obviously those were difficult days for everyone in Berlin.'

It took him a moment to work out the real message in the carefully chosen words. 'So basically anything with a taint of Jewishness had to be disposed of or destroyed.'

'That's correct, or . . .' For the first time Magda Ross looked less than confident and Jamie raised an eyebrow, half certain what was coming. '. . . or certain artefacts might have been of interest to, er, certain members of the regime.'

'Items linked with the occult, you mean,' he persisted.

'Yes,' she said carefully. 'So you understand the significance of what I am saying?'

'That if the Reichsführer-SS, Heinrich Himmler, believed the shrunken head of a South Sea savage and probable cannibal could aid his search for the homeland of the Vril, he wouldn't have hesitated to have it, shall we say, borrowed for his collection.'

Now it was her turn to raise a perfectly curved eyebrow. 'You're very well informed, Mr Saintclair.'

The statement contained an unspoken question, but one that would take much too long to answer. 'Is there any way of finding out where it went?'

She went back to her computer, frowning as she typed. She shook her head. 'There is no record of its disposal. I'm sorry; it is as if it just vanished.'

Jamie hid his disappointment. He stood up and handed over a dog-eared business card – he really must get some new ones now that he was in funds. 'If you do happen to come across any more information, please give me a call.'

'Goodbye, Mr Saintclair.' Magda accepted the card and they shook hands again. 'I'm genuinely sorry I wasn't able to help you.'

As Jamie made his way to the lift, the scent of Magda Ross's perfume in his nostrils, he released a long breath. Very occasionally in life your path crossed with someone who could have a fundamental effect on your future. Unfortunately, it was usually the wrong time and the wrong person. He tried to focus on Fiona's face and be thankful he'd just dodged a bullet.

Magda Ross watched from the office window as her visitor walked towards a black Mercedes limousine that stood idling by the museum's main gate. When it drove off she lifted the phone and dialled the international number that had been in her head since Jamie Saintclair announced the real target of his search.

An hour later, Jamie attempted to shrug off the melancholy the museum visit had inspired by spending the rest of the afternoon browsing art galleries and dealerships along Auguststrasse. Partly, it was disappointment that he'd reached a dead end in the search for the Bougainville head so quickly, but it went deeper than that. For some indefinable reason that had its roots with Adam and Eve, Magda Ross exerted a kind of magnetic influence on him. The thought of calling

Fiona temporarily raised his spirits, but he worked out that if it was early evening in Berlin it must be the middle of the night in Sydney.

As dusk approached he wandered back to the hotel by a circuitous route. When he entered the lobby it was filled with after-work drinkers and people gawping at the giant fish bowl. He decided against eating in the restaurant and went straight to his suite. Inside, he shut the curtains in the lounge and went to do the same in the bedroom – and froze. It wasn't anything he could see, not yet, but an indefinable something had changed. The maids had cleaned the room while he was having breakfast, so it should have been exactly as he'd left it, but . . .

Since embarking on his alternative career in art recovery he'd developed certain habits designed to give him peace of mind in a new world littered with moral contradictions and shadowy, sometimes dangerous characters. Not security, as such. Nothing could stop someone putting a bullet in your head, or even a knife in your back if they were determined enough. Not security, but something to give him an edge. It wasn't the kind of thing he'd mention even to his best friend, because it made him look paranoid, but it had worked in the past and it worked now. For instance: the shoes he'd left that looked as if they'd been carelessly abandoned had been at an exact angle to each other, and placed just so to triangulate with the power point. Now they didn't. The book on the bedside table with the business card marking the page and the pen perfectly touching the edge of the cover. The pen was still in place, but whoever had moved the book had been so absorbed in getting the pen right, that he'd been careless with the business card.

Someone had searched his room.

VIII

Bougainville 1943

Kristian Anugu sat in the depths of the *bikbus* listening to the sound of his pursuers crashing through the undergrowth like water buffalo. A tall, spare man with arm muscles like tree roots and handsome, almost Aryan, features, his hair flared in a wiry, untamed bush and his skin appeared so black it could almost be called purple. He carried a long spear in his right hand and the *yelopela* treasure under his left arm. He knew it must be treasure because the white soldiers who unwittingly supplied him with his belt and loincloth carried similar *kes* and they protected them with unusual vigilance for men usually so careless. His theory had been confirmed one day when he'd watched them worshipping the contents of the *kes* as they talked to God on the *dit-da* machine that travelled everywhere with them.

Curiosity had drawn him to the crashed flying machine and the *yelopela* king who looked as if he was asleep. There'd been many things from the machine he'd have liked and had it not been for his natural wariness he would have taken them. Property ownership was not a concept familiar to Kristian Anugu, a warrior of the *Koki*, a sub-clan of the Naasioi people who populated Papa'ala, in the southern centre of the island. He was the son of Osikaiang, the queen, who owned the land, the sky and the sea. Osikaiang owned, and Kristian Anugu fought to keep. That was the way it was and the way it had always been. If a man could not protect what he had and a stronger or more cunning man managed to take it away, then he deserved nothing. He'd first been attracted to the *yelopela* king's long knife with its glittering handle and silken braid. Yet even as he reached for it something made him pause. The way the dead man's hand still gripped it confirmed his instinct that the king's spirit was still strong and one of the *ensels* who surrounded God was guarding the long knife. Kristian Anugu considered himself one of the most cunning warriors on the island, but that didn't make him foolish enough to mess with the *ensels*. He'd been watching from the bush when the *yelopela* soldiers came with their long guns with knives on the front. Once, beneath a full moon, he'd seen two *yelopelas* holding a man from another tribe while a third plunged the gun-knife into his body. He had no wish to be discovered by them and treated in a similar fashion.

Unlike other islanders who made alliance with one or the other, Kristian saw no difference between the *yelopelas* and the white soldiers who always stared at the sky through the *glas bilong kaptens* he coveted. They were outsiders and nothing to do with him, or his clan. If they trespassed on his lands on big mountain he would kill them if he believed they were weak, or avoid them if they were too strong. Sometimes the *yelopelas* would destroy crops or burn houses, but that didn't change his attitude to them. More food might always be found and it was simple enough to build another house. Kristian's attention had been drawn to the treasure by the chief *yelopela* who had quartered the crash site like a dog marking out his territory. He'd seen him worship the body of the *yelopela* king before going to the *kes* and spending much time furtively studying the contents. At first, Kristian had feared the man would remove the treasure. His heart had thundered like the waves on Loloho beach as he'd watched the soldier's indecision before leaving the precious *kes* where it lay. When he'd been certain the men were gone he recovered the *kes* and set out for the longhouse on big mountain.

That was when he made the mistake. His way had taken him past the road where God sometimes rained fire on the *yelopelas*, who appeared to have incurred His wrath more than the white soldiers they hunted. He believed this must be the case because the whites were left untouched. Or perhaps they were too few and insignificant? Normally a man might cross the road with ease, because there were not enough *yelopelas* to guard it properly. Today he'd been delayed by the same soldiers who had surrounded the crashed machine.

After some thought he took a different route, using the bed of a stream a little to the north. By the time he reached big mountain he could hear the *yelopelas* and their Black Dogs, the native Bougainvilleans who supported them, not far behind. He was not overly concerned, he could outwit the *yelopelas* easily enough, but the Black Dogs were a different matter. They might be salt-water people from the coastal settlements, but even their limited skill would allow them to track him back to the longhouse. He must not let that happen. Maintaining his pace to stay just far enough ahead, he considered his position. If he abandoned the *yelopela* treasure it was possible he could talk his way past them, though it would cost him some pride. Normally, they did not kill without reason, however insignificant that reason might be. But he sensed that the crash of the flying machine and the death of their king would make the *yelopela* soldiers more murderous than usual, and, in any case, the treasure fascinated him. He would continue, he decided, and lure them away from the longhouse until he decided what to do.

The patch of thick jungle was like a hundred others and he had no idea why it attracted him. He burrowed deep in its centre with the treasure under his arm and the sounds of the hunters closing in. Once he was settled, Kristian closed his eyes and sought to make himself as insignificant as possible. When the sonorous voice began to echo inside his head it seemed entirely natural and proper.

Not far away, he could hear the *yelopelas* blundering through the brush, crushing twigs and leaves underfoot and making more noise than the wild pigs he often hunted. Sometimes he could smell them – the *yelopelas* – before he could see them. They perspired freely in the sultry jungle conditions and the scent of their bodies was acrid in his nostrils, along with the rice-cooking odour they carried with them. But the sounds in closest proximity were much stealthier: the soft, wary treads of a barefoot hunter. The Black Dogs were almost upon him.

You must trust in me, the voice of his long-dead grandfather advised. *I will be the cloak that shields you from the* yelopelas *and their Hat Men. Hold the treasure of their king to your chest and sing me the song of the fire dance that was never sung and without which I will never be at peace.*

At first, Kristian found the advice perplexing. Logic told him his grandfather was long dead and to make a noise would be fatal. The old man had been killed in a blood feud that had only ended, according to family tradition, when the *jemeni polis* hanged three members of each clan from the same tree. Kristian's mother, the queen, had always preached respect for their ancestors, but it was the mention of Hat Men that convinced him to comply with the old man's wishes. The Hat Men had been the Black Dogs of the *jemeni polis* in the days before *yelopelas* and Big War, but they had not been generally spoken of since long before Kristian was born.

Sing, the voice insisted, *and I will sing with you.*

In the sultry depths of the bush Kristian closed his eyes and the rhythm of the ceremonial drums filled his head, the click of wood on wood sharp and rapid. He could feel the flames all around him, could see their flicker as if through the eye slits of a ceremonial mask. The drone of the fire dance song filled his throat and his grandfather's strong voice echoed his, the sound spiralling around the jungle grove where it hung like a protective fence against the outside world. As he sang, Kristian Anugu's fingers worked at the straps of the *yelopela* king's treasure and removed a thin sheet from within. On it were strange scratchings that looked like a five-toed bird had danced across a sandbank. Kristian knew this was how the outsiders communicated with their gods.

Now you understand, his grandfather whispered. *But there is another task you must fulfil before I am freed.*

The drone died in Kristian's chest and he blinked as if he were waking to a new day. Birds twittered in the bushes around him and their voices told him he was alone. An intense sense of release made him want to leap in the air in imitation of the fire dance, but it was immediately overwhelmed by the responsibility he had felt when he replaced the god words in their leather *kes*. He ran a hand over the rough surface and nodded to himself. Yes, he understood everything.

IX

Jamie was staring out of the hotel window over the oily waters of the Spree when his cell phone chirped. The vibrate setting made it dance across the bedside table and he had to grab it before it fell. He studied the small screen. The incoming number wasn't one the phone recognized.

'Yes,' he said tentatively.

'Mr Saintclair?' The female voice surprised him and his heart gave an involuntary flutter when he realized the identity of the caller.

'Dr Ross,' he managed to keep his tone neutral, 'I didn't expect to hear from you again.'

'And I didn't expect to be calling *you*,' she laughed, but it sounded a little forced to Jamie's ears. 'It seemed very unlikely that I could help. But your puzzle intrigued me and I did a little more digging. I think I may have something.'

'Yes?' He doubted the laconic monosyllable was the reaction she expected, but the prospect of meeting Magda Ross again caused mixed emotions. He wasn't sure how he should react and her next suggestion only compounded his confusion.

'I thought perhaps it might even be worth you buying me lunch.'

Jamie blinked. 'Did you have anywhere in mind?'

'Yes, but I hope you are not a vegetarian.'

The Grill Royal turned out to be not far from the hotel, on a riverside terrace just off Friedrichstrasse, by the Weidendamm Bridge. It had been across the Weidendamm that Martin Bormann, Hitler's right-hand man, made his fateful and ultimately fatal bid to escape Berlin. Jamie couldn't look at the bridge without seeing the single Tiger tank roaring forward into an ambush of Soviet anti-tank guns, followed by thousands of terrified refugees and soldiers. Most of the escapees had been mown down by the pitiless soldiers of the Red Army.

As he walked into the understated foyer he reflected that a Tiger tank might come in handy to protect him during the coming meeting. Not so much from Magda Ross, but from himself. In spite of being, he considered, a perfectly intelligent specimen of the male of the species, women – Abbie Trelawney apart – had somehow managed to remain a constant mystery to him. He wasn't altogether sure why. He hoped that would change with Fiona, but there were times when he felt hopelessly out of his depth. What was worse, even on short acquaintance Magda Ross had the same effect. Just being in the same room with her had been a drug on the senses.

He'd done a little research on the venue after he'd agreed to the meeting. His first thought was that Dr Ross didn't get out much, because she was certainly making the most of the opportunity. The Grill was part art house, part restaurant, and part place to be seen if you were a certain type of Berliner: the type with more money than you knew what to do with. Jamie had plenty of experience of upmarket restaurants in London and elsewhere, but the £150 steak was a new personal high – or low, depending on your point of view. If Magda had the same taste in wine she did food, Keith Devlin's retainer was in for an interesting afternoon. He only hoped it was worth it.

Undeterred, he marched briskly into the restaurant thinking virtuous thoughts that were immediately banished when he was confronted by the table she occupied. Magda Ross sat with her back against the wall directly below a larger-than-life picture of a pretty girl with her left nipple hanging provocatively from her top. Jamie was far from inexperienced with women, but the combination caused his steps to falter. His smile froze and even though he kept his eyes firmly on the woman at the table his expression must have told its own story. Magda turned and craned her neck to look at the picture on the wall behind before facing him with a wry grin.

'Don't get any ideas, Mr Saintclair,' she warned. 'This is none of my doing. You can blame it on the drooling waiter across there. He claims this is the last seat in the house, but I have my doubts about his motives.'

Taking his seat with as much decorum as he could

82

muster, Jamie looked over his shoulder to where a heavy-set young man in a white shirt did indeed only have eyes for table number nineteen. That would have been understandable even without the attraction of the mammarian study on the wall. Magda Ross looked as if she'd just stepped off a catwalk. She wore a suit of shimmering raw silk that exactly matched her hair, and the opaque ivory of her complexion and scarlet lips provided a startling contrast to the dark material. The effect was striking. No, it was more than striking. She was the most beautiful woman in the restaurant by a long way, and her expression said she knew it.

He realized he was staring and the red lips twitched into a smile. 'If you find the picture a distraction, I can always ask to move table again,' she suggested. 'If they can't come up with something perhaps we could go somewhere a little less formal?'

'Not at all.' Jamie returned her smile. 'It's not a part of the anatomy I'm unfamiliar with. In any case, my table companion eclipses anything that adorns the walls of this fine establishment.'

He'd intended to sound like a man of the world, but he found himself the focus of deep brown eyes and knew he was in trouble. 'Are you flirting with me, Mr Saintclair?'

'We hardly know each other, Dr Ross.' He struggled to hold her gaze and his nerve. 'All I did was state a simple truth. And please call me Jamie.'

'Is there a significant other in your life, Jamie?'

The enquiry was so unexpected Jamie wasn't sure he'd heard right. 'That's a very direct question.'

'You'll find that I'm a very direct lady.'

It was a relief when the waiter interrupted to take their drinks order.

'*Eiswasser, bitte*,' Magda said.

'Oh, you can't come to a steak restaurant and drink water.' Jamie smiled, struggling to regain the advantage. He turned to the young man. 'Do you have a bottle of Nuits-St-Georges premier cru?'

'Of course, sir, the 2005 or the 2007?'

'Which was the best year?'

'I'll check with the sommelier, sir.' He placed two menus on the table in front of them and moved away.

'I get the feeling you're trying to impress me.' Magda's eyes narrowed in mock suspicion. 'But you haven't answered my question.'

'You've lured me to this wonderful restaurant,' Jamie pointed out. 'It would be very mean of me if I couldn't repay you with a glass of rather special wine. Besides, my client is paying. To answer your question: yes, there is a significant other in my life, and we're very happy together.'

'Good,' she said. 'I'm glad we got that out of the way. Now we can both relax.'

'Why did you ask?'

'Because you're an interesting and quite attractive man, and in other circumstances we might have spent a bit of time together while you're in Berlin. But I have a policy of not encroaching on other people's lives. In any case,' she smiled, 'I appreciate your compliment. She scrubs up well, as my old dad used to say.'

'And I appreciate yours.' Jamie laughed, glad to be

back on safer ground. 'I've occasionally been called interesting, but seldom attractive. Scrubs up well? My grandfather used to say that about my mum. She hated it. Where did your dad come from?'

She hesitated, as if she was unsure where to start and how much to tell. 'My dad's originally from Scotland, but we travelled a lot. He was a Royal Navy helicopter pilot based in Somerset, which was where I was born. Later on he became a military attaché. He was posted to Athens, Prague and a few other places and he insisted I attend local schools so I could get an ear for the languages. I never took to Czech, but some of them stuck . . .'

'German?'

Magda shook her head. 'My mother is German and we spent almost every summer holiday with *Oma* just outside Hamburg – hence the accent. I was pretty much fluent by the time I was twelve. Dad's retired now and they have a nice little place near the coast in Somerset.'

She paused as the waiter returned, along with a second man carrying a bottle of wine who bowed and introduced himself as the sommelier. 'I am afraid we didn't have the 2005, sir, may I recommend the 2003 as an alternative.'

'That will be excellent, thank you.' The waiter took their order while the sommelier opened the bottle with almost religious reverence. Jamie waited until he'd poured two glasses. 'You were saying?'

'Basically, I grew up a nomad.' She sipped her wine and nodded appreciatively. 'Very nice. I suppose the most interesting thing about me is that I was once held hostage in what the British Special Air Service call the Killing House at their base in Hereford.' She saw his look of surprise. 'Impressed, huh?'

'Very,' he admitted. 'Not many people get the privilege. If sitting in a room with live bullets flying around can be called a privilege.'

'It certainly gets the adrenalin flowing,' she grinned. 'I was about seventeen and dad was being sent to Yemen, so he had to go on a hostage recovery course. He took me along for the ride. A very handsome sergeant showed me a neat trick. "Just hold your hand like this, love",' she produced a very passable Geordie accent and held up her fist with the second knuckle protruding, '"and punch him as hard as you're able on his Adam's apple. He'll die spitting blood in five minutes." He said the trick is to punch through something not at it. So be very careful, Mr Saintclair. You are dining with a killing machine.'

'Then I'm in safe hands.' He raised his glass in a mock toast, warming to Magda Ross even more. 'How did you end up doing what you do?'

'When it came to choosing a university degree I closed my eyes and stuck a pin in a list and ended up an anthropologist. What about you?'

He shrugged. 'Not half as interesting, I'm afraid. What you see is a product of my mother's ambition. No, it's true,' he countered the brief look of disbelief, 'she even changed our name from Sinclair to Saintclair because she thought it would help me get on at university.'

'And did it?'

'The other grammar school students laughed and the posh ones sneered. My mother wanted me to do languages, but I was interested in the arts; in the end I did both.'

'What about your dad?'

'I never had one.'

He was glad the food came before she had a chance to ask him to elaborate. It was so perfect that neither had much to say beyond expressions of pleasure for the next forty minutes. Afterwards the waiter approached to clear the table and ask if they wanted to order a dessert. Jamie looked to Magda and she shook her head, but said she'd have a coffee. 'Make that two.'

He smiled. 'The company's been so fascinating I'd almost forgotten why we're here.'

Magda raised her glass with the last of the wine. 'To the Bougainville head.'

'The Bougainville head.' He mirrored her toast. 'You said you might be able to help me?'

Her expression turned thoughtful. 'When you left I thought that was the last we'd ever see of each other. Then again, the disappearance of the shrunken head from our collection is a puzzle and I like puzzles. You talked about a client?'

Jamie nodded. 'I should have been more honest with you,' he apologized. 'My reasons for helping return the head to Bougainville are not entirely altruistic. The tribal chief who wants his ancestor back is also in possession of certain documents that are important to my client. It means the head has a commercial value to him, and therefore to me. If you can help and we're successful, it would mean a donation – a substantial one, I suspect – to the museum. And there would also be a more personal award.'

'I'm not interested in your money, Jamie,' she laughed. 'But I am interested in what happened to the head. Remember that three-month window we talked about?'

'Of course, but we've no idea what happened in it.'

'What if we could find out?' She had his attention now. 'Last night I talked to a few people who have a better understanding of what was happening in Berlin at that time. One of them is in his nineties but still does some research work for us.'

'So he would have been around in the Thirties?'

'Exactly,' she confirmed. 'And he remembered that in the years before the war it wasn't uncommon for senior Nazis to use the museum service as what he called a "gift shop". The disgrace of it still annoyed him.'

'Gift shop?'

'Party officials would take visiting dignitaries on a tour of a museum and if they showed an interest in something it would be handed over as a gift at the end of the tour. Not the really good stuff, but things with a certain novelty value.'

'And he thinks that's what might have happened to the head.'

'He believes it's possible, yes.'

Jamie sipped his coffee and turned the new information over in his mind. 'I suppose the next question is who the dignitaries were?'

She nodded. 'I think we're probably talking about

members of foreign delegations. People who provided the regime with greater legitimacy in world terms. They wouldn't be minor government officials, because by nineteen thirty-six the Nazis had Germany completely sewn up and didn't need to impress anyone.'

'So if we can discover which delegations visited Berlin between November nineteen thirty-six and January 'thirty-seven, it would give us a potential target for the next step forward.'

'That was my understanding.'

'But how do we go about that?'

The smile she gave him could only be called enigmatic. 'I believe I have an idea.'

X

When he'd paid the bill, Jamie offered to call Max, but Magda insisted she needed some fresh air. 'Why don't we walk to the U-Bahn instead?' she suggested. 'That lovely wine has gone to my head.'

As they made their way south down the endless shop-lined canyon of Friedrichstrasse, she unselfconsciously slipped her arm through his. The unexpected physical contact gave Jamie a moment of guilty panic, but he quickly relaxed to enjoy the sensation of being with a beautiful woman who made men's heads turn even in a city filled with beautiful women. It occurred to him that for a self-confessed wanderer she seemed utterly at home and he could sense her smiling as they walked.

When they reached the underground station Magda stepped forward to buy the tickets and led the way un-erringly down to the platform. It wasn't until they were sitting together on the half-empty train that she gave a hint of their destination.

'In nineteen thirty-six Goebbels would have hailed every visit by a foreign delegation as an affirmation of

Nazi culture.' She raised her voice to be heard above the clatter as the swaying carriage picked up speed and thundered through the tunnel. 'By that point every news outlet in the city was under his control or, at the very least, his malign influence, so it's probable there would have been some sort of newspaper coverage of the events. Does that sound plausible to you?'

'It seems likely enough,' Jamie conceded. 'I get the feeling Goebbels would have insisted on a full page with pictures on everything from Franco inviting Hitler over for a beach party to a visit of the Buenos Aires ladies free-style crochet champions. But doesn't that make it more difficult for us? If they trumpeted the arrival of every overseas visitor it could run into dozens, even hundreds, and that's if we could find any records.'

Magda's reply was lost as they rattled into a station and the train slewed to a halt. Jamie saw her frown and it was only then he noticed the platform was filled with hundreds of young men wearing various combinations of blue, black and white. When the doors opened they were deafened by a wall of chanting as a group of twenty or thirty forced their way into the carriage.

Magda leaned across so her lips were against his ear. 'Perhaps the U-Bahn wasn't such a great idea after all.' He gave her a reassuring smile and they sat back, trying to ignore the jostling mass that thankfully took station at the far end of the carriage to the sound of beer bottles being opened.

'*Schwarz-weiss-blau. Haa-ess-fau. Schwarz-weiss-blau. Haa-ess-fau.*'

'Hamburg fans,' Magda shouted above the racket. 'There must be a Bundesliga game tonight.'

Jamie nodded and glanced towards the chanting supporters. The instant his eyes locked on the teenager with close-cropped hair he knew he'd made a mistake. It was no surprise that every male in the carriage would be drawn to Magda Ross, but these eyes burned with hatred. As he watched, a snarl of feral savagery distorted the young man's features before he turned back to his friends. He must have been giving instructions because other faces turned towards them and Jamie saw one or two of the Hamburg supporters nod.

'Trouble,' he said, pulling Magda to her feet.

The chanting faded as if his movement had triggered an off-switch and the phalanx of blue-and-white-clad men began to move purposefully towards them. In the hush that followed it seemed the entire carriage held its breath.

'Get behind me and stay there.' Jamie didn't wait for an acknowledgement and he was thankful that Magda Ross wasn't the kind of woman to argue or hesitate in a tight situation. He had no idea what had caused the young man's reaction, but he knew they were in danger. The other passengers were the usual mix of young and old, tourists and backpackers, but unfortunately not any gun-toting Berlin cops. A middle-aged couple looked up, the man's face twisted with frustration and anger. Jamie could tell he wanted to intervene, but wouldn't risk putting his wife in any danger. The others kept their heads down as if, because they didn't see what was about to happen, it was none of their business.

The young man with the burning eyes took the lead. He wore a dark blue replica football shirt with the words 'Fly Emirates' on the front and a curious badge of a black and white diamond on a blue background. Gym-toned muscles rippled beneath the material of the shirt and he approached with the steady, measured pace of a man with a job to do. His right hand hung over his jeans pocket like a gunfighter about to draw and Jamie tensed as he understood what the pose meant. Behind him, one or two of his supporters carried beer bottles by the neck. They were smiling.

As Jamie backed away he searched his memory for a reason. This was no spontaneous attack. The supporters had been boisterous and intimidating when they boarded, but any violence was being kept for their rival fans. No, it had all started when the young man had recognized him. The last time he'd been in Berlin he'd been kidnapped by neo-Nazis from a group called the Vril Society, but there'd been a reason for that and the reason was long gone, tortured to death in the shower room of Jamie's Kensington flat. A shiver ran through him. He felt fear, but he wasn't frightened. In some men, fear slowed the reactions and froze the brain. Others – and Jamie was one – learned to channel that fear and turn it into energy and speed.

He reached the point where the narrow corridor between the seats widened into the open area at the doors. 'Magda?'

'Yes.' Her voice came from next to his right ear and the determination in her tone lifted his spirits.

'This is as far as we go. Get to the door and stay there. How far to the next stop?'

'A minute, maybe two.'

He looked up at the wall of blue and white less than five paces away now. All he had to do was survive for a hundred and twenty seconds and pray that they could get out of this death trap. He dropped into the classic self-defence crouch, hands bunched into fists and ready to react. Jamie Saintclair had learned his gutter fighting from an expert, a Royal Marine commando instructor who could kill you with a single finger but advocated tearing your opponent's throat out with your teeth if that got the job done more quickly.

Jamie grinned at the memory, and there was a momentary hesitation in the blue and white ranks.

'*Holen Sie ihn!*'

'Look out, Jamie!'

Jamie expected the young man at the front to lead the attack. He was fairly certain his opponent had a knife, but he'd fought knives before. If he could get a block in he might be able to disable the knifeman and use him as a barrier against his followers. But they had other ideas. At the command, the leader stepped into the space between two seats and the others surged past him to overwhelm Jamie. The Englishman got in a couple of good, solid punches, but the weight of the attack was too much and he was down before he knew it, curled up in a ball to avoid the fists and boots that sought him out.

'Get him up,' a voice ordered in German. Jamie was dragged to his feet and he found himself pinioned between two of the big Hamburg fans. Helpless.

'Hold him steady.' The young man produced a flick knife that opened with a sharp snick to reveal a four-inch blade of polished blue steel. Jamie struggled and kicked, aiming for the knife hand. The thug dodged the flailing feet and pulled his arm back, ready to plunge the blade into his victim's unprotected body. 'Hold the bastard still,' he snarled. 'This is for Berndt Hartmann.'

'What?' The name was so unexpected Jamie did nothing to protect himself. His disbelieving reaction made the knifeman hesitate – but only for a split second. Jamie saw the moment his eyes went cold and cried out in anticipation of that wicked blue spike piercing his body.

'No!'

The shout came from the angry passenger as he launched himself at the knifeman regardless of the thugs who stood back to watch Jamie's murder. As he struggled with the bewildered teenager his partner rose in her seat, lashing out with a handbag that must have been filled with rocks if its effect on the football supporters was anything to go by.

The thugs backed away under the onslaught and Jamie heard a shriek of pain. He looked up to see long fingers with scarlet nails clawing at the eyes of his right-hand captor. Momentarily, the pressure eased, and he tore himself clear, pivoting to bring his fist in a scything, roundhouse punch that sank into his remaining detainer's groin. The impact was accompanied by a satisfying oomph of agony and he found himself free. Some instinct told him the U-Bahn train had arrived at the station and he scrabbled past the writhing man towards the doors. A hand dragged him upright and hauled him past more blue-and-white-clad football fans where he collapsed on to the station platform. He looked up and found Magda Ross studying him with a puzzled look in her eyes.

She was about to say something when someone reached down and helped Jamie to his feet. His anonymous saviour from the train dusted him down and nodded approvingly. The man's wife stood to one side, smiling sheepishly and still holding the handbag as if she expected to need it again.

'*Danke.*' Jamie couldn't think of anything else to say. The man nodded.

'You're welcome,' the man said in heavily-accented English. 'Perhaps next time you should take the bus?'

XI

They emerged from Kochstrasse station, close to what had once been the most notorious location on the Berlin Wall, a place of high-risk spy swaps, hair's-breadth escapes and tragic failures, which seemed appropriate in Jamie's view. Everything was a bit of a blur. He dazedly noted that Checkpoint Charlie had been turned into a tourist attraction: a hut surrounded by sandbags, a few warning signs and an opportunity to have your photograph taken with a grim-faced actor in a DDR border guard's grey uniform. It seemed a demeaning end for such an iconic piece of history, and he couldn't help thinking it would have been better if it had been swept away with the rest of the Wall.

'Who is Berndt Hartmann?' Magda asked. 'The boy with the knife said "This is for Berndt Hartmann" when he was going to . . . going to stab you.'

A grinning goblin face swam into view and Jamie remembered the awkward hump of a hunched back that didn't seem to slow the owner when they'd been running for their lives. 'Just someone I knew.'

'Come on, Jamie.' The words exploded from Magda, revealing a new and formidable dimension to her character. He realized then that he'd gravely under-estimated the steel that lay beneath the designer couture. 'Somebody just tried to kill you. I deserve more than that.'

'I'm sorry. It's . . . He was a former SS man, part of a team who stole art treasures and . . . other things . . . for Heinrich Himmler.'

'Did you kill him?'

Jamie remembered Bernie Hartmann's irresistible grin. 'No.' He smiled wearily. 'I tried to save his life. He died in a plane crash, but if I read the situation correctly no one told his former comrades. There was a Hamburg connection. I think it must have been a coincidence and the leader recognized me.'

'I thought you were just a jumped-up errand boy,' her tone took the edge off the words. 'But there was a moment on the train when you were enjoying yourself. I think you might be a dangerous man to be around, Jamie Saintclair.'

There didn't seem to be an answer to that, so they walked on in silence for a while. 'By the way,' he said, 'why didn't you use your SAS trick on him?'

She had to think for a moment before she came up with a reply. 'I didn't feel like killing anybody today.'

They emerged into a square dominated by an enormous modern office block thirty or forty storeys high with the word *Morgenpost* emblazoned across the roof in neon letters ten feet tall. Above the doorway a slightly more modest display announced that this was the

Axel Springer building. Jamie knew Springer had been the German equivalent of Rupert Murdoch, a media mogul who had monopolized German newspapers for four decades until his death in the Eighties.

They checked in at the front desk where a receptionist telephoned Magda's contact to confirm the meeting and issued them with temporary badges authorizing their presence in the building. A few minutes later a blond-haired girl in a smart business suit appeared at the entrance barrier and greeted Magda with an exclamation of delight.

'This is my friend Uli.' Magda smiled as the other woman used a swipe card to open the barrier. 'She's a feature writer on the *Berliner Morgenpost* and quite the famous one, aren't you, darling?'

Uli blushed, but Jamie could see she was pleased by the praise. 'As you know very well, Magda, a byline does not make you famous. I'm only as good as my next story. Herr . . . Saintclair, isn't it?' She held out her hand and Jamie shook it. 'That is the way it is in newspapers. Please.'

She led the way to the rear of the building and a brightly lit cafe, where a number of the tables were occupied by groups of three or four, mainly older men and young women. The women were dressed universally in jeans and T-shirts and the men looked as if they'd emerged from a Seventies time warp when beards and moustaches were still in fashion. 'Our sub-editors are on a lunch break,' Uli whispered with an indulgent smile. 'Geniuses with words most of them, but their dress sense? Ugh!'

She left them sitting at a table with a scarred top and returned a few moments later juggling three china mugs filled with steaming black coffee and a handful of sachets of sugar and milk. When they'd sorted the drinks out to individual preference she turned to Jamie. 'Magda said you are interested in the newspaper's records?'

'That's correct. For a certain period in nineteen thirty-six and 'thirty-seven.'

Uli frowned. 'Before I came to meet you I checked our computer system, but there are no comprehensive computerized archives available to us for the period before nineteen forty-five . . .'

Jamie stifled a groan. 'Does that mean they were all destroyed during the war?'

'Not necessarily,' she said, raising his hopes again. 'But you have to understand that the owners of this newspaper are not proud of the *Morgenpost*'s record during that period. When the Nazis came to power they immediately introduced a policy of *gleichschaltung* – that is, coordination – which may sound quite innocent, but in effect created a one-party state and outlawed all criticism of that party. One of the consequences of *gleichschaltung* was that the propaganda ministry under Josef Goebbels took over complete editorial control of all German newspapers.' Uli was obviously uncomfortable with this part of her profession's and her nation's history. The words tumbled out in a flow of pure passion and she had to take a deep breath to compose herself. 'If you were an editor who questioned the party line, you were replaced by a Nazi. If you were a journalist and wrote the wrong thing you would be fired, and quite possibly end up in a concentration camp. It did not matter whether you were part of an anti-Nazi organization or just a moderate expressing an alternative point of view, you were the enemy. Hundreds of journalists were imprisoned and many killed because they voiced opposition to the regime.' She paused to drink from her coffee.

'They were very brave,' Jamie said.

'Yes, Mr Saintclair,' Uli's eyes held a challenge, 'there were brave Germans who stood up to the Nazis, not many, but some. But from nineteen thirty-three to 'forty-five the *Morgenpost* was essentially a Nazi mouthpiece. Its pages hailed the Night of the Long Knives – when Ernst Rohm and his Brownshirts were murdered – as the putting in its place of a gang of criminals. It celebrated *Kristallnacht* and the persecution of the Jews as throwing off the shackles of centuries of Zionist oppression. The *Anschluss*, the annexation of the Sudetenland, the invasion of Poland, and every German victory that followed were the subject of unquestioning devotion and hysterical applause. Is it any wonder the owners do not wish to make the record of those years too readily available to the public? Some archive material *was* destroyed during the bombing, but much of it survived. Although I said there were no *comprehensive* records, a restricted computer database is available to historians and researchers, but Magda led me to believe you would prefer to see the originals, yes?'

Jamie exchanged a glance with Magda Ross. 'We'd be very grateful.'

'Then come with me.'

She led them through the glass doors of the cafe and across a broad brightly lit hall to the lifts. Inside the lift she hit a button marked B and they descended in silence until it bumped to a halt and the doors opened. B stood for basement car park and they walked through the lines of partially filled parking bays across concrete streaked with tyre marks, until they reached what looked like a wooden hut at the far end. Uli removed a key from her pocket and unlocked the door, flicking a switch that illuminated a series of striplights as she entered.

'Our archives,' she announced wryly. 'Some of us still fight to keep our history alive.'

A damp, musty scent – a combination of old-age and decay – hit them as they followed Uli into the hut. It was lined with wooden frames crammed with thick tabloid-size volumes in blue-marbled covers. Some were virtually pristine, with the embossed name of the paper and the year outlined in gold; others seemed to be held together by string and what looked like sticking plaster. Three narrow tables of rough wood ran down the centre of the shelves and two of the ragged volumes already lay there. 'Nineteen thirty-six and 'thirty-seven,' Uli confirmed. 'They are not in the best of condition, as you see.'

She stepped back. 'I have work to do, so I will leave you to your research. You shouldn't be disturbed, but if anyone asks just show them your passes and tell them you're my guests. I'll come down and see how you're getting on in an hour.'

'Thank you.' Jamie was already removing his jacket. 'I'm very grateful for your help.'

'Maybe it would be quicker if we took a volume each,' Magda suggested.

'Aren't you a little overdressed for this?' He pointed to the dark silk of her suit.

'You're talking to someone who's been up to her armpits in a Melanesian cesspit.' She pulled up the jacket's sleeves. 'Never let it be said an anthropologist was afraid to get her hands dirty. If there's any permanent damage I'll take it up with the House of Chanel.'

'All right. If you check January nineteen thirty-seven, I'll do the winter of 'thirty-six.'

'Why don't we broaden the search a month either side of our window, just in case?' she suggested.

'Good idea.' Jamie opened the thick volume so the weight of the paper slapped back against the wooden surface, raising a small cloud of dust that made his nose twitch. 'A pity they didn't provide gas masks.'

He leafed through the dog-eared pages until he came to October. Front page after front page carried pictures of Hitler, Goering or Goebbels saluting long columns of marching men, shaking hands with other Nazi bigwigs or attending enormous rallies of cheering Hitler Youths. Apart from what seemed an odd fascination with the United States, the stories had a familiar theme. They focused on the success of the regime, vilification of Jews and saboteurs, and how well things were going in Spain where Franco was preparing for an offensive against Madrid. The never-ending diet of Nazi propaganda left him cold, but Jamie forced himself to focus on every paragraph. The only reference he could find of any interest was the arrival of a military delegation from Japan for talks with their *Wehrmacht* counterparts late in October. The true reason for the visit was revealed a few editions later. On 25 November, the Japanese ambassador to Germany, Kintomo Mushakoji, and the host nation's foreign minister Joachim von Ribbentrop signed the Anti-Comintern Pact, committing the two countries to deter the expansion of Communism. Jamie reflected that by November 1936 the Nazis were well experienced on that front, given the number of Communists they'd already killed. He turned back a few pages to an article he'd noticed earlier: the beheading on 4 November of the activist Edgar Andre, rounded up during the anti-Communist witch hunt after the Reichstag fire three years earlier. It would be just like the Nazis to have staged the execution to impress their Oriental guests. Turning back to the page that announced the arrival of the Japanese military mission, he noted down the names of the officers involved. He looked up to find Magda studying him intently. 'Do you have anything?'

She shook her head. 'I've been though every edition twice and the only thing I can find for January and February is a visit from a low-level US trade delegation.'

'Nothing else?' Jamie frowned.

'Do you have anything particular in mind?'

'There's something missing. Can you look again, but take it as far as April?'

'What am I looking for?' she persisted.

'The Anti-Comintern Pact with Japan was about

turning back the tide of Communism. Communism meant Stalin.' He picked up the 1936 volume and took it across to her table, opening it at the picture of Mushakoji and von Ribbentrop. 'It was a diplomatic initiative that would have generated a diplomatic response. Japan and Germany signed the pact in November, but they would have been negotiating the detail for months in advance, that's why we have a military mission in Berlin in October. It's a sure bet the GRU – the Soviet intelligence directorate – would have been keeping Stalin informed. Despite their mutual distrust, relations between the Soviet Union and Nazi Germany were very polite and formal. The *Wehrmacht* and Luftwaffe had only closed their secret Russian training schools three years earlier. Once the treaty had been signed – forming an alliance that threatened him with a possible war on two fronts – the first thing Stalin would have done was send some kind of mission to Hitler to protest and assure him that the Comintern was no threat to Germany.'

Magda frowned before returning to her volume. 'Is it possible Mushakoji was presented with the head?'

'I'd been wondering that,' Jamie admitted. 'My instinct says not. It would be a poor offering for someone who'd just signed such a momentous document. Besides, he'd been in Germany for years, so he'd had plenty of time to visit the local museums.'

Twenty minutes later Uli reappeared at the door. Magda glanced at Jamie and shook her head. *Nothing.*

'Have you been successful?' the blond girl asked.

'We have one or two leads.' Jamie pulled on his jacket

and put the notebook in the pocket. 'But apart from that it's been very helpful in adding some context to my research.'

They thanked her and left the building, walking un-hurriedly in the direction of Friedrichstrasse. Jamie pondered what they'd learned and hadn't learned and where the next move would take him.

'Where does that leave us?' Magda's question cut across his thoughts.

'Trying to track down your Americans and my Japanese.'

'You can do that?'

'I think my client can.'

'And then?'

He shrugged. 'Find the head . . . or not.'

She stopped and faced him. 'How will you know it's the right head and not some clever fake?'

It seemed a silly question and Jamie smiled. 'There can't be that many shrunken heads on people's mantel-pieces.'

But she was deadly serious. 'You'd be surprised,' she said coolly. 'Melanesia is my territory, Jamie. I've seen more shrunken heads than you've seen Rembrandts. To a layman, the picture you showed me looks like a dozen others. I've been offered an exact replica carved from a coconut with hair woven from a dog's tail.'

'All right,' he capitulated. 'So I'm not an expert. What are you saying?'

'That I can help you. That it doesn't have to end here. One of the places my father served in was Tokyo. I speak a little Japanese, which might be helpful. In any case, I've been to Bougainville. It's my territory.'

Jamie shook his head and laughed. 'Even if I find the head, I'm not going anywhere near Bougainville. They have snakes there.' He turned to walk away, but she persisted and the tilt of her head said she wouldn't move until she had a decision. 'All right,' he raised his hands in surrender, 'I'll think about it, but the final decision will be up to my client.'

'Good.' She reached into her handbag, pulled out a business card and placed it in his hand. 'Call me.' As he watched her walk away, the confusion he felt was compounded by an odd feeling of loss.

XII

London, November 1942

The tall, distinguished-looking man in the naval commander's uniform marched through the parquet-floor corridors as if he owned them. His habit of working late into the night had long endeared him to his peers, particularly the man who was now his ultimate superior and who exhibited the same trait. Of course, it helped that they were old chums of the same class and with the same connections. It made people wary of challenging him, but things had changed recently, and even in his uniquely privileged position he understood his situation was quite precarious.

After three years of war, the resilience of his countrymen astonished him. He'd hoped for an early accommodation with the Nazis and a swift return to peace once the folly of incurring the wrath of Adolf Hitler became clear. Instead, Britons shrugged off defeat at Dunkirk and the horrors of the Blitz with the same equanimity they'd accept a setback for their local football team. They'd dug in, drawn breath and now they were fighting back. In North Africa, Rommel had just suffered a decisive defeat at some dusty railway halt called El Alamein and an Allied invasion force had landed at Oran in Algeria. Only last week the Russians had launched a counter-offensive on the Volga front to encircle German forces at Stalingrad. The conflict was at a tipping point. In the Far East, in a war he'd done everything in his power to stop, there was stalemate on Guadalcanal, but a sense that the mighty American industrial machine had only just begun to flex its muscles . . . exactly as he'd predicted.

It had started with a chance meeting, a shared interest – in this case aviation, in which he was regarded as something of an expert – which developed into an unlikely friendship and an admiration for a culture that had so much more depth, and, yes, more integrity than his own. He'd barely noticed as a few shared personal confidences – *keep it under your hat, old boy, but so and so is . . .* – developed into something more. Eventually, it had blossomed into a relationship that, on his part, was designed to ensure peace between the two countries closest to his heart.

And so it might have stayed if it hadn't been for his gambling debts. A chap had to accept help where it was offered, particularly when it was help from an old chum. It came as rather a surprise when it emerged such generosity might have a price.

Minor commercial information from his own department had been enough at the start, but somehow they'd always wanted more. He'd wriggled, of course, when he realized what was happening, but once one accepted the reality of one's situation it was so much easier. His greatest coup had been a decade earlier when he had supplied his – yes, let us be frank – his employers with the plans of a top-secret float plane in the earliest stages of its development. If he thought about it at all, it was with pride that he'd helped to shape a nation's military future. When that future came to pass at a terrible cost to his own country and others he'd watched with neither guilt nor shame.

Finally, he reached the office he was looking for. He pulled out a bunch of keys secretly put together over the years, which allowed him access to every room of any importance in the building.

They'd posted guards in the main corridors of the upper floors soon after the fighting began in 1939. In contrast, security in the basement levels was more or less nonexistent, especially here where the scrap paper from the typing pools was stored before burning. He slipped into the room and locked the door behind him. It was amazing what you could find when you knew where to look. Once the war started, technical details were much harder to come by and he'd thought his usefulness might be at an end. It turned out his masters were even more interested in the thoughts of those in power, and the political undercurrents that dictated their strategy, particularly those involving the great ally.

He stopped and listened again, ears tuned to any potential danger. Fortunately, the sacks of paper were stacked methodically in their usual places. He went directly to the one that would contain draft copies of the minutes of high-level government meetings. It was sealed, of course, but he'd managed to take a wax copy and a contact had helpfully run him off duplicates. It was the work of seconds to unclip it and untie the string at the neck of the sack. Finding the kind of information he sought took longer, but he willed himself to stay calm. Experience had taught him to identify documents of interest among the piles of turgid dross about potato quotas and provision for the return of evacuees. He found a partial minute of a War Cabinet meeting about the dispatch of African troops to the Burma front, which would be of interest, and pushed it into the buff file he carried on these expeditions. One more. Just one more and he would leave. He leafed through the sheaves of paper, skim-reading the first line and discarding them one by one. And froze.

'TO BE STAMPED TOP SECRET'.

'. . . Source X . . .'

Who was Source X? His hands shook as he realized the implications of what he was reading. He was finished. Source X was in Tokyo, but this information had been corroborated *by other means*. Every word he read increased his certainty. *Other means* meant intercepts, and if they were reading intercepts that meant they'd broken the code. They *knew*, or if they didn't know they would know soon. His first instinct was to thrust the paper back into the sack, seal it and walk out, never to return. Still, he hesitated. A little voice reminded him that the information it contained, allied to the knowledge that his employers' codes had been broken, was priceless. It might even change the course of the entire war. More importantly, it would buy his freedom. He scanned the paper again, marvelling at the utter ruthlessness of what he was reading. Could his old friend have really been so callous? But there it was in the final two words. NO ACTION.

He hurriedly placed the page in the file and resealed the sack, replacing it exactly in its original position. After waiting with his ear to the door for a few moments to ensure the passage was empty, he walked swiftly back through the warren of corridors and tunnels, then up two flights of stairs to his own office in the Admiralty. He was sweating profusely as he pushed the file into a leather briefcase and donned his dark blue overcoat. Taking a deep breath to steady himself, he switched off the light and walked smartly down the stairs to the front door, passing the familiar pictures of long-dead admirals and watery battle scenes clouded by gunpowder smoke.

When he reached the entrance hall he could feel the eyes of the chief petty officer at the front desk on him. Normally the old sailor would have wished him a friendly goodnight, but tonight there was something different about him. The tall man's steps faltered, but somehow he recovered. Two Royal Navy guards stood, one to each side of the porticoed steps, their rifles at the port. All it would take was one word and a search of the briefcase and he'd end up in the tower. He could already feel the rope tightening around his neck.

'Excuse me, sir?'

His guts turned to ice. Christ, he'd lived this moment a thousand times, waking and dreaming, and now it had come. Very slowly he turned to face his accuser.

'Don't want to be going out on a night like this without an umbrella, sir.'

He blinked. Yes, it was raining. Pouring, in fact. 'Of course.' He managed a rictus of a smile, accepting the black brolly the man thrust in his hand.

'Goodnight, your lordship.'

'Goodnight, Stevens.'

He emerged past the guards and raised the umbrella in the shelter of the portico before walking into the rain. As he walked up Whitehall he was filled with a strange mix of exhilaration and terror. In his briefcase he had the greatest secret of the Second World War. It would buy him his freedom and dictate the fate of thousands, but it also contained his doom. It was only a matter of time.

XIII

'The officer in charge of the mission in 'thirty-six was a Major Kojima Yoshitaki, of the Imperial Japanese Army,' Jamie said into the phone. 'According to the article, he attended a joint Luftwaffe–*Wehrmacht* exercise while he was in Germany, but if I was laying odds I'd say the real reason he was in Berlin was the Anti-Comintern Pact. He was accompanied by a couple of lieutenants, but if the Nazi foreign ministry was handing out gifts, he was the man receiving them.'

'What about the Americans you mentioned,' Keith Devlin demanded.

Jamie flicked through his notebook for the names Magda had provided. 'Richard Parker and Hal Roberts the Third, two US State department officials who were given the grand tour by Goebbels' propaganda ministry. The report in the *Berliner Morgenpost* mentioned museum visits, which makes it interesting.'

'Agreed,' the Australian growled. Jamie could imagine him looking out of the office across to Sydney Harbour like Zeus surveying the mortal world from

Mount Olympus, aware of, but not part of the world below. 'Something's bothering you?'

Jamie blinked. Was the man bloody psychic? 'Two things, actually.' He mentioned his theory about a Soviet mission in the wake of the Japanese–Nazi alliance.

'I have a few friends who may be able to help out with that. Leave it with me. The other thing?'

'America. Japan. Possibly Russia. Unless I'm mistaken, Mr Devlin, you have people in all those countries who are much better placed than I am to move this search on. They'll know their patch; they'll have contacts in all the right places.' He waited for a reaction, but all he could hear was soft breathing at the other end of the line. 'What I'm saying is that we know the Bougainville head was still in circulation in nineteen thirty-six and if it still exists it's likely to be in one of those countries. Maybe this is where my part in this ends?'

'I hear what you're saying, Jamie son, and I can understand your point of view. You're keen to get back to those lovely girls of yours. I've no problem with that at all. But maybe I'm in a better position to see things than you are.' Devlin paused as he considered his next words. 'You see, it's not just your talents I need, son. It's your instincts and that thing that keeps you going when other men would have stopped long ago. The thing that helped you track down the Raphael and in all those other little mysterious shindigs I'm not supposed to know about. Yes, we have proof the head was still around in 'thirty-six, but even if we track it down to one of these people, what are the chances they still have it after sixty-odd years? No, you stick with it. I'll get back to you on the Soviets and the Yanks, after that it's up to you. Just let me know what you need and you'll have it by return.'

Jamie considered telling Devlin his room had been searched, but some instinct decided him against it. 'All right,' he said finally. 'I'll wait for word. There is one other thing. I've had an offer of help. A professor at the museum who's an expert on the Melanesian islands. They say there's a possibility of confusion in identifying the head.' He shrugged. 'Apparently they all look much the same if you're not a specialist and they're known to have been faked in the past.'

'I can understand that,' the Australian agreed. 'We need to be certain of the goods. What's he offering?'

'Er, he's a she, and she's offering to come along to provide support and expert advice. She also speaks Japanese, which could come in handy if we end up going down that road.'

Now it was Keith Devlin's turn to let the silence drag. 'Well, mate, I reckon the final decision has to be up to you. I don't have a problem with anything that makes it more likely we succeed and I won't mention it to the lovely Fiona if you won't.'

'It's not that—'

'Only kidding, son.' Devlin chuckled. 'What's she asking, this . . . expert?'

Jamie managed to curb an urgent need to tell his client to stick his didgeridoo where the sun doesn't shine. 'Nothing yet, but she seems very keen to help out.'

'Maybe in that case it's better that you have her close,

so you can keep an eye on her. Ask her how much she wants per diem, plus a bonus if she verifies the head as the genuine article, then offer her half and we'll see how keen she really is.'

'Of course, Magda, that will be perfectly acceptable, and obviously my client will make a donation to the museum to compensate for your absence. I'll be in touch once he gets back to me with the details.'

A gentleman doesn't haggle with a lady and anyway it was Keith Devlin's money. In all honesty, Jamie had to admit he'd never been comfortable with the haggling side of things, which was a bit of a drawback in the art business. It might even have been one of the symptoms of Saintclair Fine Arts' glacial cash flow before the lovely people at the Princess Czartoryski Foundation had come up with their Raphael finder's fee. The thought of all that money now languishing in his bank account just waiting to be splashed out on obscure but interesting works, that might, or more likely might not, be worthy of the investment gave him the warm glow of a gambling addict standing at the entrance to a casino with a hatful of chips. The mood only lasted until he finally listened to the little voice from his left shoulder demanding to know what the hell he thought he was doing. *Well, actually, little voice, I'm doing what Jamie Saintclair always does, I'm flying by the seat of my pants.* So what if the little voice pointed out that flying by the seat of his pants had almost got him killed several times in the past?

One part of him worried that, subconsciously, he

wanted Magda Ross along for reasons that were less than altruistic. Yet it was more than that. Some instinct told him his meeting with Dr Ross, Melanesian expert and authority on shrunken heads, was no accident. The same instinct said she had a part to play somewhere down the road. In any case, she'd made it clear she didn't get in the way of other people's relationships. Fiona's face swam into his head and he swore this would be a professional partnership and nothing more. So why did the image of the gambler return, except this time he was down to his last chip and red was calling him like a siren to a shipwrecked sailor?

Devlin called back the next morning. 'The US angle is a dead end, and unfortunately for those two diplomats I mean that literally. Seems they hung about in Germany for an extended vacation and eventually stopped off in Frankfurt, where Parker had relatives.'

'That doesn't sound as if it would be fatal.'

'No, but they made a fatal decision when they chose their method of transport to go home. Does Frankfurt, May 'thirty-seven ring any bells with you?'

'I don't think so.'

'The Hindenburg?'

'Ah. So if they took the head back with them it's gone.'

'That's right. Which leaves us with the Japanese dele- gation . . .'

'You're not going to tell me Major Kojima Yoshitaki lived in Hiroshima?'

'That's quite a sense of humour you have there, Saintclair,' Devlin said after a dangerous pause.

'All part of my lovable personality, Keith.'

'Yoshitaki's dead,' Devlin continued, 'but his family still has property in Tokyo. I suggest that's your next port of call. The Japs are very particular about family heirlooms, so if the major took a liking to the chief's head, there's a good chance they'll still have it.'

Not if they have any taste. 'Won't that make it more difficult to get it away from them?'

Devlin laughed. 'With your charm and my cheque-book they don't stand a chance, mate.' Behind the faux joviality, Jamie suspected, lay the unspoken assurance he'd discovered in several powerful men. If, by any chance, the Yoshitaki family resisted the combination of charm and chequebook, Keith Devlin would do whatever it took to get his hands on the Bougainville head.

'There's an Etihad flight from Tegel to Tokyo tomorrow night,' he told the Australian. 'Can you get your people to book two seats on it? Any class will do as long as they're together.'

'You'll be on it. I'll also have my PA find you a good hotel. One room or two?'

'I think you know the answer to that perfectly well, Mr Devlin.'

'Don't be so touchy, son. Two rooms it is. The Hyatt's as good as any in central Tokyo if you don't mind the waiters looking down on you, and local middle management and their hookers.'

'You haven't mentioned the Soviets.'

'There's nothing yet. If a Russian delegation met Hitler in the spring of 'thirty-seven, it was sent in secret.

119

It's what you'd expect from Stalin,' Devlin chuckled admiringly, 'he was a bloke who liked to keep his cards close to his chest. Finding out will take a little longer than I expected, but if it happened we'll know about it in the next couple of days.'

Jamie thanked him and rang off. He called Magda Ross's cell number. 'We're going to Tokyo,' he said. 'The flight leaves from Tegel tomorrow at six p.m., so if it's convenient I'll pick you up around three.'

'Sounds great,' she said cheerfully. 'It will be good to visit Japan again, especially if someone else is picking up the bill. I lived there for two years when I was four-teen, but I haven't been back since.'

Next morning Jamie rose just after five and fifteen minutes later he was outside the hotel in shorts, T-shirt and trainers. He'd done some research the previous day and discovered a patchwork of walkways by the Spree that would make a good run. If his suspicions about being watched were correct, a phone was ringing some-where and someone was frantically throwing on some clothes. He waited, doing some stretches in the street, glad that at this ungodly hour there was no one to see him. Sure enough, after a few minutes a car appeared round a corner to his left and drew to a halt a hundred paces away. He smiled.

He'd chosen his route quite deliberately. First through the park opposite the hotel and past an impressive statue of two grim-faced, bearded men that he belatedly realized were Karl Marx and his brother in arms, Frederick Engel. He'd known Berliners were forgiving, but personally he'd have been tempted to melt the

120

fathers of modern Communism down and strike a posthumous medal for the hundreds of men and women who'd perished in the death strip of the Wall trying to flee the ideology they created.

He kept his speed to a gentle jog as he crossed the paved plaza at the centre of the park, knowing that the driver of the car was already facing a dilemma. If he followed on foot he'd stick out like a rose on a dung-heap. If he followed in the car he risked losing Jamie down a one-way street or on one of the narrow alley-ways that Berlin was provided with in such abundance. What happened next would be revealing. If Jamie's pursuer was an employee of a major security organ-ization he'd be able to call up further resources: more cars, perhaps another jogger. If he was on his own? Well, that told its own story. Once through the park he crossed a wide road, still keeping a steady pace. The car reappeared at the periphery of his vision and he turned right towards the Spree, giving his watcher a chance to get as close as he liked. Just as he reached the bridge he darted left down a set of concrete stairs that brought him to the riverside path. Now the driver of the car, if he was alone, as Jamie hoped, didn't have any choice in the matter, as the screech of brakes a few moments later confirmed. The smile turned to a grin and he picked up the pace just a little. It looked like being a good day.

When he returned from his run, Jamie breakfasted at the hotel, studying street maps of central Tokyo on his laptop. Then he set out to enjoy the sights of Berlin. He'd arranged a late checkout and Max picked him up at just before three. As they drove out to the address

Magda had given him, Jamie noticed the limo driver's eyes on him in the rear-view mirror.

'How's your day been, Max?'

'Pretty busy, Herr Saintclair – early start.' He stifled a yawn. 'Maybe I'm not as young as I used to be, huh?'

'You should try to get a little more exercise. A man your age can't afford to take any chances.' He noticed the eyes narrow in a pained grimace and he sat back with a feeling of contentment: after his hours of jogging first thing, he'd managed to fit in a flurry of museum visiting and a trip to the top of the Fernsehturm TV tower using the stairs – all 926 of them. The tower had been a late addition to the sightseeing schedule. He hoped Devlin had paid Max well for spying on him.

Magda Ross emerged from her apartment block dressed in loose-fitting trousers and a long black coat. Her wheeled suitcase was of modest proportions and confirmed Jamie's opinion of her: confident, organized and self-reliant. He suspected she'd always have a bag ready with a toothbrush, a passport and a spare change of clothes. His own packing preference tended to be more the 'Oh Christ I'm late, throw in the first things to hand and then find the passport's out of date' variety. He got out of the limousine to greet her with a kiss on the cheek as Max took her luggage and put it in the trunk of the big Mercedes S-Class.

She looked over the car with approval before she slipped into the rear seats. 'You certainly travel in style, Jamie Saintclair,' she said with a smile. 'If I'd known I would have put my rates up.'

'This is Max,' he introduced the driver. 'He may not look it, but he's a keep-fit fanatic.'

Max muttered something under his breath and put the car in gear, but he acknowledged Magda's 'Hello Max' with what passed for a smile.

'So, Tokyo.' Her eyes gleamed. 'What happens when we get there?'

'Well, if my plan comes to fruition, we visit Major Yoshitaki's relatives, you identify the head, my client wires a substantial cheque and we spend the rest of our visit wandering around and eating the finest sushi on the planet.'

'Be serious for once, Jamie.'

'All right. If I'm honest, there are a few flaws in my plan.'

'Such as?'

'Such as: a) we have no idea whether Yoshitaki ever had the head; b) if he did, we have no idea whether he passed it on to his family on his death, and c) if they do have it, we have no idea if the family will part with this precious, if rather unsavoury, heirloom even for the kind of cash my client is prepared to pay. The Japanese have an odd sense of honour, just ask anyone who was their prisoner during the war. There are a few more potential flies in the ointment, but those—'

He broke off as the phone chirped in his inside pocket. He studied the number and his first thought was that Keith Devlin didn't get much sleep: it had to be past midnight in Sydney. 'Saintclair.'

'I hope you're not on the plane, old son,' Devlin's

gravelly tones were unmistakable, 'because there's been a change of plan.'

'We're just on the way to the airport. I—'

'Just tell the driver to turn round and get you to Schönefeld . . .'

'Hold on.' Jamie relayed the instruction to Max, and the driver nodded. Magda Ross witnessed the exchange with a look of alarm. 'Okay, give me the details.'

'There's a flight to Moscow leaving in under an hour,' Devlin continued, 'but the security people won't close the gate till you get there. Someone will be waiting at the Aeroflot baggage desk with your tickets.' Jamie almost lost the phone as Max performed a tyre-squealing U-turn at the next intersection. 'The Russkis don't run to First Class, but there'll be something to wet your whistle when you get on board.'

'So the mission . . . ?'

'That's right, top secret, direct from Stalin to Hitler on Christmas Eve nineteen thirty-six. We don't have the details yet, but we're working on it. One of my blokes will have a file waiting for you when you get to Sheremetyevo. I'll let you know if I hear any more before your scheduled take-off time. Happy hunting, old son.'

The phone went dead and Jamie took it away from his ear and studied it as if it was some strange artefact from the future.

'Is there a problem?' Magda's voice mirrored his own bemusement.

He turned to her with a wry smile. 'I'm afraid sushi's off the menu. I hope you like *borscht*.'

XIV

A serious, bespectacled young Englishman from the Devlin Foundation introduced himself as Daniel and eased their way through customs at Moscow's Sheremetyevo airport. Once they'd collected their baggage and been shown to the customary black limousine he handed Jamie a slim file.

'It's not much, I'm afraid,' he apologized, poking his head through the gap in the front seats from his place beside the driver, a fit-looking older man with a tan that suggested he spent as much time under a sun lamp as he did behind the wheel. 'We weren't given a great deal of warning and, truth be told, our Russian friends are still a bit coy about their relationship with the Nazis before the Second World War. At the same time they were flexing their muscles against each other in Spain, Stalin and Hitler conducted what was more or less a mutual admiration society, which doesn't sit very well with the mythology of the Great Patriotic War. They'd prefer not to talk about the Molotov–Ribbentrop Pact or the deal to partition Poland.'

He paused in his briefing and Jamie skimmed through the contents of the file while Magda fidgeted impatiently beside him. When he had all the details fixed in his mind, Jamie nodded for Daniel to continue.

'You also have to understand that this was at a time of enormous suspicion and fear. Even though Stalin's Great Purge had just got started and would only have been the subject of whispers, the men selected for what on the surface was a hugely important mission would have been well aware of the danger. The slightest hint of mistrust and it would be the gulags at best or more likely a bullet in the back of the neck in the basement of the Lubyanka. Any official reports would have been very guarded,' he ended apologetically.

'The mission consisted of two diplomats and a couple of low-ranking clerks who are likely to have been NKVD minders,' Jamie read aloud for Magda's benefit. 'They flew from Moscow to Berlin by way of Konigsberg in December nineteen thirty-six after a personal briefing from Stalin, and held talks over a two-week period.' He grunted in surprise. 'It says here they met Hitler and von Ribbentrop in the Reich Chancellery. No official record of that meeting survives.'

'That's correct,' Daniel confirmed. 'The Moscow versions were probably destroyed around the time of Stalin's death in nineteen fifty-three, possibly the Berlin ones, too, if they didn't burn in 'forty-five.'

'But who were these men?' Magda demanded impatiently. 'And what happened to them when they came back. Surely they must be long dead now?' She saw the look that passed between Jamie and Daniel and her dark eyes widened a little. 'Surely?'

'Gennady Berzarin,' Jamie continued, 'first secretary in the Department of Foreign Affairs under Maxim Litvinov, headed the mission, accompanied by his second secretary, twenty-five-year-old Dimitri Kaganovich. Berzarin survived the war, but died in Krasnoyarsk, Siberia, in nineteen eighty. Kaganovich,' he tried and failed to suppress a grin, 'according to this, is still alive.'

The hotel, as with all things associated with Keith Devlin, was impressive – a broad, glass-fronted palace in the shape of the bridge of an ocean liner – and Magda was duly impressed. As she studied the sumptuous lobby, Daniel whispered to Jamie. 'This is probably the best hotel in Moscow, the one Mr Devlin usually stays in. We've booked you into his suite. It should be very convenient for you.' Jamie studied the owlish face for any hint of innuendo, but found no trace. Evidently, the young executive didn't think much of his chances with Magda Ross. On a certain level, Jamie found that downright insulting.

A concierge took their luggage and Daniel escorted them to the check-in desk. When they'd completed the formalities, Magda thanked the young man with a smile. 'I hadn't expected this kind of luxury. When I'm on a research trip the choice is usually between a cockroach-infested hostel and a damp tent. The tent is normally much more comfortable, and decidedly cleaner.'

Daniel watched them as far as the lifts before he headed back to the car. 'Was that okay, Mr Stewart?' he asked tentatively as he took his seat beside the driver.

'You did great, son,' Doug Stewart assured him. 'From now on we'll leave it to our usual people. Make sure they report direct to me,' he yawned, 'but not for a couple of hours. I'm getting on a bit for this globe-trotting lark. I'm off for a quick bit of shut-eye.'

The presidential suite at the Lotte Hotel seemed to stretch for miles in every direction and made Jamie's rooms in Berlin look like a mountain shack. The concierge ushered them into the palatial living room with a view across the western Moscow skyline. He offered to have their cases unpacked and their clothes stored away, but they declined.

'I'm not sure I would like them comparing my poor rags with those of the kind of royalty who normally use this place.' Magda smiled after the Russian had given them the obligatory tour, including the suite's private bar and kitchen, marble bathroom fit for the Queen of Sheba, and explained the intricacies of the digital control panel: 'with one switch you can work the lights, air conditioning, heating, curtains, TV and audio. It will give you today's weather forecast and whatever tourist information you need, oh,' he said almost as an afterthought as he reached the door, 'and you can use it to set the alarm clock.'

Jamie returned Magda's smile. 'I suspect, like hotel staff the world over, they've seen just about everything there is to see, unless you have something very exotic in there?'

Magda's 'room' turned out to be a self-contained

suite of its own, but she vowed to use the facilities in the palatial main suite instead of, as she put it, 'slumming'.

'I'll make a coffee,' Jamie offered, and set off for the kitchen.

'Don't we have someone to do that for us?' she demanded, and they both burst out laughing.

When he returned, Magda walked to the window with her coffee and stared out. Jamie saw a troubled look cross her face.

'Is something wrong?'

Her lips formed a sad half smile. 'My dad spent years living in big houses and mixing with rich people, but he was always a socialist at heart. I thought I took after him, but there's something seductive about sitting here in all this luxury, set apart from the *ordinary* people down there living their *ordinary* lives. Of course, it is only an illusion, a dream, like Cinderella in the story. When the clock strikes midnight I'll be sitting on a pumpkin, the concierge will turn into an old farm horse and I won't even have a glass slipper to show for it.' She slipped away from the window and sat beside him, so close her eyes seemed to swallow him up. 'But what about you, Jamie?'

The question and her proximity unsettled him. His first instinct was to hide behind a flippant, throwaway reply, but he decided she deserved better.

'When this is all over I'll go back to my partner and her daughter and we'll spend an idyllic couple of weeks on my client's private island. Then I'll give up being a knight in shining armour for good and turn into a boring art dealer again.'

He thought he saw a shadow cross the dark eyes, but it was gone before he could decide what it was. 'Your client must be someone very special?'

Again, there was more to the question than the words implied, and Jamie gave it some thought before he replied. Till now, as far as Magda Ross had been concerned, the client was just 'the client', but it had always seemed a rather pointless subterfuge. Anyone who really wanted to know who Jamie was working for only had to get a look at the flight and hotel bills. That trail would presumably take them directly to Devlin Metal Resources, the Devlin Foundation, or one or other of their many spin-offs. Magda was on the team, she deserved to know who was paying her wages.

'He's probably someone you've never heard of,' he said eventually. 'An Australian mine owner by the name of Keith Devlin?' She shook her head. 'He has interests all over the world, including the Solomons, but his negotiations have run into trouble because of some stolen documents and the intransigence of the local chief. The Bougainville head is the price of the chief's cooperation. I suspect it's worth a very substantial amount to Mr Devlin, given the money he's paid out so far to fund the search for it.'

'First Class all the way and no expense spared for the intrepid Jamie Saintclair, and his ever-so-fortunate assistant?'

'That's the way it looks.'

'So what happens tomorrow?'

He'd been thinking it over, but had avoided bringing up the subject because he suspected his decision would sound patronizing. He had a feeling Magda Ross was a woman you patronized at your peril.

'According to Daniel, Dimitri Kaganovich lives in an old people's home in one of the workers' housing projects just inside the outer ring road. He must be close to a hundred years old now. I think, in the first instance, I should visit him alone . . . sound him out. Apparently, he suffered a great deal under the old Communist regime. It's likely to be quite a long, possibly a difficult conversation, entirely in Russian, so you'd probably be bored and—'

'Jamie,' Magda laughed, 'all you had to say is it would be more sensible for me not to come along. I'm not going to be much use to you if I don't speak the language. Besides, I have better things to do.'

'You do?'

'Of course.' She grinned. 'I'm in one of the world's great cities. I'll go shopping. I packed for Japan, remember, and it's a lot colder in Moscow. If we're here for a few days I'll buy something a little warmer. If you let me know your size, maybe I could get you a jacket?'

'That would be great.' Jamie cursed himself for sounding like a gushing schoolboy. 'Naturally, Mr Devlin will be paying, so don't hold back.'

'Naturally.' Her lips twitched. 'And I wasn't going to. Now,' she got to her feet, and he rose with her, 'I have to go to bed.' She kissed him on the cheek and though it was only the faintest touch of her lips he felt as if he'd been branded. He watched the door close behind her, sighed and picked up his mobile phone. If it was bedtime in Moscow what time did that make it in Australia?

*

It took less than an hour by taxi to get from the Lotte Hotel to Kapotnya, but by the time the driver turned off the MKAD, Moscow's outer ring road, Jamie was convinced he'd been transported to another planet – one made entirely of concrete and steel. For the last third of the journey the highway was sandwiched between huge factory complexes, steel foundries, cement works and petrochemical plants. Daniel had described Kapotnya as a workers' housing project from the Fifties. What he hadn't mentioned was the air of defeat and destitution, or the sprawling oil refinery – all belching chimneys, giant tanks and gas flares – that squeezed the enclave against the bank of the Moskva as if it were a medieval army bent on pushing the squat, rust-stained housing blocks into the river. Low, leaden clouds leaking a thin, sulphurous drizzle helped turn the scene into the back-drop of some gloomy post-apocalyptic disaster movie; a Philip K. Dick adaption, only without the belly laughs. Jamie began to understand the look the taxi driver had given him when he'd mentioned the address: a cross between disbelief and pity. Another turn took them into a tree-lined avenue flanked by two of the giant apartment blocks, a concrete chasm with a tarmac floor. Normally, Jamie associated trees with freedom, the open countryside, or even little London parks that gave you the illusion of being out in the fresh air when your lungs were being clogged with petrol fumes. These trees felt like prisoners, just like the dusky-skinned teenagers who sheltered from the rain beneath them. The separate groups had been eyeing each other dangerously until

132

the white Mercedes caught everyone's attention. He heard the driver curse beneath his breath and he had the feeling the man was a second away from refusing to go any further, but a quick check of the satnav showed the destination to be so close as not to make any difference. Another turn and another concrete canyon. Halfway along, a path led to the entrance of the block on the right and the car slowed to a halt.

'This is it.' The driver sniffed. Jamie studied the doorway. There was a sign beside it, but it didn't look like any old people's home he'd ever seen.

'You're sure?'

The man shrugged, what difference did it make to him?

'You'll wait for me?' Jamie asked, more in hope than expectation. A half grunt, half laugh that meant 'Are you fucking kidding me?' confirmed his theory and he counted the agreed fare into the outstretched hand. The car was in gear almost before he managed to close the door.

Conscious of the predatory eyes of the teenagers sheltering under the trees, and a group of older men he hadn't noticed earlier who sat smoking and playing cards, Jamie hurried up the path and through the doorway. The block caretaker's office had been converted into a reception area. It was empty and after a brief hesitation he walked past it and through a double door that led to a long corridor. The stench of excrement, stale urine, unwashed body and the bitter tang of fresh vomit hit him like a slap in the face. On either side of the passage the original ground-floor apartments had been converted into wards. Their doors lay open, revealing dank, gloomy rooms illuminated only by the light filtering through ragged curtains and what seeped in from the dimly lit corridor. In the first room, each of the six beds was occupied by a grey-faced male in pyjamas or a dressing gown. The men lay on filthy blankets stained with weeks or months of anonymous bodily fluids, their heads back and mouths open, breath wheezing in their chests or rattling in their throats. Eyes flickered and bony hands twitched as if they were in the grip of some terrible living nightmare. A sound alerted him and a thin stream of urine dripped from the bottom of one of the beds. He watched it form a small pool before trickling towards the doorway and he stepped back in disgust.

'*Napoi-it*,' a voice as brittle as sea ice whispered. 'Water.' A feeble, blue-veined hand waved from the bed at the back of the room.

Jamie hurried out into the corridor and called for a nurse, but no one answered.

'Water.'

He returned to the room and searched in vain for a tap. A door on the far side opened on to what had once been once a tiny kitchen, with a bed containing another semi-comatose figure taking up most of the space. The only utility remaining of the room's former use was a rust-stained sink filled with unwashed cups. He gingerly picked one up and turned the tap to rinse it, but the only result was a dribble of brown liquid.

'You have to let it run for a while,' a voice from be-hind advised.

He turned to find one of the men from the card game leaning against the doorway.

'One of your patients wanted a drink – I take it you are a nurse?'

'Sure.' The man grinned. 'That will be old Nikolai. He's due his fix. Are you visiting? Only you don't sound as if you're from round here and we don't get many. Visiting time is . . .'

The water finally ran clear and Jamie swirled it round the cup. 'Here,' he said, handing over the cup and displaying a handful of hundred-ruble notes. 'I'm looking for a resident here. A man called Dimitri Kaganovich.'

'Resident?' The man's grin grew broader. 'Sure, Dimitri's still a resident. There's a special place in Hell waiting for Dimitri, but the tough old bastard's determined to keep the Devil waiting. He's like that, Dimitri, never happier than when he's pissing somebody off. I think the Devil may not be in charge for long when Dimitri eventually gets down there, know what I mean?'

'Just tell me where he is.' Jamie tucked the notes into the nurse's top pocket.

'Third door on the right. He'll be the one who's awake, unless he's died. Never takes his meds that one.'

Jamie walked to the door then turned, as if he wanted to imprint the scene on his mind; the concrete floor, with its recent history mapped out in stains of brown and yellow; the filthy, rusting ex hospital beds carrying their cargoes of chemically comatose living dead to a destination most of them probably longed for. 'Maybe Dimitri has decided he's already in Hell. Don't you ever clean this place?'

'Why?' The nurse seemed genuinely surprised. 'They just dirty it again. What's your worry? Nobody cares about these people. Only Mikhail.'

As he walked out and along the corridor Jamie heard a soft scuffle. 'Come on, Nikolai, time for your pill.'

'No, please . . .'

XV

The third room on the right showed even fewer signs of life than the previous one and put Jamie in mind of an impromptu morgue. It took a moment before he sensed chests rising and falling in the heavy, stinking darkness and made out the figures of sleeping men. He waited, seeking some sound or movement that would identify the man he was looking for – *He'll be the one who's awake* – but heard nothing but the faint hiss of laboured breathing.

'Dimitri? Dimitri Kaganovich.' The whisper cut through the doom-laden silence like a buzz saw. At first it evoked no reaction, but soon Jamie felt a chill run through him. In a single instant something had changed. Something indefinable, then not. Previously the atmosphere in the room had been oppressive, now it contained a definite hint of danger. His eyes sought out the source, drifting across the gloom and finding nothing – until he detected the faintest gleam in the far corner to the left of the window, away from any light source. Not one gleam, but two, reflecting the dull glow from the corridor lamp. A pair of eyes, watching him, wary, but not frightened; malevolent, hateful eyes that wished him dead.

'Dimitri?' Jamie pushed carefully through the beds until he was standing at the foot of the one occupied by the watching man. A hollowed-out face showed above the blanket. Skin stretched tight across bones like knife blades, a razor-lipped mouth collapsed over toothless gums, the high dome of the bare scalp etched with an elongated wine-stain. The face of a dead man. Apart from the eyes.

'Six one two five seven four Kaganovich.'

'What?' Jamie barely caught the hoarse growl.

'So you've come at last?' The old man struggled with each word as if it were the verbal equivalent of a blacksmith's anvil, and the sentences that followed were punctuated by the wheezing breaths of an asthmatic. 'About time. I have been waiting for you. I am ninety-eight years old and I've been waiting to die since before you were born. Don't hesitate. Come closer.' The tone changed and it took Jamie a moment to realize the next words were thoughts he wasn't supposed to hear. 'Yes, come closer, you bastard. If this had been twenty years ago, or even ten, I'd have my hands round your neck or my fingers in your eyes. If I still had my teeth, I'd rip your throat out, but you smashed them in with a hammer, didn't you?' A long sniff. 'So take your fucking Tokarev and put the barrel on the back of my neck so I can feel the cold steel. Look, I'll turn my head away to make it easier. One bullet, one corpse, that's the Cheka way. Just the right angle, up and into the skull.'

'I haven't come to kill you.'

In the suspicious silence that followed, Jamie could almost hear the wheels turning in the old man's brain. 'Why not? Am I of so little danger to you now? Not that I ever was, of course, but that didn't matter to you. A denounced man is a dead man, isn't that what you used to say?'

'I'm not the secret police. I only want to talk to you about the old days.'

'You have cigarettes?'

The abrupt change of subject was designed to give the other man time to think, but Jamie was happy to accommodate him. He fumbled in his pockets. Knowing the fondness of elderly Russians for the kind of cigarette that would choke a donkey, he'd bought two packets from the hotel bar. Still, he thought it was worth pointing out the 'no smoking' signs that decorated the walls.

'Pouf,' the old man grunted. 'You think a nail is going to kill me now? Or any of these old fools I share this cell with. If anybody objects I tell them to go and fuck their mother.' Jamie shrugged and handed him one of the thin cardboard tubes and produced a cheap disposable lighter, tucking the lighter and pack beneath his blanket when he'd done. The Russian inhaled with a long, whistling appreciative sigh and the thin lips twisted into a smile.

'What were we talking about?'

'The old days.'

Kaganovich choked on a cough of chesty laughter. 'When you are as old as I am there are many old days. Do you mean the old days when I was young and

139

fought in Manchuria? Or when Stalin himself noted my facility for languages and made me a diplomat and sent me to meet the beast Hitler?'

'Yes, I—'

But Kaganovich wasn't going to be interrupted. The voice became harsher. 'Or when I came back and was denounced by that crooked bastard thief Berzarin? Berzarin, who had me sent to the gulag, ruined my life and destroyed my family. I always vowed that one day I would piss on Berzarin's grave, but it is too late for me now. Maybe I will tell you what you want if you promise to piss on it for me, huh? Is it Dimitri the human mine detector you want to hear about? Or Dimitri the war hero who smashed the *Fascisti* on the Seelow Heights and marched into Berlin. Or perhaps it is Dimitri the traitor to the Motherland who ended up working in the same mines as the *Fascisti* he had been killing, because that cocksucker Stalin remembered his name, may he rot in a thousand hells.'

His strength spent, Dimitri lay back with his eyes closed and the cigarette drooping from his lips, the smoke spiralling up in wispy ribbons to form a cloud below the nicotine-stained ceiling.

Jamie gently removed the cigarette. 'Why don't you tell me about Hitler and Berzarin?'

It must have been five minutes before the old man started speaking.

'I can't remember taking a piss in the morning,' he began in a voice that shook with effort, 'but I remember those days like they were yesterday. It was just after that bastard Hitler had made his backstabbing treaty with the Yipponski, the Japs. Berzarin, who was my chief, called me into his office and told me we were both ordered to the Kremlin. I remember his hands were shaking and the sweat was pouring off him,' the haggard features took on a semblance of a smile at the memory, 'not that I wasn't shitting my pants myself. This was at the start of the Great Purge. There were already plenty of rumours going round about people, loyal people, being pulled in and never being seen again. So you have to imagine us, Berzarin and me, shaking in our shoes as we drive there in one of those fancy new ZiLs—' He was interrupted by a shout from the bed by the door, followed by a string of muttered curses that died away to be replaced by a desperate gasping struggle for breath. Jamie automatically turned to help the other man. 'Do you want to hear my story or not?' Dimitri rasped. 'He'll soon be dead, and good riddance.' Reluctantly Jamie turned his attention back to Kaganovich. 'Good.' The old man nodded. 'We saw Litvinov first. He wasn't a bad fellow for a Jew, but all he told us was that our mission was deadly secret. We must reveal its existence to no one, not even our wives – not that I had one then. The Boss would tell us the rest. So we're feeling a little braver when we go in to see him, knowing we're not going to the Lubyanka after all. He's in a good mood, the Boss, all jovial and friendly. There's been a big mistake, he says, the fucking Yipponski have persuaded the Nazis we're some kind of threat to them. You're going to Berlin to convince Hitler different. Tell him that Stalin is his best friend and that the Soviet Union has no interest in German spheres of interest (which wasn't entirely true, because everyone in the Foreign knew the Boss had his eye on Bessarabia and so did Hitler). We'll share technology and we'll share information for an assurance that the Anti-Comintern Pact has no military dimension.' He smiled at the memory and the ravaged features resembled a crow-pecked skull. 'He has this big deep belly laugh, and he does it now. Hitler doesn't like German Communists, he says, I don't like them either; tell him we don't care how many of them he kills. In fact, we'll give him a list if that's what it takes. Hitler's a pragmatist, he says, he's not going to rock the boat for a bunch of Mongolian by-blows.' There followed a long silence, but Jamie knew better now than to hurry the old man. Sometimes it seemed he was finished, but eventually he would take up the story again, as if he'd only been drawing a long breath.

'Then it's back to Litvinov for the details,' Kaganovich continued. 'More or less what the Boss had said with the rough edges smoothed off. Next day we flew to Berlin in time for Christmas, which, let's face it, even for a party loyalist like me was a fucking sight better than a freezing Moscow apartment with a couple of old farts and a family with four kids.'

His chest started to heave and he was racked by a paroxysm of coughing that shook his whole body, wave after wave until Jamie thought he would surely die. Slowly, it subsided to a dry wheeze and the old man hacked something from his throat and spat it beside the bed.

'Not long now,' he whispered. 'The last doctor these

lousy Chechens brought to examine me said a build-up of fluid is putting a strain on the heart and pressure on the lungs. Next step renal failure. Of course, that's if the black bastard knows what he's talking about.'

'You were talking about meeting Hitler.'

Kaganovich nodded. 'They kept us waiting for a week.' He grunted what might have been a laugh. 'Meetings with clerks and endless visits to their fucking boring museums. Some secret, eh? Everywhere we went they offered us things. Free tickets to the theatre. A Swiss watch. Hampers of food. Jewellery for the wife or girlfriend. Even bits and pieces from the museums if you saw something that took your fancy. I didn't touch a thing, but Berzarin was a man with deep pockets, as they say. Nothing was too small or too large for him. He thought it was Christmas every day. Stupid bastard. Of course, I reported everything to Sergeev, our NKVD minder. What—'

'Do you remember what sort of things Berzarin chose from the museums?'

'I thought you wanted to know about Hitler?'

'Later.'

'Mostly gold, but other small portable stuff.'

'Anything from the South Sea Islands?'

'Who knows, at my age you expect me to remember the details? They sometimes split us up, but you could bet one thing: if it had value Berzarin wouldn't refuse it. He hid his loot in a big chest he thought I didn't know about in our apartment off Wilhelmstrasse. I couldn't figure out how he was going to get it all home until much later.

143

'One day a car drew up outside the apartment, complete with an SS driver and a Hauptsturmführer with a Death's Head badge on his uniform cap. He was square jawed and blond, like you see in the pictures, and he looked at us as if we were shit on his shoe. Berzarin had more clout than me and he didn't like it much, but he knew this was the day, so he kept his fat mouth shut. Well, they took us to the back door of the Reich Chancellery – the old one, where they built Hitler's bunker under the gardens. We were escorted up endless flights of stairs to a big office where a Nazi bigwig called von Neurath was waiting. Berzarin managed to hide his disappointment – we'd been briefed that von Neurath was already on the way out, and Ribbentrop was the man to get results – but he said his piece. He was just finishing when a door opens and this figure dressed in a grey business suit walks in. You want to say that when you first met Adolf Hitler the room went cold, or he gave off an aura of terrible power.' He shook his head. 'Just this ordinary fellow in a suit, with a silly moustache. "You must tell Comrade Stalin that Germany and the Soviet Union will always be friends," he says in this quiet voice, not like the newsreels at all. "The pact is a purely diplomatic instrument, with no military dimension." He made to leave, but turned back for a second. "Tell him I believe we have much in common, he and I." Then he was gone. The Great Dictator? Adolf Hitler was more like a used-car salesman, and just about as honest, huh? So we had what we came for and we went home to Moscow. Only Kaganovich didn't get home.

As soon as we got off the plane they took me to one side and opened my luggage. Surprise, surprise, eh? What do we have here, Comrade Kaganovich? Gold coins. Nazi propaganda. Hashish. "It seems you are a Nazi spy, comrade." I turn to Berzarin and Sergeev for help, but they're looking at me as if they knew all the time, and then Berzarin smiled – a sort of I-told-you-so smile.' He shrugged. 'They walked away and I never saw either of them again. I denied it, of course, but in those days they just beat you and beat you until you admitted anything just to make them stop. A two-minute trial and twenty years' hard labour. Only the war came. I ended up in a punishment battalion where I was expected to atone for my crimes by becoming dead. But Kaganovich fooled them. Kaganovich lived and in time Kaganovich the survivor became Kaganovich the legend, then Kaganovich the hero. Four wounds and you were sent back to a regular unit. When I knocked out three machine guns holding up the regiment's attack on the Seelow Heights, they put me in for the Order of Lenin. Of course, I think that's it, Kaganovich is back, but Stalin had a long memory. They came for me as soon as the war was over and it was back to the gulag for another eight years for my impudence, and then the next thirty spent scraping a living any way I could find without the right papers. Shit jobs every one, and then,' he emitted a harsh cackle, 'just when you don't think life can get any worse, you end up in a fucking place like this.'

'Do you know what happened to Berzarin?'

'I'd like to say someone put the bastard's nuts

through the ringer like they did mine, but Berzarin the betrayer naturally prospered. When I was released from the gulag I looked for him, but all I know is he ended up running some district out east, where no doubt he robbed honest men blind and had his hand stroked by the other crooks. He's dead now, of course, but I find it comforting to think of him spending a few years lying in his own piss like me, before he went.' He closed his eyes. 'Now I'm tired. Unless you have another packet of nails, please fuck off and leave me to die.'

'Thank you for your time, Mr Kaganovich.'

'*Yob tvoyu mat.* Just remember. If you find Berzarin, you will piss on his grave for old Kaganovich.'

XVI

Jamie was so focused on Kaganovich's testimony that the issue of his lack of transport didn't occur to him until he walked through the doors into the open air. He reached into his jacket for his mobile phone, thinking that at least the hotel would send a car. In the meantime he had the choice of standing in the open under the wolfish and no doubt acquisitive eyes of the teenage gangsters he'd seen earlier or returning to the sweet-scented corridors of the care home, neither of which was terribly appealing. It wasn't until he punched in the hotel's number that he realized he was alone in the open space between the flats. Where there had been fifteen or twenty youths and four or five older men under the trees, all that remained were empty beer cans and fast food wrappers blowing in the breeze like tumbleweed.

Was the stillness in the air, or inside him? As he saw it, there were two possibilities. Either they were waiting for him somewhere, alerted by Mikhail who had been so impressed by the fistful of rubles, or something had scared them. And if something had scared the locals, self-preservation suggested that maybe Jamie Saintclair should make himself scarce too. He scanned the area for the threat he was certain was out there and he didn't have to wait for long. A big Mercedes SUV slid round the corner where it had been shielded by the trees and drove slowly towards him. He backed towards the doorway, but the sharp snick of a lock being engaged told him he'd find no sanctuary there. He looked to his left, in the opposite direction to the approaching Mercedes and cursed as a second car emerged from a car park between the blocks of flats.

On one level the big Mercs provided a certain reassurance. Nobody driving a quarter-of-a-million-ruble car was going to cut his throat for the contents of his wallet. On the other hand, in his experience, big cars meant big trouble. Just because they were wearing Moscow number plates didn't guarantee they contained Russians, even if, on balance, it was the most likely probability. That left one of two possibilities.

The first Mercedes drew up in front of him and two men didn't so much step from the car as flow from it; one from the front passenger door and the other from the rear. Hard men in smart suits, confident in their ability to deal with any situation, but alert just the same, the suits cut just so to accommodate the pistol of choice in a neat little holster under the left armpit. They stopped in front of Jamie, one a little to the right, the other to the left, pausing only to glare at the driver of an ancient rust-bucket of a Lada that cruised past.

'Mr Saintclair? You will come with us please.'

The words were in English with a distinct Russian

accent, and they came from behind him. He must be losing it. He hadn't even heard them get out of the other car. The man on his left moved aside and nodded towards the rear door of the Mercedes, but Jamie stood his ground.

'Perhaps you'd care to identify yourselves first. My mother warned me about getting into cars with strange men.'

Just the right tone. Polite, but firm, with a little bit of humour to keep the situation from turning rough. A miscalculation as it turned out. The fist that caught him in the right kidney sent a bolt of lightning into his brain and paralysed him in the same instant. With an ease that said they'd done it a hundred times, the two men in front caught him as he fell, taking an arm each and dragging him towards the car, the toes of his shoes scraping across the concrete. Another man was waiting inside the back of the Mercedes with two pairs of manacles. Before Jamie knew what was happening, his wrists and ankles had been shackled. The manacles were linked by a chain and the man hauled it tight until the prisoner's hands were between his knees and fixed it to a bolt on the floor of the car. Black leather seats, he noticed through the waves of pain that still flowed outwards from his lower back, ever so handy for cleaning up after an accident.

Someone pulled a hood over his head and he felt a moment of claustrophobic panic. It wasn't as if he was in a position to see where he was going, looking at his toecaps as he was, but that wasn't why they'd done it. It was part of the softening-up process. And that was what made it all the more frightening. Softening up for what?

Two options. In Russia that meant the State or the Mafia, which was actually a combination of options each more unpleasant than the one that went before. But the chilling monosyllabic professionalism and, let's face it, relative restraint, told him he was in the hands of the State. And that meant, for the moment at least, there was no point in howling indignation or demanding to see the British consul, even if he'd been foolish enough to risk another kidney punch. The men in dark suits were just low-level functionaries doing a job and it didn't matter to them who he was. Smart hotel or not he was part of the state system now, the same system that had swallowed Dimitri Kaganovich, chewed him up and, unlike several million less fortunate Russians, spat him back out again. OGPU, NKVD, NKGB, KGB were just a series of bland initials if you weren't aware of the brutal reality behind them. Now they had been succeeded by the FSB, the Federal Security Service. For the people who'd lived under the old Soviet Union they were, and always had been the Cheka, the faceless secret police. Even now a knock at the door at the wrong time of the night triggered a moment of terrifying uncertainty.

Just to make sure you got the point, the FSB continued to use the old KGB headquarters complex at Lubyanka Square where tens of thousands of men and women, many of them innocent of any crime, had screamed their guilt to their torturers before walking the long basement corridors anticipating the bullet that would end their lives. To most tourists the Lubyanka meant the big honey-stoned edifice facing the square, but the true functional hub of the FSB was an anonymous grey lump of Stalinist concrete on the north-west side and Jamie guessed that was where he would eventually be taken. He hoped they'd get there soon.

The worst of it was the pain in his wrists and ankles where the metal edges of the manacles rubbed against bone with every turn of the steering wheel. He heard one of the men grunt something about a tail, and he was puzzled until another joked that it would save them a lot of trouble if it followed them all the way home. Eventually the familiar stop-start rhythm of inner-city transportation told him they'd left the ring system. A few minutes later the car descended what felt like a steep ramp and came to a halt, before the squeal of another set of tyres confirmed the arrival of the second Mercedes.

Someone unshackled him from the bolt and the ankle irons were removed, but the hood stayed. Hands that were almost considerate guided him from the car and along a series of corridors, a bewildering maze of lefts and rights, until he heard the sound of a metal door opening. The hands guided him four steps forward and worked at his wrists to remove the cuffs, making him gasp as the circulation began to return. His watch and the contents of his pockets were removed. Another pair of hands lifted the hood from his head and he almost staggered as the light blinded him. It took a few moments for his surroundings to swim into vision: a bare cell, perhaps eight feet by six, the floor and walls of flaking grey concrete. To one side stood a metal bed with a thin mattress and a single sheet. The toilet in the corner and the tiny sink attached to the wall told him he must be in the VIP wing, which was a relief for several reasons. A single bulb in the ceiling provided light, set behind inch-thick glass so you couldn't break the bulb and use the shards to cut your wrists. One of the dark-suited men from the Mercedes stood watching him, beside a stocky figure dressed in black uniform trousers and a white shirt with the sleeves rolled up. The second man gestured to Jamie's jacket.

'I would like to protest at this totally unwarranted arrest and detention,' Jamie said as he removed the coat and handed it over. A finger pointed to the belt of his tan trousers and he repeated the process. 'I am a British citizen and I demand to speak to my country's consul.'

The word 'demand' provoked the faintest shadow of a smile before dark suit led the other man from the cell. A shiver went through Jamie's heart as the door shut with a clang that reverberated along the corridor. He stood for a moment staring at the bare steel with its single spy hole and felt very alone. He removed his shoes and lay down on the bed. The sheet smelled of damp. He'd been in worse fixes, of course. The *Obergruppenführershalle* in Wewelsburg Castle for one, where the Neanderthal foot soldiers of the Vril Society had tried to kick him to death. A certain mansion on the shores of Lake Zurich where a team of East European mercenaries had done their best to incinerate him. But this cell, naked of even the obscene graffiti that livened up such places, had an air of permanence not dissimilar to a marble tomb.

Why? That didn't really matter, he'd find out soon enough. It couldn't be about the Bougainville head, which had no value to anyone but Keith Devlin. He was fairly certain it had nothing to do with Kaganovich – an almost-centenarian former gulag inmate was hardly a threat – and Berzarin was dead, so his reputation didn't require protection. On second thoughts, the past had ways of catching up with Jamie Saintclair. If Berzarin had clout then perhaps Berzarin's offspring had clout too, and were protecting their father's memory. The only other Russian he'd had any contact with had been a late-lamented billionaire oligarch. The fact that he'd already been dead when they met seemed to rule out that particular line of inquiry.

His thoughts turned to Magda Ross. She'd be puzzled when he didn't return in mid-afternoon as he'd intended, but she wouldn't become truly alarmed for a few more hours. He'd left her Daniel's number, so Devlin would find out soon enough. The first places they'd look were hospitals and the morgue, because that's what sometimes happened to tourists in Moscow, especially people silly enough to visit places like Kapotnya. Jamie had a feeling that the Devlin Foundation would have the kind of contacts to be able to track him down eventually. What mattered then was whether Devlin had the influence to get him out. And that depended on why he was here, and probably more pertinently, who'd put him here.

He lay back on the bed and closed his eyes. He'd

always had the facility to put his immediate concerns aside when no amount of thought was going to solve them. In these circumstances the only thing you could do was conserve your energy for the tests to come. Within three minutes he was asleep.

XVII

'Up!' Jamie woke instantly at the combination of the order and the talon-like fingers biting into his shoulder. He rolled off the bed and stood to attention as if he was still enduring the two short weeks at Sandhurst that had put him off the army for life. A big man he hadn't seen before stepped back warily at the sudden movement and the shirtsleeved jailer stood by the door holding a pair of the familiar steel manacles. His eyes drifted to Jamie's feet. 'Put your shoes on.'

Jamie complied and held out his wrists for the manacles, not that cooperating was going to win him any Brownie points judging by the bite of the cuffs. The two men laid hands on his shoulders and guided him out into the corridor, turning left and then left again, to where a set of iron stairs led upwards. Another corridor and a door that opened on to a bare, windowless room with a metal table and two chairs. Table and chairs were fixed to the floor and the men sat Jamie in one chair and chained the cuffs to a bolt in the centre of the table. They left him alone and he tried to calm his racing mind. Something told him that bluster and bluff weren't going to do him any good here. He needed a clear mind, even though his surroundings weren't exactly conducive to rational thinking. No amount of scrubbing had been able to remove the stains of past indiscretions from the table and dark patches on the floor bore witness to the room's unfortunate previous occupants. On the walls, lighter areas in the concrete showed where some equipment had been fixed and then removed. Given the place's history it didn't take a lot of imagination to guess the nature of that equipment. The fact that it was no longer deemed necessary was momentarily comforting, which probably said more about his state of mind than the circumstances.

They kept him waiting for around twenty minutes – to concentrate his mind, he heard his captors thinking – before the angry man walked through the door. He took the seat opposite and placed the mandatory grey file just so on the table. You knew he was angry by his posture, which was stiff and upright, his narrowed eyes, and the pent-up aggression in the jerky movements of his hands. Not that he was angry at you. No, it was the situation you'd placed him in. He had much better things to do than sit here trying to teach this foolish tourist who had flaunted his country's hospitality the error of his ways. Eventually, he spoke, straining to keep the impatience from his voice. His eyes were fixed on the contents of the file. 'You are using the name James Saintclair?'

'That's the name on my passport, I would be very foolish if I didn't use it,' Jamie replied carefully.

'And you speak and understand Russian?'

'I do – I assume our conversation is being recorded and I am currently a guest of the FSB?' A slight shake of the head indicated the pointlessness of the question rather than a negative answer. 'In that case, I wish to protest in the strongest terms at my arrest and confinement without charge. I am a British citizen . . .'

'That is still to be decided.'

'. . . and I request to see the British consul. I would also be grateful if you could remove these chains.'

'I'm afraid that is not possible. As I'm sure you understand, we have very strict protocols here. Freed from your chains, but you do not demand to be freed from custody immediately? Surely that would be the act of an innocent man?'

'I am an innocent man, old chap, but I'm also a pragmatist.' Jamie managed a consoling smile. 'As the representative of a civilized country I assume you have your reasons for holding me. I am certain that, given the opportunity, I can convince you that those reasons are mistaken. I would also like to protest at the unwarranted assault on my person by one of your heav— . . . operatives.'

'Were there any witnesses to this *unwarranted assault*?'

'Only the men who accompanied the perpetrator.'

'Ah yes.' His interrogator picked up a sheet from the file. 'The men who state in their arrest report that the suspect refused a lawful request by representatives of the state to accompany them to their vehicle, thereby resisting arrest and requiring restrained physical persuasion. Did you refuse to go with state *operatives* as you call them?'

'Yes, but I—'

'And did you suffer any injury during your restraint?'

'Not permanent, no.'

'Then perhaps we can stop wasting both our time and discuss the serious matter of the allegations against you.'

'I wasn't aware that there were any.'

The FSB man pulled another sheet from the file and placed it in front of Jamie. 'Have you ever seen this man?'

The paper was a printout of a passport and Jamie would never know how he kept his face from betraying his shock. The answer was yes, but to admit he recognized the ever-so-familiar face he saw in the mirror every morning, only with a heavy stubble and a decent tan, was to excavate a hole he'd never dig himself out of. He shook his head. 'No, I can't say I have.'

'Are you certain?'

'Absolutely.'

'His name is Mohammed al-Awali, a wanted terrorist – an Al-Qaida bomber, in fact – he was last seen in New York last October, part of a team who blew themselves up in a Manhattan hotel . . .'

'Then I think you have your answer to why he disappeared.' Jamie risked another smile.

'Oh, al-Awali was not among the casualties, Mr . . . Saintclair, but you are correct that he disappeared. You were also in New York last October, were you not?'

Jamie froze. 'I'm not sure where you got that information, but it's no secret. I was recovering an artefact for a client.'

'And which hotel did you stay in?'

'Is that really relevant?'

'If you want to get out of here, I would say it is.'

'Then I didn't stay in a hotel, I stayed with a friend.'

The Russian picked up a ball-point pen. 'And this friend's name and address is?'

Jamie sighed. 'I'm afraid I can't give you that information until I've asked he . . . them whether they're happy to have it revealed.'

'Even if it means your detention might be extended?'

'That would be disappointing. Look, I'm doing my best to cooperate. I would really be very grateful if I could make a telephone call to the British consul.'

'I'm afraid you are not in an English feature film, Mr Saintclair, there is no one phone call allowed. This is Russia and what happens to you is entirely dependent on what you tell me. Who were you visiting in Kapotnya? It is rather far off the tourist track for one staying in the presidential suite of the Lotte Hotel.'

Jamie sensed danger in the sudden change of tack, but he had no choice but to answer truthfully. 'I was interviewing an elderly resident of the care centre as part of an investigation for a client. His name is Dimitri Kaganovich.' The interrogator wrote the name down on a piece of paper and went to the door, handing it with a whispered instruction to the young man guarding it. 'Look,' Jamie let his frustration show, 'I really have no idea what all this has to do with me. I'm partly here to work and partly to enjoy your lovely country. If I did anything wrong when I was arrested it was because your people took me by surprise and refused to show their identification. For that I apologize, but I haven't done anything illegal.'

The other man shook his head. 'Do you think we are fools, Mr Saintclair, the Englishman who looks so similar to Mr al-Awali? You will have heard of the Christian converts to Islamic terrorism who being white have a much greater chance of operating in certain countries without being detected? Your friend Mr al-Awali is one such. He is a known associate of certain radical elements from the Caucasus region who are sworn enemies of the Russian Federation. But, of course, I am telling you nothing new. One of those elements is a Chechen who we believe was part of the planning team for the Moscow theatre attack. We received information only a week ago linking him to an apartment in Kapotnya, in fact, in the very block you visited. Does that surprise you?'

Jamie felt as if all the breath had been kicked from him. Mohammed al-Awali had been the invention of his one-time friend and occasional megalomaniac Adam Steele, who'd tried to frame Jamie to cover up his own bid to stage a military coup in Britain. Steele was long gone and Jamie had thought al-Awali was long gone with him. 'Look here,' he protested, 'I—'

He was interrupted by a knock on the door and the interrogator raised a hand as the young guard entered and whispered in his ear.

'How very convenient for you, Mr Saintclair. Dimitri Kaganovich was found dead a few minutes after your visit. I do hope you find your cell comfortable. I don't believe you'll be going anywhere soon.'

'We lost him.' Doug Stewart could almost feel the heat of Keith Devlin's fury as he explained what had happened. 'Well, not quite lost him.'

'How can you lose somebody, but not lose them?' the Australian raged. 'Am I employing complete incompetents?'

'Our man followed him out to the shithole where the old Russian lives. Saintclair spent more than an hour with him. When he came out they were waiting for him.'

'They?'

'Some kind of security outfit. They took him to the Lubyanka.'

'Christ!'

'What do you want me to do, Keith?'

A long pause followed while Keith Devlin considered his options. 'Nothing,' he said eventually.

'Nothing? But—'

'If we start asking questions the Russians are going to want to know why. Maybe they want in on the Bougainville deal, maybe not, but I'm not going to open the door for them. Saintclair will have to take his chances. But, Doug?'

'Yes.'

'If he does resurface, make the arrangements for Saintclair's two little ladies to join us on our trip.'

XVIII

Despite the paltry blanket and the chill in the room, Jamie's shirt was damp with sweat the next time he woke. He was instantly aware that something had changed, but not certain what had caused it. Only when he felt the draught on his cheek did he realize someone had opened the cell door. Slowly he turned his head.

'I didn't like to disturb your beauty sleep. There is something quite admirable in a man who can sleep in a place like this.' The slight figure leaned against the door jamb dressed in a black leather bomber jacket and jeans and with the laid-back air of a slightly older and wiser James Dean. A movie star smile didn't quite reach his eyes, which were an icy-blue spotlight into a soul that Jamie suspected was just as cold. The young man threw a bundle that turned out to be Jamie's jacket and belt on to the bottom of the bed. 'Your wallet, phone and the rest of your papers are inside.'

'What do you want?' Jamie ignored the clothing.

'You don't recognize me? The man who did you such a big favour down Ketrzyn way?'

Jamie recognized him well enough – he even remembered his name: Vatutin. They'd last met at Hitler's Wolf's Lair in what had formerly been East Prussia. Vatutin had walked into his life and asked several puzzling questions about a painting of which Jamie had no knowledge. Before they'd parted the Russian had also taken care of an awkward problem that involved several dead bodies – but that didn't mean Jamie was going to trust him. Vatutin waited a while for a response then shrugged when one wasn't forthcoming, not taking offence. 'It turns out this has all been a big mistake,' he continued. 'The FSB, they want to put Jamie Saintclair's feet in the furnace and find out what he knows about the Chechens. We've explained he is a friend of the Russian people and no terrorist.'

'That's very kind of you, but who is this "we"? From our previous meeting I'd gathered that you represented a . . . shall we say private enterprise company? But here you are at the very heart of your country's state security organization. You'll forgive me for being a little suspicious of your motives.'

The smile broadened. 'Suspicious is good, I would not want it any other way. But truly we are here to help. It would surprise you to know how often in Russia the interests of private enterprise and state organizations combine. We are Communists no longer; even the FSB must balance its books, as you say in England.'

'You still haven't told me who "we" are,' Jamie pointed out.

'That's for later, but first we get you out of here.' Vatutin stepped back from the door and held out an arm, like a sixteenth-century courtier ushering an aristocrat into the presence of the monarch.

Jamie studied the grey walls. Last night he'd wondered if he'd ever get out of this place. Now a ghost from the past had turned up with the keys to the castle. So why was he so reluctant to take the step? Because with people like Vatutin there was always a price to pay, and sometimes that price was higher than you were comfortable with. Every instinct told him to stay and take his chances. Then again, if Vatutin and his shadowy 'we' had the clout to get him out of the Lubyanka, they also had the clout to ensure that his stay would be painful and more than likely permanent. Jamie Saintclair would become a Moscow accident statistic. He sighed and rolled off the bed, slipped on his shoes and walked to the door, picking up his jacket and belt as he went. He paused in the doorway. 'I'll miss the old place.'

The Russian let out a snort of laughter. 'Yeah, sure.'

Vatutin led the way down to the basement garage and a black BMW 7-series. For all their professed dislike of the Germans, Jamie mused, the Russians had a thing for their motors. As they approached the big car, two men got out. One opened the rear door for Jamie as Vatutin made for the front seat. Jamie looked at the Russian, who shrugged: *Don't make a fuss; this is the way it must be.* The Englishman hesitated for a split second, wondering how many victims had been lulled into a false sense of security by their assassins' good manners. But what choice did he have? He ducked in to the rear of the BMW and took the centre seat, with one man on either side, comforted by the fact that at least this time he wasn't manacled to the floor.

They drove up the ramp and a guard lifted the barrier to let them out into the thin autumn sunshine of a Moscow afternoon. The BMW turned right and drove through the square and along a broad street that took the car past the Bolshoi theatre complex. When the driver turned into the long drag of New Arbat Avenue, Jamie felt a jolt of elation that Vatutin was returning him to his hotel. But the optimism faded when they continued past the turning and crossed Novarbatsky Bridge and the glittering expanse of the River Moskva. They were heading westwards. After a mile or so an enormous obelisk appeared on a height to the left of the road, and Vatutin turned in his seat.

'Victory Park up on Poklonnaya Hill,' he said with a tourist guide's smile. 'You should go there some time. Lots to see. It was as close to Moscow as Napoleon got.'

Not far ahead they turned off the road into a wooded area dotted with occasional brightly coloured dachas, the holiday homes where well-off Russians came to stay in the summer months. Eventually, it led to a long driveway with gravel crunching under the car's tyres. Jamie scanned the trees to left and right until an unnatural angular shape drew his attention. A moment later he caught sight of a soldier in a camouflaged uniform staring at the car. He wasn't sure whether the fact that the man appeared to be carrying an assault rifle was reassuring or otherwise.

'Stalin had a dacha not far from here,' Vatutin said

without turning his head. 'But this house belonged to Lavrentiy Beria. You have heard of him?'

'Of course.'

'Naturally, Stalin didn't trust him and he didn't trust Stalin, so they kept each other close. The Boss used Beria and the NKVD to clean up for him, and when he'd done the job, pouf, he got cleaned up too. He was a very tidy man, the Boss.'

'Naturally,' Jamie echoed drily. 'I appreciate the history lesson.'

'Oh, the most important lesson is yet to come, Mr Saintclair,' the Russian said with a conviction that sent a shudder down Jamie's spine.

At last they arrived at a large wooden house with a wide veranda. The two men escorted Jamie to the door, where they patted him down with professional courtesy.

'I'm sorry.' Vatutin shrugged apologetically. 'I know you were searched at the Lubyanka, but it is protocol. Nothing that could be used as a weapon and no recording devices.'

Jamie felt his heart beat a little faster. Now he was intrigued, the anxiety that had been growing with every mile outside Moscow replaced by curiosity. His destination had always been a mystery and his fate, despite Vatutin's apparent affability, uncertain. But here – along with the military guards and their carefully camouflaged armoured cars in the trees – was the first sign he was meeting someone significant. The two heavies stepped back and Vatutin waved him towards the door. 'Please,' he said.

The decoration in the large hall was much sparser

inside than the exterior of the building had hinted, with a pervading smell of recently applied varnish. A few pictures, mostly Moscow scenes, adorned the green-painted walls. One was a stern portrait of a man familiar to anyone who had seen television news pictures of Russia over the last decade or so. This was a place that had a function, Jamie decided, but not one that was lived in, at least not regularly. The Russian led the way through to a room where a log fire flickered between two broad windows that looked out over a stretch of garden lawn in dire need of attention.

'You will wait here, please.' Jamie sensed a hint of nervousness in Vatutin's voice as he left the room. The sensation transferred itself to his stomach, which felt like a ball of mating snakes had taken up residence. In the silence that followed his eyes automatically swept the doors and windows looking for the quickest escape route if things happened to go wrong.

He turned at the sound of the door opening and his mind froze at the sight of the man who walked briskly into the room.

'Please be seated.' The voice was much gentler than Jamie had expected. When he appeared on TV at the side of the man whose portrait hung in the hall he always looked the slighter of the two, but that turned out to be an illusion. In reality he was as tall as Jamie and the dark jacket and blue open-necked shirt hid a soldier's physique. The appraising eyes were grey and close-set beneath heavy brows. Deep lines dragged the corners of his mouth downwards as if he'd long forgotten how to smile. In the casual clothes he might have been an off-duty businessman, or a surgeon between shifts. In fact, if Jamie was to believe CNN, he had a direct connection to one of the most powerful men on earth.

'Please,' the man repeated, gesturing to the chair. 'Thank you for coming,' the Russian welcomed him gravely. 'Of course, neither of us is really here at all.' He smiled.

In other circumstances Jamie might have argued the point, but something told him it would be impolitic, not to say dangerous. 'Of course,' he agreed, 'but naturally I'm a little curious to know *why* I'm not here.'

The other man nodded slowly, as if people were shanghaied and dragged to meet him all the time and should be grateful for the opportunity, which was a thought. 'You are enjoying your trip to Moscow?'

'It has been very interesting so far,' Jamie replied with gross understatement. Why did he have a feeling that the poker face he was trying to project was more of a village idiot's vacant smile?

'Yes.' The lips twitched a hair's-breadth upwards, which seemed to record satisfaction. 'You are a man of culture, Mr Saintclair, a graduate of Oxford University.' Well, it was Cambridge, actually, but you didn't correct a man like this. 'You understand the passions that can be inspired by art. The way a painting or a sculpture can raise goosebumps on your skin, and composition and style can seem to talk to you of a talent beyond the realms of ordinary men or women; a genius unparalleled in any other aspect of life.' As he made his unlikely observations, he studied Jamie with an almost lizard-like concentration. 'I have a friend who feels the same passion.' The bushy eyebrows rose slightly and Jamie nodded to confirm he understood just which friend was the subject of this conversation. 'It has always been my friend's vision to bring great art to all Russian people,' the man continued. 'For many decades the appreciation of such works was suppressed and the repercussions of that suppression still exist today, do you not agree?'

Coming from a former high-ranking officer of the KGB who had undoubtedly done his share of suppressing during the twilight years of the Soviet Union, this was a ticklish subject. Jamie responded with an answer that was at once general and hopefully harmless. 'Yet you have always been fortunate in having some of the world's finest museums, and I believe Soviet children were encouraged to visit them from an early age even during the, er . . . difficult years.'

The almost feminine lips twitched into what might have been a proper smile until you noticed that looking into the grey eyes was like staring into the depths of an Arctic ice hole. 'Ah, our museums. They have a particular interest for you, I understand?'

Suddenly Jamie felt like the rabbit who'd become an object of fascination for a sleek brown creature with sharp teeth and a twitching nose. So much for avoiding the trap. 'As a student of fine art,' he said carefully, 'how could they not?'

'Yet this interest is in items with a very specific origin.' The eyes narrowed and took on a knowing look. 'You are a hunter, Mr Saintclair, and as a fellow hunter I can appreciate the attributes that have made your talents so sought after.'

'I—' A raised hand instantly stilled Jamie's protest.

'For instance, your rather specialized sphere of the art profession brought you into contact with a friend of my friend. You were seeking an artefact known as the Eye of Isis, I believe?' Jamie found he didn't dare breathe and the closest window was beginning to look more inviting by the second. 'Did you ever find it, I wonder? I have evidence that it spent a number of years in what was then the Soviet Union, and that the Russian Federation might have a claim on an object whose origins are, let us agree, so very obscure.' The Eye was a priceless diamond the size of a goose egg that had been the centrepiece of the Crown of Isis. Jamie hoped the Russian wasn't hinting that he wanted it back, because some careless sod had turned the enormous gem into about a million shards of crystalized carbon.

Fortunately, the next words seemed more reassuring. 'However, my interest is not in some gem, no matter how valuable, it is in a piece of art that my friend loaned to *his* good friend Oleg Samsonov and which went missing after his untimely demise . . .' In the cartoons they see stars, Jamie saw golden flowers in a glazed green pot against a nondescript background, last seen in Oleg Samsonov's safe room as the billionaire businessman's blood spread across the floor of his London mansion. 'Mr Saintclair?' He realized the other man had continued speaking. 'I said I want you to track down the person who took my friend's painting and negotiate its recovery.'

170

'I'm not sure I can do that.' Jamie felt himself go pale. 'The British police . . . diplomatic channels . . . a much better chance of finding the . . . the painting. I already have a commission that may take some time to complete.'

His host listened to him wrestle with the words, his head cocked slightly to one side, face immobile and the eyes watchful and penetrating. 'As for the commission, I believe I can help you accomplish at least part of it. You are seeking links to a man called Gennady Berzarin? Well, Gennady had a son, Arkady, and this Arkady lives a rather reclusive life. Not an easy man to reach, but of course I can help you reach him if you wish. You might even carry a message to him from my friend.' He smiled. 'Yes. Tell Arkady that his old friend Sergei from university sends his regards. That will get his attention. You talk of time? I have all the time in the world, Mr Saintclair. All that matters is that the only remaining version of Van Gogh's *Sunflowers* in private hands is restored to its rightful owner. As for the police and diplomatic channels, this is not state business, but personal. Oleg and my friend had an arrangement, which he would prefer to remain private, just as this meeting between us must remain forever between the two parties?'

It wasn't a question requiring an answer, but Jamie decided to answer it anyway. 'Naturally.'

'Then we are agreed.' That twitch of the lips again. 'You will track down the Lausanne *Sunflowers* at your leisure and negotiate its return to the rightful owner. Mr Vatutin will be our point of contact and he will be in touch from time to time to discuss your progress. Should there be any problem with the negotiations he will prove invaluable to you as he always has been to me.'

Even as Jamie's brain screamed *No*, he knew there was no way out. This was one of the most ruthless men in the world. With a click of his fingers Jamie Saintclair would be back in the Lubyanka, his future at best uncertain. Even if he agreed and walked away with no intention of carrying out the instructions it would be a small thing for these men to destroy him. He suspected death would be the least of it. First they would kill his reputation.

'You are considering your fee, of course. On discovery of the painting you will—'

'I want no fee, sir,' Jamie stepped in quickly. The last thing he needed in his muddled and often inscrutable records was an enormous payment from a dodgy off-shore account in the Cayman Islands. 'It would be my pleasure to find the Van Gogh and ensure its return.'

The other man took time to consider this, and for a moment Jamie wondered if he'd delivered a mortal insult. 'Very well.' The Russian repeated his slow nod. 'But honour demands there should be some kind of quid pro quo. We talked of artefacts in Russian museums that might be of interest to you? These establishments are run by conservatives who believe every artwork either on display or in storage is there by right, no matter its origin. Any object recovered from, let us say, Nazi Germany in the early part of nineteen forty-five is regarded as legitimate war reparation for the destruction done to the Motherland over the four preceding years. Of course, you and I know that many of these objects were confiscated from people who were themselves victims of the Nazis. The surviving relatives have legitimate claims upon their property. On receipt of your signature agreeing to track down a *painting of unknown provenance*, I will pledge to do my best to identify these artworks. Once this has been achieved, I will negotiate their release and pass them on to Saintclair Fine Arts for eventual repatriation to the families of their former owners on terms agreeable to both.'

The avaricious segment of Jamie's brain computed the value in money and prestige of what he'd just been offered – and, let's face it, dared not refuse. At the same time, a part-admiring voice in his mind screamed a warning. This is what makes this man so dangerous. He has looked into your soul, identified what you most covet and handed it to you on a golden plate. An image of a hissing serpent in an apple tree replaced the man opposite, and he saw a hand reaching out for a shining piece of fruit. As seductions went it was up there with the best. And of course the gleam of the apple hid the little worm burrowing away at its centre; the worm that went by the name of *your signature* and meant that the seduction was the first step towards a lifetime on your back in a brothel.

He looked up as some hidden signal heralded Vatutin's return, bearing an official-looking document and a gold pen. The Russian was grinning.

'Welcome aboard, comrade.'

173

XIX

It seemed to Jamie that Magda Ross had taken his absence with surprising equanimity.

'I thought you might have been worried,' he said after Vatutin – first name Alexei now that they were comrades – had dropped him off outside the hotel in a state close to bewilderment. 'At least a little bit.'

Magda laid down the Japanese grammar she was reading by the window and uncoiled herself from the chair. 'I was a little bit,' she admitted as she walked past him to the coffee machine. 'But I trust you to know what you're doing. Besides, Daniel popped in to let me know you might be out of circulation for a couple of days.'

'He did?'

'He did. I was a little curious as to why, but he couldn't tell me.'

The statement held a question but Jamie was busy trying to figure out how Daniel could have known without having inside information from the Lubyanka. 'Dimitri Kaganovich was a dead end.' He gave her a reassuring smile to cover up the guilt of not telling her just how dead, or his suspicions that he might have been responsible in a sort of second-hand, semi-detached kind of way. 'But he pointed me towards some other people and they came up with an address for the family of his dear-departed old chum Gennady.'

'And these people would be . . . ?' she asked too sweetly.

'It was all a little bit mysterious.' Jamie felt the heat in his cheeks as he evaded the question. 'But that happens sometimes in my line of work. They looked up the files and *voilà*: Gennady Berzarin gave up the diplomatic service and moved out to Siberia . . .' Magda blinked at the unexpected geographical twist and forgot the cross-examination she'd planned. 'He became a leading citizen, and eventually mayor of a place called Krasnoyarsk, which I'm told is a mining town on the Yenisei River.'

'We're going to Siberia?'

'*I'm* going to Siberia.' The words emerged of their own volition, but his instinct told him he was correct. He was swimming with sharks now and he had no right to ask Magda Ross to accompany him into this potentially lethal part of the ocean. 'Krasnoyarsk isn't the kind of place for the unprepared with winter coming on.'

But Magda had other ideas. 'Do you really think you're dumping me here?' Her tone was a mix of incredulity and determination, a sort of low-pitched warning signal mirrored by a narrowing of flashing walnut eyes. 'You lured me all the way to Moscow with your South Sea puzzle and your promises of First Class all the way, so don't think you can suddenly leave me behind. I've an investment in the Bougainville head too and I want to be there when you find it. Where you go I go, Jamie Saintclair, even if it means travelling solo.'

She stood there with her chest heaving with passion and he struggled to maintain his conviction in the face of such a major distraction. 'Siberia isn't Moscow, Magda.'

'No, but it's halfway to Tokyo, which is where we were going originally, in case you'd forgotten.'

'I hadn't forgotten but—'

'Please, Jamie, don't do this.' She was pleading now, and he had the odd sensation that this was a different Magda Ross. 'You've no idea what it was like in the museum with all those dusty old men and simpering office girls. When you walked into the museum and mentioned what you were looking for it was like a storm blowing away the cobwebs of my life. An opportunity to have an adventure after five years of staring at mind-numbing reports on computer screens. I've contributed nothing yet, but I know I can help. Just give me a chance.'

Sharks or no sharks, a man could only take so much. Despite his reservations Jamie's resolve crumbled and Magda saw it written on his face. Her mood transformed as if the sun had just come out from behind a cloud.

'All right,' he growled, trying to regain the initiative. 'But you can forget going solo. From now on we stay close and cover each other's back. Unless you'd be uncomfortable with that?'

It was the only time he'd seen her blush. 'I may have exaggerated for effect.'

'The first thing we need is some proper cold-weather clothing.'

'Of course.' She disappeared through the connecting door into her suite and returned a moment later with a pair of enormous bags with the name of a prominent Moscow store printed across the front. From the first, she pulled a heavily padded and obviously expensive jacket – it was too stylish to call an anorak. 'I wasn't sure of the colour, but dark blue seemed neutral enough. And I got you a couple of thick woollen sweaters and some winter socks.'

'Good, we can stop off somewhere and buy some, er . . . thermals.'

'Thermals?' Her eyebrows went up along with her voice. 'Do we have some kind of expedition planned? Mammoth hunting? A camping trip on the steppe?'

'All I have to get us close to Arkady Berzarin is an address that could be in the middle of nowhere and what might be called a verbal letter of introduction,' Jamie explained patiently. 'If that doesn't work we might have to try something a little more unorthodox than knocking on his door.' He shrugged, remembering he could have been back sunning himself with Fiona on Bondi Beach instead of chasing shadows in Russia. 'In my experience, it's the things you don't take that you end up needing. And there are certain extremities I'd prefer not to expose to frostbite.'

'Well, I can understand *that*,' she laughed and turned towards her suite. 'I'll start packing for the flight.'

'Er, I'm afraid there won't be a flight.' She froze in the doorway and he quickly explained. 'I tried to book a plane, but apparently there have been severe electrical storms and everything between here and the Far East is effectively grounded. The only option is the train. I'm afraid we're in for a rather extended trip.'

'Just how extended is extended?' Magda frowned.

'Think of it this way: we'll have plenty of time to get to know each other.'

As it turned out they didn't have much choice. Jamie thought he'd booked a luxury private berth, but at Yaroslavsky station their tickets led them to a cramped second-class compartment filled by four bunks and two other people. The scene resembled an old-fashioned English farce as Jamie stood in the doorway with tickets in hand and their luggage blocking the corridor. Meanwhile, the elderly Russian occupants sat on the left-hand bench staring stolidly at the far wall. Jamie checked the compartment number with the tickets, but there was no doubt it was correct.

Magda stuck her head round the door to take a look. 'First Class all the way with Jamie Saintclair?'

'There must be a mistake,' he grimaced. 'Look after the luggage and I'll check with the carriage attendants.'

The two young women *provodniks* who looked after the carriage listened impassively and shrugged. There were no first-class compartments in their section, but they would send for their superior. When the uniformed conductor arrived fifteen minutes later he explained that the few double compartments had been booked months in advance. He could do nothing about it now, but should they wish to continue on from Krasnoyarsk he would see what he could do. In the meantime, he'd arrange for their extra luggage to be stored elsewhere. Jamie tipped him lavishly to ensure he remembered and the Russian nodded gravely. 'On this train all service is First Class,' he insisted without irony. 'You will be very comfortable.'

By the time Jamie returned to the compartment, Magda was seated opposite the two Russians and their travel essentials were already stored in the capacious luggage racks above. 'Boris and Ludmilla have been very helpful.' She smiled at the mismatched pair on the far bench. Boris had the build of a wrestler and the deep, unfathomable eyes of the Russian east, while Ludmilla reminded Jamie of a little brown sparrow, drab and desperate to blend in with her background. He guessed they were both in their sixties. 'We've been getting by in a mixture of German, English and sign language,' Magda explained. 'Apparently, it's customary for the male to have the upper bunk unless he's subject to objectionable levels of flatulence.' Jamie darted a wary glance at Boris and Magda grinned. 'Hopefully that's not the case here.'

Jamie explained the situation with the compartments, and she laughed again. 'Don't get all uptight, Jamie. I was only kidding about First Class all the way. This is nothing new for me. I travelled a lot when I was younger and, believe me, I've been on worse trains than this.'

The coach jerked into motion and a junior conductor

came for their main luggage, which was still in the corridor. He handed over a numbered chit to be presented when they reached their destination. Jamie asked when the dining car opened and was told another three hours. The conductor imparted the news with a rueful shake of the head that, in hindsight, didn't bode well.

Jamie sat down on the leather bench and nodded to their travelling companions, whose enthusiasm for conversation seemed to have been exhausted for the day. Magda leaned back and closed her eyes and Jamie watched the Moscow suburbs slip past, the residential blocks and factory buildings soon replaced by a vast forest that stretched away to his right, until, with bewildering suddenness, they were back among development again. By the time they reached the countryside proper Magda's head was on his shoulder. He smiled at the Russian couple, but they only stared impassively, like male and female versions of the largest and smallest matryoshka dolls. They were still in the same position when he woke, with darkness outside the window and Magda Ross's pale features reflected in the glass.

'I didn't have the heart to wake you,' she apologized. 'But my stomach tells me it's time to eat.'

Her words seemed to trigger the two Russians into movement. Without a word Boris reached into a voluminous bag on the nearest luggage rack and pulled out a large brown paper parcel and a jar of pickles. He handed two mugs to his wife and Ludmilla whispered an apology as she brushed past Jamie's long legs and opened the door into the corridor. Jamie stretched and yawned. 'I don't much fancy picnicking with Boris and Ludmilla even if we had the wherewithal so we should probably try the dining car,' he suggested.

Magda picked up her handbag to join him. When they emerged into the corridor Ludmilla was at a samovar filling the mugs as they passed. '*Priyatnogo appetita, ser i ledi*,' she said and bowed. Jamie smiled and thanked her, explaining to Magda that the Russian woman had wished them bon appetit.

They made their way to the dining car past a mixture of Russians, some of them cheerfully drunk, European tourists and a handful of either Chinese or Mongolians. It was roomy and comfortable, with plush red seats and polished wooden tables laid with snowy-white cloth. A waiter handed them an extensive menu filled with what appeared to be mouth-watering dishes. They studied the options, but the man quickly disabused them.

'Tonight, everything is off the menu, apart from the soup, potatoes, ham and cabbage, and cake for dessert. If you order now, there is a chance . . . later?' He shrugged.

Jamie expected to be as disappointed by the food as the choice, but the soup was vegetable and wholesome, the potatoes, ham and cabbage about what you'd expect from potatoes, ham and cabbage, and the cake, accompanied by some sort of fruit liqueur, surprisingly good. As they ate, Magda made him laugh with her stories about train trips across Europe in her teens, fending off elderly Italian Lotharios, and sleeping in the luggage rack of an express between Calcutta and Delhi. He was reluctant to move, but a waiter explained that the table was required for the next sitting so he paid the bill and left a handsome tip.

When they returned to the compartment, Jamie opened the door and ushered Magda inside. As he moved to join her, she stopped abruptly. In other circumstances they might have backed out and laughed in embarrassment that they'd walked into the wrong compartment. Only it was the right compartment, except Boris and Ludmilla had been replaced by an equally mismatched pair of burly Chinese gentlemen.

XX

The two men occupied exactly the same seats where Jamie and Magda had left the two Russians, but someone had made up the four bunks. They'd also drawn the blinds, leaving the occupants entirely isolated from the outside world.

In this case it wasn't the physique that made the two men mismatched, but the facial expressions. The intruders appeared to have inherited their DNA from the Buddha. Rounded, plump-cheeked faces sat above dark suits stretched over similarly rounded torsos. Jamie decided instantly that, in the man on the right at least, it would be a fool who assumed that rounded meant chubby or flaccid. He had a flat, lipless mouth, and the unblinking eyes of a cobra stared out from beneath a seaman's cap of black hair. His hands were clenched in a way that hinted every muscle was ready to explode into the kind of violence you only see in Jackie Chan films. The overall effect was more than chilling. This man had assassin written all over him, and Jamie had a feeling he and Magda might both be dead by now had it not been for the presence of his smiling companion.

In contrast, the second Chinese lay back in his seat with his hands folded across his stomach as if he was in his favourite chair listening to Mozart on the radio. A benevolent smile wreathed his face and his eyes twinkled as if he, and he alone, was privy to the humour of the situation. Jamie saw Magda's jaw set and before she could make a move he closed the carriage door and steered her to her seat. He had a feeling that as long as the man kept smiling they would be safe, but he had no illusions about how dangerous he could be. It was like sitting opposite a panda with fangs.

'Jamie, I . . .'

He laid a hand on her arm. This wasn't the time for questions. From what he could see, all of Ludmilla and Boris's luggage was still in place. That made their absence unlikely to be permanent, which he presumed was good news for Jamie and Magda as well as Ludmilla and Boris. Someone had paid them to disappear and that someone was sitting opposite. Now he waited for someone to let them into the secret of why.

At some unseen signal the assassin rose to his feet with his eyes on Magda and nodded towards the door. Jamie felt her bridle and her right fist clenched with the knuckle protruding in a way that suggested she wasn't going to go quietly. The cheerful man noticed it too and the smile widened. 'Please, Dr Ross, you will be perfectly safe with Mr Lee, I assure you.'

Her eyes widened at the familiar use of her name. 'Jamie?'

'I'm fairly certain these gentlemen don't mean us any harm, Magda.'

After a moment's hesitation she nodded and reluctantly followed the assassin into the corridor.

When they were alone, Jamie stared at the man opposite. The Chinese met his expectant gaze with the kind of humour in his eyes you knew would still be present when he put a bullet in you.

'A remarkable young lady.' The soft voice was immediately recognizable. 'Such beauty and such depths of determination. I genuinely fear for Mr Lee's safety.' The snub nose twitched as if he'd remembered something distasteful. 'My apologies for the surprise, Mr Saintclair. But it is always difficult to find somewhere to have a private word on a train, don't you think?'

'I'm not sure what we have to talk about, Mr Lim,' Jamie said carefully. 'Old acquaintances who turn up unexpectedly can't always be sure of a warm welcome. Especially when those old acquaintances appear with such increasing and unlikely frequency.'

'Ah, Mr Lim of fond memory.' The Chinese chuckled as if his former self no longer existed. 'It is much too long since your most stimulating, if ultimately frustrating address in Dresden. I assume the other old acquaintance of whom you speak is the dreadful Russian gangster who facilitated your exit from the Lubyanka and introduced you to your highly placed new friend.' If Mr Lim's smile had been any wider the top of his head would have fallen off. Jamie opened his mouth to protest, but the other man silenced him with a shake of the head. 'We – at least I – have no interest in the Russians and their rather uncivilized pursuit of gain. Who would have forecast that Communists would become the greediest of capitalists?' A twitch of the lips made Jamie wonder if the Russians were the only greedy Communists Mr Lim had in mind. Before he could enquire, the Chinese moved swiftly to the subject that had brought him. 'My only interest, as it was at our last meeting, is in the most efficient and fruitful exploitation of my country's resources at home and abroad. For instance, there may be a possibility that the interests of Mr Keith Devlin and myself coincide in certain areas. Would that surprise you?'

Given that Jamie was fairly certain Mr Lim was an official of China's Ministry of State Security, nothing would surprise him about the man. Nevertheless, Keith Devlin's name came as a shock. He took time to consider his next words.

'It's a little difficult to see how that would be the case.'

'But why? Mr Devlin has mining interests across the globe. The Chinese government has mining interests across the globe. In certain areas it is true that these interests compete, and we are, shall we say, friendly rivals, but in other regions it is perfectly possible for us to be partners.' He paused as the train thundered through a long tunnel. Jamie had time to reflect that if this had been a film the lights would have gone out and when they flickered back on again one of them would have added a knife to their list of unwanted accessories. Mr Lim's smile never faltered. 'China is the largest consumer of iron ore on the planet, Mr Saintclair, but most of the world's iron ore deposits lie outside China. For that reason it is essential for us to pursue global partnerships, which we have done successfully for many years. We have interests from the Arctic to the Antarctic and on almost every land mass between.'

'I thought mining was banned in the polar areas.'

'Of course,' Mr Lim nodded gravely, 'but the ban will be reviewed in 2048. Who knows what will happen then? You would be surprised by the nations who wish to work with us in these areas, but I digress. My point was that it makes sense for Mr Devlin to work with China. Our current greatest need is copper, and the Panguna Mine on Bougainville has the potential to be the world's largest copper producer. Ideally, we would like to have overall control of the mine, but for political reasons this is currently not possible. Therefore, we see a partnership as the best way forward. We would even be happy for him to retain the rights to the mine's gold deposits. You see, we would like very much to work with Devlin Metal Resources to see the mine reopened.'

'I can understand that,' Jamie conceded. He could also see why Australia and China's other Pacific neighbours wouldn't want to see her in control of a massive strategic resource on their doorstep. 'But I don't know what it has to do with me. Given your obvious knowledge in other areas, you will know I am employed by Mr Devlin in a purely freelance capacity. My main interest is in the recovery of stolen art, Mr Lim. Not in mining or *resources*.'

The Oriental huffed. 'What is art, once it has been created, but a commodity; a *resource* to be bought and sold? For instance, what if there was a man – perhaps in Germany, perhaps not – who had access to several billion dollars' worth of artworks stolen during the Second World War? An art dealership specializing in the return of such works would surely be interested in the name of that person, or his location?'

'That is just speculation, Mr Lim,' Jamie protested. 'Pure fantasy. Those rumours have been going the rounds for years.'

'True, but—'

'In any case, if such a person existed, why would anyone offer his name to the hardly venerable or even, let us admit, particularly well-esteemed Saintclair Fine Arts?'

'Perhaps because the not particularly well-esteemed Saintclair Fine Arts has something to trade.'

'I'm sorry, I can't see how that would be the case.' Jamie felt a little like he'd just been pushed into a minefield wearing a blindfold.

'You are seeking a certain . . . artefact, for Mr Devlin.'

'I can't talk about my commission. I'm sure you understand that, Mr Lim.'

'Oh, don't be coy, Mr Saintclair.' The smile was a grin now. 'Mr Devlin pays for the world's best experts to safeguard his communications and his information technology network. But the world's greatest experts in these fields do not work for corporations, they work for governments. Specifically the governments of the United States, China and the Russian Federation. I see a blink of patriotic outrage that I do not mention the

United Kingdom. Surely you are aware that since the Second Gulf War your GCHQ has been nothing but an out-station for America's National Security Agency? There are even several isolated colonies of United States settlers in your country, working under United States rule of law, paying American taxes and shopping at Walmart. They carry guns on British soil and they pay American prices for their gas. But once more I digress. So Mr Devlin upgrades his communications security, and we, the Americans and the Soviets circumvent it. All of us spy upon our friends and our enemies alike. It is a game, of which Mr Devlin is well aware he is an integral part. You will find the artefact, and Mr Devlin will arrange the exchange, is that not how it works?' Jamie didn't trust himself to speak as the Chinese agent's voice turned serious for the first time in their conversation. 'But I want you to consider this, Mr Saintclair. What if Mr Devlin's motives for the Bougainville exchange are not what he wishes you to believe? What if they are not in the interests of, let us call it, the world community? In that situation, possession of the artefact might be embarrassing, or even dangerous.'

'Now you're talking in riddles. If you have something to say, why not just say it.'

Lim shook his head solemnly. 'No, this is something you must work out for yourself. I'm aware you do not trust me, and you are quite right not to do so. In this affair you cannot afford to trust anyone.' The Chinese stood up in a single fluid movement that was a better illustration of his capabilities than his bulk. 'Perhaps we will meet again, Mr Saintclair, perhaps not, but bear in mind what I have said. You will come to a fork in the road. Take one road and there will be perils; take the other to find rewards. Only one man can decide.'

The door opened as he reached it, and Mr Lim stepped out past Magda Ross with a polite bow. She ignored him and virtually threw herself into the carriage.

'What was all that about?' she demanded.

'I'm not sure.' Jamie stared at the closed door. 'But I doubt if it's going to make things any easier.'

XXI

Bougainville, April 1945

Tomoyuki Hamasuna felt a surge of emotion as he checked the fit of the *senninbari* thousand-stitch belt his wife had given him on the eve of his departure for Manchuria. Each stitch on the white cloth had been lovingly sewn by a family member or the wives of Hamasuna's workmates in Nagasaki. The belt had seen him through the Manchukuo campaign, the invasion of Malaya and three months on Guadalcanal before he'd been posted to Bougainville. Sitting in the cramped, heavily camouflaged bunker, he was aware that he stank. His body and his tattered uniform were permeated with the stench of stale sweat, old urine, caked excrement and fear. Yes, fear. None of them had dared go out even for a shit since the Australians had started sending their dirty cannibals to roam the lines each night. The blacks moved like ghosts in the darkness and the first a man would know of them was a knife in the throat before his head was added to their collection.

191

Hamasuna had been condemned to this stinking hellhole since the 'senior naval presence' banished him back to the infantry for failing to secure the Yamamoto crash site. He'd wanted to explain about the missing briefcase and the bare footprint he'd found in a patch of sand nearby, but the admiral's raw, almost demonic savagery had left him speechless with terror. He'd done what he could to impress the man with his diligence during the crash investigation, leading endless patrols to keep the natives from the site. One patrol had captured an Australian Coastwatcher, who died under Hamasuna's knife screaming that he knew nothing of a plane crash or missing wreckage. He'd had the body secretly buried along with the spy's still living Bougainvillean bodyguard.

But Hamasuna's efforts had come to nothing. On the morning the admiral left he'd stood shaking as his own commanding officer questioned his integrity, his competence and his loyalty in an interview that was as frightening for its remoteness as it was for the implied threat of summary justice. In the end, he felt fortunate to be transferred to the infantry and placed in charge of a company digging in on the Buin road against the imminent American invasion.

Three years on they occupied the same stinking, airless bunker in the same stinking patch of jungle, only his 'company', which had started out with a hundred and fifty men, now numbered fewer than forty. The Americans had kept them waiting another six months before surprising General Hyakutake, Bougainville's commander, with a landing at Empress Augusta Bay.

Within hours the invaders had wiped out the bay's few hundred defenders and established a bridgehead.

By the end of November, despite desperate counter attacks by Seventeenth Army, the invaders had built an airfield capable of sending bombers to hit the main supply base at Rabaul. Unless the Americans could be thrown off the island, the Japanese garrison of Bougainville would eventually be starved out. For four months Hyakutake had contented himself with pin-prick attacks, but in late March Hamasuna and his men had been roused from their bunker to take part in a full-scale counter-offensive.

What followed was three weeks of terror, hunger, exhaustion and death as he and his comrades launched attack after attack against the American-defended hills protecting the bridgehead. They spent endless nights throwing themselves at the entrapping coils of barbed wire through an invisible wall of lead from the heavily dug-in positions. As the first waves were cut down, the survivors clawed their way over the bodies of the dead and wounded to grenade the dugouts and work themselves into the enemy trenches. Once through the wire it was bayonet to bayonet, knife to knife and man to man, screaming and hacking at the enemy until he was a bloody caricature of a human being. Then on to the next trench and the next, until only a visceral determination to survive – to live through this unbelievable horror and eventually return to his loved ones – gave a man the strength to lift his arm and strike the fatal blow. Daylight brought the inevitable bombs and artillery fire that shook the earth and turned the tree canopy into a blinding, eviscerating blizzard of shrapnel and splinters from torn branches. Soon it would be followed by the thunk-thunk-thunk of mortars that heralded a new barrage and the inevitable counter-attack. Then it was your turn to cower in the trenches and fire your machine gun until the barrel became red hot, and the bodies were piled three deep across your front. In twenty-one days they took the same hill four times only to be driven off again. Not once had they come close to breaking the main American line. Eventually, even Hyakutake realized it could not be done and ordered a withdrawal. He'd started out with twenty thousand men. By the time he pulled out five thousand were dead, with three thousand wounded and no medical supplies to care for their injuries.

Hamasuna and his depleted company had stumbled, exhausted, back through the jungle to their bunker complex overlooking the road, and waited for the inevitable counter-stroke. But the Americans, it seemed, were content to hold what they had. Instead of attacking they decided to allow the Japanese garrison to starve, which they duly did. For months Hamasuna had been kept alive by cups of watery rice eked out with stringy, bitter strips of vegetation and unwholesome squirming grubs the medical officer claimed were nourishing. Beriberi, dengue fever, malaria, typhus and a curious enervating, wasting disease that came in many forms that the men simply called jungle fever caused more casualties than the enemy in the miserable hunger months that followed. But all that changed when the barbarians came.

The barbarians wore slouch hats and were aggressive even to each other. Since they had replaced the Americans five months earlier they had given Hamasuna and his men no rest. The barbarians patrolled by day and sent their cannibals by night. Half-starved and exhausted, each day that passed left the Japanese defenders weaker and less able to counter the constant probes and patrols by the Australians and their native allies. When General Hyakutake's health began to fail he'd been replaced as commander of Seventeenth Army by General Matasane. With the enemy advancing steadily down the Buin road, Matasane decided he had only one course of action.

Which was why Lieutenant Tomoyuki Hamasuna was preparing for his last day on earth.

He'd been hoarding the paper and ink for this day and now he picked up the brush. His tired features creased in a frown of concentration that made the mix of dried sweat and dirt that coated his face fall away in tiny flakes.

The first was easy. A simple farewell to his wife and his family that had been written several times already in this war, but he had a feeling this would be the last. Once he finished it, he carefully folded the paper and wrote the family address on the front. The second letter required more thought.

'Not long now, sir . . . Oh, I apologize,' Murayama turned away as he saw what his lieutenant was doing.

Hamasuna ignored him and began writing, tentatively at first, but soon in bolder more confident strokes. 'I Lieutenant Tomoyuki Hamasuna, 1st battalion, 45th

Infantry regiment, 6th division, 17th Japanese Army wish to confess to a crime. On 18 April 1943, I was first to discover the crash site of Admiral Isoroku Yamamoto's plane, south-west of Aku. I wish to state that I failed to report that the admiral was in possession of a briefcase, which I failed to secure, and subsequently lost to a native inhabitant. The contents of the briefcase contained the following information . . .'

When he'd completed the letter he felt as if an enormous weight had been lifted from him. He folded up the sheets, addressed it to General Kanda Matasane and placed it, along with the other, in the water-proof map case he had taken from a dead American. One last check of the thousand-stitch belt, a pull at his legging cloths, hands automatically testing the draw of his *katana* ceremonial sword and the flap of his holster. The other men in the bunker had finished their preparations and were waiting for him by the entrance. He met their eyes one by one and was gratified by the determination he saw despite their weakened state. '*Banzai*,' he whispered and they chorused the word in reply. With a last glance at his watch he nodded and one by one they slipped out into the night.

The soldiers formed up with the other survivors of the company and moved off northwards. Around them, the jungle was alive with the sound of movement. Matasane had ordered an all-out attack on the Australian positions. The First and Second battalions were tasked with taking an enemy strongpoint five miles ahead that prisoners had identified as Slater's Knoll. Even for the hardened jungle fighters of the Sixth Division it took more than three hours to reach the assembly point as they stumbled through swamps and over gullies, fording waist-high rivers. An hour into the march a spine-chilling rush through the air above heralded the beginning of the artillery barrage that would hopefully destroy the enemy wire. The flash of bursting shells followed almost instantly, lighting up the night sky and creating terrifying shapes on the jungle floor. A moment later they heard the crump of the 75mm shells landing far ahead. Hamasuna's men grinned nervously at each other in the bursts of pale light, taking comfort from the show of Imperial power, but they knew the barrage would also warn the enemy an attack was on the way. The only question being the timing of it. He thought of the soldiers waiting for him on the knoll ahead. He had seen Australian prisoners being marched back for interrogation, big men with brutal, angry faces, fearful of their fate and resentful of their captivity. They would be exhausted and frightened, but at least they wouldn't be hungry. The thought of food made his stomach grumble. Westerners ate like dogs from tins of greasy canned meat, but after months of privation even that was incentive enough.

Word to halt came back from the unit ahead and an orderly appeared, whispering for the officers to go forward. Hamasuna found the other company commanders at the bottom of a steep gully huddled around Captain Minoru, the battalion's most senior surviving officer. Soldiers shielded the men with coats and with a pen torch Minoru identified their position on a crude map. 'We attack up this slope,' he said in a hoarse whisper, indicating a feature about two hundred metres ahead. 'A banzai charge of all companies. The signal will be a blue flare. Make sure your men are ready in ten minutes. Banzai!'

'Banzai.'

XXII

Jamie froze at the soft knock at the compartment door and for the first time on Keith Devlin's mission he wished he'd brought some kind of weapon. He motioned Magda back to the window and stepped warily to one side as the knock was repeated. Very carefully he pushed the door a few inches, then opened it fully to allow Boris and Ludmilla to enter. They'd changed into pyjamas and thick robes. The husband avoided eye contact as he laboriously climbed the ladder to the top bunk, lay back and stared at the ceiling. Ludmilla handed Jamie a brown paper bag before taking her place below her husband.

'*Spasibo*, Ludmilla.' He nodded his thanks, opening the bag to find a pair of sweet pastries. Magda caught his eye and he shrugged. 'They had nothing to do with it. Our visitors probably made them an offer they couldn't refuse to stay away for a little longer while they were changing for bed.'

'So I'm just supposed to forget the fact that I had to spend quarter of an hour within reach of Harry the

Hatchet's twitching fingers?' She shook her head and the raven hair shimmered. 'No way, Jamie. I want to know what the hell is going on.'

'Now?' Jamie lowered his voice to match Magda's.

She frowned and glanced across at Ludmilla, who was already snoring gently. 'I wouldn't want to disturb them.'

'We could go out in the corridor,' he offered.

'We might wake them when we come back in.'

'Tomorrow then.'

She took a deep breath and pinned him with dark eyes that told him that tomorrow there'd be no wriggle room. 'First thing.'

They slept fully dressed, just in case. Lying in the darkness, the rhythmic clatter of the train's progress east was a faint backdrop in his mind and the gentle side-to-side motion of the carriage barely noticeable after nine hours. Jamie could hear the sound of regular breathing from the bunks opposite, but he guessed Magda was still awake below him. He sensed her frustration, but the delay suited Jamie because he needed some time to make some sense of what had happened.

He'd first encountered the enigmatic Mr Lim a few years earlier when they'd discovered a mutual interest in the Sun Stone, a peculiar leftover from a fallen meteorite that had opened up the possibility of controlled nuclear fusion and a source of unlimited power. They'd struck a deal in a Munich airport coffee house but, unknown to Mr Lim, it had been of the one-sided variety. Fortunately, when it turned out the Sun Stone was lost forever amongst a million tons of rubble buried beneath Dresden, Lim hadn't seemed too put out. And that was that.

Now Lim had appeared out of nowhere to present Jamie with another infuriating riddle, matched to a tantalizing offer: *What if there was a man – perhaps in Germany, perhaps not* . . . Twice in two days Jamie Saintclair had been offered the Holy Grail of the art world, and he had no doubt that each of the two men could deliver what he had promised. So why did it feel as if he was in the middle of a frozen lake with the sun on his back, the ice creaking louder with every step and dry land a mile away in any direction? Because the Russians and the Chinese both wanted a piece of him. In the first instance, he didn't have any option; he could still feel the chill in his bones from that Lubyanka cell. In the second, it looked as if the choice was somewhere down the line, which meant he would just have to make it when it came. On the face of it, only one of his new allies was interested in his commission for Keith Devlin, and Mr Lim seemed happy for him to carry it out . . . to a point. But could he really believe the Russians? Even if they'd been sincere, how would they react when they discovered – as they undoubtedly would – that their faithful new comrade had spent fifteen cosy minutes alone with a high-ranking agent of the Chinese Ministry of State Security?

Then there was the question of just when Mr Lim and – he smiled at Magda's description – Harry the Hatchet had begun taking an interest in Jamie Saintclair. Certainly since Moscow, because that was where they must have boarded the train. But if Lim was telling the truth about the level of surveillance on Keith Devlin, it was possible they'd been tracking him since Sydney. Jamie had no doubt Devlin's man Max had followed him in Berlin, but had Lim searched the hotel room? He tried to remember what had been in his suitcase. His laptop, but it had only the few basic details that had brought him to Germany. He hadn't yet made the connection with Tokyo, but that didn't matter either, because he and Devlin had talked openly on the phone about the possibilities, which presumably meant the Chinese knew as much as he did.

The constant rhythmic jolt and clatter of the train seemed to eat into his mind, numbing one sector at a time into a relaxed trancelike state. His last thought before the darkness closed in was that Keith Devlin's quest was far from the joyride it had seemed in Sydney, accompanied by a pang of guilt that he hadn't contacted Fiona.

His first thought when he woke was that he must phone her. If it was 7 a.m. here – and here was some-where between Kirov, where they'd stopped two hours earlier, and Perm, another five hours up the line – his best guess was that, with Sydney time eight hours ahead of Moscow time, and Krasnoyarsk four hours ahead of Moscow, the time in Sydney was probably just after lunch, give or take a few hours either way.

He heard a rustle from the bunk below and knew Magda was awake too. They lay in bed waiting awkwardly while the Russians emerged from their bunks and wrapped themselves in their thick, all-encompassing dressing gowns. Ludmilla cheerily announced that there were always long queues for both of the bathrooms in the morning, but that was what she and Boris were used to. They'd be happy to allow the *sir i ledi* to go first. The next step was finding breakfast, but judging by last night's experience with the restaurant car there seemed little point in looking there. The immediate problem was solved by Ludmilla's gift of pastries the previous night accompanied by tea in polystyrene cups purchased from the *provodnik* trolley. When they'd eaten, they followed Boris's example of folding the bedclothes and stowing them on the upper bunk, and settled for another day of confinement that the schedule said would be punctuated by a single stop at Perm.

Jamie suspected Magda was still desperate to discuss the events of the previous day. His first priority was to call Fiona, but when he checked his phone it was out of battery. Annoyed he hadn't thought of it earlier he looked vainly around the tiny compartment for a power source to recharge the machine. It meant that, as well as having no phones, which was bad enough, there'd be no access to the computer or the internet for at least two more days, which for some reason was worse. It felt like having one hand cut off.

Eventually Magda could stand it no longer. 'We need to talk about our visitors,' she hissed, drawing a glance from the two Russians.

'All right,' he conceded warily. 'Let's go and stretch our legs.'

Outside in the corridor someone had opened a window, which only emphasized the oppressive heat and fetid atmosphere in the compartment. Washing facilities in the train bathrooms were utilitarian at best, with just a trickle of water. In those conditions it didn't take long for the scents of four people sleeping, eating and in Boris's case – he'd started sucking at a bottle of vodka after breakfast – drinking together to become overwhelming. They stood in front of one of the viewing points, Jamie leaning on the rail and Magda clutching it as if it was the handle of a life raft. A tiny village with redwood walls, green tiled roofs and an onion-dome church flashed past like something out of a dream, to be replaced by the endless steppe.

'So?'

'It turns out,' Jamie explained hesitantly, 'that the Chinese have an interest in Mr Devlin's mining project neither of us was aware of.'

'Okay,' she said in a way that told him it wasn't okay at all. 'But what kind of Chinese? Harry the Hatchet didn't look like your average trade delegate.'

'I'm not sure what kind,' he said, which was the truth, even if he could make a pretty good guess. 'Businessmen, or possibly some kind of state official. I know his bodyguard looked intimidating, but the chap I spoke to was very reasonable.'

The words were accompanied by what he hoped was a comforting smile, but the early-morning Magda Ross appeared to be immune to his charms. 'What did he say, specifically?'

'It's a bit difficult, to be honest, because he played the inscrutable Oriental to the hilt. All he wanted to do was to let me know of their interest and that they would be . . . I think monitoring is probably the best word . . . monitoring our progress.'

'And that's all there is to it?' She didn't hide her disbelief. 'They bribe our Russian neighbours and scare me half to death to give you a message they could have sent on a postcard?'

'That's it,' he insisted. 'I suspect they left the train at Kirov, but there's a possibility someone stayed on board to keep an eye on us. It doesn't really matter, because we can't change anything until we reach Krasnoyarsk in another thirty-odd hours.' He sensed she still wasn't convinced. 'You said you wanted an adventure,' he pointed out. 'Well, here you are travelling across Russia on the Trans-Siberian Express, pursued by inscrutable Chinese agents and sharing a cabin with the Posh and Becks of the steppe. What more can you ask?'

'What more can I ask?' She shook her head and finally smiled. 'Only that when we leave Krasnoyarsk, whatever direction we are going in, we do it in a plane. For some reason the Trans-Siberian Express has lost its allure.'

'I guarantee it.' Jamie grinned. 'In fact, I'll fly the bloody thing myself if it comes to it. No more Minsk, Pinsk, Chelyabinsk in the second-class compartment from Hell for us. If we find the Bougainville head in Krasnoyarsk, we'll take off for Sydney to hand it over to Devlin, then enjoy a bit of R and R. I'll introduce you to my family on Devlin's private island. If not, it's off to Tokyo and our appointment at the Last Chance Saloon.'

Magda's face turned serious again. 'What do you

think our chances really are of finding the head in Krasnoyarsk?'

'Realistically? Probably less than fifty-fifty,' he admitted. 'We know Gennady Berzarin was in Berlin at the right time and he wasn't averse to taking sweeteners from the Nazis. The problem is that for a man whose primary motive was to make a profit, the head wouldn't be a big prize.' He remembered what had been said in the Moscow dacha. 'And then there's the family. They came from a cultured background; Siberian aristocracy who survived the October Revolution and what followed by living on their wits. Is a shrunken head really something the Berzarins would have passed down from father to son?'

'If it's such a wild-goose chase, why are we here?'

'Because the one thing I've learned in this business is that you take nothing for granted. Maybe Berzarin never had the head, but we won't know for certain unless we ask the right questions of the right people.' And, he thought with a familiar twinge of guilt, a certain person wanted me here for reasons I don't understand and can't tell you.

They spent the rest of the day reading and dozing and chatting. By now Boris was more or less comatose. Jamie learned from Ludmilla that the couple were on their way to Irkutsk where, much to their annoyance, their eldest son, an aircraft engineer, was to marry a local Siberian girl. Yes, she was pretty, in that doe-eyed eastern fashion, but what good was a wife who could not bake a loaf or boil an egg, *ser*? She shot a sly glance at Magda who sat by the window staring out at the never-changing flat, featureless landscape. 'You will marry some day?'

Jamie spent a moment studying Magda's reflection in the glass. 'I've asked her a hundred times,' he shook his head solemnly. 'But she won't marry me until I learn to cook.'

Magda turned at the Russian woman's bark of laughter. 'What did you say to her?'

'I told her the tractor factory joke,' he lied. 'It has them rolling in the aisles every time. Nikita points to a red tractor and says to Ilya—'

'Idiot,' she said and slipped past him to the door. 'I think I'll freshen up.'

'Suit yourself, but you don't know what you're missing.'

She was gone for fifteen minutes and Jamie was just becoming concerned when the door slipped back. He knew something was wrong the instant he saw her face. She was breathing hard and the blood was high in her cheeks. It took a moment before he realized she wasn't frightened, just very angry.

'What happened?' He got to his feet and helped her to her seat. Ludmilla closed the door and looked on apprehensively, clucking like a mother hen.

'A man was waiting for me outside the bathroom.' Her eyes hardened at the memory. 'He was drunk and he asked me for a cigarette. When I told him I didn't have any, he started to interrogate me. Was I a tourist? Where was I from? What was I doing on the train? Was I with anyone? I tried to get past him, but he wouldn't let me.' She met Jamie's eyes and shrugged. 'What was a girl to do? I used my knee where it hurts the most and he won't be bothering anyone else for a while. The only problem is,' her face turned serious again, 'I don't think he was as drunk as he acted.'

'Chinese?' Jamie asked.

She shook her head.

He went to the door and checked the corridor to right and left, but no one was in sight, drunk or otherwise, and he closed it again. 'From now on,' he said, 'we stay in the compartment unless it's strictly necessary, and when we do go out we go out together. Okay?'

Ludmilla cut in with a machine-gun rattle of Russian demanding to know what had upset Magda. Jamie explained what had happened. She looked at her snoring husband with a look of pity, but when she spoke her voice was heavy with contempt and she shook her head. 'Ach, vodka.'

XXIII

Bougainville, April 1945

Hamasuna found his way back to his men and issued his orders. As he waited for word to move, the finality of the situation struck him like a sandbag thrown from a great height, weakening his legs and loosening his bowels. He dug his nails into his palms so he could focus on the pain and not what awaited him, cloaked by the night, a few hundred paces ahead. The Australians would have been strengthening these positions for weeks. There would be barbed wire, trip wires and mines, machine guns sited to converge on the likeliest assault points, mortars that could be vectored on to any potential weak spot, and grenades, ready to be showered in their dozens on the attackers. In addition, the supporting artillery would probably be zeroed in on the exact point where Hamasuna stood. Their tanks, though vulnerable in the jungle, were devastating defensive weapons. They were brutes, the Australians, but they weren't fools, and they had proved tenacious, deadly opponents. Many of the men breathing heavily in the surrounding darkness would not be returning to their bunkers tonight. Yet they would die, if not cheerfully, then at least willingly, and not for their Emperor, because such romantic notions had long faded, but for their families. On this night the Buin road on Bougainville was the front line in the defence of their homeland. Every man who died knew he would be honoured by his family and his community and his name would be recited at the Yasukuni Shrine in Tokyo. Hamasuna pictured his family at the shrine and the image gave him strength and resolve.

'Forward.' He moved automatically, surprised to find he already had his sword in his right hand and his pistol, the comfortably familiar Taisho, in his left. Beside him Murayama and the others began to shuffle forward, their unwieldy Arisaka rifles at the port, the twenty-inch bayonets dulled by soot to stop them glinting in the shell bursts. They moved in almost total silence; a thousand men a mere shadow flowing and spreading across the jungle floor accompanied only by the soft rustle of disturbed vegetation. After a few moments they passed through a line of kneeling men. Hamasuna recognized the short stubby barrels of grenade launchers that would provide the attack with close support. The sight made his heart pound because it meant the moment of no return was near. He could feel the tension all around like a physical presence and he had to force himself to breathe. The sound of a soft breeze blowing through a pine wood was followed by a sharp pop and the blackness above turned bright blue.

'Banzai!' The initial cry came from the officers and was echoed immediately by a thousand throats. The mass of infantry moved forward in a rush with Hamasuna and his company at its heart.

'Banzai!' The scream tore his throat and he felt a God-like invincibility. He was a Samurai, a warrior of old, with a thousand-stitch belt that would ward off the weapons of his enemies. All around him the air sang with the howls of men channelling their own fear to strike terror into the hearts of their enemies. The pace quickened and the ground began to rise. More flares, this time from the enemy, and now Hamasuna could see the men around him as clearly as if it were noon, their shoulders hunched, pot helmets low over snarling faces and their rifles clutched tightly to their chests. Slater's Knoll was a key feature of a long ridge defended by the Australians. From left and right came the steady rhythmic clatter of Vickers machine guns, and Hamasuna imagined the heavy-calibre bullets cutting swathes of death through the flanking battalions. The guns were answered immediately by the thunk of grenade launchers and the quick-fire rasp of the Type 96 as the Japanese support platoons opened up in reply. He felt the ground beneath his feet change and he was climbing, the slope steep and slippery beneath his rubber-soled shoes, struggling to maintain the pace of the men to his left and right. Up above, the sharp snap of rifle fire, the sound of screams and the crack of grenades signalled that the leading companies had reached the enemy line, but Hamasuna could see nothing but jungle and the backs of his comrades. A heavy machine gun opened fire somewhere close and suddenly men were falling all around him. He gritted his teeth and a growling sound came from his throat as he forced himself on. He stumbled on a body wriggling in a tangle of barbed wire. Twenty metres ahead he could see the first sandbags of slit trenches and his body automatically tensed, ready for the bullet that would end his life. But these positions had already been over-run, the Australian defenders huddled dead in the bottoms of their foxholes or cut down where they'd tried to flee.

'On!' Hamasuna urged his men, only now noticing that the forty he'd started with were down to twenty or less. Ragged, panting scarecrows with eyes a hundred years older than their faces, leaning on their rifles like cripples.

'On,' he screamed again, and the cry was taken up by Murayama, who kicked and pushed his comrades in to motion. Another patch of thick jungle and suddenly they burst into open. By some miracle of nature, night had turned into day and Hamasuna could see barbed-wire emplacements to their right and a line of foxholes ahead. Somehow they had veered round in a half-circle to come in on the flank of the second defensive line. He didn't hesitate.

'Banzai!' He launched himself at the rifle pits, exulting at the site of startled faces beneath the steel helmets. A rifle came round to meet his charge, but before the owner could fire Hamasuna had pumped three bullets into his chest. The company must have been joined by at least one other, because Japanese soldiers were swarming through the position. A big man with three white stripes on the arm of his shirt rose up in front of Hamasuna with his hands raised in surrender and terror in his eyes. In that moment the Australian soldier became the embodiment of everything Hamasuna hated. The government who had torn him from his family. The enemy who had killed so many of his friends. The senior officers who had forced him to endure the last three hours of terror. With a single convulsive movement he brought his sword down across the man's neck, carving diagonally across his chest and ribs, heart blood staining the air pink. The soldier gave a terrible shriek and collapsed slowly backwards.

Hamasuna stood shaking over the body, his bloody sword in hand and his eyes darting left and right seeking the next threat or the next victim. The cacophony of war suddenly became overwhelming, like a wave that threatened to swamp and drown him. Men screaming for their mothers or their wives; terrible cries in a language he didn't understand; rifles, machine guns and grenades combining in a devil's concerto. It paralysed him. His legs wouldn't move. He had to . . .

A savage shove in the back broke the spell. 'Get moving, you bastard, or I'll kill you myself.' He found himself staring bewilderedly into the snarling face of the battalion commander, the pistol in his hand aimed at Hamasuna's heart and his finger on the trigger. 'Your objective is over there.' Minoru pointed. 'Your comrades are dying while you stand here pissing yourself.'

'*Hai!*' Hamasuna bobbed his head and sprinted in

the direction of the pointing finger, screaming at his company to form on him. They reached a path that took them through some kind of plantation, and within moments it opened out on to a clearing. The sight that met his eyes almost shocked him to a standstill. No time for thought. 'On,' he screamed. 'Forward.'

The open space was lined with tight-strung barbed wire and dominated by a long ridge. Hundreds of Japanese soldiers – dead, wounded and alive – were trapped in the bowl beneath a score of machine guns. The living struggled to break through the wire and reach their enemies, being cut down in their turn by streams of tracer bullets that swept the clearing like fiery whiplashes. Despite the carnage, hundreds more men struggled to join them in the blood-soaked arena below the crest. Hamasuna found himself surrounded by snarling comrades, all fighting their way forward into the cauldron.

'Forward!' Even as he screamed the word his whole world turned red and he was at the centre of a kaleidoscope of jagged shapes; like being in a fire surrounded by a hundred smashed mirrors. When his mind cleared he was lying on his back staring at leaden clouds. He was alive, and very slowly his body informed him he wasn't badly hurt. Men and parts of men lay around him, and to his left a smoking crater in the earth showed where the shell that killed them had struck. His helmet was gone, and he'd lost his sword and his pistol. As his hand groped for the sword someone pulled him to his feet. Minoru's screaming face filled his vision. Hamasuna watched the mouth work with disembodied interest, unable to hear a word until the captain slapped him hard on the cheek.

'Tanks,' Minoru screamed. 'We cannot break through here. Withdraw your men and assemble with second company by the big bunker in the enemy front line. We'll find a way to outflank them. There are drums of petrol . . .' Minoru's left eye turned black, then red, and in the same instant the back of his head exploded like an over-ripe pumpkin as the Australian sniper's bullet exited his skull. The captain dropped like a stone at Hamasuna's feet.

'Back,' Hamasuna screamed at the men around them. 'We've been ordered back.' He pushed his way to the rear, gathering what men he could. Most ignored him, driven mad by the strains of battle, the suffering they'd witnessed, and an almost inhuman lust for revenge. 'Back.'

He was nearly clear of the wire when someone punched him in the lower back and he was on his hands and knees, staring at the churned-up ground. His eyes drifted along the underside of his body to his abdomen and a bloody mess of flesh and torn cloth just above his left hip. *I've been shot*, he concluded with a detachment he knew was caused by shock. A voice screamed at him to seek help, but Hamasuna could feel no pain. Logic told him that if he could feel no pain and still stand he must try to gather his men for a new attack. He pushed himself to his feet and stood swaying amid the storm of a battle that was still at its height. An exit wound must have an entry wound, but that seemed of secondary importance at the moment. There was very little bleeding, which meant . . . His brain couldn't quite work out what it meant. He staggered towards the rear through a confused chaos of bodies and wounded men, wire and equipment.

Hamasuna's next conscious memory was of being in the jungle and alone in the darkness. He woke with his back to a tree tormented by a thirst so intense his whole body seemed to have been sucked empty of liquid. His hands scrabbled to his waist and he almost cried out as he discovered the metal canteen on his belt had miraculously survived unscathed. Somehow he managed to unscrew the cap, lift it to his lips and drink deeply. The water was tepid, but as welcome as chilled sake, and provided instant benefit. A fire raged in his lower torso. He looked down expecting to see liquid leaking from his wound, but what little bleeding there had been seemed to have dried up.

Oddly, his mind felt clear. It was telling him to go home, but where was home? His last home had been the bunker he'd shared with his men and he determined to return there. His legs wouldn't hold him upright, but it didn't seem too difficult to crawl and he set off with a certainty that would have concerned him if he'd been more rational. His stomach felt bloated by the water he'd drunk. But the liquid sloshing around his insides wasn't water, it was blood. The bullet had nicked a major artery and it had been leaking into his stomach cavity since he'd been shot. When he found the bunker what seemed a few minutes later he hauled his pain-tormented body inside, making a bed of the leaves and straw to lie on.

Slowly, the realization dawned that this isolated bunker had been abandoned months ago and the jungle had already begun to reclaim it. But that didn't matter; all that mattered was that he was alive. His fingers sought out the precious map case and he hugged it to his chest. He would see Takako and the girls again after all, and he would inform the general personally about the Yamamoto briefcase. Comforted, Hamasuna lay back and closed his eyes, the rise and fall of his chest becoming increasingly shallow, until, with a fitful sigh of regret, it ceased altogether.

XXIV

When the train pulled in at Krasnoyarsk's immense palace of a station Jamie felt a sense of release, as if he'd been freed after a five-year jail stretch. It wasn't so much the confinement as a desperate need to get away from his fellow inmates. Boris's charms had faded with every hour he drank. By the previous night he'd been unable to make the ascent to the top bunk. Instead, he'd sat, an unseen but malevolent presence, at the bottom of his wife's bed, leaning his head on the small table, alternately muttering curses to himself and emitting enormous farts that filled the cramped berth with their putrid odour.

Now, the Russian stared red-eyed as they packed their travel cases in silence. Jamie said a quick Russian goodbye, but Ludmilla surprised them by jumping to her feet and hugging Magda. '*Mozhet ostal'noy chasti vashego puteshestviya v bezopasnosti i doroga ustlana lepestkami roz.*'

Jamie translated. 'Ludmilla says may your journey be safe and the road strewn with rose petals.' From behind her back the little Russian produced a single rose in a plastic pocket, which she pressed into Magda's hand.

'I don't . . .'

'I should have remembered, the Russians are very big on gift-giving. Do you have anything small you can give her in return?'

Magda rummaged in her capacious handbag, but found nothing suitable. She exchanged a glance of panic with Jamie before a solution presented itself. Her hands went to her neck and untied the silk scarf she wore. She offered it to Ludmilla, but the Russian woman looked horrified.

'What have I done?'

'She thinks it's too expensive.'

Magda smiled reassuringly. 'Tell her I would be honoured if she wore it to her son's wedding.'

Ludmilla listened to Jamie's explanation with a frown, but gradually her faced relaxed and she stroked the brightly patterned scarf. '*Spasibo*.' She accepted the gift with a little curtsy.

The bone-chilling Siberian cold hit them the moment they left the train. As the long line of coaches rattled off for Taishet another three hundred miles east, they stood on the platform amongst their luggage and watched with a feeling almost of nostalgia that lasted all of thirty seconds.

Jamie instructed the taxi driver to take them to an internet cafe where they could charge their laptops and phones. He made a mental calculation and decided that, give or take a few hours either way, Fiona would probably be in her bed or just getting out of it, and decided to wait until later to get in touch. It was too early to book into a hotel, so they lingered in the cafe and drank hot coffee and nibbled at the ubiquitous sweet pastries. Magda checked out flights from Krasnoyarsk to Sydney and Tokyo and discovered that the only connections were through Peking or Moscow, but they decided to delay making a decision till later.

Jamie sipped his coffee and pondered their next important step. 'I was thinking that for security reasons we should book a twin room wherever we end up. After the visit from our Chinese friends and your drunk Russian, it would seem sensible and safer for us to be . . . together.'

Magda's eyes narrowed with mock suspicion. 'I hope you're not propositioning me, Jamie?'

He rubbed his unshaven chin thoughtfully. 'For an English gentleman that would naturally be unthinkable and probably a flogging offence into the bargain. I just thought that since we'd shared a six foot by eight foot cell for three days and managed not to intrude too much on each other's modesty, we could probably manage it in a hotel room for one night.'

She considered for a moment. 'All right, that's fine with me, but only as long as I get first chance at the shower.' She pulled at her blouse. 'I feel like this thing is part of me. You really think we can get this done in one afternoon?'

'If we get access to Arkady Berzarin I don't see why not.' Jamie finished off another pastry. 'Either he has the head or he doesn't. If he has, either he'll agree a price or he won't. If he won't we'll walk away and leave the negotiating to Devlin.'

'And what makes you think he'll see us?'

'Because I have a message for him from an old friend.' Guilt froze the smile on his lips, but Magda didn't seem to notice.

She looked around at the figures hunched over the cafe's computers. 'I'm glad,' she said. 'For all its un-doubted charms, Krasnoyarsk isn't the kind of place I want to hang around in.'

Jamie knew what she meant. The moment they'd stepped off the train he'd sensed that Krasnoyarsk had an atmosphere unlike any European city. It radiated all the confidence and immediacy of a place that was going somewhere fast, a boom town, but with an added element. The only way he could describe it was the feeling a lone cowboy would have had riding into a western frontier town during the Gold Rush: a sense of adventure laced with a considerable dash of vulnerability, if not outright danger.

Once they'd booked into their hotel they searched for a taxi and Jamie handed over the address provided by his new best friend Alexei. They drove out through a mixture of factory districts and thickly wooded suburbs into the hills west of the city centre until they reached a well-paved road unlike most of Russia's potholed public thoroughfares. It wound upwards through a long, tree-lined valley and ended at a high wall surrounding what appeared to be an enormous country estate. It was only when the driver slowed well short of the wall and he noticed the sweat on the man's brow that Jamie realized this might be just as hazardous as his experience in Moscow.

'Impressive,' Magda said.

'Mmmmh.' Jamie's eyes were on the barrier outside the estate's main gate a hundred metres ahead. The last time he'd seen anything like it had been in a TV documentary about the Green Zone in Baghdad, where it had been designed to stop suicide bombers. Excessive was the word that came to mind. Then you noticed the gun-toting guards whose eyes never left the approaching taxi, and the little towers where you could almost feel the dark eyes of the rifle muzzles on you. Camouflage parkas, combat trousers and boots. Not military. Not with the array of designer sunglasses on display and the sophisticated communications equipment normally only seen riding shotgun for presidential cavalcades.

The taxi braked sharply as one of the men stepped into the road and raised a hand that was as effective a stop sign as any red light.

'Here we go again.' Magda gave Jamie a familiar look, the one that said: *What have you got me into this time?*

The guard held his rifle – it looked like the latest variant of Kalashnikov – pointed almost carelessly in their direction. While they waited Jamie noticed a tiny red light in the shadow of one of the watchtower openings. Some kind of high-tech camera was analysing the car and its number. 'Don't worry,' he reassured her. 'They're just checking us out.'

Two or three minutes passed before the guard

waved the car up to the barrier. As they reached it the driver lowered his window. 'Your business?' the man in camouflage demanded. The driver nodded to Jamie and Magda and the guard backed away slightly to give himself some rifle room. The barrel of the AK twitched. Jamie took it as a signal to get out of the car and Magda emerged behind him.

'Your business?' the guard repeated.

'We would like to talk with Mr Berzarin on a personal matter,' Jamie said. Beside him, Magda gave a little hiss of exasperation and he realized how lame it sounded.

The guard thought so too. His lips twitched into a smile. 'I do not believe Mr Berzarin is receiving today,' he said solemnly. 'Not to discuss personal matters.'

'His old friend Sergei from university sent his regards and assured me he would be pleased to see us.'

'I don't think so.'

They stared at each other for a few moments, Jamie's image bright and clear in the lens of the sunglasses, his breath misting the chill air. A Mexican stand-off – in the middle of Siberia. The other guards stood chatting to each other and he sensed the man's patience waning. He looked back, ready to return to the taxi, only to hear the engine rev and the tyres squeal as it reversed and drove away up the long road between the trees.

'Oh, Christ,' Magda groaned.

'Enjoy your walk,' the guard dismissed them and turned away.

Magda waited till they were out of sight of the barriers before she exploded. 'That was it? We would like to talk to Mr Berzarin on a personal matter. That was Jamie Saintclair's grand plan to bust into Siberia's answer to Fort Knox?'

'I was assured that mentioning Sergei would get us inside,' he said defensively.

'Only if you'd warned me in advance I'd have faked a ladylike faint and distracted their attention while you slipped past all the machine guns and cameras and God knows what else.'

'I don't think you're taking this seriously, Magda.'

'Seriously?' She stood with her hands on her hips. 'We spent days on that miserable train only to drive half a dozen miles and just walk away because of one little setback?'

'I wouldn't call a dozen men with machine guns a little setback. What else do you expect us to do?'

'I thought you might at least try to climb the wall.'

Jamie noticed that when action was required 'we' had suddenly become 'you'. 'I have an allergy to machine guns,' he said. 'There will be at least fifty more inside those walls, and that's without the infrared beams and the noise sensors and those hidden cameras you mentioned. Oh, and seeing this is Russia, the anti-personnel mines.'

'So what do we do now?'

'We walk. It's about six or seven miles back to the city if we don't freeze to death first.'

'And?'

'I'll think of something.'

She cocked her head to one side and he stared at her. 'I think you'd better do it fast,' she said.

Jamie heard the sound that had alerted her, the rumble of a car's engine. They stepped off the tarmac as a large green Jeep emerged from the trees and drew up beside them. Jamie tensed as the mirror window slowly descended.

'Mr Berzarin will see you now.'

XXV

'I should shoot you now before you cause any more trouble.' The words were in English, which had been established as their common language, but the sentiments and the force with which they were produced were unquestionably Russian. 'There are five hundred square miles of Siberia out there and the wolves are hungry. Your bodies will never be found. Tell me why I shouldn't do that?'

'Because your old friend Sergei would advise against it,' Jamie suggested.

'I don't give a fuck about my old friend Sergei,' their host snorted. 'I have a policy of not mentioning that bastard's name in this house. You never know who is listening. But we know who we're talking about, yes? Someone who has whored himself to the drug lords and the war lords and spy lords.' Jamie nodded. He sensed Magda's consternation but now wasn't the time for explanations. Fortunately, the other man didn't seem to notice the change in atmosphere. 'What are you? FSB? Not with that accent. CIA? No, you're one of those cock-sucking English homos from the SIS or MI6 or whatever they're calling it these days.' He looked Jamie up and down, shaking his head in disbelief. 'Her Majesty would weep if she could see what had happened to James Bond. The English secret service couldn't wipe its own arse without American help. Oh, yes, I've met your Queen, a true lady, lovely and honest, not like those shits in Westminster; clever, too, unlike most of the rest of her brood.'

Arkady Berzarin, son of the former diplomat Gennady and, as it turned out, sole proprietor of Siberia's aluminium industry, sat back in his chair and sipped tea from a china cup. Casually dressed in a dark blue T-shirt, jogging pants and sports shoes, a fluffy white Samoyed hound lay across his feet with its eyes closed, breathing softly. He was fifty-five, but looked ten years younger, with a full head of mouse-brown hair, narrow, shrewd features and a slim build. Opposite him, Jamie and Magda attempted to look equally composed on a couch of soft white leather so broad they'd have had to send semaphore signals if they'd sat at either end. It was all a bewildering contrast to their welcome a few minutes earlier in a sterile metal box inside the gates when they'd been individually strip-searched – by a female guard in Magda's case – and body-scanned for electronic bugs. Now the warm glow of polished pine surrounded them in a large room at the heart of an enormous and particularly opulent Swiss-style chalet. The wooden floor was scattered with dense Persian carpets in vibrant hues and an explosion of what looked to Jamie like genuine Jackson Pollock paintings filled an entire wall. Great spattered vortexes of shape and colour filled with hidden messages, they threatened to swallow you up if you stood too close. Studying them, Jamie was reminded of Keith Devlin's 'collection', and he reflected distractedly that great art was to the billionaire what the Ferrari was to the futures trader, a sort of giant phallic banner waved from a hilltop. Not exactly a fresh or particularly relevant insight, he admitted to himself, but a genuine enough reflection of the new reality.

A beautiful girl in a tailored business suit appeared from a disguised entrance. She handed the Russian a brown paper envelope and whispered in his ear before exiting by the same route. Berzarin weighed the package in his hand.

'Your passports,' he said. 'Apparently genuine, or somebody has built you a very good background. It wouldn't be the first time.' He shook the contents carelessly on to the low glass table that separated them.

'Genuine, sir, I can assure you.' Jamie picked up the maroon oblong with the gold lion and unicorn coat of arms. Odd how comforting it felt to have it back in his hands. He handed the second passport to Magda, and she smiled her thanks.

'So, Mr Jamie Saintclair, art dealer, and Dr Magda Ross, museum curator, you have come to talk to Berzarin about his father,' the Russian nodded absently. 'That is curious enough in itself, but Berzarin would be wise to ask himself why his visitors think it is good manners to force themselves into his presence by the use of a threat?'

'I don't believe we threatened anyone.' Jamie covered his defensiveness with the upper-class Englishman's disdain he'd learned at Cambridge. 'If anything, it was the other way round.'

'So you don't understand that the use of the name Sergei is a threat? That for Berzarin it is the equivalent of a bullet in the mail or a horse's head in the bed?'

'No, I—' Magda's voice reflected her bewilderment, but Berzarin cut her off.

'Sergei was the work name he used when he was a KGB recruiter at the St Petersburg State University – it was still Leningrad State, then – and it was as feared then as his own name is now, at least in certain quarters. Sergei would get you by the balls and he would never let go; I can feel the grip of his cold fingers yet.' He sat forward with a long sigh and the dog at his feet moaned in sympathy. 'Do you understand how difficult it is to be both honest and rich in today's Russia? To hold on to what you have without taking on the form of the creatures who would kill to take it from you?'

Jamie couldn't hide a blink of amused disbelief. Berzarin noticed and went on the attack. 'I saw you looking at my paintings, art dealer, sneering at a rich man's conceit; but let me tell you what they mean to Berzarin. For me they are Russia after the fall: vast, confused and chaotic, but full of potential if a man can only read the messages hidden there; valuable enough to provoke envy, even perhaps to kill for. Like my country, they are the product of a flawed genius, who was eaten alive by the things he loved. What Russian would not like to make such an end, driving his car into a tree

229

with a quart of whisky inside him while his girlfriend gave him a blow-job?' The billionaire laughed, but his eyes betrayed a zeal that revealed the true Berzarin. 'I look at those paintings and I see Siberia twenty years ago. If you don't understand what you are looking at they are just a big mess that it is impossible to make sense of, and therefore of no value to you. But if you can visualize the patterns behind the confusion, the genius of the construction, and discover the treasures hidden beneath the surface, then . . .' the words had tumbled out like rocks in an avalanche and he was forced to pause for breath '. . . then you have something that is literally priceless.'

He ended with a long sigh and called for another pot of tea and three cups. From the hidden entrance came the sound of someone filling a kettle. 'I would offer you something stronger,' he apologized, 'but I no longer have alcohol in this house. It was altogether too seductive for me and I saw the destruction it caused among my countrymen.' When the tea arrived they drank in silence and nibbled at the dainty almond cakes that accompanied it.

Jamie took advantage of the lull to change the conversation's direction. 'Your father was in Berlin before the war. He met Adolf Hitler.'

Berzarin's eyes narrowed, and for a moment Jamie felt like a fish wriggling on a spear. To tell, or not to tell – what would his answer be? Any other man of his class would have thrown them out for their impudence, but it seemed that Arkady Berzarin needed to prove he was different from his peers. He nodded.

'He did not reveal this until many years later. Gennady Ivanovich Berzarin travelled to Nazi Germany in the winter of nineteen thirty-six as part of a secret delegation to assure Hitler that the Soviet Union had no aggressive intentions against any other part of Europe. Stalin regarded the mission as a great success, because my father returned with a suggestion from the Führer that would bear fruit a few years later.' He saw Jamie's eyes widen. 'Oh yes, Mr Saintclair, the destruction and subsequent partition of Poland was conceived on the day my father met Hitler.'

'But Kaganovich—'

'Ah,' Berzarin snorted, 'you have spoken to The Rat – that's what my father called him. I thought he would be long dead but hatred can be an elixir in the right kind of man. Of course,' he shrugged with an eloquence that was almost French, 'this means I can tell you anything and you will not believe me. What did he say about my father?'

Jamie hesitated. 'That he led the mission; that he was a greedy man who took everything the Nazis offered. And that he betrayed him.'

Berzarin nodded slowly. 'All true, apart from being greedy – Gennady Ivanovich was under orders from Litvinov not to reject any gift from the Germans in case the rejection caused annoyance or upset – and that any hesitation to report Kaganovich to the NKVD would have been viewed as treason. I see you still doubt me. My father used to say there was no greater patriot than Dimitri Kaganovich when he was sober, but when he was drunk his mouth had a mind of its own. Gennady

Ivanovich warned him, but the Germans would deliberately get Dimitri drunk. He would tell them everything he knew about the mission and, worse, criticize Stalin and the leadership. Of course, my father reported him, and of course, he helped the NKVD watchers incriminate him, but he also helped save his life at the risk of his own.'

'Did Dimitri know that?' Jamie was trying to reconcile what Kaganovich had told him with this new version of the Berlin story.

'I doubt it,' Berzarin admitted. 'He was a prime candidate for a bullet, but at that time there was still a semblance of Soviet justice and my father was allowed to give a character reference. Later, when Dimitri was sent to the gulag, my father arranged his transfer to the Krasnoyarsk ITL – you would call it a corrective labour camp, I think – where he could ensure he was not badly mistreated. How else do you think such a man survived all those years in the camp system?'

'He said he was a hero.'

'There were many heroes of the Great Patriotic War, but quite a few ended up in the camps. Unlike Kaganovich the majority did not live to enjoy their freedom. My father too was a hero who marched into Berlin and what he took from there laid the foundation for all this.' He waved a hand at the paintings and the house. 'Oh, yes, Mr Saintclair and Dr Ross, I hide nothing from you. My success, such as it is, is based on gold looted from the Nazis. Should I be ashamed of that? I do not think so.'

'Did he tell you what he brought back from his first

visit to Berlin?' Jamie tried to get the conversation back on track.

'Trinkets,' Berzarin shrugged, 'things of little value. He handed them all to Litvinov. For all I know they ended up with Stalin. He had a liking for things that glittered.'

'Nothing from the South Sea Islands?'

Berzarin laughed. 'You think the Nazis presented my father with a canoe.'

'I was thinking of something a little more personal. An artefact with a history.'

The Russian shook his head. 'Nothing.' Jamie couldn't hide his disappointment and the billionaire sighed. 'You see, I cannot help you. I can hardly help myself. And now Sergei wants to take it all away from me and give it to his gangster friends. How would you feel about that, Mr Saintclair? How would you feel if everything you had worked for every day of your life was about to be robbed from you by a man who has betrayed every value he ever possessed?' He rose from his seat and went to the broad window that made up most of the rear wall of the room, beckoning Jamie and Magda with him. 'Bomb-proof glass mirrored on the outside so no one can send me an RPG for breakfast.' He extended an arm to take in the bare expanse of tundra that stretched more than a mile before it turned to dark green forest. 'Everything you can see from here is mine, but I almost lost it all in the crash of 2008. The only reason I still have it is because I was negotiating with the same fools who caused the disaster in the first place. It turned out the banks were in a weaker position than I was. They backed off when they understood I would never give up what was mine without a fight. Now I must fight for it again and my opponent is a man without morals or pity who will use any weapon to get what he wants. Just as he is using you.'

'It seems we have been wasting your time,' Jamie said carefully.

The Russian turned away from the window, his face thoughtful. 'Perhaps. Perhaps not. Did he send any message?'

'No. All my contact said was to say that your old friend Sergei sends his regards.'

'Then *you* are the message.' Berzarin's voice turned harsh. Suddenly, the man who had wheeled and dealed and fought his way to control one of Russia's strategic industries was revealed. 'He knew about this artefact you seek?'

Jamie thought back to his meeting in the sterile dacha outside Moscow; the feeling that the Russian had been able to see into his soul. 'I believe so.'

'Then he would know that my father never had it. That means he has sent you on what you English call a "wild-duck race" . . .'

'Goose chase,' Jamie corrected automatically.

'. . . or there is some other reason.'

Jamie felt himself the focus of two sets of eyes, the one appraising, the other filled with a mixture of confusion and anger. This was the first time Magda Ross had heard about his meeting and it would take some delicate diplomacy to convince her he'd been right to keep her in the dark. But that would have to wait. The question now was would Vatutin's shadowy boss send them all the way to Krasnoyarsk simply to increase the pressure on his enemy? Berzarin himself had said he would use any weapon, so it was possible, but there could be another explanation.

'Were you acquainted with the businessman Oleg Samsonov?'

Berzarin frowned at the change of subject. 'Of course. Sometimes we were allies and sometimes rivals, but always we were friends. I was genuinely devastated by what happened to him and Irina.' He glanced sharply at Jamie. 'Was it Sergei's doing?'

'No,' the Englishman assured him. 'The shootings were the work of a disgruntled employee.' He hesitated. 'I only wondered if you were aware of his interest in art?'

The Russian had a way of becoming very still, which wasn't threatening until you realized it was the stillness of a hunting leopard just before the pounce. 'Why would you ask such a question?'

'Because,' Jamie looked past Berzarin's shoulder to the central Jackson Pollock, a monstrous kaleidoscopic spatter of reds and blues like the eye of a hurricane, 'Sergei's messenger mentioned he had a similar interest.' He ignored the billionaire's disbelieving snort. 'In fact,' he went on carefully, 'he suggested that a certain recently acquired painting in Oleg Samsonov's collection was a loan between friends. When Oleg died, it appears there was some confusion about the picture's origin and it went missing, purloined, claimed or otherwise placed in the custody of a person, or persons, unknown.' Jamie allowed a sympathetic smile to touch his lips; the odd things that happened to billionaire art collectors. 'Apparently, Sergei was quite put out and he's very keen to get it back.'

'And he believes I have this painting?'

'He didn't say as much, but the possibility crossed my mind.'

'Come with me, both of you.' Berzarin marched from the large room and up a set of wide stairs to a pair of double doors that led to the bedroom suite, an even larger space with a raised bed about the size of a tennis court in the centre. Other doors led off to what must be dressing rooms, showers and, for all Jamie knew, an Olympic-size swimming pool. His eyes searched the room for the explosion of gold that would release him from the Faustian contract he had struck, but if it was here it was well hidden. 'He knew I had always admired it.' The Russian stopped in front of an alcove that would be the first thing the bed's occupant would see when they woke in the morning. 'Even so, I was surprised when the attorney called to let me know I'd been left it in his will.' He moved aside to allow his guests a view of the contents and Jamie stepped forward eagerly – only to be disappointed. Not the only copy of Van Gogh's *Sunflowers* in private hands that would get him off Sergei's carefully forged hook, but a rather drab-looking portrait of a plump, arrogant man wearing a velvet doublet and with his hands on his hips.

'It is wonderful,' Magda Ross whispered, and, looking closer, Jamie had to agree. The artist had encapsulated the sneering man's entire personality in that expression and that stance; his disdain for the proceedings, the near violent feelings he had for his tormentor and the raw physical strength hidden by the shining cloth. A substantial gilt frame surrounded the picture.

'The papers are entirely in order,' Berzarin growled. 'If Sergei wants it he'll have to fight me for it. There is a full company of ex special forces soldiers in the grounds and I can have a battalion here within the hour. Let him come with his gangsters. He will find that Siberia is not Moscow.'

'Oh, I don't think you'll have to worry about that, old chap,' Jamie assured him. 'Though I've no doubt he'd be interested if he knew about it. One of *Meinheer* Rembrandt's better efforts, I think.' Berzarin's lips clamped in a thin smile at the artful dismissal of *Portrait of a Man, half-length and with his arms akimbo*, which, to Jamie's certain knowledge, had captured a record price for the artist from an anonymous buyer at Christie's a couple of years earlier. Their eyes met and he searched the other man's for any sign of a lie, but found only wary defiance. 'On the other hand, if you happen to be offered a temporarily mislaid Van Gogh, please give me a call.'

'So, we are done,' the Russian said. 'The only concern now is how I dispose of you.'

XXVI

'I'm glad Comrade Berzarin's English wasn't entirely up to scratch,' Jamie said as he and Magda shared a table at the internet cafe near the hotel. 'Just for a moment I thought we were going to end up buried in a Siberian bog with a bullet for company.'

He accompanied the observation with a wry smile that wasn't reciprocated. In fact, there was something quite intimidating about the way his companion was playing with her bread knife. Almost as intimidating as the scowl she'd worn for the past hour and the silence that had accompanied it.

He sighed. 'You're not still angry about the Sergei thing? I told you,' he carried on with what he considered was impeccable logic, 'it was nothing to do with the Bougainville head. An entirely separate issue. A loose end left over from a previous commission. In any case,' he sought out her hand, but she whipped her fingers away, 'there are some things it's better not to know. I didn't want you involved.'

'I can look after myself, Jamie.' The brown eyes

238

skewered him. 'But don't you think I deserved to be kept informed after the visit from your Chinese *acquaintances*?' She let her eyes drift across their fellow customers. 'If I'd known someone like that was taking an interest it might have explained the familiar faces I keep seeing from the train.'

'What familiar faces?' He followed her gaze.

'Not here.' She shook her head. 'On the streets. They're mostly men, but at least one woman. I think one of them might have been the drunk who questioned me on the way from the bathroom on the train.'

'Coincidence.' He ignored her withering look. 'Krasnoyarsk is one of the more scenic attractions on the Trans-Siberia route. You'd expect tourists to stop off here for a couple of days.'

'These men aren't tourists. I think they're following us.'

'It might have been helpful if you'd mentioned it before.'

'I didn't know then that a very intimidating person was in partnership with my travelling companion.'

'Would it help if I apologized again?'

'No.'

'Not even if the good news is that I've booked us first-class tickets to Tokyo.'

Her eyes turned suspicious. 'If that's the good news, what's the bad news?'

'The flight's at four tomorrow morning.'

'I suppose that puts paid to my beauty sleep again.' She sighed. 'It's a pity this was all such a waste of time.'

'Not at all,' Jamie said cheerfully. 'It's how the business

works. Sometimes you end up chasing shadows, but you don't know it's a shadow until you've caught it. We might have walked into that room and found the Bougainville head on the mantelpiece between his Jackson Pollocks. "Take it away, Mr art dealer Saintclair, Berzarin is fed up with it and needs to make room for a Ming vase." All right, it didn't happen, but we'd never have known without being here.'

She smiled at his passable imitation of Berzarin's voice. 'So tomorrow night we'll be in Tokyo and out of the clutches of Sergei's annoying followers.' The knowledge clearly invigorated her because her eyes glittered with excitement and Jamie reflected that she appeared to have as much invested in this quest as he did. The thought gave him another twinge of guilt.

'Look, I really am sorry I didn't tell you . . .'

'You're forgiven, but from now on we're proper partners. No more secrets, right?'

'No more secrets.' He stood up and went to pay the bill, hoping she was right about the minders, but not entirely convinced. That wasn't the way it usually worked out for Jamie Saintclair.

They walked back to the hotel along one of the city's broad avenues and she linked her arm through his, suggesting he really was forgiven. Even through the padded jackets he could feel the curve of her breast against his bicep and he tried to think of Fiona back in Sydney or wherever she would be at this time, which reminded him he still needed to phone her. If it was 8 p.m. in Krasnoyarsk what time did that make it in Australia? He was still trying to work out the time difference when the drunk stumbled into him with a slurred '*yob tvoyu mat*' and it wasn't until the man was past that Jamie realized he'd felt a sharp sting in the hip at the exact moment of collision.

He stopped and looked back in confusion as the man disappeared into an alleyway.

'Is something wrong, Jamie?'

'I don't know.' He pulled up his jacket and shirt and in the light of a streetlamp tried to check the area of flesh where he'd felt the sting, but the angle and the bulk of the coat made it too awkward. 'Can you see anything?'

Her face was already pale in the artificial light, but he could have sworn it went even whiter. The dark eyes filled with concern. 'I think . . .'

'What?' he demanded.

'It looks like a puncture mark.'

For a moment Jamie's head spun and he felt like vomiting. Breath became hard to come by and Magda acted as a prop as she helped him to a nearby doorway. It was a combination of shock and fear – or was there something coursing through his system turning his blood to tar? Pull yourself together, idiot, it was just a drunk. But a drunk on the train had harassed Magda. Was it the same man? After what she'd said earlier surely she'd have recognized him? But this one had been wrapped up in a winter coat with a cap low over his face. Jamie had an image of a bald man lying back on a hospital bed, patches on his chest and tubes and electrical leads hanging from his emaciated body. What had his name been? Litvinenko, that was it. Alexander Litvinenko. A former FSB officer who'd fled to London seeking asylum, he'd accused his former masters of arranging the Moscow theatre siege that had left a hundred and thirty people dead, along with forty Chechen terrorists. He'd also accused high-ranking members of the government of complicity in the death of a prominent Moscow journalist. Someone had poisoned him with a radioactive isotope and it had taken him three painful weeks to die.

'Can you walk?'

Christ, he'd forgotten where he was. 'I think so.' Magda took his arm and they stumbled in the direction of the hotel. What reason could anyone possibly have for . . . ? He thought back to his conversation with Berzarin. If the FSB had somehow managed to get a bug into the aluminium mogul's living room had he revealed too much to Sergei's sworn enemy? No, it wasn't possible. But what about their new friend Berzarin? For all his comradely bonhomie – *Do you understand how difficult it is to be both honest and rich in today's Russia?* – he was a ruthless tycoon who'd built his fortune on the bodies of lesser men, some of them undoubtedly in the ranks of the Russian mafia. Maybe Berzarin had decided it would be more convenient to get rid of the nuisance away from his home?

Jamie's head had cleared a little by the time they reached the hotel and he was able to walk up the steps unassisted. They took the lift up to the third floor and Magda opened the door to the twin room. When they were inside Jamie staggered to the toilet and was sick into the bowl.

'I'll get the front desk to call a doctor,' Magda said as he emerged, wiping his mouth with a paper towel.

'No. I don't think so . . . If you do that I'll end up in hospital where they'll want to do tests and keep me under observation. I could be there for a week and I don't fancy a week in a Russian hospital. I'm feeling much better now. We have to get out of here tonight.' He saw her face harden and shook his head. 'I think it's only shock and over-reaction. Get them to book a taxi to the airport and set the alarm for one a.m.' He stripped off his jacket and threw it over a chair, pulling the tail of his shirt and opening his jeans so he could study the mark she'd seen. There it was: a tiny dark spot surrounded by about an inch of reddened skin. A thin line of watery blood wept from the puncture. No dark lines reaching out from it, which had to be good news. He returned to the bathroom and washed the wound before applying copious amounts of antiseptic cream. His vaccinations were up to date, which should rule out hepatitis and tetanus. If the needle had been infected with HIV there wasn't a lot he could do about it, and if someone had injected him with Polonium or whatever they'd used on Alexander Litvinenko, he was already dead, which was a cheerful thought. There was only one thing for it. He lay down on the left-hand bed and closed his eyes. 'In the meantime, I'm going to try to get some sleep.'

Magda stood over him, waiting for his breathing

to regulate. When she was certain he slept, she went to the door and silently opened it before slipping out into the corridor. She returned a few minutes later and contemplated the two beds for a moment before lying down fully clothed beside Jamie and pulling a coverlet across both their bodies.

XXVII

They arrived in Tokyo two days later after an overnight stop at Beijing airport. Jamie's hip throbbed and he barely registered the low descent over the grey waters of Tokyo Bay with the city's soaring skyline a spiky, gap-toothed rampart painted stark against the low hills beyond, and both dwarfed by the snow-dusted vastness of Mount Fuji in the far distance.

When they reached the multi-storey Hyatt hotel in Minato, Magda insisted on sending for an English-speaking doctor to examine him and a young Japanese man arrived at their suite within thirty minutes. He probed the area around the puncture mark with a gloved finger and frowned at it for a while before asking Jamie to remove his shirt and checking his heart and lungs. Then he wrapped an inflatable bandage around the Englishman's arm to take his blood pressure. Another study of the wound was necessary, this time with the help of what looked like a pair of binoculars, before he made his prognosis.

'I think you'll live, Mr Saintclair,' he announced,

with what Jamie felt was a rather casual air given the circumstances. 'Your blood pressure is a little low, which would account for the lack of energy you're feeling, but that's probably a result of the shock you had and I've no doubt it will pass.'

'You'd have been shocked too if you'd been stabbed by a hypodermic syringe of unknown origin.'

The doctor picked up his odd-shaped binoculars again. 'I don't think either the dimensions or the characteristics of the wound would suggest a syringe. It's also quite shallow. You're worried about HIV, I take it?'

'Wouldn't you be?' Jamie said.

'I suppose it's possible that someone could contract HIV from something like a nail, or more likely the pin of a belt buckle.' He shrugged. 'On balance, I'd say the odds are against it. I'll take a blood test, of course, but . . .'

With a wince, Jamie remembered the jacket the drunk had been wearing when he barged into him – the one festooned with straps and buckles. He ignored Magda's raised eyebrow.

'That won't be necessary . . .'

'Oh, I insist,' the young man said gravely. 'I wouldn't be doing my duty as a medical practitioner otherwise. It won't take long. If you'll just roll up your sleeve again.'

Magda waited until the doctor was gone. 'Buckle?'

'You were the one who said it looked like a puncture,' Jamie complained. 'How was I to know what caused it, especially with all that stuff about people following us?'

'You should be glad someone is keeping their eyes

open on this trip.' She tilted her head to study him. 'Am I right in thinking the patient is about to make a re-markable recovery?'

'Oddly enough, he is.' He smiled. 'All down to the wonders of medical science and your nursing skills.'

'In that case, we should get back to business,' she said decisively. 'I noticed they had some decent maps of the city down in reception. Why don't you give Fiona a call while I get one? She must be wondering what's hap-pened to you?'

Jamie looked at his watch. It would be early evening in Sydney. Worth a try. He punched in the mobile number, but the phone immediately went to a disembodied voice that informed him the person he was attempting to call was not available to answer. Disappointed, he tried again, with the same result. Given that Fiona had probably had similar problems phoning him in Russia, the lack of communication didn't seem anything to worry about. Still, he thought he'd mention it to Devlin. He called the Australian to let him know they'd arrived in Tokyo and a secretary informed him the mining tycoon was in an important meeting. She promised to call Jamie back as soon as Devlin was available.

The phone went while he was still in the shower and he shrugged on a robe.

'Saintclair.'

'What have you got for me?' Jamie detected an abrupt edge to Keith Devlin's voice, but he replied in his usual amiable tone.

'Russia was a dead end, I'm afraid. We've just arrived in Tokyo.'

'Why am I just hearing this now?'

'Because we had a few problems in Krasnoyarsk.' Jamie explained about the drunk and his fears he'd been attacked.

'And that was all?'

The disbelief in Devlin's voice was clear. Jamie frowned; this was beginning to feel like an interrogation. 'Why should there be anything else?'

'I had this Berzarin bloke checked out.' The other man didn't hide his anger. 'It turns out he's in the same business as Devlin Metal Resources. If he happened to get wind of why we really want the head he could be a problem.'

'I think you're over-reacting, if you don't mind me saying so.'

'Well I bloody do mind,' Devlin was plainly unconvinced. 'I didn't get what I have today by letting other people make the running. From my point of view he's like a little bit of grit under the eyelid. You always feel better when it's removed.'

A long silence followed while Jamie contemplated the significance of the word 'removed'. 'Look, Mr Devlin,' he said slowly, 'I'm sensing an undercurrent to this conversation I don't very much like. If you don't trust me all you have to do is say and I'll be on the first plane back to Sydney.'

'Don't get all shirty with me, son.' The tone changed instantly and the old chirpy Devlin reappeared. 'I apologize if I've been abrupt, but it's been a tough day. Remember, you owe those little ladies of yours a bit of pampering.'

Jamie frowned. 'By the way, I haven't been able to get in touch with Fiona. Do you know how she is?'

'Last I heard she was having a great time with a couple of aunts out in Perth and the kid was being treated like a princess. You just leave them to me and find that fella's bonce and get straight back here.'

Jamie assured him he'd get to work the next day. 'All I have is an address. I was under the impression that one of your people was going to meet us with more information.'

He heard Devlin grunt. 'There's been a change of plan,' the Australian said. 'We've had a little trouble in one of our Philippines operations and my man's had to fly to Manila to sort it out. Turns out he didn't have much to give you anyway. This Yoshitaki crowd are proving a harder nut to crack than the bloody Russians. Your major became a war hero, but when it was all over he disappeared into obscurity. Turns out it happened to a lot of prominent Japs. They couldn't stand the dishonour of defeat, so they gave up public life. The last he's heard of is in a short and not particularly revealing obituary after his death in 'fifty-five. We might have been able to squeeze a bit more out of the Tokyo cops if Bill had still been in town, but to be honest he wasn't hopeful. The address is the only thing we have for the Yoshitaki family, and that could be out of date by as much as a decade.'

'You're not exactly raising my expectations.'

'I'm just telling it like it is, son.' There was a moment's hesitation and Jamie had a feeling that, on the other end of the line, Devlin was smiling, and not in a nice way.

'Maybe you'll have to go an extra mile just to prove or disprove whether the head is in Tokyo.'

'What do you mean by that, Mr Devlin?' he said carefully.

'Just that you have a reputation as a resourceful man, Jamie. From what I hear you had to cut a few corners when you were going after that Raphael painting. Maybe even crossed a line or two.'

'The one thing I've learned, Mr Devlin, is that when you cross that line you have a tendency to also be putting your neck on a block. Maybe I was prepared to do that for a hundred million pounds' worth of Old Master, but I'm not sure a smelly old shrunken head is worth the same risk, no matter what you're prepared to pay for it.'

'Well, that's for you to decide, Jamie boy,' there was an emphasis on the last two words and Devlin's voice held a hint of something indefinable that might have been menace, 'but when you're making your decision just spare a thought for those two little ladies of yours.'

'What is that supposed to mean, Devlin?'

'Just what I say, Jamie boy. If you don't come up with the goods over the next few days I have a feeling that Fiona and Lizzie are going to be a mite disappointed in you, and we don't want that, do we?'

The phone went dead in Jamie's hand and he sat for a moment tempted to throw the oblong of plastic against the wall. He wasn't one hundred per cent certain what he'd just been told, but instinct told him the stakes had just got a lot higher than he'd bargained for.

'Jamie?'

He looked up to find Magda in the doorway. 'Something has changed,' he tried to explain. 'I have a feeling my client in Sydney doesn't trust us. Maybe he didn't trust me from the start. If I'm right he knows I went off the radar in Moscow. Possibly he knows about our Chinese visitors too. Suddenly he may not be the only player in the game. A man like Keith Devlin isn't going to take that lying down. I'm pretty sure he just threatened Fiona and her daughter.'

'Why would he do that?' She sounded sceptical.

'I don't know,' he admitted. 'It's as if what started as a game has suddenly turned much more serious. I took a look at the business pages in the paper earlier and Devlin Metal Resources shares are about as popular as the Black Death. There are rumours of an announcement, which is generally a bad sign.' He went to the window and looked out over the skyline towards the distant mountains. 'Remember what Berzarin said about almost going bust in the crash. What if Devlin is in the same position? What if this Bougainville deal isn't about putting a jewel in the crown of his glittering business career, but survival? Devlin might be close to losing everything he's worked for and the company that's been in his family for three generations?'

When he turned she was staring at him with a frown of indecision. For a moment he thought she might be about to say something important, but eventually she just shrugged. 'That might be enough to push him over the edge. But what can we do?'

Jamie picked up the map she'd brought from reception. 'We can knock on the door of the Yoshitaki place first thing tomorrow morning and suggest that the late major's relatives might want to send the head back to its homeland.'

She looked doubtful and he didn't blame her. He had a distinct feeling Devlin was right. He was going to have to go the extra mile before the job was done. But if that's what it took to keep Fiona and Lizzie safe he knew he wouldn't hesitate.

XXVIII

The former home of Major Kojima Yoshitaki turned out to be in a fairly unremarkable part of Tokyo, with the usual high-rise apartment blocks, but more than its share of detached homes and several institutes and museums. The taxi driver negotiated his way through a series of narrow back streets and drew to a halt beside a blank seven-foot wall with a steel gate and entry-phone system. Beyond the gate stretched an area of extensive woodland, which *was* remarkable this close to the city centre. Jamie's heart sank as he recognized the kind of security set-up favoured by rich men who had things to hide or people to keep away. It didn't bode well for a warm welcome.

'Ask him if this is the right address.'

Magda hit the driver with a quick-fire burst of Japanese and received a longer version in reply.

'He says there's no mistake. Apparently this would once have been an estate belonging to a *daimyo*, a Japanese lord. It looks as if the Yoshitakis have been important people around here for centuries. He's asking if we want him to wait for us.'

'Tell him no. I have a feeling the fewer witnesses we have the better.' He saw her frown. 'Anyway, we shouldn't have too much trouble finding another cab around here.'

Jamie got out of the car and wandered nonchalantly across to the gate. Reinforced steel, with retractable supporting bollards behind. Heavy enough to stop anything but a proper tank. No doubt there'd be a surveillance system, which meant they were being watched.

'What do you think?' he asked Magda.

'I'm hoping you've come up with something cleverer than Krasnoyarsk.'

'Like all the great generals I intend to use the most effective weapon in my armoury,' he said airily. 'Actually, I was wondering if you might like to have a try this time.'

Her lips pursed and he braced himself for the expected backlash to this craven abdication of responsibility, but eventually she nodded. 'Okay.' She studied the gate in her turn until she spotted the almost invisible button on the left-hand pillar with a little mesh grill above it.

As she reached for it, a car parked fifty metres to their left suddenly growled into life and drew out into the roadway. They tensed as it inched its way towards them, and they found themselves the focus of the two hard-eyed young Japanese men. Jamie sensed they were memorizing every molecule of his features. As if that wasn't proof enough, as the car drew level the man in the passenger seat raised a camera to the open window and the quick-fire click-click-click of the automatic shutter announced he was taking multiple images. When the photographer was satisfied he said something to the driver, the engine revved and the car sped off.

'What was that all about?' Magda wondered aloud.

Jamie watched the car disappear round a corner. 'I'm not sure. The police, probably. They saw us mooching around and decided to take a look just in case we had larceny in mind.' Unless, of course, they were watching the place for a specific reason. But what that reason might be, and why they should want pictures of visitors, was anybody's guess. He was certain of only one thing: it stank to high heaven. He could see she didn't believe him, but there was no point in speculating.

Magda stepped up and spoke into the microphone and there was a long pause before a male voice emerged from the speaker with a reply.

'What did you say?'

'Simple. I asked if this was the home of the Yoshitaki family and told him we're interested in shrunken heads.'

'And?'

'It looks as if the feminine approach works.' She tilted her head and gave him a superior look. 'They want to know whether we're buying or selling.'

'You're a genius.' He grinned.

Before she could reply a mechanical whirr sounded as the bollards retracted and the massive steel gate slid open to reveal a tarmac road leading into the trees. For an instant Magda seemed reluctant to move, as if there was something momentous about the next step and it would take her over an invisible line. Jamie sensed her hesitation and wondered what caused it, but there was no going back now. He reached out to touch her hand. 'Nothing to fear but fear itself, as a wise man once said. This is what we came for.'

The contact seemed to break the spell. She took a deep breath and they walked side by side through the gate and into the shadow of the trees.

'I think our chariot awaits.' As the gate closed behind them Magda pointed to an odd vehicle parked in a bay to their right. Painted green and gold, it looked like an over-sized golf buggy with six seats under a canvas roof, four wheels, but no engine or steering mechanism that they could see. 'What do you think?'

'I suppose it must be here for a reason,' Jamie agreed.

They took the two front seats and waited, feeling slightly foolish until, without warning, it moved into gear with an electronic whirr. With a hiss of rubber tyres the buggy followed the road as it wound its way through the open woodland that Jamie pointed out on the map as an island of green in one of the most populated cities on the planet.

'This must be one of the most valuable pieces of real estate in Tokyo,' Magda broke the silence. 'Most of these places would have been turned into parks.'

'You have to hand it to old Yoshitaki,' Jamie agreed, 'somehow he managed to save all this while the rest of the city drowned in concrete. He clung on to his heritage through war and famine and financial disasters that brought ruin to millions. That's evidence of not just money, but power.'

After another hundred metres they turned a corner

and Magda said quietly, 'Does this thing have a reverse gear?'

Jamie was thinking something similar, but it was too late to turn back now. He struggled to evaluate the building at the far end of the neatly maintained lawn. Long and low, the grey concrete structure reminded him of a Second World War bunker. Whoever built this house had security in mind. The massive frontage – he assumed this was the front – was made up of three storeys of overlapping layers of concrete, each thick enough to stop a rocket-propelled grenade, and with not a pane of glass in sight. It might have been a factory or a military installation with its aerials and satellite dishes, but two horses in a paddock on the far side of the lawn were evidence this was someone's home.

The cart slid to a silent halt in front of the building and two oriental men in dark suits stepped out from a hidden guard house to meet them. Meet, but not greet. Not a word was spoken as they motioned Jamie and Magda from their seats and indicated they should raise their hands to be searched. Jamie complied without protest and the leaner of the two began to pat him down, but Magda spat a stream of Japanese at the man facing her. Built squat, low and solid as a brick outhouse, the most emotionless eyes she'd ever seen stared out from a flat, moon face and his only reply was to step back and fold his arms over his massive chest.

'I think he's trying to tell you that you're not going anywhere until he searches you,' Jamie pointed out.

'And you think I'm going to let him?' She glared.

'Look at them. They're professionals. All we are to them is a potential threat.'

'I don't want some Japanese pervert running his filthy hands all over me.'

'Actually, he looks more Korean. And look at his left hand.'

The man stood patiently with his arms crossed, the fingers splayed out against the fabric of his jacket. 'You mean he's missing a finger?' She smiled sweetly at her confronter. 'With a face like his I'm surprised that's all he's missing.'

'It's a very specific injury,' Jamie continued. 'The top joint of the finger has been removed. I think he probably cut it off himself.'

Magda frowned. 'Why would he do that?'

'Because he's Yakuza.'

Without another word she handed her bag to the thin guard and raised her arms above her head. As the stocky Korean approached her, she whispered something to him in Japanese. The man stared at her for a long moment before his face split into a grin. Three minutes later they were being escorted down a corridor of polished concrete under the unblinking red eye of a pair of security cameras.

'What did you say to him?' Jamie asked.

'I told him that if his hands got out of place even once I'd add something else to his list of missing parts.' She studied the corridor's bare walls. 'What really interests me is why a Japanese gangster would agree to see us?'

'It has to be the head,' Jamie said. 'It confirms this house is connected to Major Kojima Yoshitaki and whoever now owns it is intrigued enough to open the doors of his citadel to us. The chiefs of the Yakuza crime clans like to think of themselves as civilized businessmen, regardless of the evidence. He obviously thinks he has nothing to lose by meeting us.'

'You seem to know a lot about them for an art dealer.'

'I've come across them a couple of times in Europe,' he confessed, 'though without really knowing who I was dealing with. The Yakuza is an international organization. They're as happy trafficking stolen artworks as drugs or Korean sex slaves, so I had to learn a bit about them. On one level they run an incredibly sophisticated operation, a sort of global criminal octopus whose tentacles reach into every country and at all levels of society. On another they're just a brutal gang of thugs, with almost medieval rules and traditions.'

'The human battering ram there with his missing finger?'

'Exactly. If a lower ranking member of a clan offends his boss in some way he has to cut off the top of his finger and send him it as a sign of apology. And if our friend there was to take off his shirt I can just about guarantee you'd find his torso covered in tattoos that signify his status in the organization. It's a matter of honour among the Yakuza to have it done the traditional way – what they call "hand poked" – by an expert using a sharp stick rather than a machine.'

Magda looked over her shoulder at the human battering ram, who stared back with a half-smile that made her wonder if he was as dumb as he made out. 'Tough guys, huh?'

'Tough guys indeed.'

'Did I ever tell you about my tattoo?'

Jamie was still laughing as they climbed a set of wide white stairs that led to the second level of the building. When they reached the top he understood why the outside of the building had no windows. It had been designed as an open square, with a central area as large as half a football pitch. The second and third storeys had inner walls of glass looking out on to an immaculate Japanese garden, complete with streams and waterfalls and fishponds, miniature temples and ornate bridges. Somehow the temperature and humidity in the garden must have been regulated because, despite the season, all sorts of flowers and trees were still in bloom, creating a blaze of colour from azure-petalled irises, pastel-painted orchids, delicate pink cherry blossom and flame-tipped azaleas. They barely had time for a glimpse before their silent escort led them to a room furnished with chairs and couches that looked as if they'd been carved from concrete, but which they discovered were actually fabric.

After a few minutes an electronic door in the far wall slid open and the thin guard ushered them through to a large office. Jamie gradually became aware of another presence. A woman stood partially hidden in the shadows staring out of the window at the garden. Slim and straight backed, her long dark hair was pulled back in a ponytail and she wore a white blouse and tight riding breeches. Her hands were clasped behind her back in a pose that was more European than Oriental and her whole bearing had an air of strength and authority.

They waited for her to turn and acknowledge them, but she seemed in no hurry and Jamie allowed his eyes to drift over the room. The first thing that drew his attention was a large oak desk on which a long Samurai sword lay horizontally on a cushion of blue velvet. For all the formality of its display it was a functional weapon: a soldier's sword. It had a well-worn leather grip and the naked blade was long and slightly curved, the edge glinted blue from regular sharpening. Something told him its purpose wasn't purely ornamental.

'My grandfather's sword.' The words were addressed at Jamie and in English without a trace of accent, but they emerged from features that could not have been more Japanese. Her face was made up of planes and shadows with barely a curve to mar the symmetry. Deep-set dark eyes stared from beneath long lashes above cheekbones sharp enough to rival the sword blade on the desk. The eyes radiated an intensity and a ruthlessness – you might even call them pitiless – that made Jamie wish he'd stayed in Australia. Feminine lips, but a hard mouth; a thin, humourless line that might have been etched by a knifepoint. She must have been close to fifty but her body had the angular athleticism of someone twenty years younger. Everything about her said this was a woman not to be underestimated.

'You must be very proud of him to display it so prominently.' Magda's voice demanded acknowledgement and there was a moment of almost electric tension between the two women, as if two alley cats had met unexpectedly at a street corner.

The Japanese looked the anthropologist up and

down and a dismissive smile flickered on the thin lips.
'Of course.'

'And your grandfather must be Major Kojima
Yoshitaki?' Jamie took over the conversation with a
warning glance at his companion.

A slight nod. 'He ended the war as major general in
charge of homeland defence.'

'Then it was fortunate he never had to command his
forces in battle.'

'Believe me, my grandfather did not think himself
fortunate.' The words were almost contemptuous. 'He
would have fought on even after the nuclear bombs the
Americans dropped on our cities. A million casualties
was his estimate of the cost of an invasion of Nippon.'

'On which side?'

'You have a sense of humour, Mr . . . ?'

'Saintclair. Jamie Saintclair.'

'It can be an admirable trait, but in Japan we have a
saying: *Silence surpasses speech.* Sometimes it is better
to say nothing than to say the wrong thing. My asso-
ciates also think you are very rude. You do not bow, nor
hand over your business card to effect an introduction.'

'I apologize if we have offended you,' Jamie said. 'We
are unfamiliar with Japanese culture. Dr Ross and I
have only just arrived in Tokyo, Miss . . . ?'

'You may call me Madam Nishimura.' She walked to
the desk with an elegant flowing stride and slipped into
a leather executive chair. The moment she was in position a black cat squeezed its way through a narrow gap
in the window and crossed the room to jump into her
lap. Nishimura scratched its head and it began to purr

gently as she stroked the gleaming fur. Jamie was re-minded of a scene from a Bond film and something told him that was the effect she had intended. 'Please,' she said, indicating a pair of chairs by the door, 'perhaps we can get down to the purpose of your visit.'

Jamie took his seat with Magda beside him. 'Prior to the Second World War,' he explained, 'your grandfather was a diplomat as well as a soldier. We are here to talk about an artefact he may have brought back from a visit to Berlin in the nineteen thirties.'

'No, Mr Saintclair, you are mistaken.' The dark eyes glittered with malice and the cat lifted its head to add its own glare of annoyance. 'You are here because I do not like loose ends. You mentioned a shrunken head, which I presume is the artefact to which you refer. For reasons of my own, I found the importance of such an unlikely item to you of interest. Under certain circumstances the fact that you brought this subject to my attention might be considered a threat. Someone in my position cannot afford to ignore a threat. Do you understand?'

Jamie smiled politely at the unspoken implication the threat might have to be neutralized, or perhaps even eliminated altogether, but the room had suddenly grown a little cooler. He hesitated before replying, noticing for the first time that the regular shadows lining the walls were in reality small niches. 'You have been very frank and I hope you'll forgive me for being equally so.' Nishimura's eyes narrowed but he was committed now. 'Firstly, let me assure you that Dr Ross and I pose no threat to you. I have been commissioned to track down a relic of a primitive culture which my client intends, for reasons of natural justice, to return to its original owners. It is possible, given your relationship to Major Yoshitaki, that you are in possession of this relic. If that's the case my client is prepared to pay substantial compensation for your loss. We are talking about a straightforward business transaction.'

'Straightforward, Mr Saintclair?' Madame Nishimura smiled coldly. 'Do you really believe there is anything straightforward about your current predicament?' She leaned forward and pressed a button on the desk. Lights flicked on to illuminate the contents of the mysterious recesses.

'Oh, my God.' Jamie heard Magda's hiss as his heart seemed to stop.

Thirty. His mind must have counted them of its own accord. Thirty hairy shrivelled orbs each the size of a small coconut.

XXIX

The mind took time to come to terms with the fact that they had once been living breathing human beings. A photograph of the Bougainville head did nothing to convey the obscene reality of the blind, half-shut eyes, leathery brown skin and protruding, oversized fleshy lips and noses. If Jamie hadn't known what they were he might have convinced himself he was looking at the last remnant of some long-lost bastard union of men and monkey. Their hair was lush and thick, as if they'd died only yesterday, and ranged in colour from black to brown to a startling straw-blond.

He turned to Magda to see if she'd identified the Bougainville head among the twisted anonymous faces. Her eyes were fixed on a single part of the wall, but the expression on her face surprised him. Magda Ross was a scientist, an experienced anthropologist endowed with all the best traits of her kind: objectivity, professionalism and an ability to see the evidence for what it was, unclouded by her personal feelings. In their short acquaintance he'd come to admire not only her style, which was confident and self-assured without a hint of arrogance, but also the fearless objectivity with which she faced potential hazards. The sight of the heads was undoubtedly a shock, but what would make a woman who'd probably handled hundreds like them react this way? Suppressed fury touched every part of that beautiful face, and though she was trying to hide it there was murder in her eyes. Jamie only hoped Madam Nishimura didn't notice it, or the high colour that rouged her cheekbones.

'Are you all right?'

The dark head nodded briefly, as if she couldn't allow herself to speak.

To his relief Nishimura acted as if Magda wasn't even in the room. 'So you see, Mr Saintclair, your shrunken head, even if it is among the exhibits you see here, is not just something to be bought and sold on a whim. It is part of a carefully assembled collection that took many years to bring together.'

'How . . . ?'

'In his youth my grandfather spent some time in the South Seas. He became fascinated by the native practice of removing an enemy's head and creating an ornament of it. He studied their methods of war and the different ways they achieved this end. The Maoris of New Zealand retained the skulls of their dead enemy chiefs and preserved them by removing the brain, eating the eyes then boiling the skull slowly so the skin tightened around it.' Jamie felt his stomach lurch at the thought of that awful feast; soft white globes and God knows what else disappearing down someone's throat.

Nishimura noted his distaste with a cold smile. 'He found these grinning headpieces to be unsubtle. In his view, the true genius of the art was to be found further north in the Solomon Islands and Papua New Guinea. Here they removed the skulls and used the skin to create the essence of its former wearer. It was a remarkably delicate procedure that required great skill. The heads needed to be repeatedly heated and cooled with stones and sand to achieve the proper lasting effect you see here. When he travelled to Berlin in nineteen thirty-six the last thing he thought to discover there was a shrunken head of the utmost perfection. His hosts recognized his admiration for the relic and immediately offered it as a gift. He believed it was his destiny and, as you see, it created a lifelong interest, which resulted in this collection.'

Jamie had to half-admire as proud a tale of ancestral acquisitiveness as he'd been privileged to hear. He could just imagine one of the red-faced old colonial scions of the Hertfordshire manor houses he occasionally visited recounting something similar. *And this is the fuzzy-wuzzy my great, great grandpater bagged at Omdurman. Put up a splendid fight. Been in the family since eighteen ninety-eight, you know.* 'My client is prepared to offer half a million dollars.'

'Really, Mr Saintclair, do I look as if half a million dollars will make a difference to my life?'

'A million.'

Nishimura laughed. 'Is he really such a philanthropist that he would pay so much to repatriate a piece of dried-out flesh to a group of savages? I think not. Perhaps if I

267

knew the identity of your client we could come to some sort of arrangement?'

Jamie understood she was playing with him the way her cat would play with a mouse. For now the claws were sheathed; for now . . . Nishimura would never willingly part with the Bougainville head, but if she had Keith Devlin's name she would find a way to extract money or favours from him. The time might come when Jamie could use that as a bargaining chip one way or the other, but it wasn't now.

'I'd have to consult with my client on that,' he said firmly.

'Please.' She rose from her seat without warning and the cat leaped acrobatically from her lap to land on all four feet. 'I will happily leave you in private for a few moments while you discuss it with him.'

Jamie hesitated. The opportunity had appeal, because it would allow them to inspect the heads and certain other things about the room that interested him, but did the risk outweigh any potential gain? He turned to Magda. Her face was still set in that angry mask, but she nodded. 'It can't do any harm.'

Jamie turned back to the Japanese. 'As long as I have your assurance that my conversations will not be monitored in any way?'

'Come, Mr Saintclair, what benefit would it provide for me to bug my own office?'

'In that case, thank you.'

Nishimura touched a hidden button on the desk that opened a second door in the wall to her left. 'I will give you ten minutes.'

When she was gone Magda rose to her feet and walked to the wall, staring at one particular niche.

'Which one is the Bougainville head?'

'Shouldn't you be phoning Mr Devlin?'

'There'll be plenty of time for that later.'

The compartments were ranged in two lines one above the other, at around head height. Three feet separated the individual alcoves, each of which was lit by a single recessed bulb that showed the doleful features of its unfortunate occupant to best effect.

'This is it.' She pointed to the upper niche in the centre of the line. He went to stand beside her and looked into the leathery features. The first thing he noticed was that the skin was much darker than the other examples and the hair was a ball of tight curls of pure black. Long, almost feminine lashes curled up from the empty eyes and the face had a soulful, resigned expression.

'I don't think he likes me. You're sure it's authentic?'

'You can never be sure without a DNA test,' she said tersely. 'But this is the only Melanesian head in the collection. If the Dragon Lady's grandfather brought a shrunken head back from Berlin this is the only one it could be. Now, are you going to phone Devlin?'

'No, you are, but first you're going to find me a safety pin from that bag of yours.'

She looked mystified, but did as she was ordered, rummaging in the leather bag until she found something that suited. 'Will this do?' She held up a small paper clip.

'Let's hope so.' Jamie took it from her and walked to the window. 'Go to the door and pretend to call Devlin.

We've traced the head, made the offer, but our principle won't proceed without knowing who the buyer is. Devlin's wary, he wants to talk about it in detail. Got that?'

'Sure.' She frowned. 'But what will you be doing?'

'Me?' Jamie grinned, crouching by the narrow gap in the sliding window. 'I'll be keeping our options open.'

He'd just completed what he'd planned when the door reopened and Madam Nishimura entered the room four minutes ahead of schedule, with the thin guard at her back.

'Well?' she demanded.

'I'm sorry,' Jamie said evenly, 'but my client needs more time to think about your request. He's not certain it's in his best interests to be identified at this time.'

Her expression hardened. 'When you talk to him again you will tell him it is a demand, not a request; a prerequisite for any further negotiation. And I will wish to know the true reason for his interest in the head. I am trusting by nature,' Jamie smiled at the blatant lie, 'but I do not believe in fairy stories. It may be that once I am aware of all the facts we can come to some sort of agreement. Perhaps not a sale, but an agreement that would suit both parties nonetheless. You will tell your client this?'

'Of course.' Jamie bowed his head. 'I will also assure him of your good faith and let him know of the warm welcome we received.'

Madam Nishimura snorted. 'Be careful, Mr Saint-clair. One day that sense of humour will get you into serious trouble.' She walked back to the desk and pressed a hidden button that opened the door behind them. She waved a hand towards the entrance in a way that made the invitation to leave more of an order. 'I sense your client's interest in my collection goes beyond philanthropy. We will meet again, Mr Saintclair.'

'What did you think?' he asked Magda as the buggy carried them silently back through the woods.

She glanced over her shoulder to where the grey concrete block was disappearing among the trees. 'I think the Dragon Lady is the most loathsome woman I've ever met.'

'I noticed you wanted to claw her eyes out, but I doubt that would have helped the negotiations. I meant about our situation.'

'It was always a long shot. Now I think it's insane. Whatever the Dragon Lady says and whatever your Mr Devlin decides, you cannot negotiate with these people. They're gangsters, Jamie, and when things don't go their way they'll clean up the mess the way they always do. Jamie Saintclair will end up in the foundations of Madam Nishimura's next bijou residence or going for a swim in Tokyo Bay with a concrete block tied to his leg. If you've got any sense you'll call Keith Devlin, tell him where the Bougainville head is and get on the next plane home.'

Jamie nodded slowly, accepting the logic of the argument if not the suggestion itself. 'Did you think there was anything strange about the heads?'

'You've been doing this too long, Jamie.' She stared at him in disbelief. 'What isn't strange about a shrunken head?'

'It's just that I got the feeling that the Bougainville head was the odd one out,' he tried to put his suspicions into words, 'at least apart from the blond one. I suppose that could be explained by a liaison between some traveller and a native girl way back when. The others were all similar to each other, but not to it, if you see what I mean. They had different complexions, their hair was different, and, unless I miss my guess, they'd been preserved by a different, and not quite so skilled, technique.'

Magda stared stolidly ahead. 'There's no single standard for shrunken heads.' He was a little hurt that her tone seemed to infer that only an idiot could think there would be. 'They don't come off a conveyor belt. Generally, across cultures, the head will have been preserved by the warrior who won it; or should I say the warrior who killed its owner and cut it off. How it comes out would depend on the individual's skill and the materials he had to work with. The Bougainville head is Melanesian, but there are different decorative styles and fashions across the region. They differ from those of Micronesia and Polynesia, where the practice was implemented to a lesser extent. It also differs greatly from the *tsantsas* of the Shuar, Achuar, Huambisa and Aguaruna, Jivaroan peoples of Ecuador and Peru, which are much more easily obtained and probably make up the bulk of the collection.'

Jamie had smothered enough awkward clients in an avalanche of detail to know that his companion was using her argument to distract him from pursuing his hypotheses, which he found interesting. But not quite as interesting as the fact she'd never once questioned his nefarious use of a paper clip back at the Dragon Lady's concrete mansion. Or that when she'd urged him to get the first flight home she hadn't mentioned taking one herself.

That was something that would bear thinking about.

XXX

Arkady Berzarin smiled as he settled into the back of the armoured Mercedes S-Class, one of a fleet of six from which to choose at random whenever he needed to travel. He'd decided on the big V12 because it was the preferred method of transport of various Middle East potentates who had tested its bomb- and bullet-proof qualities to the very limit. A second identical car started up behind them, and a third was already waiting at the gate to act as the point vehicle. He pressed the intercom linking him to the driver's compartment.

'Is everything arranged, Lev?' He already knew the answer, but he'd learned over the years that it never did any harm to ask.

'Sure, chief.' The driver grinned. Lev had been with Berzarin for ten years and knew his boss's habits better than any man on the protection detail. 'We'll have a motorcycle escort from the outskirts of Kras, but they'll stop at the airport gates. Security know to let us through to the apron to wait for the plane to land. Andrei will walk down the steps and straight into the car.'

'Good. Good.' The billionaire nodded. He hadn't seen his son for more than three months apart from the odd video conference, and he was frightened the boy was growing apart from him. The school in England looked after him well enough and he was doing well, but . . . Berzarin worried about the influence of that bitch of a second wife, though he'd never mention it to Andrei. They had three weeks together and he intended to spend every possible moment with his son and to hell with the aluminium industry for once. 'Who's in the lead car today?'

The driver frowned, ticking off the security detail in his head. 'Mikhail and the Bulgarian, Serov.'

'Good,' Berzarin repeated. 'They know their business. Okay, let's go.'

They drove out of the underground garage into the sunlight, a low Siberian sunlight that could scorch your eyeballs if you weren't careful. Lev plucked a pair of Ray-Bans from the dash, flipped the arms open and placed them expertly with one hand.

'You want the sun visors down, boss?'

'Since when could I get too much sun?' Berzarin chuckled and the driver smiled. It was unusual to see the boss in such a cheerful mood these days. The boy would be good for him.

The road wound across the tundra in tight loops, narrowing where it was flanked by concrete pillars that would slow any intruder who managed to get his car or truck beyond the gate. It was designed to give the house guards time to reach their defensive positions long before an attacker could get there. Lev had driven it a thousand times and took the corners smoothly. It was two miles from the house to the gate and he called ahead to make sure the guards were ready for them.

In the back of the car Berzarin tried to study share movements in the metal and minerals industry on his personalized iPad, but found he couldn't concentrate. He flicked to a weather website. It was a little late in the year, but maybe he could organize a fishing trip with Andrei up one of the tributaries of the Yenisei. Catching his first *taimen* with his old man would give them something to remember for a long time. One of the guiding companies had just started to use mini-hovercraft to get up into the headwaters, which would be something new for the boy. Yes, that's what he would do. Of course he'd run it past Andrei first. You couldn't dictate to a fourteen-year-old.

His mind drifted back to the strange visit from the Englishman and his girlfriend. When he'd had time to consider, it seemed to him that fate had brought them to his house. They'd provided him with an opportunity that was unlikely to occur again and he had put things in motion to take advantage of it. He wondered if Andrei's impending visit had influenced his decision, and decided it probably had.

As they approached the gate Lev saw one of the security SUVs speed off down the road. He glanced in his mirror to check if the boss had noticed, but Berzarin was engrossed in his computer. With a mental shrug he decided they'd find out if there was some sort of problem soon enough.

Up ahead, the guards watched the big black car

approach. They held their machine pistols casually, the way a workman holds the tools he has wielded for half a lifetime, and their eyes were hidden behind the ubiquitous mirrored sunglasses. One of them, Yuri, the big ex Spetsnaz from Omsk, waved the car down and Lev lowered his window.

'What's up?' the driver demanded. 'The boss won't want to be late for the kid.'

'We had word of two men by the roadside a mile south of here. Probably just hikers, but Ivan and Vitaly are checking it out. It should only take a minute.'

Lev scowled, but put the automatic to park and waited for the inevitable reaction. Arkady Berzarin heard the click and looked up from the fishing website he'd been studying. 'What's happening?'

'Nothing, boss. Just security starting at shadows, but that's their job, eh?'

Berzarin grunted and sat back in his seat. 'We'll be late for Andrei,' he growled after a few minutes passed. 'Fuck shadows. Let's go.'

Lev looked up at the security man and shrugged, but Yuri shook his head. 'It's not worth taking a chance,' he said quietly. 'You can make up the time.'

'Security says no, boss. Better to be safe—'

'Who pays their fucking wages?' Berzarin exploded. 'I say when it's fucking safe and when it's not.' He reached for the switch that lowered the window separating him from Yuri. The guard watched emotionlessly as the mirrored glass began to slide downwards, anticipating the blast from within.

Lev frowned. 'Boss, I . . .'

Berzarin ignored his driver and glared at the guard. 'Did you hear—'

Yuri stood with his legs slightly apart and in a crouch so he could see into the rear compartment of the Mercedes. He held the AK-9 machine pistol at a thirty-degree angle, barrel downwards and with his right hand on the butt, and his left gripping the black plastic stock just behind the barrel. It was the work of a millisecond to twitch the barrel upwards and bring his finger to the trigger in the same movement. Berzarin saw the muzzle come up and fell backwards with a cry of terror, raising his hands in a futile attempt to fend off the stream of bullets that was about to erupt from the black tunnel. Yuri had loaded the AK-9 with armour-piercing rounds and they shredded the Kevlar vest Berzarin put so much faith in with the same efficiency they shredded the raised hands. By the time he took the pressure from the trigger Berzarin was already dead, but Yuri was nothing if not professional and he fired the last four rounds into the former oligarch's head even as the bullets of his comrades smashed him sideways away from the car window.

As he lay on the ground the cries of the guards faded and all he could hear was the tick-tick-tick of a cooling engine and what his dying mind believed was the soft murmur of the Siberian wind, but in reality was the sound of his last breath.

XXXI

'So, in a nutshell, she has the head and I don't think she'll willingly part with it,' Jamie explained warily.

'But she wanted to know your client's identity?' Keith Devlin sounded outraged.

'That's right.'

'I hope you bloody well didn't tell her.'

'Of course I didn't.'

'And you're certain she's Yakuza? From what I hear they don't go in much for women bosses.'

Jamie shrugged. 'She as good as admitted it. I got the feeling she was proud of the fact.'

There was a long silence at the end of the phone and Jamie had a feeling he'd been put on hold while the other man discussed the situation with a third party. Eventually, Devlin came back on the line.

'All right, son. This is where we're at. Time's getting short due to some factors of which you're not aware. We need the head now, and you're gonna get it. It's time to go the extra mile.' Jamie felt the breath catch in his chest and he couldn't have spoken even if he'd known what to say. 'So you're going to go right back in there and fetch that little treasure back for your Uncle Keith.'

'And get myself killed?'

'C'mon, Jamie mate,' Devlin sounded positively jovial, 'you're a player. You've done this kind of stuff before. You can do it now. Besides, son, you've never had a better incentive.'

'What do you mean by that?'

'Well, those girls of yours, they're gonna be rooting for you for a start.'

An image of Fiona and Lizzie locked in a cell at some remote mining complex in the Australian bush filled Jamie's head and he felt a thrill of panic. 'What have you done to them?'

'Nothing at all, son,' Devlin assured him, but the words *not yet* were there by implication. 'They're being well looked after. We're on a little exotic holiday just like we planned from the start.'

Jamie heard a muffled squeal in the background and thought he recognized Fiona's voice.

'Let me talk to them.'

'Tell me you'll think about it first.'

'All right, I'll think about it. Just let me talk to Fiona.'

'Jamie?'

'Yes, darling, it's me. Are you and Lizzie okay?'

He heard her take a deep breath. 'Yes, we're being treated well enough. He said we were going to the Gold Coast, but we're on some kind of tropical island. It's horrid, the whole place stinks and there are men with guns.'

'Where—'

'I think that'll do for now, son.' Devlin's voice returned to the phone. 'Your girls are just fine and I'll make sure they stay that way as long as you cooperate. The guns are for their protection, and as long as I'm with them we'll be fine.'

Jamie tried without success to keep his voice anger free. 'All right, Devlin, what do you want me to do?'

'Just exactly what's in your contract, Jamie. You find the head and you bring it to me.'

'What if I can't get it? What if . . . ?'

The Australian lowered his voice to a whisper. 'If I read your obituary in the *Tokyo Times* your little lady and her lovely daughter will be flown back to Oz none the worse for their holiday. Likewise, if you end up in a Jap jail. All I want to know is that you've given it your best shot, son.'

'And if by some miracle I do get the bloody thing, what then?'

He could almost see Devlin's grin. '*When* you get the Bougainville head, all you have to do is let me know and I'll make sure you get to where you need to be. Are you still there?'

'Yes, I'm still here. And Devlin . . .'

'Yes, mate.'

'Just so we know exactly where we are, if you harm a hair on either of their heads I will hunt you down and I will kill you. Do we understand each other?'

Devlin's mocking laughter echoed in the earpiece. 'You just bring me the head, son, and we're quits. I might even forget what you just said.'

The phone went dead in his hand.

He looked up to find Magda Ross staring at him. 'What's going on, Jamie?' she demanded.

'It seems my esteemed client is in more need of the head than I'd realized.' He explained what Fiona had said about a tropical island and armed guards.

'You mean he's holding them hostage? That's unbelievable.'

'Unfortunately it's not. I think Devlin means exactly what he says and he's not the kind of man to let morality get in the way of his objectives.'

'You should call the police,' she said, but without any conviction.

Jamie nodded distractedly. It was the logical thing to do, but he had a feeling Keith Devlin would have planned for that contingency. It was too big a risk. Instead, he said: 'I think it's time we did some late-night shopping.'

Platinum Street – *Gaien-Nishi-dori* – lived up to its name and Jamie's Presbyterian instincts winced at the amounts he shelled out as he ticked off the mental check-list in his head. Small black rucksack from some Italian designer fashion house – seventy thousand yen. Tight-fitting leather jacket in black, with zipped internal hood, Hugo Boss – ninety thousand yen. Jeans, black. Cashmere roll-neck, black. Sport shoes, black. Still, he rationalized, it would all go on Keith Devlin's expenses bill, and if not, the Princess Czartoryski Foundation's little windfall would tide him over.

'When you said *we* should do some shopping, I actually thought you meant *we* not *you*. Why this sudden interest in dressing like James Dean? Couldn't you have waited till we got back to the hotel to change?'

As he'd shopped, Jamie had exchanged each item for a piece of clothing he was already wearing so he'd gradually metamorphosed into something approaching a silhouette of his former self. It was only when they exchanged the designer shops for a hardware outlet that realization dawned. She shook her head as he added a head-torch, a hammer, a large pair of pliers, pepper spray and fifteen metres of climbing rope to the contents of the rucksack.

'Are you crazy?' she whispered. 'You have no idea what kind of security they have in those woods. You'll get yourself killed.' The thought had already occurred to Jamie, which was why he'd discarded his original plan of buying a black ski mask on the grounds he was less likely to get shot if someone could see the terror on his face. 'And even if you get there,' she added unnecessarily, 'do you really think the Dragon Lady is going to let you walk into her house?'

'No, I don't. All I know for certain is that I have to try, and there's only one way to find out.'

'You look far too wholesome to be a burglar.' She gave him a shrewd look. 'Do you have any experience of breaking and entering?'

He considered for a moment, remembering the intimidating darkness of Himmler's Hall of the Generals at Wewelsburg Castle, the snarling hounds in the long grass outside Max Dornberger's mansion and the unique terror of having a gun barrel pressed against his forehead at a Teutonic castle in the Sierra Nevada Mountains. In retrospect, none of those episodes had turned out quite the way he'd intended. 'A little,' he admitted eventually. 'But it's not something I do every day.'

'Then you're going to need all the help you can get.'

'What do you mean?' he said suspiciously.

'I mean I'm coming with you.' There was no arguing with Magda Ross when she'd made her decision. She walked back into the store and returned moments later with an oblong box from a multicoloured stand by the door. Jamie nodded appreciatively as he saw what she'd bought.

He pushed the box into the rucksack and they set off for the complex. A road flanked much of the walls, with buildings on the opposite side. He chose an area that hopefully shielded him from any security cameras covering this part of the wall.

'All right, tell me what you had in mind for these?' He reached into the rucksack and brought out the multi-coloured box Magda had bought in the hardware store.

'If you're going in there, you're going to need some sort of diversion.' Magda kept her voice low. 'I'll find a way to the opposite side of the complex – somewhere close to a camera – and set these off at intervals along the wall.' Jamie opened his mouth to protest that she'd be deliberately putting herself in the firing line, but she continued: 'I'll be safe enough. The best chance you have is if the people watching screens up at the Dragon Lady's concrete palace are looking the other way when you go in.'

'All right,' Jamie agreed reluctantly. 'But don't take any more chances than are absolutely necessary.'

She didn't reply, but gave him a look that reminded him who was about to put their head into the lion's mouth.

He tore open the box to reveal a string of firecrackers, four or five rockets and a range of anonymous tubes with bright starbursts on the side. 'There should be enough here to keep them interested for at least half an hour if you play it right, but for God's sake don't start any fires. Most of the houses around here are made of wood and I don't want to burn down half the bloody city.' He kissed her on the cheek and she reacted with a rueful smile. 'I won't move until I see the first rocket or hear the first bang. Don't rush it. Don't cut any corners. Go right to the far side of the complex before you start anything. We'll meet up back at that twenty-four-hour coffee shop we passed. Okay?'

Magda nodded and Jamie watched her jog off down the street. When she was out of sight he closed his eyes and leaned against the wall of the building. One more thing to worry about. How in the name of Christ did he keep getting himself into these things? He studied the wall on the far side of the road. At seven foot high he'd have no problem clearing it but he could see no sign of the usual refinements that protected the homes of the rich, the famous or the criminally inclined. And that was a puzzle in itself. Yes, they had the security cameras at the gate, but where was the electrified wire that would turn the wall into a formidable and – depending on the voltage – potentially lethal barrier? The wall itself ran in a long curve, which ruled out any laser or ultrasonic beams. Maybe Madam Nishimura didn't want to advertise her presence by living in a fortress, but the Dragon Lady was a major player in a, quite literally, cut-throat business, and she hadn't become that by being careless with her security. No, there must be something else. The wall was the first line of defence, therefore its purpose was not to deter, but to detect. So, some kind of pressure pad running round the top, or just inside the wall where an intruder would drop when he slipped across. A problem. But not an insurmountable one. All he needed was to find the right tree.

When she was certain she was past the gate, Magda returned to the road running round the wall. She followed it until she estimated she was more or less diagonally opposite where Jamie waited. The surrounding streets seemed to be devoid of life, which was fortunate, and the few cars she could see appeared unoccupied. A security camera was fixed to a tree in the woods opposite, but that didn't bother her. Her entire purpose was to be seen.

She strung the firecrackers along the top of the wall and left the fuse dangling. When she was satisfied with their position, she pressed the rocket's wooden stick into a patch of soft earth so that the rocket was angled just over the wall. Her preparations complete, she struck a match and lit the firecracker fuse first, immediately followed by the rocket. The twisted paper glowed and a worm of fire ate its way upwards. Without warning the rocket rose on a column of sparks before accelerating with a long whoosh to rip through the air almost faster than the eye could follow. As it soared into the night sky the first firecracker went off with a tremendous bang that made her heart stutter, instantly followed by ten more in quick succession. A buzz-saw ripple of violent explosions. The awed silence that followed was broken by an almighty crack as the black void above was flash-lit by the expanding blossom of sparks from the exploding rocket. For a moment she was too stunned to move, but after a few seconds she put the box back in her bag and hurried away to the left as the lights in the apartment block behind began to flick on.

Even though he'd been waiting for it, Jamie was startled by the flash of the rocket above the trees. He stood outside the wall opposite the tree he'd chosen, a big cedar, hundreds of years old and with a wide cleft where the trunk split at just about the right height. From the rucksack he withdrew the rope and attached the hammer with a pair of half hitches. The tree was perhaps fifteen feet inside the wall and the cleft maybe eighteen or twenty feet up, giving him just enough rope to play with. He positioned himself six or eight feet back from the wall and dropped the coiled rope at his feet. Taking a length of rope in hand he swung the hammer in an arc and allowed it to sail out, arching upward towards the cleft only to fall slightly short. He winced at the sound of the steel hitting the trunk; the echoing clatter as it rattled on to an unseen root. Cursing under his breath he carefully retrieved the rope.

After three more failed attempts sweat ran down his back and he tried to ignore the sharp little bangs from the far side of the complex that told him he was running out of time. The split in the trunk widened the higher he went. Did he have enough rope? There was only one way to find out. He swung again, released and opened his eyes just as the rope sailed through the gap. With a panic-stricken lurch he clamped his left hand on the cord as the last five feet uncoiled. Very gently, he pulled the rope back towards him. This was the key. Was the cleft narrow enough to stop the hammer sliding straight back through? He felt the line tighten and increased the pressure. Would the knot hold?

He shrugged on his rucksack and used the taut rope to help him walk up the wall until he was balancing on the balls of his feet on the very edge. Remember what the instructors told you: left hand as high as you can get it, right hand above and pull your knees up, all in one smooth movement. He felt himself sailing into space, saw the gnarled trunk speeding towards him and allowed himself to drop to the ground just short, fortunate not to break his ankle on a twisted root. The hammer dropped to the ground on the other side of the tree carrying the rope with it.

He allowed himself to breathe again. And that was the easy part.

Jamie untied the hammer and recovered the rope, coiling it neatly into the rucksack. When it was safely stowed he took out the head-torch and slipped the band over his brow. The only other item he retrieved was the small canister of pepper spray he hoped would be proof against any guard dogs that roamed these woods. He had a horrible memory from a couple of years earlier of a slavering pair of fangs and jaws with terrible strength; he didn't want to repeat the experience.

He waited a few moments, allowing himself to become accustomed to the whisper of the woods; the sound of branches rubbing together, the soft breeze through the leaves and, in the distance, the faint hum of a generator he hoped would lead him to his target. When he was ready, he set off, moving silently in a low crouch. All he could do was pray Magda's diversion had done its job. If they spotted him he would know soon enough, because the Dragon Lady's deadly guardians would be on him like a pack of wolves.

While one part of his mind concentrated on silence and survival, the other turned to Keith Devlin. Mr Lim had hinted on the train that there was more at stake than mining rights, however rich. *What if Mr Devlin's motives for the Bougainville exchange are not what he wishes you to believe?* That hint had latterly taken on an element of prophecy. What incentive was so powerful that Devlin thought it was worth abducting an innocent woman and her daughter to force Jamie Saintclair to steal an ancient body part? Fiona had said they were being held on some kind of tropical island and the more he considered it the more he understood the answer had to lie somewhere on Bougainville.

He slowed when he came to a roadway and had one foot on the tarmac when the faintest hum in the air made him hesitate. With a convulsive heave he threw himself backward as one of the electric carts rounded the corner and swept silently over the ground he'd been about to cross. A glint of light on a gun barrel and they were past, leaving Jamie lying in the damp roadside ditch with his heart pounding in his chest. When he was certain they'd gone he raised his head – and froze.

XXXII

A painted devil's face with dark, glaring eyes pinned him in position, the narrow slit of a mouth twisted in a contemptuous sneer. It took him a heart-stopping moment to realize it was some kind of ceremonial mask pinned to the trunk of a cherry tree. A joke or a warning, but enough to paralyse him for a few moments after the close call with the buggy. He lay back and fought to recover his composure, the rucksack digging into his body and his hand clutching the pepper spray. At least it hadn't been a bloody Rottweiler.

He used the time to visualize the lay-out of the massive concrete house. If he had it right most of the protection and security would be to the front and rear, so his best bet would be to come at it from the flank. He only had one plan, and its success depended on certain factors that were now beyond his control and the rudimentary equipment he'd managed to put together. On instinct he stowed the pepper spray where it was least likely to be found.

A few minutes later he was within sight of the house

and he made an arcing run that brought him, hopefully, unseen, to the low concrete cliff that was the east wall of the Dragon Lady's bunker.

It was only when he stood with his back against the wall that he fully understood the challenge facing him. It rose sheer for something like thirty feet and ended in a flat roof. The only consolation was there appeared to be no cameras covering it. If this was the movies the hero would have been equipped with Spider-Man suction cups to help him climb the wall, sonic gizmos to disable the listening devices and, for all he knew, holograms to fool the cameras. All he had was a rope, a pair of pliers and a hammer, and he had a feeling the hammer had done its job.

Pleasantly surprised no one had yet come to welcome him with a 9mm Glock or a Heckler MP7, he stepped away from the wall and looked upwards. A concrete cliff all right, but against the night sky he could just identify the rim of the object he'd spotted when they'd driven up to the house. From what he'd seen there was no way of gaining entry to the place from the exterior without the use of a small army and/or half a ton of high-explosives, neither of which was available. But the internal courtyard and that beautiful Japanese garden were different. Jamie had the distinct feeling this was where the Dragon Lady escaped the day-to-day cares, murder and mayhem of your average Yakuza crime baron. It meant it was a place where she valued her privacy, so no intrusive cameras. Her cats had leave to come and go, which, he hoped, meant there'd also be no invisible security beams to hamper the potential interloper. Of course, he could be wrong and the cameras were hidden and the cats locked up for the night. Sometimes you just had to wing it and accept the painful consequences later. He'd worry about it when he got there. The question was how to get there?

The simple answer was a grapnel. With a grapnel hooked over the sill of the roof he could've shimmied up the wall in about five seconds flat. But the hardware shop and the outdoor store appeared to have run out of grapnels. So, no grapnel, and the hammer and the pliers wouldn't answer on the flat roof. That meant falling back on a skill he'd learned a long time ago and which he prayed he hadn't lost.

He uncoiled the rope from the rucksack, remembering winter nights curled up on the sofa beside his grandfather watching old black-and-white cowboy films. Jamie had vowed to learn how to use a lasso and had practised incessantly without much success. Then his grandfather, a former Anglican missionary who'd amassed an odd array of skills during his time in the Church, had taught him how to rope a kitchen chair with an old clothes line. He'd improved upon the skill until rope spinning became an unlikely, but much-admired party trick at Cambridge. He just hoped to God it hadn't deserted him now that he needed it in earnest.

He curled the rope to create a loop bound by a simple slip knot. It had to be a substantial loop to encircle the object he'd noticed earlier. He was pinning his hopes on a medium-sized satellite dish just within range and strong enough – he hoped – to provide an anchor point. The only problem was that he'd never roped anything quite this high and it was difficult to get the technique right. He spun the loop around his head, using the wrist action to keep the circle open. He tried a practice throw that was well short, but shrugged off his disappointment because he knew he could do better. His first serious throw was off to the right and the second hit the wall just below the roof edge and crumpled back at his feet. Magda's diversion had ended at least fifteen minutes earlier and it was only a matter of time before the investigating party returned and then the game was up.

A couple of steps back flattened the angle and this time the loop fell perfectly over the dish. He felt a surge of relief as he tightened it over the holding arm, using his full weight to test it before beginning the climb. He was nearing the top when he felt the holding arm begin to give, accompanied by an awful, terminal creaking groan. Desperately, he increased his pace, knowing that if the arm snapped it would send him plunging twenty-odd feet to the concrete. Inch by treacherous inch the curved silhouette of the dish moved out over the edge of the wall as the holding arm gave way. By the time he reached the top it could only have been held by a single screw, but somehow he managed to throw an arm over the lip and drag himself to lie wheezing on the roof.

No time to rest. He pulled the rope after him and snaked on his stomach to the far side. The courtyard below was steeped in darkness and the only light from the landing at the top of the stairs where he'd stood earlier. Fortunately, the stanchion for some sort of radio aerial gave him the solid anchor he needed and he threw the rope over the edge and let himself gently down on to a gravel path. This was the point of greatest danger. All it would take was for someone to walk into one of those rooms and turn on the light and he'd be spotlighted like a bug under a magnifying glass.

He moved towards the room with the gruesome collection of heads, wincing at every crunch of gravel beneath his feet. Would the window open? The catch was a simple hook that dropped into place when the floor-to-ceiling panel slid shut. He'd used the paper clip to hold the catch in a position he hoped would prevent it engaging completely while still providing a satisfactory click when the window closed. There'd also been two locks at the top and bottom that made it a much more serious proposition, but he hoped someone with a cat constantly running in and out wouldn't bother with them too much. He said a little prayer as his fingers closed on the handle and pulled.

The window slid back with the slightest hiss and he almost died of fright as something small and black brushed against his legs. Bloody cat, he whispered to himself, if I get hold of you you'll need every one of those nine lives. He unslung his backpack and slipped inside, closing the window behind him.

He switched on the head-torch. Something about the room was different, but he couldn't place it. The beam ran over twin rows of shadowed niches taking in the tortured faces until he reached the one with the Bougainville head. Dark pits in the wizened face marked where the eyes had once been and he shivered as he imagined them blinking open to trap him in their stare. He reached up, and paused, not quite able to bring himself to touch the leathery human flesh. Who had he been, this shell of a creature that had once breathed and thought and hoped? Get a bloody grip, Saintclair. You don't have time for this. He grasped the curly dark hair, surprised at how soft it felt despite its wiry appearance.

It was only then that his subconscious mind fixed on what was different about the room.

The samurai sword was missing from its cushion on the desk.

When the lights clicked on it hardly came as a surprise at all.

'You will replace the head in its position, Mr Saintclair, drop your backpack, put your hands on your head and turn around.' The voice was the soft rustle of silk running over the edge of a blade, but the words contained a menace that told him not to argue or protest. Very carefully he put the head back into the niche, placed his hands on the back of his neck and turned.

His focus should have been on Madam Nishimura and the sword she held, or on the thin guard from their morning visit and the pistol pointed at his heart. Instead, he felt a stab of almost physical pain at the sight of Magda Ross in the grasp of two more guards. Her hands were tied and a piece of duct tape had been placed over her mouth. Despite the hopelessness of the situation she struggled against her bonds, snarling behind the gag, and he felt a surge of pride beneath the panic.

'I think—'

'You will speak only when you are spoken to or your companion will be the one who suffers.' Madam Nishimura nodded to one of the guards to emphasize the point and Magda let out a muffled squeal as he twisted her arm. Jamie clamped his mouth shut.

'Search him.'

The thin guard who'd conducted the same search earlier in the day patted him down; torso first then arms and finally legs. When he was happy, he kicked the rucksack across the room to nestle beside Magda's shoulder bag, which lay at her feet. Jamie obediently put his hands back behind his neck.

'It was most amusing to watch you test my security,' Madam Nishimura continued. 'The door to the courtyard is, of course, alarmed so we knew you were coming, but I wondered how you would reach the garden. Your use of the rope was most ingenious, but I caution you against trying any further tricks. Did you really believe you could break into *this* house undetected? My people followed you every step of the way and when your foolish companion hopped over the wall it was the work of a moment to scoop her up.'

Jamie wondered what he'd see now if he met Magda's eyes. She'd had strict instructions to stay outside the complex, why would she risk her neck? Nishimura misread his puzzlement for defiance and stepped forward to place the blade of the sword under his chin so he could feel the chill of the metal against his flesh. 'Your naivety is touching. But, as you will discover, it comes at a cost.'

The question why she'd allowed them to get this far was on Jamie's lips, but the threat against Magda was all too real. He had a feeling he'd find out soon enough. He was right.

'Your presence here is an insult to my grandfather's memory.' The words were spoken without rancour, but he understood they had a meaning beyond the mere statement. Just to ensure he got the point the blade stayed tight against his skin, held there by a rock-steady hand. A single flick of the wrist was all it would take to tear his throat out.

But Madam Nishimura was in no hurry. For the moment she seemed content to bore him to death with her family history. 'When it was over. After the . . .' she hesitated, hardly able to bring herself to utter the word '. . . surrender, he vowed that no white man would ever set foot on this estate, the land of my ancestors. My grandfather was samurai. He followed the code of *bushido* and would have fought to the end. Instead, he was forced by duty to accept the collective humiliation of defeat. Afterwards, he considered *seppuku*, but with Japan led by weaklings he decided he must sacrifice his honour to maintain the flame of the warrior among his people; the flame he had nurtured throughout his lifetime.' A cold smile flitted across the alabaster features, but Jamie felt a wave of relief as the sword dropped away. Nishimura picked up a framed photograph of two Japanese soldiers from the desk. The men, one older and presumably Major Yoshitaki, stared at the camera with a look of disdainful superiority as they stood with their hands resting on their scabbarded swords. 'My grandfather and his comrade Lieutenant Kajimoto in Nanking during the Chinese disturbance of nineteen thirty-seven. You have heard of Nanking?' Jamie nodded. 'You may speak.'

'Yes, I've heard of Nanking. If I remember rightly it was referred to as the Rape of Nanking and several hundred thousand innocent Chinese were slaughtered there.'

'A fabrication of the western media,' she said dismissively. 'My grandfather and his comrades were in China purely to exercise and protect Japan's ancient and inalienable right to passage through the region. They were opposed by bandits and those bandits had the support of certain members of the population. Of course, the authorities must take action against them and naturally my grandfather was ready to step forward and do his duty.' She flicked the switch on her desk to illuminate the thirty recesses. Jamie was overwhelmed by a sense of impending horror. 'He and Lieutenant Kajimoto became famous for their competition to eliminate the greatest number of bandits using only a sword. They set a target of one hundred.' She met Jamie's eyes and he followed her gaze to the first of the heads.

'No.'

'Yes, Mr Saintclair. Unfortunately, he found it difficult to perfect the preservation technique and these are – How should we describe them? – the survivors of his haul. Each of them his own creation. Each of them beheaded by this sword, all but one.'

'The Bougainville head.'

'Of course. You would like to reveal your client's name now?'

'I don't think so.'

She shrugged. 'It does not matter. I'm sure we could elicit an answer by causing your companion more pain. There are certain refinements my grandfather perfected . . . But we are not barbarians. All that is required is to remove the stain on his memory.' She rapped out an order in Japanese and Magda Ross squealed behind the tape. He turned to find her eyes wide and her head shaking. He only understood why when the thin guard left the room and returned a few moments later.

When Jamie saw what he was carrying the blood in his veins turned to ice water and his legs threatened to give way beneath him.

'No, I—'

The sword point at his throat silenced him. 'You must think of it as an honour, Mr Saintclair, a form of immortality. I am sure we will do you justice. We are much more practised now.' The edge of the blade switched to his neck so he could feel the blood in his carotid artery pulsing against it. 'And of course, it is virtually painless. Much preferable to dying by inches of cancer in your hospital bed.'

The thin guard spread the roll of plastic sheet he'd brought across the carpet at Jamie's feet.

'Kneel.'

'I'd prefer to die on my feet, if that's all right with you.'

'Kneel or I will have them cause your friend pain.'

'You're going to kill her anyway.'

'Yes, indeed. But I promise you she will not suffer. Kneel.'

Jamie shot a last desperate glance at Magda. Christ, he should be fighting for his life; putting his fist through the bloody woman's face and tearing at the guards with his teeth. But for all his mind screamed at him to act, his body wouldn't obey. He felt completely numb as he complied. This must have been what it was like for the men and women who queued obediently at the gates of Auschwitz waiting to die: a feeling of utter helplessness and inevitability. Nishimura issued another order. One of Magda's captors left her to take Jamie's arm while the thin guard took the other. The touch of their hands at last prompted some resistance, but it was too late. The more he struggled, the tighter they gripped.

'Bow your head.' Her voice had turned almost seductive. 'It will be over in a moment.'

He froze as he felt the edge of the blade on the nape of his neck. His mind turned to his own grandfather, Matthew, the Anglican missionary who'd turned out to have fought in the SAS during the Second World War. The image of the old man gave him new strength. Matthew wouldn't give in and allow himself to be butchered like this. Matthew would have fought to his last breath. 'By the way,' he turned his head to look up into his executioner's face, 'I don't think your grandfather was a hero. I think he was a coward and a murderer who slaughtered innocent civilians for his own pleasure. Even your own government has dis-owned criminals like him, who encouraged the type of bestiality the Japanese Army perpetrated at Nanking. If

301

there's a Buddhist hell that's where he is now, and that's where you're going.'

'It is a testament to your own fear,' Nishimura smiled, 'that you think to provoke me into prolonging your life, even if it costs you a great deal of pain. I'm afraid that will not work, Mr Saintclair.'

The guard on Jamie's left forced his chin round so he was staring at the plastic sheet, the one designed to protect the expensive carpet from his spurting blood. In the same moment he felt them angle their bodies away from him, loosening their grip just a fraction. The movement gave him the chance to rotate the object clutched convulsively in his left hand.

XXXIII

Jamie closed his eyes, counting down the seconds and knowing he would only get one chance. He could feel Madam Nishimura's presence looming over him, the sword lifting, the dark eyes picking the precise point of impact between two vertebrae. The guard holding his right arm edged an inch further away to avoid being splashed by the inevitable flood of gore. Magda's muffled scream told him the sword was ready to fall.

Now! He pressed the button on the little canister of pepper spray he'd retrieved from the hood compartment of the expensive jacket, praying that his aim was true. A distinctive smell made his nostrils prickle and he felt the faintest touch of vapour on his cheek. The guard screamed as the stream of fiery liquid turned his face into an inferno. Jamie jerked down hard on the arm that held his, throwing himself left to bring the man into the line of the arcing blade. A sharp slapping sound and the scream changed in pitch to a long shriek of mortal agony. Jamie opened his eyes to see a jumble of blood-spattered plastic as his momentum continued to take him left. As he'd intended, his shoulder rammed into the remaining captor's ribs as the man clawed for the pistol beneath his jacket.

The plan, if there'd been one, had been to disable him with the pepper spray, but it was already too late for that and he sensed Madam Nishimura manoeuvring for a killing blow. Almost of its own volition his right hand wrestled with his captor's as the guard tried to get the gun from its underarm holster. A sharp crack seemed to paralyse the Chinese for a moment and he fell away with a soft mewing sound, leaving Jamie in sole control of the gun. He wrenched it from the holster and fired a second round that left a smouldering hole in the guard's jacket and passed close enough to freeze Madam Nishimura in position with the sword ready to bring down on him. Struggling to hold it steady, he moved the barrel until the muzzle was pointing at the centre of her chest. The sound of a struggle told him Magda must be doing what she could to occupy the remaining guard, but he didn't dare look.

'Tell him to let her go and drop his gun,' he rasped. 'I'd sooner shoot you than not and the chances are that if he puts a bullet in me I'll fire anyway.'

Nishimura hesitated, glaring her hatred through narrowed eyes, before snarling the order to the guard. The man must have objected, because she had to repeat it twice. Jamie almost collapsed with relief as he heard the sound of a gun hitting the floor. The adrenalin pulsed through him and he had to relax the pressure of his trigger finger in case he shot Madam Nishimura by accident. Not that he'd mourn her passing, but he had plans for her. He bent to pick up the pepper spray and slipped it in his pocket. 'Good. Now tell him to very slowly move with his back to the wall round into my field of vision. And you can put the sword down. Nice and gently, if you please.'

Nishimura complied, her volcanic gaze never leaving his. Magda moved into view and used the sword blade to slice through the ties binding her wrists. When she was done she tore the tape from her mouth, glaring at the other woman and looking for all the world like an avenging Amazon in designer jeans. 'If you have any sense you'll shoot that bitch now.' Her voice shook with emotion. 'She was going to cut your bloody head off.'

'It's tempting.' He managed an awkward grin. 'But I don't think I will. It could make things more difficult later and she might come in handy.'

She looked down at him and her expression changed to concern. 'Are you hurt?'

For the first time he noticed the blood spattered across his new jacket from shoulder to waist. 'No, it's all his.' He pointed at the guard who lay twitching like a beached fish in a widening pool of gore. The sword had taken him diagonally across the back from shoulder to ribs, slicing his spinal cord. It didn't seem likely he'd ever walk again if he lived at all, but that was his problem. The other guard wouldn't be running a marathon any time soon either, not with what looked like a bullet through the pelvis.

Jamie removed the first guard's pistol from its holster and took mobile phones from the inside pockets of both. He dropped the phones to the floor and crushed them under his heel. He nodded to the unwounded guard, and the man complied with the wordless suggestion, throwing his mobile to Magda, who gave it the same treatment. She snapped a command in Japanese and he threw a second object, which she put in her pocket. As an afterthought she went to the phone on Madam Nishimura's desk and ripped the cord from the wall.

'Why don't you suggest to our friend there that he looks after his chums, and then get the head?'

Magda passed on the order and the guard glanced at Madam Nishimura for approval. He received a curt nod and grunted before going to crouch beside his comrades, muttering to himself as he tried to staunch their wounds.

Meanwhile, Magda picked up the rucksack and approached the line of niches. She hesitated in front of the Bougainville head. For a moment he thought she was experiencing the same feeling of dread he'd suffered earlier, but when she eventually reached up it was to cradle the blond-haired head to the right.

'Not that one.'

She turned to stare at him. 'This is what I came for.' The words were spoken with a mixture of defiance and pride and he realized belatedly that he'd seriously underestimated Magda Ross. With something close to reverence she placed the head in the bag, only then adding its Bougainville counterpart.

'Don't . . .' Jamie twitched his pistol to where Madam Nishimura was edging her way towards the door. He strode to where the Japanese woman stood and took her by the shoulder, putting the gun to her head. The guard looked up from helping his comrades and tensed as if he were about to spring to her defence.

'Tell him that if I see his fat face outside this room in the next half an hour I'll shoot you.'

'Very well.' She turned her head to stare into his eyes and her expression was almost amused. 'You do realize all of this has been for nothing. Nothing at all. You will never get out of Tokyo alive.'

'I suppose I could increase our chances by pulling the trigger,' he suggested.

'I don't think a man like you would do that, Mr Saintclair. You are too much the English gentleman.'

'Try me,' he said, screwed the barrel a little deeper for emphasis and pushed her towards the doorway. 'It's not every day someone tries to chop off my head.'

He nodded to Magda to follow. 'We'll talk about this later,' he assured her. 'First we have to get out of here. We can't use one of those electric buggies, but Tokyo Rose here must have some other transport handy.'

Magda reached into her pocket and pulled out the car key the guard had thrown her. 'A big Toyota SUV. It's parked out front.'

'Can you handle it?'

'I think so. What happens when we get to the gate?'

'We'll worry about that when we get there.'

Keeping Madam Nishimura in front of him, Jamie made his way cautiously to the stairs. He wasn't too worried about a reaction to the gunshots, the first report had been muffled by the muzzle's proximity to the victim, and in any case he doubted if the occasional bang was anything unusual in this house.

'How many guards?' he demanded.

'Another five, but you need not concern yourself while you have me. They have instructions never to place my life in danger. Your real problems will start when you discard me, Mr Saintclair, as you must do at some point. Japan is an island nation and you must leave by air or sea. Whichever method you choose we will be waiting for you. By the time I have finished with you, you will be begging for the edge of my grandfather's sword.'

Two more guards waited by the entrance, the big men in dark suits and white shirts he'd seen earlier in the electric buggy. They raised their guns the moment they realized what was happening, but at a snapped order from their leader they laid the weapons on the ground, contenting themselves with glares of frustrated, smoke-eyed hatred.

'Good lads.' Jamie returned their gaze. 'Let's keep it that way.'

The SUV was parked a few feet to the right of the guard house. Magda pointed the key and pressed a button and the door locks clicked open accompanied by a blaze of light as the headlamps automatically illuminated. 'You get in first and start the engine,' Jamie told her. 'Put the rucksack on the front seat.'

Keeping the gun barrel against Madam Nishimura's neck he waited until Magda was in the car before he went to the near-side rear door and used his free hand to open it, backing into the angle between door and seat.

'All right,' he said to the Japanese, 'this is what we

do. Turn round to face me.' Madam Nishimura did as she was ordered and Jamie took the gun from her neck and put it to her forehead. 'Now, I'm going to back into the car and you will follow me. If you try anything I'll kill you.'

Their eyes were less than two feet from each other and he saw the moment of revelation, quickly followed by a moment of decision.

'I really don't think you will do that, Mr Saintclair. I am calling your bluff.' She edged backwards with an almost ethereal mocking smile. For a split-second he was undecided, then he realized he really didn't have any option. His finger tightened on the trigger and he felt the kick of the recoil as he threw himself backward into the car. The last thing he saw was the look of disbelief on the pale face. 'Drive,' he roared.

Magda risked a glance in the mirror as she floored the accelerator. All she could see was a group of men in dark suits clustered around a body lying in the road. 'I thought you said you weren't going to shoot her?'

'Circumstances change.' Jamie hauled the door shut as they bounced across a grass verge and on to the exit road. 'Actually, I didn't, but she must have thought I had. I figured that the sound of the shot would cause a bit of confusion and give us an edge.' He looked out of the back window to where the guards had run back to pick up their weapons. 'But it looks as if that edge is about to run out.' They heard the faint stutter of automatic weapons and something spanged off the rear window leaving a starred chip about an inch across, then they rounded the corner by the lake and were out

of sight of the house. 'Bullet-proof glass. That's handy.'
He squirmed his way between the backrests and moved
into the passenger seat. 'It'll take them a couple of
minutes to come after us . . .'

'Jamie, I should explain . . .'

'I don't think this is quite the time, love. I'm sure you
had your reasons, but it isn't going to make a blind bit
of difference unless we can get out of here.' He reached
inside his jacket and checked the other pistol, grunting
with satisfaction when he saw it had a full magazine.
'Hey,' he grabbed the door handle as she threw the big
car into a corner, 'take it easy. There's no point in out-
running them if we hit a bloody tree.'

She glared at him, but lifted her foot off the accelerator
a fraction.

'Are you complaining about my driving?'

'Wouldn't think of it,' he grinned; 'merely proffering
an opinion. After all that it would be awfully silly to be
killed in a car crash.'

'I haven't thanked you for saving my life. I thought—'

'No thanks required.' Jamie glanced in the wing
mirror for any sign of pursuit, but they were still on
their own. 'My neck was on the line too,' he felt the
sword edge on against his flesh and shivered, 'quite
literally, come to think of it. If you hadn't kept that third
bloke occupied while I was sparring with the Dragon
Lady and her chums it might have been different. It
would hardly have been worth the bother if he'd put a
bullet in my back.'

'No, I meant I always knew you would.' She sensed
his surprise and shrugged. 'You give the impression

that you get into these things by accident, but you always have something up your sleeve. I knew you'd get us out of there . . .'

'Bugger.'

'Should I slow down?'

'No. Put your foot down. I think this time it's neck or nothing.' A hundred metres ahead someone had toppled the electric golf buggy to block the road and Jamie could see at least three men behind it. Hurriedly he buckled his seat belt and winced as he saw the intermittent blink of machine-gun muzzles. A heartbeat later, bullets hammered into the bonnet and stitched the ground ahead of them. 'They're going for the tyres. Go right. Aim for the back of the bloody thing.'

Magda screamed as another burst of fire smashed into the car. 'Right?'

'Trust me. But hit it full on.'

The temptation was to try to get round the obstacle, but Magda gritted her teeth and put her foot to the floor. She aimed for a point just in front of the rear tyres where one of the gunmen crouched behind the chassis.

'Hang on.' The big car seemed to bounce as it hit and the engine surged, but the effect on the buggy and the men behind it was devastating. The entire rear of the fragile machine disintegrated and something whirled to smash off the bonnet of the Toyota and disappear into the trees. The rest of the buggy was smashed aside taking the other two men with it and they were through.

'Oh my God.' Jamie looked at Magda, wondering if

he'd need to take over the wheel, but she was grinning. 'I thought we were going to die. How did you know we'd get through?'

'I didn't. The engine in those things is either at the front or the back. I took a gamble it was the front. If I'd got it wrong we'd probably be halfway up a tree.'

'You—'

'But I didn't get it wrong.' He cocked his head and listened for a moment. 'The engine doesn't sound too healthy, but we can't be far from the gate.'

The security gate appeared as they rounded the next corner and Magda gunned the engine, prepared to ram her way through the barrier.

'I wouldn't advise it,' Jamie counselled, 'not unless you want to be the filling in a metal sandwich. That gate is designed to stop things a lot heavier than us.' She slowed and he leaned across to push a button on the dashboard. 'I suspect it normally opens automatically, but the Dragon Lady's henchmen must have disabled the mechanism. Pull up across the roadway and as close to it as you can get.'

Jamie watched the road while she manoeuvred the car into place. When she was done she handed him the rucksack and the keys. He helped her on to the bonnet, then the roof and finally across on to the top of the gate where she could jump down into the street. He heard another car in the distance, but before he followed her he walked round the Toyota carefully putting a bullet through each tyre. By the time he reached the street she'd disappeared round the corner of the nearest block and he could hear the shouts of consternation as the chasing car was forced to halt. He sprinted after her and within a few minutes they were back on the main street, breathing hard but trying not to show it.

XXXIV

'This is too quiet.' Jamie studied the street around him. 'We need to find somewhere with a lot more people and quickly.'

'If you don't want to attract attention you'd better get rid of that.' Magda pointed to his jacket, caked with what, even in the light from the street lamps, was obviously blood. He slipped the rucksack to her and unzipped the gory evidence, rolled it into a ball and pushed it under a bush in a little ornamental garden.

The sound of squealing tyres alerted them and Jamie instinctively took the first turn they came to. It led to a poorly lit alley and he wondered if he'd made a mistake. He didn't have time to worry because moments later a car drove slowly past the entrance. They ducked into a doorway before they could be seen and the vehicle moved on. Jamie would have stepped back out into the alley if Magda hadn't clutched him by the arm. 'Hang on,' she hissed. 'I thought I heard a car door.'

They waited, hoping against hope she was wrong, but knowing she wasn't. An indistinct shadow appeared at the far end and began to move warily towards them and they pressed further back into the doorway. 'Shit,' Jamie said under his breath. Two thoughts clawed their way through the panic that set his heart thundering. The first that the man was certainly carrying a gun. The second that Jamie also had one, but he didn't feel like shooting anybody else today. On the plus side, the Yakuza foot soldier was alone, and therefore vulnerable, but that wasn't likely to last for long. Jamie slipped the rucksack from his shoulders and unzipped it one notch at a time.

He put his mouth directly to Magda's ear. 'Get down low.' He felt her nod and obediently drop to a crouch. A man searching the darkness couldn't afford to look everywhere without making himself as vulnerable as his quarry, so he tended to cover his bets by looking at waist height. The closer to the ground they were the less likely to be seen. Jamie fumbled inside the body of the rucksack and recoiled as his fingers touched something leathery covered with hair. He tried again and found the neck of the hammer, but he discovered that the thought of bashing someone's head in with a hammer was even less attractive than shooting them. He delved a little deeper hoping to find the pepper spray before he remembered it was still in his jacket pocket and now nestling beside a plastic bag of McDonald's leftovers.

He had the option to let the gangster walk past, but, even if he didn't see them, they'd still be trapped in a district that would soon be flooded with Yakuza. The hammer or the pistol then. He made his decision. As he crouched down beside Magda his foot brushed something that emitted a tiny rattle and he suppressed a curse. All it would take was one sound. Their pursuer was less than fifty paces away and Jamie felt Magda tense against him. He gripped the handle of the hammer in two hands, then changed his mind. With his right hand he groped for the beer or soda can and picked it up. Forty paces. Not yet. Thirty. Wait. Twenty. Now!

With a flick of his wrist he threw the can so it clattered across the concrete about thirty feet ahead. The gangster shouted something and Jamie heard the sound of running feet. When the approaching shadow appeared in the corner of his eye he waited another second before rising silently to his feet. The running man had a pistol in his outstretched hand when Jamie came from nowhere and brought the head of the hammer down with bone-breaking force on his wrist. Jamie felt a surge of relief as his victim gave a grunt of agony and the gun dropped with a clatter on to the concrete.

He'd gambled on the pain paralysing his victim long enough to allow him a second, knockout blow. Almost any other man would have been put out of action, but this one stepped in close to thwart the follow-up strike and simultaneously slammed a left hook under the Englishman's ribs that gave a new meaning to the word pain. In the same movement the Yakuza brought his right foot round in some sort of jujitsu move that swept the legs from under his opponent. Stunned by the speed of the reaction Jamie had no defence as the gangster followed up with a body slam that crushed the breath out of him.

Too late he discovered his target was the slab-sided Korean who'd 'welcomed' them to the Dragon Lady's concrete castle the previous morning. So much for being bloody squeamish. In desperation he tried to bring the hammer round to smash the man's back and ribs, but the body on top of him was so bulky it was impossible to get the angle for a telling blow. Instead, the Korean was able to push Jamie's arm backwards and he felt fingers as powerful as an industrial vice close over his wrist, working the bone like a terrier's jaws until he dropped the hammer. At the same time a granite skull battered down in a brutal headbutt that would have smashed half the bones in Jamie's face if he hadn't managed to twist away. He felt the rasp of the Korean's stubble on his cheek and the pungent scent of his aftershave filled his nostrils. If he couldn't think of something quickly it would be the last thing he'd ever smell.

The weight and the strength of his opponent were unbelievable. As the Korean's head rose for a second butt Jamie clawed desperately at the moon face, his fingers raking the deep-set dark eyes. With a grunt of irritation the Yakuza released his grip on Jamie's wrist, bringing both hands to the Englishman's throat. There was a moment's confused hesitation as he contemplated his dangling right wrist, but it didn't last and the claw-like fingers of the left hand closed on Jamie's windpipe. Jamie scrabbled desperately at his killer's arm in a futile attempt to break the grip, but it was impossible. He heard the sound of a rook cawing and realized distantly that it was the sound of his own death.

As his vision began to blur a snarling figure launched itself at the Korean accompanied by a stream of obscene oaths. Jamie had a fleeting thought that Magda Ross must have had a more chequered upbringing than he'd realized, before the Yakuza swiped her aside with a sweep of his right arm. The only benefit of her attack was a fleeting reduction of the pressure on Jamie's throat that allowed him to take in a last whooping breath. When the world turned red and the screaming started he thought someone had opened the gates of Hell.

What seemed a lifetime later he heard Magda's voice in his ear urging him to get up. He tried to raise himself on his elbows but it felt as if someone had tried to tear his head from his shoulders. It honestly didn't seem the best idea, but she was very insistent.

Hands hauled at his shirt. 'Jamie, we have to get out of here. They'll be back.'

Reluctantly he tried again, and with her help he staggered to the nearest wall where he could recover his breath. For the first time he noticed the Korean lying on his back in the middle of the alley with a dark shadow covering the upper half of his face.

'I hit him on the head with the hammer,' she said by way of explanation. 'I couldn't think of anything else to do.'

'Good idea,' he said. 'I wish I'd thought of that.' He had a moment of recollection. 'What was the red light I saw?'

She held up a blackened cardboard tube. 'I needed to get his attention first. I think it's called a Roman candle.'

When they reached the street Magda did what she could to dust him down and get rid of the nameless filth from his clothing. It was worth a try, but he knew from the way she scowled at him that he still looked like something from a Zombie movie. Still there was no help for it. After fifteen minutes of cautious searching they found a place where the bars were still open and they could get a taxi. As they waited in the queue Jamie went over their options.

'I don't see how we can go back to the hotel. The chances are they're already waiting for us.'

'All right,' she agreed immediately, and he wondered how many other women would abandon all their clothing and jewellery so readily. 'So we head straight to the airport? Only they could be waiting for us there too.'

'That's true, which is why we won't go there directly.'

After a tense wait they got in the back of the green and yellow taxi. 'Tell him to take us to the ferry terminal down at the port. It's the last thing they'll expect,' he explained. 'We'll book a cabin on the first sailing to Okinawa. From there we can get the earliest flight out of Naha airport to Hong Kong or Taiwan and we're home free.'

She passed on the instructions and the driver pulled out into the late-night traffic. Every bone in Jamie's body ached and exhaustion threatened to overwhelm him, but he knew he had to stay awake. Little images of horrors that were and worse horrors that might have been flitted through his head. He frowned as he remembered the piece of business that couldn't be ignored.

'All right,' he turned to Magda, 'I know you've been waiting for me to ask. Who's the mystery man with the blond bob?' He nodded to the rucksack that sat between them.

'My grandfather.'

Why wasn't he surprised?

'And you knew he was there all the time?'

'No.' There was a challenge in her eyes as she turned to meet his gaze. 'But I had to find out. It's a long story.'

Jamie was conscious of the driver's eyes on them in the rear-view mirror and he lowered his voice. 'Tell me. We have all the time in the world.'

'His name was Johannes Rudiger and he was a pastor with the Basel Missionary Society in China in the nineteen thirties. When the Japanese attacked Nanking he went there to do what he could to ease the suffering. He was that kind of man. Johannes linked up with a businessman called John Rabe. Rabe was a Nazi who supported Hitler, but he was a good man at heart. Because of the Anti-Comintern Pact between the Third Reich and Japan, he had some influence with the Japanese commanders. He managed to set up safe zones for westerners and some Chinese civilians.' She had begun the story forcefully, but now she hesitated and he registered the catch in her voice. 'The zones . . . the zones were mainly successful – they managed to save about two hundred thousand people – but individual Japanese units violated the agreement. They'd claim bandits were operating in a certain section and carry off hundreds, sometimes thousands, of innocents to be executed, or raped and then killed in ways too sickening to describe. One of the worst perpetrators was a battalion led by a Major Yoshitaki.'

Light danced across her face from the garishly lit skyscrapers with their metres-high adverts for computers and photocopiers; in their glow Jamie could see the tears shining on Magda's cheeks. He wanted to hold her, but somehow he knew it would be wrong.

'I was always told my grandfather had simply disappeared in China.' Magda's voice found new strength as if she was defying the past. 'Everyone in the family accepted that story, except me. Nothing just vanishes. Not things. Not people. There's always evidence. I read everything I could about Nanking and the Japanese occupation and what I learned almost drove me mad. I was on the point of giving up when Rabe's surviving relative allowed me access to his letters and a memoir he'd written, but never published. Rabe said Yoshitaki would permit his soldiers freedom to rape and plunder, and personally select their victims. The German's protests were ignored and finally he asked Johannes to remonstrate with the Japanese commander. He never returned, but a witness testified that he had seen Yoshitaki himself taking my grandfather away under guard after he'd tried to stop his men burying a group of Chinese civilians alive.'

She paused and once again Jamie caught the driver's eyes on them in the rear-view mirror. He wondered if the curiosity was concern for a passenger's welfare or something more sinister.

'I'm sorry,' he said. 'I still don't see how believing you knew what happened in Nanking in 'thirty-seven prompted you to come along with me. Especially when there was no way you could have known your grandfather's, er, remains even existed.'

'It wasn't about his remains.' The dark eyes shone as if they were on fire. 'I knew about Yoshitaki's obscene competition to behead a hundred people and I learned about his trip to Berlin through Uli. After China he served in the Solomon Islands and I wasn't even certain he'd survived the war.' She shook her head. 'When you came to a museum and asked about the Bougainville head it was as if a vital piece of the jigsaw of my life had fallen into place. I could never have afforded to go to Tokyo even if I'd known where Yoshitaki's descendants live. What better way than to accompany Jamie Saintclair on his mad quest for an obsessed mining tycoon.' She wiped a hand over her eyes. 'Ever since I learned how Johannes died I've been desperate to find out *why*. He was thirty years old. My grandmother was only twenty. She would have joined him in Nanking, but for the fighting, and the fact she was pregnant. I wanted to know what kind of person could do such a thing to such a courageous and compassionate man. Well, I had my answer when I saw the look in that woman's eyes when she stood over you with that bloody awful sword.'

'All right.' Jamie suppressed a shiver as he relived the kiss of the blade on his neck. 'I accept that, but I'm still curious. If you knew all along that the answers lay in Tokyo, why did you let me go gallivanting around Russia?'

Magda hesitated as a police car flashed past in the

opposite direction, intermittently lighting up the interior of the taxi. By now they were crossing the city's famous Rainbow Bridge and the lights of the towers were reflected in the dark waters of the bay. He saw a moment of confusion in her eyes.

'I couldn't *know*, Jamie, not for certain, but I believed. But how could I divert you? When you got the call to go to Russia instead of Japan I could hardly stand up and shout, "No!" You'd have thought I was mad, or worse trying to sabotage your mission. No, you had to go to Russia, for your own peace of mind, if nothing else.'

He couldn't help smiling. It was difficult to equate what had happened in Moscow and Siberia with peace of mind. 'And now?'

'Now,' she said decisively, 'I'll take my grandfather home and lay him to rest, but first . . .' Jamie opened his mouth to protest, but she silenced him with a finger on his lips. 'No, Jamie, no arguments this time. You've helped me do what I needed to do. Now I'll help you. Whatever it takes.'

He stared at her for a long moment, taking in the determined line of her jaw and the certainty in her eyes. She was right, he couldn't do it alone, and there were worse things than going into a fight with Magda Ross at your back. 'Okay,' he agreed. 'But you do exactly what I tell you this time. No little freelance jaunts into no man's land.'

'Guide's honour.' She smiled.

The car slowed as they reached the man-made island the Ariane ferry terminal shared with the Odaiba

Marine Park. When they reached the terminal building, Jamie paid off the driver while Magda went inside to check the sailing schedules.

She met him in the doorway. 'I don't think this will work, Jamie. The first sailing to Okinawa isn't for another two days. Maybe we should try somewhere else?'

'Don't worry,' he reassured her. 'I'll fix it. You keep an eye on our friend there.' He nodded to where the driver was still counting his money.

He went to the 'A' Line desk, where a girl in a red and white uniform cheerfully booked him a first-class two-bed cabin for the Thursday sailing and charged him fifty thousand yen of Keith Devlin's dwindling cash for the pleasure. The transaction completed he went to the side door furthest away from the official taxis and was pleased to see his hunch was correct. Before joining Magda at the door he withdrew the maximum amount possible on Devlin's credit card from one of a bank of ATM cash machines.

'Well?'

'He's been on the phone ever since you left. He seems quite agitated and he keeps looking in this direction.'

'Good.'

'*Good?* It means they know where we are.'

'No. It means they think they know where we are. Let's go.' He led her to the side door and out into the chill air, wishing he still had the jacket he'd started the night with. About fifteen cars of varying age, manu-facture and state of preservation were parked along the road with their drivers smoking or chatting beside them. As they walked towards the line of unofficial taxis the drivers came forward smiling and offering their prices in pidgin English. 'Tell them no thanks.' Jamie grinned. 'We want that one.' He pointed to an ancient grey Honda in the centre of the line. A young man leaned against the bodywork wearing a New York Mets baseball jacket and a Yankees cap.

Magda managed a smile as she fobbed off the other drivers and pointed to the Honda, whose young driver was as surprised as anyone at their choice. The other men laughed and took the decision in good humour.

'What are they saying?' Jamie asked.

'That Kaichi will have us pushing his chariot before we get where we're going.'

'Let's hope not.'

They got in the back of the car, placing the rucksack and Magda's bag between them. 'Ask him how much it will be to take us to the airport and when he tells you, offer him twice as much if he can get us there in twenty minutes.' When he heard the terms the young man grinned and saluted. 'Yes, sah.'

'But there's no hurry until we get out of the terminal gates.'

Magda's request was received with a shrug. They pulled out past the line of cabs and turned the corner to pass the main door of the terminal. Jamie saw the first taxi driver still talking on the phone. 'Kiss me,' he said.

'What?'

'Kiss me.' He pulled her down so their faces were below the level of the window.

'I think that's enough, Mr Saintclair.' Magda pulled

herself away with a wry look after they'd travelled a hundred metres. 'Wouldn't it have been perfectly acceptable just to hide below the door sill?'

'No.' Jamie grinned. 'It had to look authentic.'

She punched him on the arm and the taxi driver leered in the rear-view mirror and said something that was neither English nor Japanese.

'What did he say?'

'I think he told us to get a room.'

For the first time in hours they were able to relax and sit back as the driver chain-smoked cigarettes and listened to what sounded like a snooker match as he weaved through the traffic. Magda asked if they could open a window and as she held the driver's attention Jamie pushed the hammer and pliers under the front seat and surreptitiously dropped the guns out on to the road. They were passing the Wangan Road freight terminal and approaching the Haneda tunnel when Jamie's mobile phone began to chirp. He checked the caller ID and before he refused the call Magda saw Keith Devlin's name on the screen.

'What was all that about?'

'I think I've had enough of Keith Devlin pulling the strings. We have the Bougainville head and if he wants it that much he's going to have to prove it.'

'What do you have in mind,' she said sweetly, 'or are you going to surprise me again?'

'Ask our friend here how much he wants for his jacket and cap.'

They entered the airport terminal building at Haneda separately and by different doors. Jamie had the driver drop him off just short of the entrance and told Magda to stay in the car until the last possible moment. When he entered the terminal he marched in, trying to look as if he owned the place, the way Americans of his acquaintance had a habit of doing. He chewed imaginary gum, kept his head up and his chest out. As well as the cap and jacket, their new friend had entered into the spirit of things by insisting Jamie take a pair of spectacles left in the car by a fare. It meant he had to peer in order to read anything, but the gesture and the broad-rimmed glasses aged him and added to the disguise. He headed for the escalator and took it up to international departures on the third floor. At the periphery of his vision he saw Magda attach herself to a group of Caucasians laden with luggage. He watched admiringly as she insisted on helping carry some of the smaller bags to the check-in area. While she stood among them Jamie made for the Cathay Pacific ticket desk. The departure board said the airline's next flight to Hong Kong was due to board in three hours.

'Two first-class tickets on the Hong Kong flight,' he requested. The beautiful girl on the desk frowned. 'It is a little short notice, sir, but of course we will do our best.' Jamie waited, trying not to fidget while she checked her computer. The frown deepened, she chewed her lip, found a solution, and her face relaxed as she smiled. 'You are fortunate we had a late cancellation and that poor passenger MacDonald who believes he is being upgraded will now find himself back in Business. Do you have any luggage to check in? No? Then have a good flight, Mr Saintclair.' She handed over the tickets.

As he set off back towards the check-in desks Jamie noticed four Japanese men – standing in two pairs – studying passengers heading for the security gates. From time to time they'd glance down at something in their hands, presumably photographs taken by the video cameras at the Dragon Lady's house. Jamie had intended they go through security separately, but the Yakuza seemed to have concentrated their watchers on the main security gate. The way they were deployed hinted they were there to snatch their quarry, not to kill, which meant Magda would be more vulnerable alone. He made his decision and went directly to her.

'Stay close and don't look anybody in the eye,' he whispered.

He handed her the second ticket and steered her towards the almost empty priority line for First and Business Class passengers. Their passports were in a side pocket of the rucksack and he retrieved them as he reached the gate, with the scanners beyond. Would the scanners show the heads for what they were, or just a couple of shapeless objects? Magda must have had the same thought because as she was ushered through she cast a nervous glance back towards the watching men. The movement drew the attention of the man nearest them and his eyes leaped between the face that swam into his vision and the picture in his hand. By the time he'd made up his mind they were out of sight, but Jamie heard a quick-fire burst of Japanese that signalled they'd been spotted.

'We're not out of it yet,' he told her. 'The chances are they'll have someone inside too. This way.' Magda followed him down through the avenues of shops, bars and cafes until they narrowed into a corridor that led towards the main boarding gates. Dozens of men and women talking on phones, but none yet with the tense watchfulness that would spell danger. Suddenly, at the far end of the corridor, Jamie noticed someone who didn't fit the pattern.

'Keep your head down,' he hissed.

The man was fifty paces away, talking into his phone and unashamedly studying every white face he encountered. Another few strides and he couldn't fail to see them.

'This way, honey.' Jamie politely steered Magda to the right where, with a flourish of their tickets, they were ushered into the sanctuary of the First Class lounge. They were safe. For now.

XXXV

'May I tempt you with a glass of champagne? Today we are serving the Dom Pérignon 2002.' The Japanese hostess hovered beside the secluded booth overlooking Tokyo Bay.

Magda hesitated. 'No thank—'

'You should,' Jamie encouraged her. 'We might be here for quite a while.'

'But those men . . .'

'Won't be able to reach us in here.' He gave her a tired smile. 'The Saintclair philosophy is that as long as you're alive you might as well make the most of it.' He saw her resolve weaken. 'Two glasses please, and can you bring us the menu?' Smiling, the hostess poured from the green and gold bottle, the liquid frothing gently into the narrow crystal stem.

'To life,' he said, lifting his glass to clink it against hers.

Her face dissolved into a disbelieving grin. 'You really are the most infuriating, illogical . . .' She gave up. 'To life.'

'May it be a little less eventful than in recent times.'

'A sentiment I'd gladly echo.' She took a sip of the champagne, wrinkling her nose at the exploding bubbles. 'Except that with Jamie Saintclair around that seems a little unlikely. What time does our flight leave?'

'The Hong Kong flight takes off in about two hours, but I don't actually plan for us to be on it.'

'But the tickets . . . ?'

'The tickets bought us sanctuary, a glass of champagne and a hot meal, but more important they bought us time. The men in the lobby and at security were here to abduct us if they got the opportunity, but their priority was to track us. By now they'll know we're holed up in here and booked on Cathay Pacific CX 6321, departing from Gate 112 at six thirty a.m.. They'll be relaxed because they have us where they want us.'

'Trapped,' she pointed out.

'Succinctly put.' The hostess returned with the menus. 'May we have another glass, please?' He smiled at Magda. 'You order for us both while I make a phone call.'

One and a half ring tones before it was answered. 'Where the fuck have you been?' An Australian accent; harsh with authority and a touch of threat, but not the mining tycoon.

'You're not Devlin. I only speak to Devlin.'

'Jumped-up messenger boys don't dictate to the boss. Do you have the head?'

'Look, old son, somebody should have told you I don't react well to threats. Why don't you put Devlin

331

on and go and work out your issues somewhere else? Either that or I can hang up.'

'You don't want to be doing that, Jamie boy.' Keith Devlin's rasping voice was full of chummy bonhomie, but Jamie felt the hair on the back of his neck rise like an angry cat's. 'Just a little misunderstanding.'

'Sure, Keith. Just a little misunderstanding that's supposed to remind me you have the heavy squad ready to wade in if I happen to get the wrong idea.'

'But the question stands, son, and this is important: do you have the head?'

Jamie let the silence lengthen before he replied. 'Yes.'

'And where are you?'

'Let's stop playing games, Keith. You know exactly where I am. The only reason you gave me the credit card was so you could track it. You know I booked two tickets for the Okinawa ferry about an hour and a half ago and you know I bought two flights to Hong Kong at Haneda airport. The trouble is that the minute I walk out the doors at Lantau it will be straight into the arms of certain people it wouldn't be healthy for me to meet.' He gave Devlin the short version of the night's events.

'So Madam Nishimura wants your guts for garters, and when she gets it, she'll take the head back and I can whistle for it?'

'Well put, except that it would be more accurate to say that she wants my head for a wall lamp. Which is why we're staying here until you get us out.'

'And how in the name of Christ do you expect me to do that?' the tycoon spluttered.

Jamie told him.

'That's the craziest thing I've ever heard. Why don't I just send you a bloody magic carpet instead?'

'Come on, Keith. You've got the money. You've got the resources. And didn't I read that the Japanese government were trying to persuade Devlin Metal Resources to invest in a scheme to extract rare earth minerals from under the Pacific? That should give you a few favours to call in.'

Devlin grumbled for a moment before making a grudging capitulation. 'All right. I'll give it a go, but it could take a bit of time.'

Jamie smiled. 'Make it happen, Keith, or maybe I'll have to negotiate with Madam Nishimura instead.'

'You're forgetting about your girlies, Saintclair.'

'No, I'm not, Keith. But this is my life we're bargaining over and we both know you won't touch a hair on their heads.'

'Don't be so certain about that, son.' He heard the hesitation in the Australian's voice. 'If you believed that why didn't you just walk away?'

'Because I like a challenge.'

He rang off and found Magda studying him with a question in her eyes.

'We could be here for another two hours or another two days,' he told her, 'so make yourself comfortable.'

'Won't they call us?'

'No, I've arranged for our tickets to be cancelled without any fuss.'

She looked as if she was about to say something. Thanks? A verbal slap on the wrist for keeping her in the dark again? He'd never know because she thought better of it and wandered over to a shelf scattered with international newspapers. She picked up a copy and began to flick idly through the pages. He saw her stiffen and was on his feet before she turned her head.

'Jamie? This . . . I can't . . .'

'What is it, Magda?' He kept his voice steady because two or three of their fellow passengers had sensed her concern and were looking towards them. Her hand shook as she folded the paper and showed him the headline: *Russian oligarch assassinated by bodyguard.*

'Christ,' he breathed. He took the paper and they went back to their seats.

'I can't believe it. He seemed . . . I don't know . . . such a *good* man. Not like the others. We had tea with him less than a week ago.'

Good. Jamie wasn't so sure. He supposed your opinion of Arkady Berzarin depended on your definition of good. A good businessman? Certainly, but a good business-man was generally a ruthless businessman. Good to his workers? Probably. Good to his competitors and rivals, definitely not. He remembered the man with respect, but he'd been glad to get out of the house unscathed, without experiencing his generosity or animosity. Still it was hard to believe he was dead.

Russian billionaire Arkady Berzarin was assas-sinated by one of his bodyguards as he drove to meet his son in nearby Krasnoyarsk.

The respected businessman, who dominated Russia's aluminium industry for decades and had commercial interests all over the world, was shot

*several times by Yuri Prasolov before the killer was
gunned down in his turn . . .*

A shadowy and hitherto unknown Chechen terror
organization had claimed responsibility, citing the
Russian's profiteering and abuse of his workforce in
the Caucasus . . . Tributes led, naturally, by the Russian
president . . . We will hunt them down wherever they
hide . . .

Berzarin had feared no one. Not terrorists, not the
Mafia, not the unions and not his rivals. Only one
person had coveted his power in Siberia. And one
person had coveted what he believed was his by right,
but which Berzarin claimed he did not have.

Why? Why didn't matter, except as it affected
Jamie and Magda. The deed was done and could not
be undone. He felt certain they'd been used in some
way, but he couldn't work out how. Maybe Berzarin
had upped his security after their visit and the cryptic
warning from Sergei. Maybe . . . No, maybe didn't
matter either. The question was: is this the end of it?
Or was there a further reckoning? He had a feeling his
good friend Vatutin was out there somewhere smiling
at the mess he'd got himself into. But was the Russian
there to protect him? Not much evidence of that, it was
true. Or – for reasons he didn't understand – had his
usefulness ended with Berzarin's death?

He flicked through to the share prices. Devlin Metal
Resources was down another five points on the Nikkei
and seven on the Dow. No wonder Keith Devlin was
getting edgy.

*

'Mr Saintclair?' Three hours after his call Jamie looked up to see a man in a dark uniform and a pilot's peaked cap looming over him. They'd used the time to take turns at sleeping on the leather couch. Magda opened her eyes, blinking against the bright light, her hand automatically reaching protectively for the backpack beneath the seat.

'Yes,' Jamie said warily.

'Mr Devlin sent us?'

Jamie looked past him to where two other men and a woman dressed in the same smart livery stood waiting. They all had the small wheeled suitcases you saw flight crews dragging through airports the world over. He smiled. 'In that case, let's get it done.'

A few minutes later he was sharing the lounge's male shower room with the corporate jet's steward, an American called Brett who hailed from New York.

'You must have some clout, man. We were heading from Seoul to pick up the East Asia director in Manila when we had word to get our asses to Tokyo. You could hear his cusses from the galley when Cap told him about the change of plan.'

'Well, you know how it is, Brett,' Jamie said as they exchanged clothes and Brett handed over the neck lanyard carrying his ID badge. 'Old man Devlin will do anything for his favourite nephew. Sorry about the state of the jacket.'

The flight attendant studied the battered Mets bomber and grinned. 'Damned if I wouldn't feel like a traitor if I wore that thing anyway. They'll have

336

something to fit me in the mall. Be pleased to take that cap off your hands, though.' Jamie handed it over and studied himself in the mirror as the other man squeezed himself into his black designer jeans. He wore a white shirt and dark maroon tie. The trousers fitted him for length, but the waistline was a little loose, though nothing that a belt wouldn't fix. He'd borrowed Brett's shaving kit and looked about five years younger without the stubble he'd allowed to accumulate over the past week. There wasn't a lot he could do about his hair, but the peaked cap would hide that. The biggest problem was the immaculately shined wingtips. The American was about two sizes larger and they were alarmingly loose. They eventually solved the problem by the age-old fix of stuffing the toes with paper towels. He shrugged on the tailored jacket and pulled the pilot's cap down at a rakish angle over one eye.

'How do I look?'

'Like you've been doing the job all your life. Just one thing . . .'

'Yes?'

'When you're heading for the plane, narrow your eyes, square your shoulders and think like a B-17 pilot heading for a trip to Berlin. I always find it helps smother the crushing knowledge that I'm just an over-paid, mile-high gofer in a snazzy suit.'

He came to stand beside Jamie and ran a comb through his thick dark hair. They were approximately the same height and build, which was fortunate. Jamie wasn't sure he could have persuaded the pilot to give up his wings. 'I hope this isn't putting you to too much trouble?'

Brett's face dissolved in a dreamy smile. 'Who wouldn't swap serving lobster at thirty thousand feet for two nights of expenses-paid R and R in Tokyo? And with Miss Perfect along to add a sporting interest.' Jamie raised a questioning eyebrow and the other man slapped him on the shoulder. 'Hell, I've got fifty bucks riding at two to one with the Cap that I can't get her into the sack by Friday night.'

When they emerged from the shower room, Magda was already there, but it took Jamie a second to recognize her.

'Wow,' he said. 'You were born to be in a uniform.'

Miss Perfect was probably a size larger than Magda's slim figure, but they'd contrived to make the skirt and jacket look as if they'd been made for her. The effect was military, but somehow she managed to give the uniform a softer and more feminine quality. A black pillbox hat perched jauntily on her raven hair completed the ensemble. 'It'll take me a while to get used to the idea of you in killer heels, though.'

'Don't push your luck, Saintclair.' She smiled. 'Though I admit you don't look so bad yourself.'

'Are we ready?' the captain urged. 'We've got the eight fifteen slot and I don't want to miss it.'

'Just one more thing . . .' Jamie took Brett's overnight case and swapped the contents with those of the rucksack. As his hands touched the wrinkled ovals something like a mild electric shock ran through him. It struck him he knew more about Magda's grandfather than the man whose remains had turned his life upside down. For the first time he was tempted to take a closer look, to see if something remained of the features that would give him a clue to the type of human being this Solomon Islander had been. But this wasn't the time. He looked up to find Brett peering over his shoulder.

'Hey, that looks kinda like—' Jamie turned and stared at him with hard eyes. 'Okay, man, I didn't mean nothing.'

The Englishman allowed his face to relax. 'Just a little present for old man Devlin. And Brett?'

'Sure?' A nervous smile.

'Don't forget to share a bottle of the Dom Pérignon with Miss Perfect before you go. The 2002 is the perfect loosener when you combine it with smoked salmon and scrambled eggs for breakfast.'

The new flight crew marched out of the first-class lounge with the captain in the lead and Jamie at his shoulder. Behind them came the tall co-pilot, chatting to Magda. They made their way through the terminal with the fixed stare of men and women for whom the human sea they traversed was indivisible from any other potential piece of cargo. Not individuals, or even people, just numbers and weights and appetites to be serviced. Neither recognized nor even acknowledged. Eight pairs of eyes saw them leave the lounge, but if they noticed anything it was the female attendant in the tight skirt who moved with all the grace of a catwalk model even on killer heels that looked a size too small.

'We normally park at the VIP terminal,' the captain muttered from the side of his mouth, 'but we have special dispensation this time round. When we get to the security desk just open your passport and wave it airily in the guard's direction and you'll find he'll barely even notice you. If there does happen to be a problem leave it to me to sort out. I filed a flight plan for Brisbane when we landed, is that right?'

'Brisbane is perfect.' Keith Devlin had wanted to land Magda Ross in Port Moresby and Jamie to continue in the executive jet to an unspecified meeting place, presumably on Bougainville or somewhere in the Solomon Islands. Jamie had insisted he wasn't going to be dumped in the middle of nowhere with the Bougainville head and a reception committee headed by a maniac who'd kidnapped his girlfriend and her daughter.

Devlin had eventually agreed he could accompany Magda to Brisbane and take a scheduled flight to the mining boss's as yet unspecified destination. That way Jamie would be assured that a whole plane load of passengers would witness his arrival and he could insist on a daylight meeting with Devlin and whoever was with him, to make the exchange.

The mining tycoon had only put up a token argument, which made Jamie's ear tingle in a way he didn't like. The thing that gnawed at him was why the head was so important and why Devlin needed *him* to take it to Bougainville. The more he thought about it, the more it didn't add up. If Devlin was being straight why wouldn't he fly them direct to Sydney, where Jamie would hand over the head in exchange for his loved ones? The original agreement hadn't specified a location for the head to be handed over, but there'd been no suggestion he'd have to travel to Bougainville. That meant either some dynamic had changed or Devlin had planned to play him false right from the start. For the life of him he couldn't believe that. The more likely explanation was that someone, somewhere had imposed a deadline and Devlin needed the head in a hurry.

A face swam into his mind; a genial panda with hidden fangs. Could the Chinese have upped the ante? It had to be a possibility. Mr Lim had hinted there was more to this than a multi-billion-pound copper mine contract, and that was high stakes by anyone's standards. It would explain the hard case Devlin had put on the phone to try to put the frighteners on him.

Well, two could play that game.

XXXVI

London, February 1943

When he sucks on his false teeth the old man looks like a bulldog chewing a wasp, Jock Colville thought affectionately, but his master's consternation was hardly surprising given how close to home this particular bombshell had struck. Colville stood before the big desk in the office-bedroom beneath the Treasury building where his master spent most of his waking hours. Surrounded by metres of concrete, on the wall beside him was a giant map of southern Britain while behind the desk hung a smaller scale map of the European mainland.

Winston Churchill looked up from the paper he was reading, the fleshy lips jutting and lower jaw sticking out like a battering ram. 'Are they certain?' he rasped.

'As sure as they can be without hauling him in and giving him the third degree,' Colville replied steadily, meaning rigorous interrogation.

Churchill winced as if gripped by some internal

cramp. 'Give me the details. I can't condemn a man on tittle-tattle.'

Not a man, Colville thought, but an old and very close friend; a confidante who has been selling you and his country down the river for decades. You were told, but you didn't listen. But he couldn't fault the old man, not really, because loyalty had stayed his hand and loyalty was one of his most appealing characteristics.

'His affection for the Japanese before the war was well known.' The other man grunted – ancient history – so he moved on quickly, reciting the facts as if he were giving evidence from the witness box. 'The security service was first alerted to the possibility of an informant close to the heart of government in the summer of nineteen forty-one after your meeting with President Roosevelt in Canada on the *Prince of Wales*. We intercepted and decoded a communication between the Japanese Embassy and Tokyo—'

'I remember,' Churchill snapped. 'Accurate transcript of the conference notes, down to the very words and phrases.'

'That's correct, Prime Minister. The investigation was inconclusive and the closure of the embassy after . . . at the outbreak of the war with Japan, meant a temporary end to our ability to read the Japanese codes, specifically Code Purple.'

'Temporary?'

'From mid nineteen forty-two we have been able to intercept messages between their embassy in Berlin and the Japanese government in Tokyo. The diplomatic communications continued to be sent in Code Purple, but the people at Bletchley Park noticed that certain others were sent in what at first was assumed to be a personal code. However, they continued to work on it and last week they were able to begin deciphering the backlog. It wasn't until yesterday they began on this.' He handed over the flimsy sheets of paper and took a step back from the desk. 'Fortunately, Brigadier Tiltman understood immediately that it must be for your eyes only and sent it to me by courier. The cryptographer who decoded it has been encouraged to apply an even greater degree of secrecy than is usual at that establishment, if that's possible. I think the words Tiltman used to the poor woman were "on pain of death".'

Jock Colville had been private secretary to Winston Churchill from the day he walked into 10 Downing Street and he had seen him confronted with many setbacks, some of them five-star disasters, but he had never witnessed him grow old in the space of a single heartbeat.

'The Americans . . .'

Colville shook his head. 'We believe the Berlin–Tokyo link is our domain. We share Code Purple transcripts, but as far as we're aware this is *our* exclusive property.'

Churchill grunted from deep in his chest, a deep bass rumble like a male lion challenging its rivals. 'Keep it that way. They are playing what Mr President calls *hardball*, whatever that is, over the Pacific transcripts, so it's what they should expect.' He hunched low over the desk, his broad shoulders around his ears. 'You know what it would mean if this ever became public,

Jock? Particularly now, when we are embarking with our allies on the planning for this greatest of all military enterprises.'

'Yes, sir, I think I do, sir.' He remembered the day he'd brought the original intelligence to the man on the other side of the desk. It had originated with a double agent in Tokyo, a man who spied for the Soviets, but who shared his take, and the requests of his masters, with British intelligence. A devastating piece of information that could save many thousands of lives. He'd expected a shout of 'Eureka' or some such and the usual explosion of energy, barking of orders and boundless enthusiasm. But he'd been wrong. Winston Churchill had studied the piece of paper for a long time, his head down and his face as sombre as Colville had ever seen it. There would be a meeting of the Cabinet inner circle to discuss it, but the decision had been taken in those first few moments. No action.

'Comrade Stalin already has his eyes on half of Europe in the event of ultimate victory. If he had this information he would demand the other half.' Churchill picked up a document from the side of the desk, scanned it and produced a harrumph of displeasure before initialling it. 'And you know, Jock, I should have to give it to him. That is how important this is.' He paused for a long moment, his eyes on some distant image before focusing once more on Colville. 'We're sure it's him?' he asked again.

'Counter-intelligence narrowed the field to two men; the other was a Commander McGrath, who was also in Japan before the war. We had them both followed, and I'm sorry to say, sir, that there's no doubt he's our man. We have enough evidence to charge him under the Treason Act.' He licked his lips. 'Presumably he could hang, sir.'

The Prime Minister of Great Britain glared at him over the top of the reading glasses he refused to let the public see in case they looked like a sign of weakness. Colville knew he had made the civil servant's greatest mistake, positing a solution unacceptable to his minister.

'No,' the other man said softly, and Jock Colville felt a twinge of distaste that the person he admired more than any other should show such a human flaw; to put personal friendship before country. But he was mistaken. 'Certainly, he deserves to hang, but he is too high, too prominent and with too many well-placed friends.' Churchill allowed himself a self-deprecating smile to acknowledge that he was one. 'The King would never forgive me, but it is not friendship that stays my hand. To drag him before the courts, even a secret court, would cause a scandal. We would alert his spymasters and, worse, those who spy upon them. I doubt we can afford that, Jock. No, I think we must promote the honourable gentleman.' He saw Colville's instinctive look of disgust and his eyes took on a mischievous twinkle, like a little boy bent on dirty deeds. His voice changed tempo, all hesitancy gone. 'A memo to the First Sea Lord. Commander is too low a rank for one so diligent and so talented. Another stripe, I think. Yes, captain sounds much better. There must be a post for such an officer in the far north. Scapa Flow, I believe, has a vacancy for a supply officer of that rank, and if it does not we will create one. Counting long johns and crates of ships' biscuits should keep him too busy to make mischief. Any refusal or demur to be met with a mandatory posting to the North Atlantic convoys. If not Scapa, Murmansk, eh, Jock? That should take the starch out of our spy. Now,' he smiled grimly, 'let us get on with the war.'

XXXVII

'Can I use my iPad on this thing?'

'No problem,' Jerry, the co-pilot, told Magda. 'There's a socket beside every seat if you need to plug it in.'

As they prepared for take-off he explained that Devlin Metal Resources' Gulfstream G650 was basically a flying boardroom. 'But there are a couple of full-size beds beyond the bulkhead if you feel like taking a nap. If you don't mind me saying so, you guys certainly look like you could do with one.'

They thanked him and he told them to help themselves to food and drink from the galley during the flight. 'Just treat it like your own home,' he said. 'We'll be landing in Brisbane in about five hours depending on the wind strength. Conditions are good and it's a damn sight warmer over there than it is in Tokyo.' He went off to join the pilot for the pre-flight checks.

Jamie exchanged a tired smile with Magda. 'I don't know about you but sleep seems like a good idea. Who knows what tomorrow will bring.'

'Maybe later,' she said, strapping herself into one of

four deep cushioned leather seats at a mahogany table. 'First of all I think you should come and sit here.' She patted the seat beside her. 'There are things you should know.'

'That sounds mysterious. Or perhaps the word is ominous?'

'I'll let you decide.' She placed her hand on top of the computer tablet as the plane taxied out towards the end of the runway. 'It didn't seem all that relevant until last night, but I think it's time you knew a little more about Bougainville, Jamie. When people say "You don't know what you're getting into" it's usually an exaggeration, but in this case . . .' She paused as the Gulfstream's engine pitch rose in a few seconds from a soft roar to a shriek and the plane gathered momentum, tyres bumping and fuselage swaying, until with almost miraculous ease it left the earth and climbed at an almost impossible angle. Jamie looked past Magda's shoulder and saw the bulk of Mount Fuji dominating the horizon through the oval window. 'Well, I think the statement is probably accurate.'

'Then perhaps it's time I found out,' he said and smiled.

Magda studied him gravely. 'Where do I start?'

The plane levelled out and a few seconds later the seat belt sign above the cockpit door turned green. Jamie unstrapped himself and went to the kitchen, removed a bottle of remarkably fine white wine from the refrigerator, gathered up two crystal glasses and an ice bucket and returned to the table. 'It's traditional to start at the beginning.' He poured the wine and put the bottle into the ice bucket. 'That seems as good a place as any.'

'Okay.' She ran her fingers across the face of the tablet, scrolling down a list of subjects. 'Let's begin with a geography lesson. Bougainville is actually not one principal island, but two: Bougainville, the larger, to the south, and Buka, to the north, separated by the eight-hundred-metre-wide Buka Passage. The main island is about a hundred and fifty miles long by forty wide. Mountains run down the spine, including one active volcano and two dormant ones. They're covered by thick jungle, and the warm, wet climate means they're cut with streams and rivers. The centres of population, generally quite small villages, are all in the coastal areas where their main employment is – was – tending the coconut plantations or fishing. You with me so far?'

'Yes, miss.' Jamie grinned. 'Somewhere to avoid at all costs. I take it the wildlife is just as welcoming.'

'Go to the top of the class. No bears or wolves. Just bats and wild pigs. Oh, and snakes, spiders and man-eating salt-water crocodiles.'

'That's very reassuring.' His face told a different story. 'I wish I'd packed my swimming trunks.'

'All right. Let's get to the population.' She brought up a new page and pointed to a picture of four or five almost naked wire-haired islanders glaring at the camera. 'Bougainville has been inhabited for something like thirty thousand years. As you can see, the native Bougainvilleans are unique to this region, being extremely black skinned – the difference is so distinctive they call the other Melanesian races Redskins – and of a very ancient and unknown origin. A French navigator called Louis Antoine de Bougainville gave the islands their name in the eighteenth century.'

'And introduced them to civilization, I'm sure.'

She nodded solemnly. 'If by civilization you mean slavery, disease, poverty and material exploitation. Oh, and religion, which is worse than any of the above. The French were followed by the Germans, who developed the copra industry – you know what copra is?'

Jamie thought back to his less than comprehensive briefing in Keith Devlin's office. 'Coconut fibre?'

'That's right. It meant that huge amounts of land that could have been used for food production became coconut plantations, and the people who had worked that land now depended on the plantation owners for a living.' She paused as the co-pilot appeared from the cockpit and walked to the galley, returning a few minutes later with two bottles of water.

'We're making good time,' he announced as he passed. When he'd gone Magda continued with her briefing.

'The Germans also joined the islands politically to Papua New Guinea, six hundred miles to the west, although their traditional affinity and trading links lay with the Solomon Islands, the nearest of which is six miles to the south. As you will see, this stored up a great deal of trouble for the future.' She took a sip of her wine. 'Any questions so far?'

'You haven't mentioned headhunting.'

Small white teeth nibbled her lip as she considered

her answer. 'Traditionally, the practice was limited and mainly confined to the defeated enemy chief. It only became widespread after the Europeans arrived . . .' She preempted his question before he'd even decided to ask it. 'Once it became clear the newcomers were prepared to pay for a shrunken head it created a market, so instead of a trophy of war it became the reason for it. Every fight created a new blood feud and eventually the Germans had to ban the taking of heads. It still went on, of course, our Bougainville head is from this period, but it was illegal.'

Jamie nodded. It made economic sense. There was no point in letting your workforce slaughter each other before you'd had the chance to work them into the ground. All this had nothing to do with Keith Devlin, of course, but he knew Magda would get to that part of the story in her own time.

'The Germans were thrown out by the Australians during the First World War.' Magda wrapped up the first half of the twentieth century in a sentence. 'The Australians by the Japanese in nineteen forty-two, and the Japanese by the Australians and the Americans in nineteen forty-four and 'forty-five. The age of colonialism was over – for the moment – and the islanders, much to their dismay, reverted to the administrative rule of what became Papua New Guinea.'

He picked up on her hint that colonialism hadn't ended for good. 'For the moment? You mean the mine?'

'The Panguna Mine,' she confirmed, and now her voice took on a new intensity. 'What none of Bougainville's past exploiters knew was that they were sitting on one of the most lucrative pieces of real estate on the planet. Enormous deposits of silver, copper and zinc were hidden beneath those jungle-covered mountains, but they would never have been found but for one thing: gold. The gold rushes of the late nineteenth century caused a revolution in mining, and in the early twentieth that revolution finally reached the island. The islanders sincerely believe Bougainville is the land known in the Bible as Ophir. They will tell you that King Solomon was led to the island by the Angel Gabriel and that gold from his mine here was used to build the Temple of Jerusalem. It's no joke, Jamie,' she reacted to his smile of disbelief, 'this is where Keith Devlin is leading you, so you'd better listen and learn, because not all that long ago Bougainville was a war zone. Think Vietnam fought out on a tiny island, but with all the viciousness, slaughter, destruction and cruelty; up to twenty thousand dead out of a population of less than two hundred thousand. The tensions that created that war still existed when I visited a few years ago and it seems your Mr Devlin is intent on stirring the pot.'

Now she had his attention. 'When did all this happen?' He was thinking Sixties, Seventies, when it would have been overshadowed by the greater conflicts in South East Asia.

'The insurgency started in the mid-Seventies. It was effective enough to close the mine in 'eighty-eight but it didn't turn into a full-scale shooting match until a year later. The last Papua New Guinea troops didn't leave the island until nineteen ninety-eight.'

'Twenty thousand casualties?' Jamie shook his head

incredulously. 'I was still at university in nineteen ninety-eight. I wanted to be a soldier and I was interested in wars. How come I never heard about this one?'

'Because the Australians, who had a major investment in the government side, didn't want you to. You and the rest of the world. The Bougainville Conflict was a small war on an island in the middle of nowhere. The only people interested were the people fighting and dying, and shareholders in the mining companies that had a stake in the Panguna Mine. It only came to international attention in nineteen ninety-seven when a company called Sandline International became involved. For thirty-six million dollars they offered to wipe out the Bougainville Revolutionary Army for the Papua New Guinea government, with a mercenary force using helicopter gunships, planes converted to bombers and the latest in military technology. The plan was only abandoned when the media found out and it almost brought down the PNG government.'

'Christ, so much for Devlin's *few labour problems and some local difficulties with community leaders*,' Jamie exploded. 'So the mine has never reopened?'

Magda shook her head and tapped the screen, bringing up a row of figures. 'Between nineteen seventy-two and its closure in nineteen eighty-eight, the Panguna Mine produced twelve hundred million tonnes of material, of which some four hundred and fifty million tonnes went through the treatment process. It produced and shipped three million tonnes of copper, three hundred tonnes of gold and just short of eight hundred tonnes of silver. All of that meant billions in profits. Half went to the mine owners, a fifth to the government of Papua New Guinea – it accounted for seventeen per cent of the country's internal revenue – and less than one per cent to the people of Bougainville . . .'

'Well, that would certainly account for the locals being a little upset and why the PNG government were so keen to keep the mine going.'

'It also caused incalculable environmental damage,' Magda continued relentlessly, hammering out statistics like a poker player slapping down a full house. 'It takes three and a half tonnes of water to process one tonne of copper. The Panguna Mine was processing a hundred and twenty thousand tonnes a day, which required about half a million tonnes of water. It was polluted with heavy metals and other chemicals and it had to go somewhere. The contaminated water destroyed the entire Jaba River system in the island's central region. Animal and fish species were wiped out. Forests were stripped bare for miles around. Spoil from the mine has made seven thousand acres unusable for agriculture or any other purpose in perpetuity. Fifteen years on there are an increasing number of unexplained birth defects and health problems that are likely to be linked to the pollution.'

'No wonder the islanders haven't let them back. I assume they're demanding an eye-watering sum in compensation before the mine reopens.'

She nodded. 'But many of the islanders don't want it to reopen – ever. They want proper independence and a return to their old way of life. That's why the conflict continues to rumble on, at a lower level and as an internal battle, because there's a faction who made money from the mine and they see no reason why they shouldn't again.'

Jamie understood it all now in a revelation as vivid as any saint's. 'Along comes Keith Devlin with his billions, his promises and his smooth talk of sustainable development. And of course his company on the brink. Give the man his due, he's an operator. He probably already has an option to buy shares in Bougainville Copper Ltd at rock-bottom prices. If he can somehow persuade the majority of the natives that Devlin Metal Resources will pay them a fair price, mine it in a way that will do no further damage – at the very least – and provide the kind of infrastructure the island doesn't have: modern schools, hospitals, well-paid jobs for their children . . .'

'But the islanders have heard all this before,' Magda pointed out.

'So he needs an edge.'

'The Bougainville head . . .'

'Or whatever is in these mysterious documents he plans to exchange it for, if they even exist.'

XXXVIII

It was raining when Jamie stepped off the Air Niugini Fokker 100 jet at Buka airport after the three-hour flight from Port Moresby, but not the kind of miserable London drizzle he was accustomed to. This rain came out of the sky like bullets and would have soaked him to the skin in seconds but for the hooded anorak he'd bought at Brisbane airport. The one compensation was that it took the edge off the sultry heat that hit him in the face like a slap the moment he left the air-conditioned cocoon of the plane.

His travel-weary mind fought to compute that it was still only nine in the morning. He'd parted company with Magda at Brisbane, where a young Devlin aide had given him his instructions. There'd been no surprise that his destination was Bougainville. The first leg of the journey had taken him to Port Moresby where he'd spent ten hours trying to avoid being mugged as he waited for the connecting flight. He hitched his ruck-sack on to his back and followed the other passengers towards the small single-storey building that constituted the Bougainville terminal. As they crossed the tarmac, the rain stopped as if someone had flicked a switch and wisps of steam rose from every surface like the essence of trapped souls escaping from the grave.

For a moment he had to fight the feeling of being very alone and far from home. Everything was unfamiliar. Exotic foliage hugged the fringes of the airport and palms and coconut trees swayed under a ceiling of puffy white cloud. Shading his eyes, he scanned his surroundings for the Devlin representative who would undoubtedly be here to meet him. A distinctive oily smell caught his throat, forcing the earthy scent of the passing shower into the background. It was the rancid aroma of some vegetable that had been lying decaying for years and just been exposed to the air. To his left was a small car park filled to overflowing with big sturdy SUVs, and beyond it a rusting corrugated-iron hangar that might have been there since the Second World War.

By the time he reached the terminal the heat had forced him to remove his jacket, and sweat poured down his back thanks to the incredible humidity. The baggage collection area was on an open veranda at the front of the building. He groaned inwardly as he saw the man in a blue uniform shirt checking passports while another made a cursory examination of his fellow passengers' hand luggage. Jamie had thought he'd been clever disguising the Bougainville head in a box that had originally contained a toy of a similar size. The only problem was that it had a perspex window, and he now realized any native of the Solomon Islands wouldn't be fooled for five seconds. Just as he reached the end of the line a hand touched his shoulder.

'Mr Saintclair? If you'd like to come with me.' Jamie turned his head and found himself the focus of a pair of ice-blue eyes. His captor was half a head shorter and thirty years older, but he wore his light tropical suit like a uniform and there was a stillness and a confidence to him that warned against taking any liberties. The man gave an almost imperceptible nod to the two guards and they stepped aside as he led Jamie through to the baggage area. 'Which is yours?' Jamie pointed to a brown leather holdall and the man picked it up. 'You travel light.'

'I'm not planning to be here for long.'

The comment prompted a faint smile and he followed his guide out into the sunshine. 'Doug Stewart.' Jamie took the proffered hand and winced as his fingers were crushed in an iron grip. He looked into Stewart's face for any sign of a challenge, but there was nothing there but steady appraisal. 'I'm Devlin's head of security.'

'That must be an interesting job.'

'It has its moments.' Stewart ignored the sarcasm. 'I take it by your reaction to the security check that what we've been waiting for is in your backpack?'

'When do I see Fiona and Lizzie?' He took a tighter grip of the rucksack's strap.

'When Mr Devlin decides.' Stewart's laugh betrayed an easy confidence in his abilities. 'Don't worry, son, I'm not planning to take it away from you; but if I was there's bugger all you could do about it.'

'What would have happened if they'd found it and you weren't there?'

The other man shrugged. 'They'd have taken it and locked you up.'

'And then?'

'Then we'd have had to persuade them to give us it back. But the whole island would know about it in less than three hours.'

Jamie noticed that getting him out of jail wouldn't have been part of the package. 'Is that such a bad thing? I'd have thought the return of an ancient artefact would be cause for celebration on Bougainville.'

Doug Stewart stopped in the street and turned to face Jamie. 'Oh, yes, Mr Saintclair, that would be a very bad thing indeed.' He looked down at his feet. Jamie followed his gaze and flinched at what looked like bloodstains on the concrete. Stewart grinned at his reaction. 'Betel juice. The Boogs chew betel all the time and the filthy so-and-sos spit it out wherever it suits them.'

Bastard.

The security chief led the way to a Toyota SUV that had been put through hard use judging by the number of bumps and scrapes. Doug Stewart motioned him to the passenger side and it was only when he was inside the vehicle that he noticed the two men in the rear seats. Like Stewart they were small, compact men with unforgiving eyes, but they were twenty years younger and decked out in jungle green. Each held a stubby assault rifle with a plastic stock at his side.

'Meet Joe and Andy,' Stewart introduced the pair,

'the boss's personal bodyguards while he's on the island, but he's loaned them to you for today. Andy doesn't say much, but compared to Joe he's a bundle of laughs.' The pair smiled dutifully at their colleague's joke. 'You'll learn very quickly that it pays to be prepared when you're on Bougainville, Mr Saintclair. This isn't your average tropical paradise. You'll have had your shots? Malaria and beriberi?'

Jamie nodded. He'd had a full set of injections for a planned trip to South America. 'Good, but just remember the mossies aren't the only pest around here. If you swim in the river a croc could take you. Swim in the sea and it'll be a shark. The people are as friendly and open as any on earth; to a European they might even seem childlike. Don't let that kid you. They welcome visitors, take them into their homes and share their food, but if you're a Chinaman who opens up a shop you'll like as not find it burned down the next morning. They're all Christians, but they believe in magic and sorcery and that you can die if a witch curses you. There are enough guns left over from the last war to start the next one, every man knows how to use them and they're not slow to pull the trigger. That's the kind of place it is. If you don't keep your eyes open you'll end up in very big trouble indeed.'

Jamie knew the litany of danger had been designed to scare him, but he wasn't impressed. 'If that's the case, why bring me here? We could just as easily have made the exchange in Brisbane.'

Stewart's face turned blank as if a shutter had fallen. 'That's for Mr Devlin to explain.'

As they drove out of the car park Jamie saw a tall, dark-haired woman wearing sunglasses emerge from the terminal building to be met by a large black man in a T-shirt and jeans. A passenger who must have been one of the last off the plane. Taking care not to show an interest, he felt a surge of what might be optimism, or more accurately hope. He wasn't alone any more.

Doug Stewart drove with the same economy of effort with which he moved and they made swift progress though the town past a mixture of coconut groves and clapboard houses with roofs of corrugated iron or plastic. Even with the air conditioning on and the added firepower of the driver's aftershave the now-familiar rancid odour grew in intensity.

Eventually, they pulled in by a dock. Joe and Andy stowed their guns in a holdall and when they got out of the car Jamie winced at the heat and the stink. Stewart noticed his reaction and grinned. 'That, my boy, is the smell of money. Copra; dried coconut husks. Those warehouses are full of it and so is the ship. Coconuts, cocoa and crazy tourists are the only things holding the Bougainville economy together right now. That and Australian aid money, which some of the locals would be happier without. The Buka Passage.' He indicated the narrow strip of water, less than half a mile wide. 'It's quicker to leave the car here and get a banana boat across than wait for the ferry.'

It took them a matter of minutes to reach the far side, and moments later they were in another Toyota, heading south along a dirt road that hugged the coastline. They passed occasional small huts where locals sold surplus produce or native delicacies cooked over an open fire. Groups of women and children smiled and waved to the car as it passed. Jamie noted that the males were less friendly and most carried some sort of weapon: either a machete or a long bush knife. They were uniformly stocky and well muscled with handsome features, tight-curled bushes of black hair and skin so black it had a purple sheen.

The trip gave Jamie a glimpse of the picture-postcard tropical paradise he'd imagined on the flight from Port Moresby. Beyond a narrow fringe of white sand an endless expanse of sea stretched away to the horizon, its waters shot with every shade of blue from the lightest sapphire to the deepest indigo, constantly altering in harmony with the sky's ever-changing moods. It was so beautiful it almost made you forget why you were here. Somewhere up ahead, Fiona and Lizzie Carter were being held against their will; dispensable tokens in whatever dirty game Keith Devlin was playing. Ever since he'd boarded the plane, Jamie had nursed a growing anger that bubbled inside him like the caldera of one of the volcanoes in those jungle-clad mountains looming to his right. The natural manifestation of this feeling would be to beat Devlin to a pulp the moment he set eyes on him, but Stewart and his two attack dogs ruled that out for the moment.

His first priority was to get Fiona and Lizzie out of this place. Keith Devlin seemed to think he could dabble with other people's lives like some omnipotent god. Well, Jamie Saintclair had a message for him: he could bugger off and think again. The Bougainville head lay comfortably in the rucksack between his feet and he had a feeling its destiny was to do mischief on behalf of the Australian mining boss. He could almost sense its desire to be home and a growing power he hoped was all in his mind. But for Fiona and Lizzie he would have thrown the head to the fishes in the Buka Passage, but he knew he had no option but to play the game out to its bitter end. There was only one problem with that scenario. On a place like Bougainville it meant someone was going to get hurt. He just hoped it would be the right someone.

Doug Stewart concentrated on the road, which deteriorated the further south they travelled. Potholes riddled the dirt surface, spinning tyres had ripped out enormous mud holes where previous vehicles had become stuck and fought their way out of the mire. Every few miles they came to a boulder-strewn stream that needed to be forded at a crawl, with the car bucking like a rodeo pony. Now Jamie understood why only a big SUV would do in this kind of terrain. He counted at least five times they'd come close to being rammed by other cars or mini-buses filled to overflowing with islanders. Andy and Joe seemed unconcerned by the near-death experiences. One took turns on watch while the other got what sleep he could in the rattling vehicle. After two hours on the road, Jamie followed their example and closed his eyes.

He was woken with a nudge from Andy. 'Grub's up, mate.'

Stewart pulled up beside a roadside shack roofed with banana leaves, set back from the road in a clearing cut from the jungle. He got out of the car and stretched. 'Christ, I'm getting too old for this.' Jamie joined him and studied the wares on display. They mainly consisted of fresh fruit, some of which he recognized and some not, small see-through bags of what looked like potato crisps that turned out to be made from banana, and a bun-like object served on a coconut leaf.

Andy bought enough bottled water and bags of banana chips for the rest of the journey. A shy, bushy-haired boy of about five peeled and sliced a pineapple using an enormous machete with all the ease of a penknife. The pineapple was sweet, juicy and refreshing, and was followed by some kind of smoked fish and finally one of the sticky buns. 'Tamatama, you likim,' the boy said, following up with what sounded like a long explanation in the sing-song dialect the locals spoke.

'Tok Pisin,' Stewart explained. 'Pidgin English. The different Boog clans have about twenty languages between them, but just about everybody can get by in English or Tok Pisin. He's just told you the recipe. Basically its sweet banana, taro and coconut turned into a paste, rolled into a ball and roasted. Give it a try, it's not bad.'

What Jamie found most interesting about the stop was the puzzling way the other men treated him. It had been the same ever since he'd arrived at Buka. These were Keith Devlin's men, and by now he thought of Devlin as the enemy. He'd expected to step off the plane into a tense confrontation, possibly to be threatened with violence and then manhandled to a meeting with the mining tycoon. Instead, after an initial wariness, it seemed he was regarded not so much as a prisoner but as one of the team. At first he'd been suspicious. Was he the turkey being fattened up for Christmas? It was a possibility, but he had a feeling Joe and Andy, at least, though consummate practitioners of their art, tactically cunning and physically deadly, weren't the dissembling type. If they acted as if Jamie Saintclair was one of the boys it was because someone, most likely Doug Stewart, had told them he was one. For the moment, Stewart himself remained an enigma, part middle management executive, part Fifties matinée idol, part superannuated assassin. It was an interesting mix.

When they drove on, Andy was at the wheel with Stewart in the passenger seat, while Jamie sat in the back beside the apparently mute Joe. To ease the boredom Jamie decided to try to tease him into conversation, remarking on the thickness of the jungle beside the road, which, frankly, scared the hell out of him.

'Jungle?' Doug Stewart snorted from the front seat. 'That's not jungle; it's more like somebody's back yard.' In the rear, Joe nudged Jamie and grinned as Devlin's security chief continued. 'You wanna see proper jungle get yourself up country to Bien Hoa in the 'Nam. It once took us three days to cut a two-hundred-yard trail through elephant grass so thick you didn't have room to swing your machete. The bloody leaves were sharp enough to shave with.'

'You were in Vietnam?'

Stewart turned to stare at Jamie.

'Hey, I'm just interested.'

'Sure, I did two tours in 'sixty-seven and 'sixty-nine.'

'What outfit were you with?'

The security chief smiled. 'Now that would be telling.'

Jamie shrugged as if he'd taken the hint. 'It's always surprised me that the Australians supported the Americans, but the British didn't.'

Doug Stewart shook his head. 'Partly politics, but mainly geography. The war was on our doorstep and the Yanks were our allies. If we didn't fight Charlie in the 'Nam what was to stop the Chinks rolling over the rest of South East Asia, and where would that leave us? Nah, we needed the Yanks more than they needed us, but they were bloody pleased when they saw what we could do. And don't you believe there were no Brits in Vietnam. I served beside a few guys who were about as Australian as Yorkshire pudding.'

An hour later the road moved away from the coast towards the mountains and they arrived at the first major road junction Jamie had seen in a hundred miles. Stewart told Andy to stop. As the Toyota rolled to a halt he turned to Jamie. 'In case you're interested, this is the road to the Panguna Mine that caused all the trouble a few years back.' Jamie stifled the urge to tell him all he was interested in was seeing Fiona and Lizzie. The road was different from the one they'd travelled because it was paved and in reasonable condition. It ran for about a hundred metres before it disappeared into thick jungle, and he could see the green-clad mountains that rose just beyond. In the foreground a dilapidated sign announced that it was a No Go Zone, and just beyond it a line of iron oil barrels reinforced the message. He shrugged. 'Thanks for the tour, but I'd really like to get wherever it is we're going.'

Stewart grinned. 'No problem. At least you won't have long to wait now.'

They resumed their journey, dropping down towards the coast again. After about ten minutes Jamie saw a sight that seemed almost surreal after the endless miles of jungle track.

'Welcome to Arawa, the Pearl of the Pacific,' Doug Stewart announced.

It was a town. Public buildings – a hospital, a school, a library – churches, paved roads, a shopping mall, open spaces filled with greenery, and a grid of streets lined by white houses and colonial-style apartment blocks sprawling across acres of flatland in a river valley running down to the sea.

'It even had its own international airport. Let Mr Saintclair have a look-see, Andy.'

The bodyguard took a left that sent them towards the town square. It was only when you looked closer that you realized this wasn't so much a town as a ghost town. Every shop and business had been gutted by fire. Most of the buildings – burned-out shells – were only held together by rusting metal beams. The windows of a thousand houses stared out black and empty like the eye sockets of as many skulls. Doors hung by their hinges, roofs had collapsed into the rooms below, and the jungle had reclaimed gardens once thriving with scented flowers, yams, sweet potatoes and taro.

Here and there were a few signs of revival. Someone

had opened a bar with a few tables outside. A couple of dozen houses had been patched up, perhaps by their former owners.

'Difficult to believe this was once the richest town between Sydney and San Francisco,' Stewart reflected. 'It had a country club with its own golf course, restaurants and a footy team, the best health facilities money could provide. This,' he shook his head, 'truly was Paradise to the people who lived here.'

'What happened to it?' Jamie asked. 'And to them?'

Devlin's security chief shrugged. 'Bougainville Copper Limited built it for the mine workers and their families. They turned a coconut plantation into the state capital of Bougainville; Government House was just up the road there. By the Eighties the place was going like a fair. It had its own power plant, shared with the mine, over at Loloho Point across there, a couple of hundred kids were born in the hospital and a couple of thousand taught in the schools. You could buy every western luxury as long as you could afford it. So there you are, the world's biggest copper mine is churning out millions a week in profit, you have some of the finest mining experts to make sure it continues that way, and probably the happiest workforce in the world. What could go wrong?'

'They'd forgotten something,' Jamie ventured.

'That's right.'

'The people.'

'You have an elite group of white workers living in all this luxury and the only look-in the Boogs get is to clean their toilets; okay, that's an exaggeration, but you get the picture. Some slick lawyers have persuaded them to more or less give their land away or if they refused the government just took it. They don't understand how big a mess this thing is going to cause, and when they do find out the PNG government doesn't give a bugger because all they can see is dollar signs and they don't care about the Bougainvilleans anyway. It could all have been sorted out with a couple of million to the right people, but by the time anybody realized it was too late. One of the Bougainville employees at the mine was a clever young fella called Francis Ona. He could see what was happening and what was gonna happen. So he started a war. One thing led to another and the mine closed down, Arawa was abandoned, the PNG defence department brought in troops to destroy the Bougainville Revolutionary Army and when that didn't work they tried to burn and starve Bougainville into submission. But the Boogs are a lot tougher than they look and here we are.'

'I don't understand,' Jamie said as Andy put the big SUV into gear. 'What will Keith Devlin do that's any different? How can the Bougainville head cancel out thirty years of history?'

'I'll let the Messiah tell you that himself.' Stewart smiled, but Jamie detected a sardonic edge to his voice.

XXXIX

Keith Devlin had set up home in a former community centre that had survived the destruction of Arawa relatively unscathed. The smell of fresh paint fought for supremacy with damp and the chemical, salt-heavy scent of the sea. The mining boss sat behind a big desk in a room that had been prepared with chairs set out in neat rows for a meeting. Jamie scanned the place for any sign of Fiona and Lizzie, but there was no hint of their presence. An open door beyond Devlin led to a second room with a bed just visible beyond the door, but whether it was his or his captives' wasn't apparent. In that moment Jamie felt an utter loathing for the other man that triggered a visceral urge for violence. He must have shown it because Doug Stewart moved in to grip his elbow.

'Steady, tiger. You've come a long way to do something stupid. Listen to what the man has to say.'

Jamie took a deep breath and Devlin looked up from the paper he was studying.

'It's been a while, son.' He smiled. 'I take it the big

371

prize is in your bag there, because if it isn't we've all wasted a helluva lot of time.'

'I want to see the girls,' Jamie insisted.

'That's not a problem. Fiona and little Lizzie are down at the beach right now having a swim and a sun-bathe.' He saw Jamie's look. 'Yes, I thought you'd be surprised. Your little ladies have been having the time of their lives. The kid's been great. You can see them in a minute, but I thought we should have a little chat. First things first, though. Let me see the head.'

Jamie hesitated for a millisecond, but what Doug Stewart had said was true. They could take it away from him at their leisure. He laid the rucksack on one of the chairs and unzipped the flap. Devlin watched curiously as he removed a brightly coloured cardboard package about ten inches high by eight wide and handed it over.

'Jesus.' The tycoon laughed, but his hands were shaking as he worked at the cardboard. It came apart and he was left with the bizarre little oval of preserved flesh and curly black hair. He looked into the long dead face and it gradually dawned on him what he was holding. With a shudder, he placed it to one side of the desk, rubbing his hands as if he was washing them. He took a deep breath and waved a placating hand towards a seat, but Jamie ignored it.

'I can understand that you're angry, Jamie,' the tycoon said. 'I can't blame you for that, but I'll try to explain what this means to me. Maybe, just maybe, you'll cut me a bit of slack.'

'I doubt it.'

'Let's see, shall we?' On the wall behind him a small

green lizard with only half a tail appeared and scuttled to head height. Jamie watched as it stopped and looked around for a second before darting to disappear into a hole in the corner of the ceiling. 'You've had a chance to see a bit of Bougainville on the way here, and old Doug's filled you in on some of the background?' At his side, Jamie sensed the security chief flinch at the reference to his age and filed it away.

'He gave me the grand tour. All green hell, potholes, rust and ashes, as far as I can make out.'

Devlin nodded. 'Not a bad description, but think of the potential. Think of what this town was like at the height of its success and multiply it by ten across the island.'

'You're crazy.' Jamie didn't hide his scorn. 'And from what I've heard the people on Bougainville would have to be crazier to allow the mine to reopen. Why should they trust Keith Devlin after what happened with BCL?'

'Because Keith Devlin would cut out the middle man.' The mining boss slapped the desk. 'A fair deal for the islanders and bugger the PNG government.'

'Won't they have something to say about that? After all, they sent in the army the last time.'

Devlin shook his head. 'They got away with it because they had Australian support – no, it was more than that – Australian encouragement. This time public opinion will be on Bougainville's side. I have it on good authority that Canberra sees independence for Bougainville, or a form of it, as a positive outcome. If Papua New Guinea decided to interfere, Australia would scrap the five hundred million dollars in aid it gives them and call on the United Nations to step in. Everybody knows linking Bougainville to Port Moresby was a cock-up in the first place. The new government of Bougainville will get the same percentage PNG received last time round, and Devlin Metal Resources, or whatever we call the company that runs the mine, will pledge a cut of its profits for infrastructure and development improvements.'

Jamie found his resolve tested by the Australian's enthusiasm, but he saw an obvious flaw in the plan. 'What about all these men with guns I keep hearing about? They fought the mine owners the last time round, what's to stop them doing it again?'

'That's a good question, son.' Devlin frowned. 'The former soldiers of the Bougainville Revolutionary Army are still a power in this land. That's why they were the first people we started discussions with, along with the Panguna landowners, of course. They were suspicious – and who wouldn't be after what happened in the Seventies and Eighties? – but I think we've managed to convince them we're sincere.'

'Sincere about what?'

'Turning this little island into the powerhouse of the Pacific and making sure that the people – that's the native Bougainvilleans – have one of the best lifestyles in the southern hemisphere.' Jamie opened his mouth to interrupt, but Doug Stewart touched his arm. Devlin continued. 'I'm not going to make any bones about it, Jamie, the three things that destroyed the Panguna Mine project were greed, arrogance and stupidity. If I can win these people round, and I acknowledge it's a big if, I don't intend to make those mistakes. This will be *their* mine as much as Keith Devlin's, maybe more so. The minute we get the go-ahead we'll recruit the first thousand apprentices from amongst the brightest kids on the island. We'll build and staff a technical college to train them, and we'll send the best of them to Australian universities to continue their education. And that'll be just the start. The family of everybody who works for the company will have the chance to move into a house with proper sanitation, electricity and running water. There'll be hospitals and schools and a decent road around the island. There'll be money in every household and that'll stimulate the economy and create more businesses. We'll reopen the airport across there for international flights. Bougainville will be back in the world community, but this time with a voice of its own.'

'The gospel according to Keith Devlin?'

Devlin ignored the mockery in Jamie's voice. 'That's right, son, but can you think of a better future? We have to find a way forward. Bougainville can't go back to the old days, the world won't let it. I'm offering progress and prosperity for all the people who suffered during that terrible war.'

'You'll be telling me next you're going to magic away all the environmental damage and the toxic chemicals in the river systems.'

'No,' Devlin shook his head, 'I can't promise them that, and I've told them so. All I can say is that we'll use the most modern methods to make sure there's as little pollution as possible. I won't bore you with all the technical details about sustainability, but we've moved on a long way from nineteen eighty-nine and we're prepared to spend money to make sure nothing like the Jaba River disaster happens again.' He walked to one of the windows and drew up the blind. 'You take a look out there. The jungle's already reclaimed whole blocks of what was Arawa and swallowed up roads and industrial plants. I say nature's going to surprise us all. That river system will recover quicker than anybody believes possible.'

Jamie had a feeling that Devlin wasn't talking to him, but rehearsing his pitch to whoever was going to occupy these chairs. He hated to admit it, but the mining boss was a persuasive, almost seductive orator. Right at that moment if Keith Devlin had told him he was going to walk across the Buka Passage without getting his feet wet he'd probably have believed him. Yet in a little hidden corner of his mind a voice whispered that it was all too pat. Too good to be true. He locked eyes with the tycoon. 'What I'm really wondering, Keith, is what's in it for you?'

'I get the satisfaction of seeing one of the world's great mines reopened.' Devlin grinned. 'I get the thanks of the good people of Bougainville. But mainly I get to make an awful lot of money. I don't see anything wrong with that, do you?'

You had to marvel at the man's charm – and his cheek. Jamie shook his head 'All right, I give in. You've convinced me that the Second Coming is just around the corner. Now can I see Fiona?'

'There's just one minor detail to sort out before you

go, Jamie son.' Devlin gingerly picked up the head by a strand of curly hair. His smile didn't falter, but an edge to his voice told Jamie he wasn't going to be laughing any time soon. 'The old boy on the mountain is a cagey sort of fella. For some reason he blames the Panguna Mine on Australia and right now he doesn't trust us one little bit. Of course, that'll change when he gets his old granddad back, but until then we need someone not linked to Devlin Metal Resources to make the delivery.' He shrugged. 'During the war – our war – he got to liking a couple of the Coastwatchers who spied on Jap planes around here. Pukka English officers, they were, not like us rough-and-ready Aussies. So that's exactly what I'm going to send him: a pukka English gent.'

It took a moment for Jamie to realize only one person in the room came close to the description of a pukka English gent. He had an image of the all-encompassing jungle they'd passed on the road. It would be a hundred times worse in the mountains. Christ, there'd be snakes. 'You can't be—'

'Oh, I am, son,' Devlin's voice was soft, but his tone said no arguments. 'You take a quick jaunt up the hill, hand over the head and bring me the briefcase the old man pinched. Easy as pie. When you get back you and your little ladies will be on the first plane back to civilization with first-class tickets to wherever you wish. There'll also be a substantial bonus in *both* your bank accounts to make up for our little misunderstanding.'

'I don't have any experience in the jungle, Keith,' Jamie pointed out. 'I'm more of a Hampstead Heath man, and then only when it's not raining.'

'I understand that, Jamie, and that's why I'm sending my best man with you. Doug will make sure you're nice and safe. He might even show you how to live for a week on a roast possum.'

'Keith, I . . .' Doug Stewart attempted to intervene and Jamie noticed he wasn't the only one who wasn't too impressed by Devlin's plan.

'Come on, Doug.' The mining boss laughed harshly. 'You're always telling me what a helluva fella and a great jungle fighter you are. Now's your chance to show it, mate.'

The word 'mate' was anything but matey and Jamie saw Stewart flinch as if someone had poked him in the chest. The security chief continued to object, but Devlin wouldn't be swayed and while they argued, Andy said he'd drive Jamie to the beach where Devlin had said Fiona and Lizzie Carter were bathing. After ten minutes he stopped the car by a coconut grove and pointed seawards. 'Just follow the track down through the trees. Someone will be along to pick you up in an hour.'

Jamie hesitated in the doorway. 'Andy, have you any idea what's really happening here?'

The guard shook his head. 'I just do the job I'm paid to do, Mr Saintclair. If you've got any questions you ask old Doug. He might be a bit over the hill, but he's been around long enough to have all the answers.' He nodded. 'Enjoy your reunion and remember you have to be ready by five thirty tomorrow.'

Jamie walked until the track ended at a long, curving beach of white sand fringed with palm trees and coconut groves. The sun was in his eyes and it took a moment before he saw the bright orange beach umbrella two hundred metres away to his right, with three or four small figures playing in the surf close by. His first instinct was to run to them. Instead, he sat down and took off his shoes and socks and rolled up his trousers to the knee before walking, shoes in hand, to the breaking waves. With the wet sand squishing deliciously between his toes he set off towards the orange marker. By the time he was halfway the figures in the surf defined themselves into one pale child in a blue bikini and three startlingly black ones. Beneath the umbrella's canopy a pair of long, tanned legs was just visible.

Lizzie looked up as he approached and her mouth dropped open. Jamie put his finger to his lips and she swallowed the shriek that was about to emerge, copying his gesture to her grinning playmates.

Jamie advanced till he could see past the edge of the umbrella. His breath caught in his throat at the sight of Fiona lying there in a black bikini barely worthy of the name that tantalized rather than covered. Her eyes were closed and the sleek golden body glistened with sun oil, all curves and hollows and tight muscled planes.

'It looks as if being kidnapped agrees with you,' he said.

Her eyes shot open. 'Jamie.' She struggled to her feet and enveloped him in her arms, so he could feel the contrasting softness and hardness of her. Kisses rained on his lips and cheeks until they finally found his mouth and he took control, ending the frenzy by holding her there for a long, long, increasingly breathless moment.

'Yuk.' A small body forced its way between them, and they reluctantly moved apart, holding each other by the arms.

'I've missed you,' she said. Her eyes were shining and his heart did a double somersault at what he saw in their shadows.

'I've missed you too.'

'Have you missed me?' a small voice demanded.

'Of course I've missed you, Lizzie.' Jamie laughed. 'Who are your friends?'

She introduced the grinning youngsters: 'Gabriel, Maria and C'melita.'

'Banana crisps for the one who finds me the prettiest shell,' Fiona announced, and Lizzie ran off, followed by the others.

'I don't know if they understand her – I think they only speak Tok Pisin – but kids have a language of their own.' She sighed. 'Now,' she said, taking his face between her hands and looking into his eyes, 'where were we?'

'Wondering why we're standing on a beach in Bougainville when we were supposed to be drinking champagne in a hot tub in Cairns. By the way,' he glanced to where Lizzie and her friends were searching through the sand by the waterline, 'someone told me there are sharks and crocodiles.'

'The sharks are further out and the crocs tend to stay in the estuaries.' She smiled. 'The locals say it's quite safe to bathe here. Come and sit down.' She stepped back and drew him into the shade of the umbrella, making a space for him on the towel she'd been using.

'I think I just left the biggest shark of all back in Arawa.' Jamie sank on to the fine sand. 'Look, I'm sorry I got you into all of this. The question now is how I get you out. Devlin's asked me to go on some daft mission into the mountains tomorrow, but I'm more than half inclined to hire a car, put us in it, and head for the airport . . .' He'd been looking at her as he spoke and he saw a range of emotions cross her face before she turned her head away. None of them were the ones he'd expected. 'Unless there's something else you'd rather do,' he ended lamely.

She stared out at the sea, taking a long time to formulate her reply. 'When I realized the plane wasn't taking us to Cairns I was angry at first, then frightened. We'd had a wonderful time in Perth and Melbourne with the aunties and cousins, and I couldn't believe it was happening. They said there'd been some sort of emergency and we'd had to divert, but I didn't believe them. But everything changed when Mr Devlin met us and explained why he'd brought us here. I think you have to do this thing for him, Jamie. The people on this island deserve all the help they can get.'

Jamie set his face in a reassuring smile designed to cover the inner confusion he felt. Christ, he thought, I'm not the only one who was seduced by Devlin's pitch. You've got it in a bad way. Bewitched, bewildered and completely buggered. There were things he could say, things he could tell her, doubts and worries, but he had a feeling they wouldn't do either of them any good. 'So you don't feel like you've been kidnapped?'

She shook her head with a little half-grin of apology. 'So there isn't anything to forgive. In a way, it's much better than it would have been on Mr Devlin's private island, especially for Lizzie. Life here is so simple. We have a house beside the family who look after us. The plumbing is basic and the electricity is supplied by a generator and goes off at ten. The TV has three channels instead of three hundred and we drink rainwater and eat the same food the locals do. Yet I've never seen Lizzie happier or more content. Our landlady, Grace, treats her as if she's one of her own, and her children like she's their sister. I've heard all about the mine and the war, but despite all that Bougainville is a special place and it can be even better . . .'

'If I help Devlin?'

'Yes.'

'Despite the fact that he – let's put a happy face on it – at best shanghaied us and brought us here against our will.'

'He told me his plans. What he can do for these people—'

'Spare me, I've heard it.'

'And then there's the money.'

'He told you about that?'

'Yes. It'll mean I can put Lizzie into a good school; give her all the things I've always wanted to but haven't been able to afford.'

Seduced and bought. Keith Devlin never did things by halves. Jamie lay back on the sand and closed his eyes.

'What are you going to do, Jamie?'

'Sleep. Wake me up when Andy gets back.'

'Andy?'

'Devlin's bodyguard. Dark hair, shoulders like a bullock.'

'Oh, the good-looking one.' He kicked her leg with his bare feet. 'So what are you going to do?' she repeated.

'Can't you leave me alone, woman? I have a mountain to climb tomorrow.' He opened one eye. 'And of course, I may have other duties to perform later.' Now it was her turn to kick him, but she lay against him in a way that said she didn't really mean it.

As it turned out, despite their joint inclination, the paper-thin walls of the guest house and Lizzie's excitement at seeing him again precluded any potential 'duties'. Jamie lay beneath the sheet with Fiona's arm across him, listening to the unmistakable concerto of the tropical night, to which she seemed annoyingly immune. The machine-gun clicks of cicadas and crickets competed with the croaking of a hundred frogs; a raucous cackle that sounded as if it should come from a hyena, but was probably a fruit bat; the buzz of tiny insects he'd been assured weren't mosquitos and the soft chirrup of the lizards that scurried around trying to have them for dinner. At one point he heard the thump-thump-thump of a heavy bass and a car screeched by with the male occupants making more noise than either the stereo or the engine. A few minutes later came the crack of a gunshot, but whether it came from the car or from someone taking issue with the noise was anybody's guess. Eventually, he slept. The last thing he remembered was the jungle closing in around him.

XL

'My grandfather served in the SAS during the war.'

Doug Stewart's head came up from the map he was checking. 'Is that supposed to impress me?'

'Don't be so bloody bolshie,' Jamie snapped as he slipped into the jungle boots Devlin's people had provided. Since breakfasting in the dark he'd become increasingly nervous about what lay ahead and it wasn't very reassuring that it appeared his supposed protector was equally jittery. 'I just meant that I knew what you were on about when you said *that would be telling* and about the Brits in Vietnam. I read somewhere about a few of them being unhappy about missing out on a proper war and taking "unofficial leave" to join in. Lessons to be learned, and all that.'

'Maybe you're not as dumb as you look, your lordship.'

Jamie stared at him. Another man had called him that not so long ago and that man had ended up dead. 'Let's get this straight. I'm not *your lordship* and I'm not your *pukka English gent*. I went to a grammar school and my mother cleaned the local bank to make ends meet.'

'With a name like *Saint*clair? Don't make me laugh. What did your old man do? A squaddie like your grand-dad? He must have been at least a general.'

Jamie concentrated on packing the camouflage-green rucksack that matched his Australian army-issue shorts and T-shirt. 'I wouldn't know; I never met him.'

'Now who's being bolshie?' Stewart let out a cackle that was interrupted as Keith Devlin marched into the room.

'Got everything you need, fellas?'

Jamie nodded. The rucksacks were filled with survival gear and enough food and water to last three days. He picked his up, surprised at the weight. He could carry it without too much trouble, but it would take a bit of getting used to. He was just glad Stewart had vetoed the tent and sleeping bags they'd been offered. 'If it comes to it, we sleep on the ground like the Boogs; and if it rains we get wet. It never did me any harm in Vietnam.' The security chief gave his boss a significant look. 'Just one more thing.'

Devlin's heavy brows came together in a frown. 'Are you sure you'll need it?'

'Better safe than sorry. You're not the one that's going out in the long grass, mate.'

After a moment's hesitation Devlin nodded to Joe who accompanied him. The guard left to return a moment later with a long leather case. He handed it to Doug Stewart. The security chief unzipped the case and whistled as he withdrew four foot of painted steel and black plastic.

'Just like the old days,' he chuckled. He turned to Jamie. 'Your L1A1 self-loading rifle is a precision weapon that is efficient and easily maintained,' he said, as if quoting from the service manual. 'Weighs a fucking ton, but it can put a 7.62mm round through a brick wall and still kill the bastard hiding behind it. Eighty rounds of ammo,' he checked the magazines one by one, 'but we're not planning to start a war, so forty will do.' He tossed two of the magazines to Joe. 'The Bougainville Revolutionary Army captured hundreds of these buggers from the PNG troops. If we do happen to shoot someone nobody's gonna be any the wiser.'

Jamie was appalled at the sight of the weapon. He'd fired it on familiarization courses during his time at the Cambridge OTC and he knew just how deadly it could be. This trip had suddenly taken on a whole new dimension. 'You can cut out the *we* for a bloody start,' he bridled. 'I'm not planning to shoot anybody. I thought this was supposed to be a quick jaunt up a mountain and back down again?'

'Of course it—'

Devlin's reassurance was cut off in mid-sentence by Doug Stewart. 'So if the buggers come at you out of the jungle waving one of these,' he whipped the machete from the scabbard on his belt with a soft hissing sound and pointed it at Jamie's groin, 'you're just gonna let them cut off your goolies?'

Jamie glared at him and Keith Devlin stepped forward

to take his employee by the arm. 'A word, Doug.' The two men walked out of the room.

'Jesus Christ, what have I got myself into this time?' Jamie muttered as he finished packing his rucksack.

'You don't want to mind old Doug,' Joe said mildly. 'I think he had a little too much of the jungle juice last night. He likes to cover all the bases, that's all. Says it's what got him through the 'Nam.'

'Somebody should tell him the war is over,' the Englishman snapped.

Devlin returned carrying something in a soft leather bag tied at the neck with a beaded cord. He handed it to Jamie. 'You'll need this,' he said. 'Remember. You don't make the exchange until you have the briefcase in your hand. Got that?'

Jamie nodded and checked the contents: the Bougainville head nestled in a cocoon of plastic bubble wrap. He stowed it in a separate compartment of the rucksack he'd left empty for the purpose.

'What about Wyatt Earp?' he protested. 'Wouldn't it be safer to send Joe and Andy with me instead? At least they don't plan to start a war.'

'It's all sorted, son,' Devlin assured him. 'I've had a word with Doug and nobody's going to be doing any shooting.'

But when they went out to the Toyota the first thing Jamie noticed was the gun case in the back seat.

Stewart drove in silence, every movement a testament to his anger at whatever Keith Devlin had said to him, each gear change accompanied by a savage howl of engine noise. They left the compound and reversed their route of the previous day until they came to the junction. Someone had moved the roadblock of barrels during the night and the security chief swept past the 'No Go Area' sign as if it didn't exist. As they drove by, Jamie noticed a man standing in the shadow of the trees with a mobile phone to his ear. His eyes never left the Toyota. At first the road was wide enough for two vehicles, but soon the jungle closed in and it became single track, rising steadily to be consumed in the lush green folds of the mountains.

'All right,' Jamie said eventually, 'I think you've sulked long enough. Now you can tell me what the plan is.'

'The plan is to get the job done and stay alive.' Stewart's tone was terse and Jamie noticed he spent as much time looking behind him as in front.

'I'd assumed that. I was hoping for a little more detail.'

He winced as Stewart changed gear with a metallic crunch to take a hair-pin bend that had a stomach-churning drop on the passenger side. 'This road was built by Bougainville Copper Limited. It takes us up to the Panguna Mine, which just happens to be close to the highest ridge in the Crown Prince mountain range. The old chief, Kristian, has a longhouse about nine miles south, down Takuan way, more or less on the same ridge line. The easiest way to get there is from Panguna so we'll leave the car there and trek through the jungle.'

'Nine miles?'

Stewart shrugged. 'The going's not too bad, except

in a couple of places. I reckon we can be in and out by teatime – if everything works out.'

Something about the way he said those last four words made Jamie wary. 'Is there any reason why everything shouldn't work out?'

The road widened again at a sweeping bend and Stewart drew in to the side of the road and switched off the engine.

For a moment the only sound was the gentle tick of cooling metal. Stewart gestured at the greenery that covered everything around them. 'What I learned about the jungle in Borneo and Vietnam is you can't fight it, you have to learn to live with it. The people most at home in the jungle are the ones who've never known anything else. The minute we step off this road we're at a disadvantage. You're an arty-farty city boy who's got lucky a couple of times and I'm an over-the-hill special forces veteran who's not so special any more.' He reached down to his feet and retrieved a bottle of clear liquid, taking a long slug before resuming. 'Good old Keith has been feeding you the sugar-coated version of Bougainville from the start, and he still is. Y'see, Kristian Anugu isn't the only person on this island who wants the head. There are at least three other factions who have an interest in it, all for different reasons, and they all outgun us. One of them is an offshoot of the old man's clan who think they have a better claim. They come from the matriarchal line, so they could have a point. Women were the traditional land holders on Bougainville up till what they call the Crisis, but now the men have the power. It's no coincidence that the

Panguna landowners' association we've been dealing with is an all-male preserve.' A few metres further up the road a large pig stepped warily into the road and Stewart paused as he watched three small piglets follow it across the tarmac and disappear into the jungle on the far side. 'That could have been supper.' He grinned, but his voice quickly turned serious again. 'Then there's the government of Papua New Guinea, who by now are aware that Devlin Metal Resources' master plan for the reopening of Panguna will cut them out of the loop. Whatever Keith tells you, these blokes are not going to give up billions of dollars without a fight. Right now, on the other side of this hill, down in the Jaba River valley, there are a couple of hundred small-scale and highly illegal gold-mining operations. About seventy-five per cent of them are run by outsiders, what the islanders here call Redskins, from Papua New Guinea. What if some of these miners aren't miners at all, but PNG spies, or worse, PNG special forces soldiers in disguise? Way back when, I helped to train some of these guys and if they find out we're on the way to see Kristian it kinda ups the ante.'

'And the third group.'

'We're not certain,' Stewart admitted. 'A few Boogs down in Arawa sticking their noses in where they're not wanted. Maybe not all the former BRA fighters are prepared to dance to Devlin's tune, or maybe they just want more money. It's the fact that I don't know that makes me more nervous about them than all the others.'

'So that explains the SLR?'

'That's right, son. You know what they say: never take a knife to a gunfight. And all of this is without taking into account the Chinks, who have their spies everywhere but tend to do their fighting in the court and the boardroom. They've already made one pitch to the landowners' association that Devlin has seen off, but it won't be the last.'

At the mention of 'Chinks' Jamie wondered whether he should mention his encounter with Lim, but decided to keep it to himself. 'What I don't understand is why Devlin didn't send us with a proper escort. Either more guards or these BRA people you keep talking about.'

The security chief responded with a bark of bitter laughter. 'The straight answer is that taking more guys like Joe and Andy would make us stick out like your proverbial dahlia on a dungheap and make us more of a target if the bad guys *are* out there. Likewise, the BRA boys might just get halfway there and decide to take the head for themselves and ransom it back. Like I say, you can't trust 'em.'

'If that's the straight answer what's the not so straight one?'

'You go down that road and you could end up in dangerous territory, Mr *Saint*clair.'

'Nevertheless . . .'

Stewart sucked on a tooth while he made up his mind. 'All right, let's just say that in the past couple of years Devlin Metal Resources has become what we might call a leaky ship. People in high places are asking awkward questions about subjects they're not supposed to know about.'

'I could see how that might make a certain party nervous.'

Stewart nodded. 'Naturally, your intrepid head of security instigates an immediate investigation and cleans out anyone who's tainted, even by association. The leaks stop, but the fact that they happened at all might make that certain party look at his hitherto trusted security chief through new eyes. Either he's past it – after all, he's getting on a bit, as you're so fond of telling him – or worse, maybe someone from outside has offered to enhance his pension package in return for privileged access. If it's scenario number two, you have a big problem. This bloke you've trusted with your deepest secrets for the last twenty-five years knows more about Devlin Metal Resources operations than any man alive, even you – you might even say he knows where the bodies are buried, and you wouldn't be far wrong – because it's the nature of things that certain aspects of the business have to be done on a deniable basis.'

'Now you're making *me* nervous.'

Stewart restarted the engine and engaged the car's transmission. 'So you should be, son.' He turned to stare at Jamie for a moment before pulling out into the road. 'Because I find it bloody strange that Keith Devlin decided to choose a desk-bound dinosaur like me to babysit Jamie Saintclair on a jaunt that's supposed to turn Devlin Metal Resources into the world's biggest mining company.'

The Toyota crested the brow of a hill and began the gradual descent into a long valley. The only signs of modern civilization since they'd left the junction had been a line of rusting electricity pylons and a few sections of battered crash barrier. Gradually, Jamie became aware of a subtle change in his surroundings. It must be the same sensation explorers felt when they came upon the ruins of a lost civilization hidden deep in the jungle. The first thing he noticed were angles when, till now, the jungle had dealt solely in curves. Then fragments of what could only be buildings appeared, throttled by twisted lengths of vine and liana, or hidden amongst vast, olive-green plants.

'Panguna,' Stewart said laconically. 'The world's biggest scrapyard.' They drove towards the centre of town and the ruins became more visible. Vast complexes of skeletal iron that had once been factories. Workshops a hundred times larger than anything Jamie had seen in Arawa, stripped of their roofs and walls, but still with the massive crushing machinery inside. His eyes were drawn to the blue-white flash of a welding torch and he saw a small group of men eyeing the car suspiciously from the shadows of some former mill or smelter.

'Looters,' the security boss announced. 'We stay out of their way.'

At last the half-buried industrial landscape gave way to wrecked and looted apartment blocks and houses, tennis courts and the empty blue rectangle of a large swimming pool that, given the climate, must have been the most popular place in town. Stewart pointed to a vast concrete building that had been the mine's administrative headquarters, but, like everything else, was once more being consumed by nature. Jamie was suddenly overwhelmed by the certainty that he was seeing the future; a chilling foretelling of the day humankind got its comeuppance and disappeared from the earth.

And that was before he saw the mine.

He'd had glimpses of bare earth and rock through the trees on the way down into Panguna town, but only now, as Stewart drew up at the side of the crater, was the true vastness of one of the world's largest industrial sites or, depending on your point of view, greatest acts of ecological vandalism, truly apparent. It was an enormous pit, big enough to swallow the entire City of London and still have room for afters. Sharply stepped inner slopes were scattered with hundreds of rusting pieces of machinery. Jamie thought it was probably the ugliest, harshest and most desolate piece of real estate he'd ever laid eyes on, yet it still contained elements of beauty that took the breath away. Half a kilometre below, in the centre of the drab brown crater, a copper-blue lake shone like a brightly polished jewel fed from the innumerable streams that carved gullies in the steep walls. These, he now saw, were also tinged with blue where the copper ore was directly exposed to the air. A row of what looked like dead beetles caught his eye and he realized he was looking at a line of parked trucks that must have been used to carry the ore from the mine to the processing plants. Stewart saw the direction of his gaze.

'There are forty-five of them and they weigh one hundred and seventy tons each. Everything was moth-balled the day the mine closed and unless it's been pinched or dismantled it's still here. Like I said: the world's biggest scrapyard.'

'It's incredible.' Jamie heard the awed shake in his voice. 'That's the only word for it. As if the world ended, but nobody told us.'

'It definitely ended for the Moroni.' Stewart accompanied the words with a bitter laugh. 'Their village was somewhere right in the middle, but about on the level with that mountain over there.' He pointed to a hill that towered above the level of the mine walls. 'The mine company – with the help of the Australian government, I might add – shipped them out lock, stock and barrel and stuck them down on the coast. A few years later they were burned out of their new houses by the PNG Defence Force. Whatever Moroni means in their language it definitely isn't good luck.'

'You sound as if you have some sympathy for them? I have to say I find that a bit unlikely.'

'Maybe it is,' Stewart conceded. 'But I have my reasons. I've got twenty-five years in this business, son.' His eyes turned solemn as they surveyed the massive crater below. 'Most of it's been spent stopping Keith Devlin's workers pinching anything they could lay their hands on. We had the occasional idiot breaking in to steal a truck or an excavator, but the mines in Australia were mostly places where there were no people. Oh, the Abos would complain that some bit of bush was their old man's special dreaming place and try to hit us for a bit of compo, but they had another fifty thousand acres to get lost in and nobody paid too much mind. They'd get an axe and a knife from stores and be on their way. This was different.' He turned to meet Jamie's gaze. 'They conned these people and stole their land, and not content with that they destroyed their way of life. The least they could do was to give them a decent amount of cash to start again and to build the kind of places BCL built for its own people. Instead, they filled the pockets of the politicians in Port Moresby, and maybe in Canberra, too.' Without warning his face split in a grin. 'And then the Boogs surprised them. They thought they could bulldoze the islanders out of the way, but Francis Ona and his mates fought back, and by Christ didn't they show them something? I'm a fighting man, Saintclair, and I respect fighters. These guys fought with spears and home-made rifles against helicopter gunships and somehow they won. They tormented the enemy by night and lured them into ambush by day. When the choppers flew in to carry out the wounded they took out the pilots or the motors. The PNG didn't have the stomach for it and eventually they left. That was when they stopped the medicines and food supplies coming in, which on a tropical island is the equivalent of biological warfare. The world abandoned the buggers, but they still stuck it out. Sure, I have sympathy for them, I even admire them, but that isn't going to do them any good in the long run.'

'So you don't believe in Keith Devlin's brave new world?'

Stewart stared at him. 'I hope I'm around to see it.'

They drove round to the far side of the mine and parked behind an abandoned shed, where they unloaded the Toyota. At this height the temperature was a little lower, but the humidity correspondingly high and by the time they'd finished Jamie could feel the sweat pouring down his back and into the band of his camouflage trousers. He shrugged on his pack and strapped on a belt with a machete and water bottle attached. Doug Stewart did likewise and hefted the L1A1, ignoring Jamie's look of disgust. The Englishman pulled out his mobile phone and was perplexed by the lack of a signal.

'You can forget that up here,' Stewart said. 'Might as well leave it behind. And before we get out into the bush we need to set some ground rules. First, water. We're going to be sweating a lot of it out so we need to rehydrate regularly. On the other hand, drinking too much can bring on water intoxication, which can kill you. So you drink when I drink, or if you feel the need, ask. Got that?'

'All right,' Jamie agreed. 'I don't see any problem.'

'We'll see.' Stewart showed his teeth in a shark's grin. 'Second, all the land around here is owned by clans, that is extended native families. As you'd expect given the situation with the mine, land ownership is a sensitive issue and they can be touchy about strangers venturing too close. Normally, I'd have contacted these people in advance, but that would have alerted the whole island. If we meet anybody, or anybody hails us, you freeze and let me do the talking. No aggressive moves.'

'I wouldn't dream of it.'

'Listen, son,' Stewart jabbed him in the chest to make his point, 'this is no bloody joke. That's the jungle out there and the jungle will kill you if you don't take it seriously. We get a scratch anywhere, even the kind of thing you'd ignore back in the real world, we smother it in ointment at the next rest stop, because, believe me, the last thing you want is a tropical ulcer. You stay close to my back and keep your eyes peeled. If we hit any really rough stuff we'll take it in turns to cut our way through.' He pulled out a compass and handed it to Jamie. 'Here, this is a spare. In case we get split up this is what you do. We're gonna head south-east for about three hours until we hit a little plain in the head-waters of the Pagana River. You'll know you're in the right spot because there are two distinctive hills to the west of the plain, like gateposts. Kristian Anugu's long-house is right between them and his clan has planta-tions and gardens scattered across the plain.'

'That all sounds deceptively easy, Doug old boy,' Jamie looked out over the rumpled carpet of jungle-clad hills that stretched for mile upon mile, 'and I'm sure you know exactly where we're going. But we both know the reality is that once we're in there we won't be able to see more than twenty feet in any direction, and the broken ground means we aren't likely to travel in a straight line.'

Doug Stewart shook his head in exasperation. 'In that case, Jamie, *old boy*, I'll make it even simpler for you. See that notch in the hills on the other side of the valley?'

Jamie screwed up his eyes and he could just make out some kind of deviation in the forest canopy. 'More or less.'

'Well, that marks an old trading trail from the Moroni days and it runs from here, through the Pagana Plain all the way to Buin. You follow that feature until you hit coconut and cocoa plantations; proper cultivated ground. Somewhere around there, you'll find people. Any one of them will guide you to Kristian Anugu.'

'But how will I ask them, I don't speak Tok what's-it?'

'Oh, it shouldn't be too difficult. All you have to do is keep repeating his name and looking gormless.'

Jamie managed a wry smile. 'I think I can manage that.'

'Then let's go. Tarzan, your jungle awaits.'

XLI

Jamie hated the jungle with all the loathing and passion he'd feared, but he decided he hated Keith Devlin even more. No matter his apparently altruistic plans for the future of Bougainville and its people, Devlin was a malignant human being who manipulated everyone within his orbit. He'd noticed it first with Nico, the successful young Australian lawyer who'd brokered his deal with Leopold Ungar. Assured and urbane, Nico become uncertain and fearful in Devlin's presence, like a dog worried the next thing he'd feel was the whip. Jamie knew he would never have dared cross swords with the odious Madam Nishimura if it hadn't been for Devlin's veiled threats against Fiona and Lizzie. And now it was happening again. He was out of his element and he knew it. For no good reason, Magda Ross's face appeared in his head. He missed the air of calm competence she brought to every tough situation and she would be familiar with the Bougainville jungle. The feeling was quickly replaced by a familiar pang of guilt when he realized that her competence wasn't the only thing he missed about her. Something fell down the back of his neck and he slapped frantically at the back of his shirt. And things were about to get worse.

It started to rain.

People talk about *the heavens opening*, but in Bougainville a shower was more like being caught underneath an emptying swimming pool. Jamie was soaked to the skin before he even had the chance to reach for his waterproof. His clothes stuck to his body as he trudged miserably on, the trail – little more than a dirt scar in the thick grass – turning to glutinous mud beneath his feet. Soon the trail wasn't a trail at all, just an emerald strip of knee-high grass between the trees, filled with ferns and shoulder-high, razor-edged spiky leaves that sliced tiny cuts in the skin of his bare arms. Doug Stewart led with his rifle at the port across his chest, setting a pace Jamie struggled to match. The conditions had no effect on the Australian and his eyes alternately scanned the ground ahead and the wall of trees and vines that sloped upwards to left and right. Every hundred paces brought a gully to struggle down or a steep ridge to climb, each thousand a river to ford, filled with slippery rocks that were ankle-breaking booby traps.

As the canopy thickened the rain faded and eventually stopped completely, the constant rush replaced by a silence vastly more unnerving. Stewart halted and raised a hand for Jamie to do the same. For twenty seconds or more he stood with his eyes closed, tasting the quiet with his ears the way a dog tests for scent with his nose. When he was satisfied, they moved on, but he repeated the exercise half an hour later.

'Five-minute rest,' he whispered.

Jamie staggered to a grateful halt, panting with exertion. Stewart unhooked the water bottle from his belt and took a three-second drink. Jamie matched him gulp for gulp and had to avoid the temptation to continue. The security boss leaned against the barrel of his rifle, drawing the breath deep into his lungs. Jamie was about to take a seat under a tree beside him when the Australian's fingers twisted into his T-shirt to drag him upright.

'Don't you know anything?' he grunted. 'If you sit down, it's only more difficult to get up again. Stand tall and suck in that oxygen. Water and air, that's your fuel, but you've got to get that air into your lungs.'

Jamie leaned against the tree instead and, imitating the Australian's actions, carefully treated every scratch on his arms. After what could only have been three minutes, Stewart straightened up and headed off down the trail. With a curse and a groan, the art dealer followed.

Jamie's image of the jungle included brightly coloured birds and potentially dangerous animals. Lizards and, he suppressed a shiver, scaly, thin-lipped, bead-eyed, enough-poison-to-kill-you-ten-times-over snakes. Yet this jungle was curiously devoid of life. All he saw was the occasional insect, although they included an ebony millipede the length of his forearm and butterflies that ranged between the size of a poker chip and a soup plate. A soft rush in the distance had just signalled the next river when the Australian froze and his eyes swivelled to the tree canopy. Jamie followed his gaze, aware that something wasn't right, but not sure what it was. They stood frozen while the seconds lengthened. Eventually, Jamie's eyes caught the flutter of a small brown bird flitting through the highest canopy.

It seemed nothing, but Stewart was already on the move, picking up the pace although, Jamie noted, not lengthening his stride pattern. The sound of the river grew louder and when they reached it the Australian stopped and beckoned Jamie close. 'When you get to the middle,' he whispered, 'you turn, walk very carefully ten paces downstream and wait for me. Got that?'

Jamie nodded. This was no time for questions. The river was close to thirty feet wide with steeply sloping banks of gravel. He scrambled into the water and complied with the directions, disturbing the river bed as little as he could. When he reached the spot the security chief had indicated he turned and watched curiously as Stewart completed the crossing. When the Australian reached the far side he did an odd little dance, moving from side to side as he crossed the patch of loose stones. Once into the grass he moved quickly, planting his feet very deliberately for fifty paces, then marching from the path up into the trees for a count of ten. Jamie watched him stop and turn. Stewart scanned the path on the Panguna side of the crossing, before even more deliberately walking *backwards* down the slope. When he reached the flat he continued, parallelling his original tracks until he reached the river again and walked downstream to reach the Englishman.

'That was very neat.'

'What are you waiting for?' Stewart growled. 'That

little parlour trick won't fool a proper tracker for long.'

'Tracker?' Jamie frowned, but the Australian was already forging downstream out of sight of the ford. Here the banks closed in and Stewart grunted approval as he saw what he was looking for. The roots of a pandanus palm had given up the struggle with the thin soil and the eighteen-inch trunk had fallen to hang precariously at head height over the flow. As they reached the tree, Stewart handed Jamie the SLR and with surprising athleticism pulled himself up to balance on the trunk. He reached down to take the rifle and carried it to the sloping bank before returning to haul Jamie up beside him.

When they reached the bank Stewart studied the fallen tree, grimacing at the wet marks their feet had left on the bark.

'Can't be helped,' he whispered. 'Follow me and for Christ's sake don't make a noise.' Picking up the rifle, the Australian ghosted his way through the vegetation without seeming to leave a mark of his passing. Jamie followed, trying, with limited success, to emulate him. As they reached the top of the bank Stewart forced him unforgivingly down among the fronds of a dense fern. They lay side by side, Jamie trying to still the arrhythmic, adrenalin-fuelled hammering of his heart and the breath that forced its way from his lungs in sobs. A minute passed, then another. Was the security man jumping at shadows? Stewart met the question in his eyes with an almost imperceptible shake of the head. *Wait*.

When they came they were like shadows, ethereal

and almost invisible as they hugged the bank of the stream, their feet barely disturbing the surge of the water as they advanced. Jamie froze at the sight of the two black men in ragged T-shirts and worn combat trousers, automatic rifles held at the ready across their chests. Another ten paces and they would reach the tree. Jamie tensed, but Stewart laid a hand on his arm. *Don't move. Relax.* Through a gap in the ferns he saw the enemy – whoever they were, their alertness and certainty of purpose definitely made them his enemy – halt. The closest, tall and athletic, with narrow-set killer's eyes and pockmarked skin, cast a final glance over the surroundings and made a twirling motion with his finger. His companion nodded and together they turned to disappear upstream as silently as they'd come.

Jamie turned to his companion, but Stewart put a finger to his lips and squirmed silently backwards, downhill and away from the stream. Only when they'd covered fifty paces away and buried themselves in the bush did he rise. Jamie hurried to catch up with him, a dozen questions on his lips.

'They were PNG,' Doug Stewart whispered, forestalling the first of them. 'Those illegal gold miners from the Jaba River I told you about. Redskins, and they must be desperate to be running around with fucking M16s in BRA country.'

'What do you think they want?'

The Australian let out a soft snort of laughter. 'Us, idiot. That monstrosity you have in your rucksack. Anything that Devlin has and they haven't.' He saw Jamie's look of bemusement. 'Intelligence,' he tried to explain. 'Just because they're black fellas doesn't mean they don't have it, and you'd better start using yours if you don't want to wind up dead. Look, Keith thinks he's got Canberra wrapped around his little finger, but there are people in Canberra who don't like Keith Devlin and would like nothing better than to see him fail. Maybe they're sympathetic with the blokes running Port Moresby, maybe not, but they won't miss a chance to do Devlin down. So the PNG government knows there's dirty work afoot and they have spies on the island because they have everything to lose. The Solomons has spies on the island because they have an interest in what happens to Bougainville. The Chinks have spies on the island because they have spies everywhere in the Pacific. And the Aussies have spies here because they need to know if the mine is going to reopen and Bougainville is going to blow up in their faces again.' He pushed his way through a stand of tall grass and Jamie struggled to follow. 'All of those people have been watching us, some of them would be happy to see us dead and most of them want to see us fail. We're on our own out here, son. Nobody's gonna help us, but us. Just like the old days, but without the fucking Jolly Green Giant to take you back to the world. Now for half a dollar I'd bugger off and leave you on your own, but that would also leave me a long way from home and without a pot to piss in. So I'll stay, for the moment, and help you get that thing back home. But you stay close and you cover my back.'

The barrage of bad news made Jamie wonder more than ever about Keith Devlin's motive in sending them out into the bush without a proper escort. He wished to Christ he'd never come anywhere near this godforsaken island and that he'd never set eyes on the Bougainville head. But most of all he wished he had a gun; a big, shiny black gun like the one Doug Stewart carried.

'We're going in the wrong direction,' he pointed out.

The ground fell away sharply to their right and Stewart tested a length of liana that would help him down the bank before he answered.

'If we try to get back to the track the chances are we'll meet them head on and they'll either ask politely for what's in your rucksack or shoot us and take it anyway. On the other hand, they might just carry on for a bit after they lose our tracks and set up an ambush.'

'That seems to presuppose they know exactly where we're going.'

Stewart grinned savagely. 'A gold watch for the clever bugger with all the answers.'

'Which means they could be waiting for us when we get there?'

'It's a possibility,' Stewart conceded. 'But Kristian Anugu's clan owns a lot of the land where we're going and they don't take to strangers much, especially Redskins. I'm gambling our "gold miners" know that and won't want to chance getting involved in a gun battle. I plan to cut down the western side of the hills until we reach the Pagana Valley, then follow it until we hit the plain. It won't be much fun and it'll take us longer, but at least nobody will be shooting at us.'

He grunted as he began to descend the crumbling earth slope, the liana in his left hand and the SLR in his right. Jamie picked another vine and followed. Within a few metres he felt something give and before he knew what was happening he was tumbling down the hill past the startled face of the other man. The trunk of a tree flashed by and it occurred to him he might break his neck and probably deserved to for not testing the vine properly. A millisecond later he landed flat on his face with an almighty, bone-shaking crunch that knocked every ounce of breath from his body. He lay with his eyes closed and experienced a mix of emotions. Relief that he was still alive and – he tested one limb at a time – more or less in one piece. Embarrassment that he had looked like a fool in front of a man like Doug Stewart. And concern that the bloody Bougainville head hadn't suffered the kind of damage that would make it even uglier than it already was. But when he opened his eyes the only thing he felt was a paralysing surge of sheer terror that made him release an involuntary cry.

It wasn't what you'd call a big snake, but when it was coiled two feet from your nose with its head held back ready to strike and its jaws gaping to show the awful fangs inside, it was more than big enough. The dull brown had slightly darker bands at intervals along the body and the serpent was a sinuous three feet long. Jamie noticed it had tiny overlapping scales that glittered with moisture from the earlier rain. He thought of moving back, but the pitiless black eyes mesmerized him and he knew the slightest movement would provoke the strike. Christ, what would it be like? His nightmares had always entailed being bitten in the leg or the arse; the face seemed that bit more awful. He'd feel the hit, and then the sting and then . . . He'd never understood the term gibber, but he was gibbering inside. Gradually he became aware of Doug Stewart's boots moving into vision just beyond the angry reptile and a thrill of hope surged through him. The machete, that's it, chop the ugly little monster into pieces. Pleeeeaaaase.

The Australian bent down and picked up the snake by the tail, holding it away from his body so the head couldn't reach him. It hissed and wriggled, attempting to get into position to strike, but Stewart didn't even flinch. Eventually, Jamie raised himself on shaking legs and brushed himself down, keeping a safe distance between him and the twisting brown body.

'Thanks.' He swallowed. 'That was a damned close thing, as the Old Duke would say.'

'It sure was.' Doug Stewart shook his head in mock sorrow. 'You might have landed on the poor little bugger. It was the same in the 'Nam. FNGs never knew a bloody thing.'

'FNGs?'

'The Fucking New Guys. If you'd done even a little bit of research about this here island, Mr Jamie Saintclair, you'd have learned that the only good thing about Bougainville is that there are no poisonous snakes. Off you go, little fella.' He threw the snake a few feet into the bushes and it slithered away into the undergrowth. 'Now stop pissing about and let's get going or Kristian Anugu will have died of old age before we get there.'

Jamie ignored him and opened the rucksack flap that held the Bougainville head. His fingers prickled with distaste as he picked it up by the curly hair and studied the ugly little face: it didn't appear any more battered than usual.

'This is the first time I've seen it close up,' Doug Stewart said. 'We're risking our necks for a fucking gonk?' He turned away and set off through the jungle, shaking his head in disgust. Jamie replaced the head and followed.

XLII

'Now this is what you call jungle.' Doug Stewart sounded as if he was enjoying himself. 'Put your back into it. You're not cutting cake.'

Jamie launched another attack on the thick stems of head-high elephant grass that blocked the way, chopping until his arm ached, but the big machete seemed to bounce off the springy green vegetation. Eventually, Stewart cursed and pushed him out of the way.

'Not like that. Like this.' He sliced the machete down at an angle in short, efficient strokes, cutting the stalks about thirty inches above the roots, allowing them to advance a few feet at a time. It had taken an hour to reach the Pagana River valley on the western slopes of the Crown Prince range. Since then progress had been slow as they worked their way upstream, halted at intervals by the thick clumps of impenetrable grass.

'All right,' Stewart gasped eventually, 'your turn.'

Jamie winced as his blistered hand closed over the machete and braced himself for another ten minutes of hell.

At one point they came across the tail section of a large plane, which Stewart identified as a B-24 Liberator. It seemed bizarre to find evidence of advanced human engineering lying in the middle of nowhere like so much discarded rubbish. 'Dozens of American and Jap planes came down in the jungle, and a lot were never found,' the Australian explained. 'The rest of this one will be spread all over the hillside. There's a Jap bomber in the jungle down by Buin that they reckon was the plane Yamamoto was in when he died.'

Jamie studied the twisted metal for any signs of a serial number. 'Would the crew have got out?'

'What do you think?' Stewart turned away and Jamie hurried to catch up with him.

The valley rose steadily upwards, snaking its way through the jungle, and Jamie lost track of time as they followed the winding contours, sometimes forced into the shallows where the jungle became too thick to penetrate, even with the machetes. Eventually, Stewart found what seemed to be an overgrown track and the going became slightly easier.

They'd gone about a mile when the Australian suddenly froze, mid-step, and dropped to one knee, gesturing for Jamie to do the same.

'Do you see it?' Jamie frantically scanned the jungle ahead for signs of life, but all he could see was trees, bushes and ferns. Stewart slowly rose to his feet and brought the rifle to his shoulder. The rising terrain had forced a bend in the trail and he walked slowly forwards and stopped a foot from the green wall. He used the rifle barrel to push aside a twisted vine and reveal a dark void beyond. 'Jap bunker,' he said.

Jamie moved to join him, astonished that even though he knew the bunker was there, his eyes still didn't believe it. It would have been well camouflaged originally, but after five decades the jungle had made the concrete structure its own.

'Perfect place for an ambush,' the Australian said admiringly. 'When the Allies landed at Torokina the blokes in the 26th Battalion would have had to come this way to cover their flank when they marched south. We can't be far east of Slater's Knoll, where they broke the back of the Jap resistance in March 'forty-five.' He laid down the rifle and unsheathed his machete, chopping at the vegetation until he revealed the angle of the bunker's side, then cut a route to the rear, where he found the entrance. Jamie followed. 'Let's take a look.'

Stewart produced a torch from his rucksack and ducked into the concrete passage. Vines had blocked the machine-gun slits and fought their way in to take over most of the interior, the roots clawing their way into the flaking concrete. The floor was thick with leaf mulch and the whole interior smelled of decay and damp. As the torch beam passed over the base of one wall, Jamie noticed what looked like a bundle of old rags.

'What's that?'

Stewart flicked back to the spot and crouched beside it. The cloth disintegrated at his touch, but not before he'd identified it. 'Jap uniform,' he said. 'Looks like the owner was still in it, but the pigs have been at him.' He dug in the leaf litter and pulled out what appeared to be part of a human jaw, plus a few bone fragments.

Jamie waited for him to throw the remains aside, but the Australian cradled them in his hand as he ducked back into the passage and out into the daylight. Without a word, he laid the bones in the grass and used his machete to dig a small hole to the right of the bunker entrance, where he placed the bones and replaced the earth. When he was done he sliced a piece of wood from a nearby branch and shaped it into an oblong three inches wide and eighteen high. 'Do you have a pen?'

Jamie searched into his pockets until he found what he was looking for and watched as Doug Stewart wrote 'Unknown Japanese Soldier' into the raw wood.

Stewart caught his look and shrugged. 'He was a Jap, but he was a soldier, and believe me, son, every soldier wants to know that when he's dead someone will send him home. I'll mark this place on the map and hopefully someone will come and check the place for more remains. At least what's left of him will get a decent burial.'

With a final glance at the last resting place of Lieutenant Tomoyuki Hamasuna they set off for the Pagana Plain and the longhouse of Kristian Anugu.

Jamie's energy-sapped mind barely registered the first burst of fire from their right front, but Doug Stewart reacted instantly, bundling the Englishman to the ground and firing single, aimed rounds from the SLR over his body. 'Find some cover,' the Australian snarled. 'That was just a warning.'

'Where?' Jamie looked around in desperation, but with his nose in the damp earth all he could see was grass. 'They're probably all around us and if you shoot back at them the next bullets will be up our backside.'

'Nope,' Doug Stewart said calmly. 'I reckon there's only three or four of them. The main party haven't had time to get ahead of us.'

'How do you work that out?'

'Because if there's more than that we're well and truly fucked.' They ducked as bursts from two or three weapons ruffled the top of the grass. 'You go left,' the Australian ordered. 'I'll work my way right and try to flank them. Soon as you hear the SLR, get off your arse and get yourself as far into the jungle as you can.'

'For Christ's sake,' Jamie cried, 'why don't we just give them the bloody head if they're that desperate for it? It's not worth fucking dying for!'

But Doug Stewart was already gone.

Reluctantly, Jamie squirmed back through the grass towards the thick jungle. When he reached it, he turned and began to crawl deeper into the foliage, moving fast up the slope, but staying low. There'd been no firing for almost a minute, but suddenly the distinctive whip-crack of the SLR broke the silence. 'You bloody madman,' he groaned. But he did as he'd been instructed. He leaped to his feet and sprinted uphill as the rattle of two or three automatic weapons combined. A hidden dip opened up in front of him and he dived into it, rolling over and over until he came to rest at the foot of the hollow.

The sound of gunfire faded and he found himself

staring at a pair of dark feet in open-toed sandals, the nails and the flesh beneath them a pale contrast to the rest. He decided distractedly that it was an odd thing to notice at a time like this, probably the mind delaying the moment of awful truth. With a feeling of terrible inevitability he craned his neck and looked up into the bearded face and flaring nostrils of a black man wearing a Jimi Hendrix T-shirt and sports pants. The face, with its betel-stained teeth, would have been fearsome enough even without the rifle – the twin of the one Doug Stewart had carried – that was aimed directly at Jamie Saintclair's right eye.

'Bugger.' He allowed his head to drop; he wasn't especially keen to see the bullet that killed him. All that effort wasted, the Bougainville head would never reach its destination and he'd never find out what was so important about all this. His final bleak thought was that the ever-so-clever Doug Stewart had been wrong and he'd been right. They'd been surrounded. He had walked straight into the people he'd been trying to run away from, which was very silly when you thought about it. But a little niggle in his brain told him there was something not quite right. Something . . .

'You're a hard man to keep track of, Jamie Saintclair. We lost you when you left the trail and almost didn't find you again.' He wondered if he was hallucinating, because, when he looked up again, the black man had been replaced by the slim figure of Magda Ross, with a hand held out to help him to his feet. His heart thundered and his mind seemed to dissolve in confusion at the sight of her. 'I'm sorry.' She smiled. 'I promised

I'd cover your back in case Devlin tried to double-cross you, but I didn't do a very good job, did I?'

He accepted her hand and hauled himself to his feet. 'I'd say your timing was impeccable.' If they'd been alone he would have hugged her. He might also say that no one had ever looked better in a pair of combat trousers and a T-shirt, but something more important occurred to him. 'What about Doug? The man I was with.' He looked up and noticed for the first time that the black man had been joined by two others, who crouched on the rim of the hollow, listening intently and peering in the direction of the ambush. 'He's down there, shooting it out with somebody.'

'There was nothing we could do.' Magda shook her head. 'My friends here were reluctant to meet him before you and I made contact. They were worried about a misunderstanding.'

Before Jamie could ask who her new friends were a fourth man appeared at the edge of the dip and spoke to the bearded Bougainvillean in a singsong burst of pidgin. The big man nodded and jogged down the slope to join them. 'He says there's been no movement down there since a couple of blokes ran off into the bush by the river.'

Jamie blinked, because the accent was pure untainted Australian and for some reason sounded odd coming from the unyielding black face with the sombre eyes.

'Jamie Saintclair,' Magda said solemnly, 'meet Michael Taruko.'

'G'day,' the black man said. 'It's a pity we couldn't get involved sooner, but we couldn't take a risk of mucking about when you were with an ex-SAS man with a loaded rifle.'

'You know about that? How did—'

'That's for later.' Michael Taruko's tone made it clear who was in charge now. 'First we have to get down there and see what's happened with your mate and those other blokes. I'd be obliged if you take the lead, because he's less likely to shoot you than anybody else. I reckon it'll be okay to go in shouting his name, but for Christ's sake keep your head down.'

Jamie clambered out of the dip and stumbled down the slope. There was no answer to his calls, but he wasn't being shot at either, which must be a good sign. 'Doug?' He repeated the cry. 'It's Jamie, and I'm with some friends. Four native gentlemen and a white girl, so hold your fire and shout out so I know where you are.'

They reached level ground and he looked to Michael. 'I think we should spread out.'

The big man nodded and issued an order to his companions who split up and entered the jungle on the far side of the track. Magda came to Jamie's side and together they advanced warily into the trees, their eyes searching the undergrowth for any sign of the missing Australian.

'You told me you had a friend on the island who might be able to help,' Jamie whispered. 'Judging by Michael and his mates' armoury, that seems to have been only half the story.'

'What did you expect me to say?' she hissed back. 'He's an islander. He was my translator when I was doing work for my Ph.D. We kept in touch. The accent comes from being sent to school in Brisbane. He was there for the entire period of the Crisis and it still shames him. The family are landowners and didn't want to get involved, but that only made them fair game for both sides. He lost close relatives. Despite that, his father insisted he complete his education. He was just out of university when I met him. In many ways he's a very formidable man, but I think he is still confused about his identity.' Her eyes sought Jamie's across her shoulder. 'There's more. Maybe he'll tell you, maybe he won't, but that has to be up to Michael, okay?'

'All right,' he agreed. 'I trust your judgement, so we'll do what Michael says.'

Magda turned to reply but something caught her eye and she gasped. Jamie's vision was partially obscured by the intervening trees, but when he moved to join her he saw that she was staring at a man lying twenty feet away with his back against a tree and his head twisted at an unlikely angle. Not Doug Stewart, but one of their ambushers, judging by the automatic rifle at his feet. The torn T-shirt he wore had a dark patch in the centre of the chest.

'Stay here.' He was halfway to the dead man when he heard the soft groan from his right. Doug Stewart lay in the foetal position, his body partially hidden by the long grass. Jamie experienced a wave of nausea as he saw the splashes of red on the ground beside Keith Devlin's security chief and the ragged exit wound low in his back that was leaking too much blood.

He knelt over the injured man wondering what to do first. Should he try to move him? At first glance the wound looked terrible, but just how bad was it? As gently as he could, he lifted the Australian's shirt to reveal a fist-sized mess of ragged flesh. Christ, it was even worse than he'd feared. What now? The first-aid kit? But it had been in Stewart's backpack and he'd clearly abandoned it somewhere along the way. Jamie wriggled out of his rucksack and searched inside for the spare shirt he'd packed, but tearing it into bandage-sized strips turned out to be more difficult than in the movies.

'These might help.' Magda handed him a small pair of scissors and he used them to cut the material. She stared at the blood oozing from the bullet wound and had an idea. From a zip pocket of her bag she came up with four padded squares in blue paper packets. 'And these.'

'Perfect.' He tore open two of the packets and positioned the sanitary towels so they overlapped across the wound. 'Can you hold them in place while I turn him over?'

'I'll give it a try.' She knelt beside him and though her face was pale, she wore a determined expression that made him proud of her. Jamie tied two pieces of shirt together so they'd encircle Doug Stewart's body at least twice. He draped the length of cloth over Stewart's lower back and Magda moved her hand so that the bandage covered the pads, then replaced it again over the cloth.

'This might hurt a bit, Doug old son,' Jamie said, though he had no idea if the wounded man could hear him, 'but there's no helping it. You know the drill. Try to keep calm and stay with it. You're making a proper mess of this bit of jungle and we have to stop the bleeding.' He manoeuvred himself into a position where he could get his arms round the wounded man's chest. 'On the count of three,' he said to Magda. 'When I get him up, you wrap the bandage round and plug the hole in front with another of your little marvels. Got it?' She nodded, but her lips were a single pale line. 'Don't worry,' he gave her what he hoped was an encouraging smile, 'he's a tough old bastard. He'll live, but we have to get him to hospital. One . . . two . . . three.'

Jamie heaved upwards. Doug Stewart gave a groan of agony that ended in a long whimper. The Australian was all bone and muscle, but there wasn't much of him and Jamie managed to hold his body until Magda could apply the second patch and fix the bandage in place.

'That's great,' he said. 'You seem to have bitten your lip.' He raised his hand to wipe the blood way only to realise it was covered in Doug Stewart's.

'It's nothing,' Magda swallowed. 'I'll go and fetch Michael. We need to get your friend off the mountain somehow.'

She ran off in the direction of the trail and Jamie lay back with the Australian in his arms. 'You really are a silly old bastard,' he sighed.

'Less . . . of . . . the . . . old.' Every word was a challenge to Doug Stewart's ebbing strength and the voice emerged as the merest whisper. 'Not dead yet.' There wasn't really much of an answer to that, so Jamie tried to make them both as comfortable as he could under the circumstances. Stewart's breath wheezed in his chest and his face was the colour of old parchment with nicotine stains under the eyes. 'Should have left me.'

'Don't be bloody daft. We've been in this together from the start.'

'You . . . hung out to dry.'

'Devlin hung us both out to dry,' Jamie insisted. 'Look, Doug, save your strength.'

But Doug Stewart's hand closed over his, the skin chillingly cold to the touch, and when he opened his eyes they were filled with some desperate urgency. 'No, don't understand, Devlin,' Jamie felt the body shudder in his arms. 'You . . .' But there was no more. The words faded and the Australian's grip tightened convulsively before the hand fell away. Jamie hardly dared look at his face for fear of what he would see, but Stewart's eyes were closed and his chest continued its uneven rise and fall as his tortured body struggled for life.

Jamie was still trying to decipher the message Devlin's security chief had been so desperate to communicate when Magda appeared through the trees with Michael. The Bougainvillean took one look at the wounded man and issued a stream of instructions to his comrades.

'We need to get him to a doctor.' Jamie's voice acknowledged the hopelessness of their situation. In the unlikely event they could carry Doug Stewart back through the bush to Arawa, the Australian would have bled to death long before they got there.

But Michael only nodded. 'We should continue along the trail,' he said. 'My grandfather's lands are not far away. I have communications there, a radio. We can call up a helicopter and have him in hospital at Buka in another hour.'

Jamie stared at him, aware that Michael's persona had taken on another new dimension. With Stewart's bandages already turning pink this wasn't the time to question the mystery of the convenient communications in a place with no phone or internet signal, and the even more convenient helicopter that appeared to be at Michael's beck and call. But he did have one question. 'Buka? Why not Arawa? Surely it's only a few minutes away by air.'

The sombre brown eyes studied him, testing . . . something: his courage, integrity? 'Because Devlin is in Arawa,' he said finally. 'I doubt it would suit either my purposes or yours for him to know that we had joined forces, Mr Saintclair.'

Jamie looked from Magda to the bearded islander.

'We need to talk,' he said, 'and soon.'

But there was no time now. Michael's three companions appeared from the jungle carrying newly cut branches, vines and palm leaves that they turned into a functional stretcher within a minute. All the niggling little uncertainties would be answered later. Their first task was to save Doug Stewart's life.

XLIII

Jamie took the right rear handle of the makeshift stretcher for the first stretch. His right palm was still blistered from his earlier session with the machete and it felt as if he'd plunged it into the heart of a fire as he gripped the raw wooden pole. Michael had the left, with two of the islander's companions on the front. The third worked his way ahead to scout out any potential trouble. Michael doubted the ambushers would bother them again; he was more concerned about the original party who'd followed Jamie and Doug Stewart from the Panguna Mine. 'My people will know the Redskins are coming, but it depends how eager they are to lay their hands on what you're carrying. They have a great deal of firepower and I've told my people not to get into a fight.'

'So you know what this is all about?'

'Of course, Mr Saintclair.' The bearded islander nodded gravely. 'Magda informed me of your interest in my ancestor's remains the day you walked into her museum. You seem shocked? But why should you be? How could she betray someone she had only just met? We had been friends for years. Why should she not inform me of an event that might be of great importance to myself and my clan?'

He glanced down at the deathly white figure on the stretcher, but Doug Stewart, if he was conscious at all, was locked away in a world of pain all of his own.

'I also have what you might call a singular interest in the activities of your friends Mr Devlin and Mr Stewart. I'm a Bougainvillean and a patriot, Mr Saintclair. Of course, many of my people are also patriots and we do not always agree on the future direction of this country, particularly in regard to the island's mineral resources.' There was a long pause as they negotiated the stretcher across a steep gully. Beyond it, the trail, if it could be dignified by the name, wound its way up the side of a steep hill and Jamie wondered if his strength would hold out. Michael hardly seemed to notice his burden as he continued. 'But many of us agree passionately on one thing. Whatever the future of Bougainville is we will never again allow it to be exploited by outside influences. It does not matter whether those influences are commercial or political or whether they are from Papua New Guinea, Australia, China, or Japan, which has shown a recent and unlikely altruistic interest in upgrading our infrastructure. A few years ago we became aware of an insidious undermining of that principle. Influential people became rich overnight and began to use their power to convince others that perhaps our stance was not in the best interests of Bougainville. Landowners who had been against any reopening of the mine suddenly changed their minds. Politicians who had spent a lifetime fighting the original mine owners became relaxed about cooperating with a potential new one. The old ways had died with the opening of Panguna, they said. We must embrace a new future.'

'Keith Devlin's future.'

'Exactly. And who wouldn't be seduced by Mr Devlin's vision for Bougainville? A South Seas utopia where everyone lives in a fine house that has access to running water and electricity; where every child is cared for by the most advanced health system in the world and has the opportunity to attend the best schools in the region; where every man has a job if he wants one; and every menial task is done by a Redskin. And all that paid for by a mine run on the latest scientific and environmental principles and creating minimal pollution.'

'It all sounds very fine. I might come and live here myself.'

They were interrupted by a hacking cough from the man on the stretcher. Jamie looked down at Doug Stewart, fearing the worst. But the Australian was conscious – and he was laughing.

'Put me down for a minute,' the wounded man croaked hoarsely. 'All this bucking about is gonna kill me.'

'Can't do that, Doug old son,' Jamie insisted. 'We need to get you to a hospital.'

Stewart shook his head. 'I've got some stuff to say and this might be my last chance to say it.'

Jamie exchanged a glance with Michael, who shrugged. He'd been about to call a rest in any case.

They laid the stretcher gently in the grass and Stewart closed his eyes. Magda brought him water, but Michael only allowed her to wet his lips with it, while Jamie checked his wounds. It was almost a minute before he began speaking.

'Never trust Devlin. Panguna's not the only mine.' The words came in short bursts, punctuated by gasps as the pain swept through him, and every one required enormous effort. It was as if Doug Stewart had decided to dictate his last will and testament and he wouldn't be silenced. 'Seven other licences already. Opportunities all over the island.' He paused to gather his strength, and there was more. Devlin planned to turn the BRA into his private army. He'd buy every politician and landowner on the island if that's what it took. Canberra was fixed, so was Port Moresby. By the time anyone noticed it would be too late. The result would be Keith Devlin's personal fiefdom, with the islanders as his serfs. By the end Stewart's voice had faded so much Jamie, Magda and Michael had to bend over him to make out the words. Eventually, with a last garbled whisper, he lapsed back into unconsciousness.

They stared at each other till Magda broke the silence. 'Is he . . . ?'

Michael reached out to touch the Australian's neck. 'No, there's still a faint pulse, but he can't last much longer.'

'How far to the radio?' Jamie demanded.

'Another half-hour. It is at my grandfather's long-house. But there are farms on the way where we can get help.'

'Then let's get going.'

They picked up the stretcher and set off up the trail.

Magda kept pace beside Jamie. 'Did you hear what he said at the end?' she asked. 'Something about the head.'

'He said: "It's not about the head".' He changed his grip on the raw wooden pole to try to make it more comfortable. 'There was more, but that's all I could make out. I think he must have been rambling. It's always been about the head. Keith Devlin is using the head to ensure the support of the tribal chief for this master plan of his.'

Now it was Michael's turn to look mystified. 'Which chief? My grandfather has been trying to have the head returned to Bougainville for fifty years, but he doesn't have any political power and he won't be bought.'

'But what else does he have to gain?' Magda was mystified.

Jamie thought back to his first meeting with Devlin. 'Kristian Anugu is your grandfather?' he asked Michael. 'That would explain your interest.'

'He never mentioned anything about the mine,' the bearded man said. 'Keith Devlin's people offered to give him literally anything he desired in return for the briefcase. Kristian said the only compensation for such a treasure could be the lost head of his grandfather, and they went away disappointed. But Devlin didn't give up. He sent you to find the head and Magda agreed to help you so that I'd know what was happening.'

Jamie felt Magda's eyes on him and tried to ignore the fact that she'd used him from the word go. All right, he'd kept her in the dark about a few things himself, but whatever Michael said it felt like a betrayal. 'So this is all about the documents that went missing during the negotiations?'

The black man shook his head. 'I've never heard about any missing documents. The briefcase dates back to a cargo cult on the island that ended in the mix-Sixties. My grandfather always referred to it as the *yelopela* treasure, so it must have come from the Japanese occupation period. He never said how he came by it, or let anyone near.'

'That's crazy,' Jamie said. 'Why would Keith Devlin spend God knows how much to get his hands on a relic from the Second World War?'

'Maybe you'll find out when you hand over the head to the old man.'

The first settlements appeared on the hillside ahead. Traditional native houses, some of them on stilts, with pitched roofs thatched with palm leaves, and walls of woven grass, surrounded by gardens or groves of coconut, cocoa or banana trees.

'We'll find someone to help soon,' Michael predicted. 'Then I will take you to my grandfather's longhouse.'

Jamie hoped he was right because his arm felt as if it was about to fall off. 'You didn't seem all that surprised by what poor old Doug here had to say about Devlin's scheme?'

'We know the licences to excavate more mines exist,' the big man explained. 'They'd be passed to him if he becomes the majority shareholder in Bougainville

Copper, so it just depends on their legal status after twenty years. Likewise, it's obvious that the island has more resources that can be exploited.'

'I meant about creating a private army. Basically buying Bougainville off the shelf.'

'That's an interesting way to put it.' The observation brought a wry half-smile from the islander. 'When I was at school during the Crisis, I was treated as an enemy; the big black Boog boy from the rebel island that wouldn't do what Australia told it. I learned to hate Australia and Australians.'

'Yet you went back to university,' Jamie pointed out.

'My father said it was my duty and I am a dutiful son.' Michael shrugged. 'He was right to send me, because I learned that not all Australians supported the war against my people, and that many were ashamed of their role in it. I studied International Relations and one of my tutors very carefully steered me in a certain direction. Looking back, I should probably be angry at the position he placed me in, but I'm not.' Doug Stewart's breath began to rattle in his throat and both men looked down at him in concern. Michael rapped out an order and the two front men picked up the pace. Jamie gritted his teeth and tried to keep up as Michael continued, grunting with exertion between the words. 'Around the time I graduated it became apparent to certain people that Keith Devlin was taking an interest in Bougainville. My tutor put them in touch with me, and it was suggested that the only way to fight the kind of power he wielded was with an equal power that I didn't have. They convinced me that the best way I could serve my people was to accept the support of the country I had once hated.'

'Would "Accept the support of" be a euphemism for "work for" or, to be more exact, "spy for"?' Michael glanced across at him and Jamie could see the sweat coursing down the black face into his beard. The dark eyes smouldered and he knew he'd strayed into dangerous territory. Still, it explained the radio and the helicopter, and if they could only get there soon, Doug Stewart might still have good cause to be thankful for them.

They tensed at a shout from further up the trail, but relaxed when the scout reappeared with half a dozen male natives followed by a group of children. 'Thank Christ for that.' Michael smiled. 'My bloody arm was about to fall off.'

Jamie felt emotionally and physically drained as he handed over the stretcher to a grave-faced black man who offered him a drink of some kind of fruit juice. The newcomers forged ahead with the stretcher and he, Michael and Magda followed in their wake.

Michael took up where he'd left off. 'If you stay long enough on Bougainville, Mr Saintclair, you'll discover that on this island there are no easy answers. My people knew nothing but war and hunger, murder and rape for eleven years; twice the span of your World War. The BRA fought off the PNG defence force, who outnumbered and outgunned them, and when they'd done it, they fought each other. The scars of that conflict are too deep to heal as long as those who fought it are still alive. I reckon it's up to the next generation to create the foundations of a new Bougainville, and if I have to sup with the devil to make that happen, it's a sacrifice I'm prepared to make. So here we are. I've been keeping an eye on Keith Devlin's activities on the island, and my friends have been keeping me in touch with what's been happening at their end. Unfortunately, there are certain people in Canberra who actively support Devlin, and others who, for their own reasons, don't have any option but to protect him.' He hesitated and Jamie felt himself the focus of the brown eyes. The art dealer turned to Magda and discovered she was studying him with a look of expectation as Michael found the words he was looking for. 'The truth is that if we're going to stop him, or bring him down, we need to have solid evidence.'

'Look, Michael,' Jamie tried to ignore the plea in Magda's eyes, 'I have every sympathy for you and your friends, but there are two people I care for down in Arawa who are depending on me to get them home. All I want is to make the exchange and deliver this mysterious briefcase to Devlin. Once we're out of here I'll do everything I can to stop him, but until then—'

'Forget it, Jamie.' Magda's words were like a dismissal and Jamie felt himself redden. 'Not everyone can be a hero.'

'Don't be too hard on him, hon.' Michael shook his shaggy head. 'Mr Saintclair got this far, and from what you tell me that took some doing. Who knows what might happen down the line?'

Jamie struggled to keep the anger out of his voice. 'If

you can keep Doug alive he may be the key to every-thing. He told me himself he knows where the bodies are buried.'

'Maybe he won't be so talkative if he stays alive.' Michael snorted through his wide nostrils. 'Right now he thinks he's dying and maybe God's whispering in his ear.'

'True enough.' Jamie looked to where the stretcher had reached the first houses. 'But I think he's more in-terested in having his revenge on Devlin than meeting his maker on first-name terms. How far to your grand-father's longhouse?'

'We're nearly there.'

The stretcher bearers stopped outside one of the grass and banana-leaf houses that had an aerial running from the pitched roof to a nearby palm tree. Michael and Magda watched as Jamie went to where the men had laid Doug Stewart and spent a few minutes talk-ing to him. In the meantime, the bearded man asked Magda to stay with the wounded Australian while his men called in the helicopter.

'Are you ready?' Michael asked.

Jamie took a deep breath and hitched up his ruck-sack. 'I think so.'

'Then come and meet my grandfather, Kristian Anugu.'

XLIV

Kristian Anugu sat comfortably on the stairs of his longhouse, eyes as old as time staring at a present of which only he was aware. His hair was a frizzy helmet of tight-linked white curls and his sparse, stubbled beard and bushy, caterpillar eyebrows matched it. The eyes were a deep walnut, buried deep beneath hooded lids in furrows on either side of a broad, negroid nose and they had a mystic quality, full of shadows and secrets and ancient knowledge. At first sight he gave an impression of fragility – of brittle bone and tough gristle held together by skin the texture of worn parchment – but that was before you noticed the arms, which, for all his antiquity were well-muscled, and the hands. They were thick-fingered and powerful; strangler's hands, Jamie thought for no reason. His only clothing was a kilt of brown material that covered his skinny legs as far as the knees, and his dark flesh was pitted and lined with old scars, each recording some long-healed wound or injury or brush with disfiguring disease. A length of frayed string hung round his wrinkled neck attached to what looked like a crumpled piece of lead. The longhouse was about twice the size of any other house in the village. Through the open doorway Jamie could see colourful ornaments and the intricately carved hollow wooden logs that he remembered from Magda's museum as traditional Bougainville drums.

'This is my grandfather, Kristian Anugu,' Michael introduced the old man. 'He is an elder of the Naasioi *wantok*, our tribe, or, more precisely, language group – and a very important person on the island.'

'Please tell him I'm honoured to meet him.' Jamie had no idea how to conduct what amounted to a negotiation in an entirely different language and culture from his own. Doug Stewart had planned to coach him on the march, but his induction had been taken over by events. Where experience was lacking, he reasoned, a pukka English gent would always fall back on cheerful good manners.

Kristian's longhouse lay in the centre of a flat bowl between the jungle-covered mountains and, like the other houses scattered across the cleared ground, was surrounded by gardens planted with sweet potato, taro, vanilla, pineapple and banana. Close by were ordered groves of coconut palms and cocoa trees, the leaves fluttering gently in the warm breeze. After the heart-stopping terror of the ambush and the long trek carrying Doug Stewart, Jamie was almost overwhelmed by the soporific tranquillity of the place and he had to fight to keep his mind clear. Kristian Anugu listened to his grandson's translation and nodded gravely, replying in a sonorous, low-pitched whisper that nonetheless conveyed great dignity, and in a language that sounded like the burbling of a mountain stream.

'He welcomes you as a guest,' Michael said. 'He sees that you carry a great burden and have travelled far through darkness and danger to return it to the land of its origin. This thing, of *his* grandfather, was always destined to return to Papa'ala, which is the ancient name for our land. He says that the land is our mother, our lifeline and our protection.' Kristian Anugu nodded sagely as if he understood the English words. 'This has been forgotten but it is time for the restless spirits of the victims of the Fighting Time to have peace. Women own the land – everything you see here belongs to my mother – but it is men who must hold the land and protect it. His grandfather assures him that only once he has become part of the land again can the healing begin. He told him this when he was young and foolish, and it was only then that he understood the responsibilities of manhood. He has been waiting for this day since the time of the *yelopelas*.'

'*Ningan ko bananiai*.' The old man smiled, showing a mouth devoid of teeth.

'He asks you to sit down beside him.'

Jamie accepted the invitation and Kristian said something to Michael that sounded like an order. The islander hesitated, his face twisted in an expression of what might have been foreboding, but he disappeared inside the hut. He returned after a few minutes with a large package wrapped in palm fronds, which he set beside his grandfather with the reverence of a man delivering a diplomatic gift.

Jamie reached for his rucksack, but Michael laid a hand on his arm. 'There's no hurry. He's waited more than fifty years for this. He says to you this is not a business deal, but an exchange of gifts between friends. Before we begin, he will tell how he came to own the *yelopela* treasure.'

Jamie listened fascinated as Michael translated the tale of how Kristian, a young man in the prime of his life, had heard gunfire in the sky and seen a red streak across the jungle canopy ending in a great fireball. 'He saw many planes fall after that, but this was the first,' the Bougainvillean explained.

Kristian had noted the position of the crash with eyes long attuned to the confusion of the island's jungle terrain. By the time he reached it he could hear the sounds of the *yelopelas* coming and he hid, watching the curious behaviour of the leader. When Jamie heard how the Japanese lieutenant had worshipped the *yelopela* king with the fine sword, he remembered what Doug Stewart had told him as they stood by the crashed American bomber. 'Yamamoto,' he whispered to himself. 'The *yelopela* king must have been Admiral Yamamoto.'

'At first he believed the treasure brought good fortune to him and his people. When the mine opened at Panguna and the white men came to the mountains with their measuring sticks, he began to have doubts. It was soon after that the disturbances and the killing began. My grandfather pitied his neighbours the Moroni, who lost everything and were forced to live with the salt-water people they despised, but they were not of our clan and it was none of his business. At first, we were left alone, then some white men from the mine came asking questions about a lost object he recognized as the *yelopela* treasure.' A small crowd of curious curly haired children dressed in football tops or multicoloured cotton dresses gathered to see the visiting white man. Long hours playing in the sun had bleached blond highlights into their dark hair in contrast to the mothers who came to shoo them away and allow Michael to continue. 'By now many island people had learned of Kristian Anugu's powerful cargo and, though he denied any knowledge of it, the white men returned to press him. When he refused to give it up, they sent their Redskins to take it and he was forced to kill some of them, and retreat to the jungle where they dare not follow. For a few years he was left in peace, but later some faction of the BRA began to ask the same question. This time when he didn't answer, they shot him from ambush.' Sophisticated and well-educated or not Jamie noticed that Michael's whole manner changed as he recounted the old man's history. It was as if he had reverted to his childhood and Kristian was a figure of awe and power. 'Fortunately, his grandfather protected him and he still wears the bullet as a charm. He had hidden the treasure where no man could find it, and by the time the fighters had stopped looking and burned the village, he had crawled to safety in the jungle.' The black man hesitated. 'What I don't understand is how a briefcase from the Second World War suddenly became so interesting to everyone? As far as the clans were concerned it was just another

439

piece of cargo with a certain amount of power. Kristian says he never told anyone about his grandfather or the *yelopela* king. Yet suddenly some white bloke puts two and two together and all hell breaks loose.'

'Keith Devlin told me he was on Bougainville in the early days of the mine,' Jamie said.

'That still doesn't explain—'

He was interrupted by what sounded like a question from Kristian just as Magda ran across from the radio hut. 'The helicopter is on its way,' she called out. 'It will be here in thirty minutes.'

'How's Doug?' Jamie asked.

'He's breathing more easily, but . . .' She shrugged.

'My grandfather would like to see his ancestor,' Michael said.

Jamie unzipped the compartment of the rucksack feeling like a man about to jump out of a plane desperately trying to remember whether he'd tightened his parachute straps properly. He'd anticipated this moment with a mixture of fear and exhilaration, but there was no going back. Keith Devlin would get whatever it was he wanted from the Yamamoto exchange and unless Michael and his friends could stop him, he would get the island too. Yet it was accompanied by a sense of relief. He was freed of the burden he'd carried since Tokyo. Fiona and Lizzie would be safe, and he could forget he'd ever set foot on a place called Bougainville. Yet, looking at the faces of the three people who studied him so intently, he knew he was lying to himself. He would never forget Bougainville and if he didn't do something about it, he would feel shame every time he heard Keith Devlin's name. He drew the head from the bag and placed it gently in Kristian Anugu's outstretched hand.

The old man closed his eyes and his thick fingers drifted across the frizzed hair and leathery features of the little coconut-sized ball of desiccated, withered flesh, the pink tips taking in the texture of every plane and every strand. A wave of emotions flowed across the weathered face and a tear left a silver trail through the stubble of one lined cheek. His chest began to pound as if some great energy was pulsing from the lifeless globe beneath his fingers.

'Grandfather?' Michael said.

'*Me'ekamui*.'

'He says, "God is Holy, the land is Holy, the flesh is Holy."'

More words, but one was mentioned repeatedly: '*Sipungeta*'.

Jamie saw Michael shake his head, patently torn between disbelief and reverence, caught between the presence of his land, the *knowing* of his birth, and the logic of his upbringing and his education. Magda placed a hand on the islander's arm and, eventually, he regained the composure to explain. 'He says that from the ashes of the fire dance Papa'ala will rise again.' The words seemed to catch in his throat. 'The earth will swallow up the great obscenity that has been wrought upon it and the forest and the grass will cover the land again. Once more, the gardens of the Moroni will bloom upon the land that is rightfully theirs. The island of sorrow will again become the island of smiles.'

Kristian Anugu nodded in time to his grandson's translation, staring into the gnarled, eyeless face that had once been his ancestor's. Michael placed a large object in Jamie's lap but the old man's monologue had so mesmerized him that it wasn't until it was in his grasp he realized it was the parcel the islander had brought from the longhouse. The banana leaves that wrapped the package were almost as old as the thing they concealed and they fell apart beneath his hands, turned to dust like the covers of a book that had been waiting a millennium to be opened. Without asking for consent he tore them away to reveal an old-fashioned leather briefcase with long straps and brass buckles made green by the damp climate. The thick hide was dried and cracked and had turned from brown to black over the years, but it was still solid enough to protect whatever it contained. But had the contents survived?

Jamie's fingers hovered uncertainly over the straps. Keith Devlin would expect him to deliver the briefcase intact, but he'd given no direct instructions not to check the contents. Even if he had, it was before Jamie discovered Devlin's true motives, and that knowledge changed everything. He looked up and found himself staring into Magda's face. Her eyes shone with anticipation and she was holding her breath. They had to know, she was telling him, because without knowing how could they understand its significance to Keith Devlin and the tens of thousands of others whose futures were affected by his plans?

'Open it.' Michael had no doubts. 'You owe it to my people.'

Jamie worked feverishly at the buckles, but the metal and the leather straps had fused into one mass.

'Use this.' The bearded islander leaned forward to hand him a Swiss army knife. Jamie opened it, resisting the temptation to use the blade to cut the straps, and instead worked it between the brass and the leather. It took minutes to free the first buckle, but the second came away more easily. He handed the knife back to Michael and released the clasp holding the flap. As he pulled it back the opened case released a draught of mildew-scented air that made him fear for what was inside. On closer inspection the contents consisted of two cardboard files that were close to disintegration but still each held two or three sheets of paper that remained remarkably well preserved. He removed a small aluminium flask from a side-pocket, along with a spectacle case and, more poignantly, a dark-haired female doll, six inches tall and dressed in a red kimono. Magda instinctively reached for the little figurine.

'Someone's daughter?' she said. 'It makes the owner of the briefcase suddenly seem much more human.'

Michael was less impressed. 'What do the papers say?' His voice was hard-edged in anticipation.

Jamie poked warily at the most prominent sheet. 'It seems to be in decent shape for having been in there for so long. I suppose we don't really have any choice, do we?' He picked it up between two fingers and gingerly pulled the document free. It slipped clear without harm, thanks to the green mildew covering the coated surface. He cleared a small section and frowned at the long columns of unfamiliar script. He handed it to Magda. 'Japanese or Chinese?'

'Japanese,' she confirmed breathlessly, reaching for the others. With a frown of concentration she rubbed away at the slimy coating and began to read. Jamie saw her eyes widen.

'What is it?'

'Let me read the others first,' she said urgently.

Michael and Jamie craned over her as she studied each in turn. She shook her head. 'It's impossible.'

'What does it say?' Jamie repeated.

Magda spread her hands and there was a wildness, perhaps even fear, in her eyes. 'Is the world ready to hear that Winston Churchill knew about the attack on Pearl Harbor a week before it happened?'

XLV

Minutes later Jamie still couldn't believe what he'd been told, but Magda was certain. 'It's all here,' she insisted. 'The part in red says: DESIGNATION TOP SECRET. The rest is dates, names of the Cabinet committee who discussed the information, some agent called Source X who provided it and Winston Churchill's insistence that nothing should be done about it. It says all this came from a highly placed spy in the British government.'

'Christ.' Jamie struggled to come to terms with the document's implications. 'I don't know how he found out about it, but no wonder Keith Devlin was so keen to get hold of the briefcase. This would be worth billions, not to mention the global influence it would give him if he offered it to the right somebody.'

Michael only shrugged. 'It is ancient history, surely? Churchill is long dead and the war was won. Who says it's even true? What does it have to do with the Panguna Mine?'

'Ancient history it may be,' Jamie admitted, 'but the fact that Britain's greatest statesman appears to have stabbed his country's major ally – the country with which Great Britain still has a *special relationship* – in the back could have major global consequences. The very threat of revealing it might be enough to force Britain to change its foreign policy so as not to lose the good will of one of its major trading partners.'

'But surely the Americans are pragmatists,' Magda interrupted. 'They'd have a huge amount to lose if they cut Britain off.'

'I'm not so sure about that,' Jamie said. 'We're talking about an ally who stood back and watched as eight thousand US sailors died, in an event that suckered their nation into a war most of them wanted no part of and cost hundreds of thousands more casualties. Tell Joe Public their boys were killed on Guadalcanal or Omaha Beach, not because America chose to send them to war, but because Winston Churchill tricked Roosevelt into it, and I don't think any US president would be able to ignore the backlash.'

Muttering to himself, Kristian Anugu ponderously rose from the step beside him and carried the head into the longhouse.

Jamie watched him go before he continued. 'You'd probably be talking about a trade boycott at the very least. Britain could be forced out of NATO, American bases would be withdrawn from the UK and without American support in the South Atlantic, Argentina could walk into Port Stanley and take back the Falklands any time they liked. And that's just the Yanks. If Yamamoto's fleet had sailed into an ambush it would have set Japan's preparations for a Pacific war back twenty years. Without those battleships and carriers there would have been no war in Burma or Malaya, Indo-China would still be French and there might have been no Vietnam War. How many people died in a war that didn't have to be fought? Indians, Africans, Malays, Chinese, Dutch . . .'

'Australians.'

'Yes,' Jamie answered Magda. 'Australians, too. How do we know it's not a fake?' He turned to Michael. 'I don't know that for certain. But everything I know about Churchill tells me it *could* be true. He was prepared to go to almost any lengths to get what he wanted and he wanted – needed – above all to get America involved in the war. He gave the go-ahead for the Dieppe raid that killed thousands of Canadians, even though he'd been warned it would be a bloodbath. He sent British bombers to bomb French cities and sank their Mediterranean fleet despite the fact they were Allies. It's perfectly possible that a man who would do that would sacrifice the American fleet, Singapore and Hong Kong to get the Yanks involved.'

'So he allowed his own people to die?' Michael said incredulously.

'Judging by this it could be worse than that,' Jamie admitted. 'He may have deliberately sacrificed them. At Singapore, Australian and British reinforcements were still arriving when the Japanese landed on Malayan beaches to the north. If he'd called them back the Japs would have known something was up. Without America in the war there'd have been no Second Front, no daylight bombing of German cities. The Red Army would have been penned up east of the Volga. At worst, the war would have been lost and the Nazis would have ruled from Siberia to Spain. At best, Europe would have gone on bleeding for an entire generation. To avoid that, I have a feeling Winston Churchill would have counted all the sacrifices a bargain. The question is what do I do with it?'

Magda handed him back the files. 'You've made the exchange, they're yours now. Nothing has changed. You still have to get Fiona and Lizzie away from Keith Devlin.'

'Now that you have Doug Stewart's testimony you can do something to stop Devlin taking over the island.' Jamie appealed to Michael.

'We still need more evidence,' the islander repeated. Magda went to stand beside him and the set of her jaw told Jamie she was laying down a marker. He remembered the dangers they'd shared in Tokyo and Siberia, and the time spent on the Trans-Siberian trapped with the monosyllabic Ludmilla and her flatulent husband. Did he really want it to end like this?

'All right,' he surrendered, 'I'll help you, but I won't do anything that will put Fiona and Lizzie in any more danger. Tell me what I have to do.' Michael bent his head so Jamie had to do the same to hear the whispered instructions. A few moments later the rhythmic whup-whup-whup of a faraway helicopter interrupted the conversation and Kristian Anugu beckoned his grandson to him. Jamie slipped the Yamamoto papers back into the briefcase.

'My grandfather has invited you to witness the fire

dance tonight,' Michael said. 'It is a great spectacle when he will burn his grandfather's remains and bury the ashes, so that his spirit will no longer roam. I'm sorry you will miss it, because it is followed by a great feast, but I've told him that you must travel with your wounded comrade. He wishes you well. He says you have a good heart, the heart of a warrior, and he thanks you for bringing the head home to Papa'ala.'

Jamie looked at the old man's grinning face and felt a momentary twinge of conscience that he'd been on the point of turning Michael down. 'Thank him for his invitation and tell him I hope to feast with him another time.'

The sound of the helicopter increased to a thunderous clatter as it appeared above the trees like a giant hoverfly and settled over the landing ground that Michael's men had marked out on a patch of clear ground a hundred and fifty paces away. Michael and Magda ran to Doug Stewart's stretcher. The pair had a brief conversation before Jamie joined them. As he approached Magda rose up and surprised him by kissing him on the cheek.

'What's that for?'

'For the good times and the bad times.' She shrugged. 'Do you think you'll ever be able to forgive me?'

She looked into his eyes and he saw hers were shining. He smiled. 'I think they just about balance each other out, so there's nothing to forgive.'

'Good,' she said. 'I hope you remember that.'

He looked on puzzled as she accompanied the stretcher to the helicopter. Michael's men lifted Doug Stewart on board and the big islander came up to say farewell. He clapped Jamie on the shoulder. 'I have to stay for the fire dance, but we'll meet up again tomorrow. I'm depending on you, mate.'

'I know what I have to do.'

Michael held out his hand. 'At noon, then,' he said.

Jamie took the big fist. 'Just don't be bloody late, mate. That's all I ask.' With a nod he ran to the chopper, bending low to avoid the whirling rotor blades, the briefcase that could change the world heavy in his right hand.

XLVI

Jamie's eyes swept his surroundings as he walked stealthily up the empty street in the shadow of the derelict apartment blocks and shops. Michael had said Keith Devlin's private army of security guards mainly kept to the area around the community centre where he'd set up his headquarters, but there were no guarantees tonight. He checked his bearings and stifled a yawn. It would be dawn in an hour. The house where Fiona and Lizzie Carter were being kept was about five blocks ahead and off to the left. Adrenalin had seen him through the last two days, but after waiting three hours in the Toyota up in Panguna his bones ached as if he'd been sleeping on a pile of concrete rubble. He needed to finish it. Now.

When the helicopter had dropped him near the mine, Magda Ross had stayed on board to see Doug Stewart safely to the hospital in Buka. He found it ironic that just when he thought he'd got to know her she'd turned out to have been playing a double game all along. But, as he'd said, even after everything that had happened

451

there was nothing to forgive. In the short time they'd spent together her strength of character and easy companionship had been a beacon in some dark times. Okay, maybe it was a little more complicated than that, but she'd become a friend and you couldn't have too many friends.

He'd left the car on the Buka side of town. It wasn't ideal, but he hadn't dared bring it any closer. Still it was in easy enough reach for his purposes. All he had to do was get to the girls.

A sudden movement up ahead made him freeze, but it was only a feral cat. It crossed the road like a wraith, stopping in the middle to study him suspiciously with glowing green eyes before moving on. When he reached the point where it had disappeared he followed its route between the houses. Fiona had said most of the occupied homes kept dogs and he hoped they'd react to the cat before they reacted to him.

The jungle had encroached on the rear gardens of the abandoned houses. It wasn't thick enough to delay him, but he took his time nonetheless. There was no point in reaching Fiona's place too early. He ran over the layout in his mind. The entrance of the apartment was at the rear and reached by a set of wooden stairs. Fiona's room was to the left and Lizzie's to the right. Every few metres he stopped to listen. When he heard the sound of a car passing nearby he crouched behind a dilapidated outhouse among the vines for ten minutes after it was gone. Not one of the old rattletraps the locals drove, something more modern. Two blocks to go. No point in taking any chances. He dropped to his belly and slithered through the long neglected vegetable patches using his elbows and knees, trying to ignore the nameless slithering and hopping things that shared his environment.

Within sight of the house he stopped again and waited, attuning himself to his surroundings. When he was certain, he got to his feet and silently approached the stairs.

'Mr Devlin thought you might try something like this.' The words were accompanied by the cold steel of a gun barrel on his neck and Jamie's heart jumped into his throat. 'As it happened, we moved the girls last night just in case, but we've had the place more or less surrounded since Joe spotted your car.' Andy's tone was almost conversational, but Jamie knew that didn't make him any less dangerous. The security man patted him down with an expert hand, the pistol never leaving his skin. 'You didn't do too badly, really. I'll be kicking a couple of arses in the morning for letting you get this far. Where is it?'

'Where's what? Ouch.' Jamie grunted as the pistol barrel rattled playfully off his ear.

'Don't get cute with me, Mr Saintclair. Where's this briefcase the boss is getting so fired up about?'

'You won't find it even if you take this town apart.' Jamie tensed for another blow, but it didn't come and he hurried on. 'Devlin can have it as soon as I have proof Fiona and Lizzie are on the eleven-thirty flight for Port Moresby. Call him now and tell him that.'

Andy spun him round so they were face to face with the pistol barrel square between Jamie's eyes. 'I admire a man who looks after his ladies,' he was grinning, but there was no humour in the deep-set grey eyes, 'but I really don't think you're in a situation to make any demands.'

'Come on, Andy.' Jamie kept his voice as steady as the circumstances dictated and prayed the safety catch was on. From where he was looking the pistol appeared to be a 9mm Ruger that would turn his head into a canoe if it went off. 'We both know you're not going to shoot me. No more games, but I'm not having Devlin bugger us about any more.'

Andy stared at him for a long moment before emitting a low whistle between his teeth and removing the pistol from Jamie's head. A moment later they heard the sound of large bodies rustling through the bushes.

'Keep Mr Saintclair nice and close,' the guard ordered. 'And if he tries anything break one of his legs.'

Andy went off a few feet and Jamie heard him whispering into a phone or radio as two men he hadn't seen before took him roughly by the arms. Andy was back within two minutes.

'Mr Devlin is not best pleased. I told him we'd be happy to use a little gentle persuasion to locate the item in question, but he's grown attached to the girls and he sees your point of view. He says to tell you that if you play silly buggers with him again he'll let us break *both* your legs.'

'So what happens now?'

Andy nodded towards the stairs. 'Now we wait.'

Four hours later Jamie Saintclair felt like the condemned man on his way to his execution as the three guards escorted him through the streets towards the community centre. He was filthy, hungry and thirsty and the feeling was compounded by the knowledge that his companions would happily form his firing squad. A door opened as they approached the building and he squinted against the sun as a portly figure dressed in a freshly pressed white shirt and tan slacks walked towards him across the potholed car park. When the man's identity slowly seeped into his sleep-deprived brain Jamie's steps faltered and he automatically searched his surroundings. Had someone rewritten the script and not told him?

'A fine morning, Mr Saintclair, if a little humid.' Mr Lim ignored the guards and his smile confirmed that all was well with his world. 'You look perplexed. Are you not pleased to see an old friend?'

'Actually, I was wondering where your acquaintance, Mr Lee, was hiding.'

'Mr Lee?' The smile turned into a frown as if the bodyguard had slipped from his memory, but only momentarily. 'Of course. Today, I have left him in Shanghai. He was never the most talkative of companions and an honest Chinese businessman requires no assistance. Besides, it saves an air fare. Do I take it from this unfortunate scene that your mission is not yet complete?'

Jamie glanced over his shoulder at the three guards and the Chinese laughed.

'I have nothing to do with this, I assure you, Mr Saintclair, though I am aware how keen Mr Devlin is to lay his hands on a certain article. My presence here was merely to make him an offer, which he has unfortunately refused. It is a pity, because had he accepted I too had a gift that might have been to his advantage. Still, in the event he succeeds I have assured him that the Chinese People's Republic will become his best customer. Of course, if he does not . . .'

Jamie felt the guards stir restlessly, but he didn't move. 'I'm not entirely sure what you're telling me, Mr Lim?'

'Oh, I am not *telling* you anything, Mr Saintclair. We are just two old friends having a chat. I must, however, express my admiration for your efforts. The fact that you have got this far against such odds is truly remarkable. I still cannot understand how you managed to escape the clutches of that terrible woman; and as for your vanishing act from Tokyo airport . . .' He shook his head. 'I would advise against any inclination to return to the East for a while, and it might be wise to avoid Japanese restaurants on your return to London, the food can be terribly spicy.'

'I generally only eat the sushi.' Jamie managed to return Mr Lim's conspiratorial smile.

'No, no. Please stick to Chinese; it would be much better for your digestion. The world would be a worse place without you, Jamie Saintclair.'

He nodded and as he walked off, Jamie could swear he heard the first few whistled bars of 'Waltzing Matilda'.

Keith Devlin was in the meeting room, seated behind the big desk flanked by Joe and another bodyguard. Andy took the stranger's place and the hard eyes told Jamie he wasn't part of the team any more.

'I thought I said we should be alone until we get the call?' Jamie said.

'So you did, son.' Devlin's lips twitched. 'But I thought I'd make it clear who's in charge right from the start. It's easier all round if we understand each other.'

'All right.' Jamie could see there was no point in arguing. 'But I hope you've complied with my other . . . request, or we might as well all go home.'

Devlin's brows came together and his lips twitched in an entirely different way. He glanced at Andy, who shrugged. 'We've searched, but we haven't found anything.'

'All right, son.' The mining boss picked up a cell phone from the desk. 'No need to get shirty. Everything's just the way you wanted it. The girls are at the airport with tickets for the next flight out.' He hit a preset button. 'Joe? Get the lady on the phone.'

He passed the handset to Andy and the bodyguard tossed it to Jamie, who caught it with his right hand. 'Fiona?'

'Jamie, where are you?'

'I'm back in Arawa. There's nothing to worry about. We have a few details to straighten out. I plan to catch a later flight and meet up with you in Brisbane.'

'But . . .'

Jamie glanced at his watch. 'Shouldn't you be boarding?'

'We're on board, but they say the flight's been delayed for technical reasons.'

Jamie looked at Devlin and the tycoon's grim smile told its own story. 'I'm sure they'll get it sorted out soon. Give my love to Lizzie.' He handed the phone back to Andy. 'The briefcase is hanging inside an empty cistern behind the old hospital.'

'Get it,' Devlin ordered.

They waited in silence until Andy returned ten minutes later with the briefcase under his arm. The security guard worked at the leather straps to open it and pushed it across the desk. Devlin's face creased into a shark's grin as he retrieved one of the papers, nodding as he read it. 'Okay, Andy.'

Andy dialled a preset number. 'Vern? The deal's done, mate. You can let the plane go.'

Jamie's legs almost gave way with relief. It was over. He looked to Devlin for some sort of acknowledgement, but the businessman continued to study the documents, frowning occasionally as he came across a symbol that tested his knowledge. With a glance at Andy, Jamie shrugged and turned away.

'Not interested in what's in here? It makes fascinating reading.' Devlin was savouring the moment, basking in the spotlight of his cleverness. *Here I am, the victor, and this is the mark of my genius.*

'I already know.'

The smile tightened. 'Of course.'

'What really interests me is what you're going to do with it.' *Play the plucky loser, Michael had said. There's nothing he likes better than crowing over the people he's beaten. Spin it out.* 'I can understand it might be worth a great deal of money. But you can't be certain what will happen when the world gets to know that Winston Churchill knew about Pearl Harbor a week

458

before it happened and didn't tell his friends the Yanks. Who knows what it will do to the economy? That sheet of paper might just be a smoking gun pointed right at your head.'

'This?' Devlin laid down the document he'd been reading and picked up the other piece of coated paper from the case. 'You think it's about this?' He held it away from his body and pulled something from his pocket with his other hand. 'But you're right. We don't want Bougainville all over the front pages and folks writing alternative histories about Yamamoto and Churchill, do we?' Jamie heard the flick of a cigarette lighter and cried out as the paper disintegrated in Devlin's hands with a bright flash. 'Clever buggers the Japs. Way before their time. Paper impregnated with gunpowder to ensure complete destruction.'

'I don't—'

'No, you don't, son. You thought you had it all worked out, but Keith Devlin was way ahead of you. It's a shame about old Doug,' he shook his head in mock sorrow, 'but he'd had his day and to be honest I was beginning to have doubts about him. Imagine getting to his age and suddenly developing a conscience. I'll see he gets a decent send-off, but it's better this way. We were worried they might have got you too and run off with the merchandise. Andy and the boys were around to pick up the pieces, but they couldn't get near you for some rogue BRA outfit. Fortunately, good old dependable, go-the-extra-mile Jamie Saintclair delivered the goods.'

Jamie somehow managed to keep his thoughts to

himself as he listened to the cynical dismissal of Doug Stewart and his half a lifetime's service to the man behind the desk. 'But it was all for nothing.'

'Not for nothing, son.' Devlin rose from his seat. Jamie waited apprehensively for his next move, but it was only to extract a cigar from a box on a side table. He lit it with the lighter and drew in two puffs before continuing. 'For progress. When I was here back in the day, I was forever looking at stuff from the war. Jap bunkers. Crashed planes and that old Sherman on Tank Corner round by Buin. The local boys used to bring me things. Old rifles, bayonets, even a couple of live hand grenades. One day they walk in with a map case they'd found with the bones of a Jap officer, and lo and behold what was in it? That's right, a letter from the lieutenant who recovered Yamamoto's body saying he'd found a briefcase with the admiral, only some Boog native had pinched it, and by the way this is what was in it.'

'If you knew all the time why didn't you use it?'

'Oh, I tried, son. I was a bushy-tailed idealist just like you in those days. I went to Canberra and spilled the beans to some po-faced civil servant. The next thing I know I'm locked in an office with a US State Department official who laughed in my face. And pretty soon I was laughing too.' He blew out a big cloud of smoke from the cigar and Andy moved half a step away. 'Why? Because they already knew. Why do you think the Yanks screwed the Brits into the ground after the war while they were pouring money into Japan and Germany and helping them rebuild their countries? In nineteen forty-six the UK was about to go bust, so

460

Westminster sent a fella called John Maynard Keynes to Washington. Naturally, they expected the Americans to slap him on the back and send him home with a shipload of gold bullion with the thanks of a grateful nation for all their sacrifices.' Keith Devlin laughed out loud at the notion. 'Only by then the Yanks had found the other copy of the Yamamoto document in some Tokyo safe. Instead of rocking the boat with the New World Order by blowing the whistle, Harry S. Truman decided to make your countrymen pay blood money for those eight thousand sailors at Pearl Harbor. They reckon Keynes looked like he'd been kicked in the teeth when he heard the terms, but the Brits had no option but to pay up. They kept on paying until five years ago, and all that time they watched the world's economies passing them by. Tragic, ain't it?'

'But there was something else in the letter you never mentioned to anybody.' Jamie suddenly saw where the scenario was taking them.

'That's right, Jamie.' He held up the second document. 'By rights this shouldn't exist. Sometime in nineteen forty-two the Japs sent a surveyor to Bougainville to check out the mineral deposits and he came back with a big fat blank.'

'But the Panguna Mine has produced billions.'

'Sure, he found copper.' The Australian shrugged. 'But it was in traces so small it was uneconomic to mine it using the techniques they had in those days. What a lot of people don't understand is that BCL took a huge gamble when they opened that mine, but it paid off.'

'Not for the Moroni and the other tribes up there.'

Devlin ignored him as if he'd never spoken. 'Only there was something else that one of their top scientists must have noticed and thought the report was worth sending to Yamamoto. The surveyor found deposits of a metal so useless he didn't even bother to name it, but when I read what he said that little Devlin alarm bell went off in my head. What's the rarest and most expensive metal on the planet, son?'

'I don't know,' Jamie admitted, happy to play Devlin's games for now. 'Platinum, maybe.'

'Not far off, but the answer is rhodium.'

'So that's what this is all about?'

'Bougainville Island is sitting on top of one of the biggest deposits of rhodium on Earth, enough to double the world's output. Just a couple of years ago it was selling for ten thousand dollars an ounce, but with the new applications they're developing for it in the weapons industry, that could double and double again.'

Keith Devlin studied Jamie with a knowing half-smile on his face and suddenly he wasn't the only person in the room with an alarm bell in his head. By now Jamie's was ringing off the scale, accompanied by a little voice that said Devlin was giving him too much information. There was only one way off the island for the man who knew this much, and it wasn't in an Air Niugini Fokker. Jamie glanced at Andy and his partner. They looked relaxed enough, but their eyes never left him and he knew they were ready for him to try anything. Even if he somehow managed to evade them, there'd be more of Devlin's bodyguards outside the door. He only had one chance and that was to play the game out to the last hand.

'If this stuff is so valuable why hasn't anybody found it before now?' He let his curiosity show. 'The island must have been crawling with geologists since before the mine opened.'

Devlin smiled. 'Either they weren't looking for it – the world only found a use for rhodium in the mid-Seventies – or they were looking in the wrong place. This document in my hand has the exact coordinates. Do you know what that means, Jamie?' Jamie knew exactly what it meant, but he also knew it was one of those questions that didn't need an answer. The tycoon's voice took on that messianic certainty the Englishman had learned meant he was lying through his ten-thousand-dollar teeth. 'It means that we can make a huge investment in the future of this island and its people and a huge investment in technology to make future mining operations more environmentally acceptable. Bougainville will be the showcase for the world of how industry and indigenous people can combine for the benefit of both. You've heard my vision for the island, Jamie. Tell me I'm wrong.'

Jamie let a smile play across his face, but his voice dripped with contempt even though he now knew for certain that every word was leading him towards an early grave. 'Sure, Keith,' he laughed. 'I've heard your vision for the island, but the one I heard didn't sound anything like that. The one I heard had a private army beholden to one man and ready to break the heads of anyone who speaks out. It had politicians bought and paid for by that same man on the island, in Port Moresby and even in Canberra.' Andy came off the wall with his fists clenched and a killing look in his eye, but Devlin waved him back.

'Let him finish,' the businessman snapped. 'He'll find out the price of his little speech later.'

'You didn't mention the seven other mining concessions, every one of them just as big as Panguna, which are just the start as you turn this island into one big hole. Or the islanders who are going to lose their ancestral lands to make way for them. All those people whose lives will depend on the company store for everything, because their coconut groves have been ripped out and they can no longer grow their own food, or fish in rivers that will all go the same way as the Jaba. Do the Rotokas people, or the Lawunuia, or the Askopan, or the Ramopa,' he listed all the tribes Michael had said would be left landless by Devlin's plans, 'know they're all going to go the same way as the Moroni, Keith? Or that they're destined to be worker ants for Devlin Metal Resources?'

Keith Devlin was still smiling, but the smile was frozen on his face. 'The funny thing about worker ants, son, is that as long as you give them a roof over their head and food in their belly, they don't even know they're worker ants.'

'It's all true?'

'Seems to me that old Doug's been speaking out of turn before he croaked. I'm getting soft. I should've got rid of him sooner.' If there was an Angel of Death his eyes couldn't have been any bleaker than the ones now focused on Jamie Saintclair. 'The rhodium's the key. All the rest would have come my way in time, but with the rhodium I can buy every politician in the Pacific. Of course, it only works if nobody else knows about it.'

'So I'm going to have an unfortunate accident?'

'I'm afraid so, son.'

'So I'm going to have an unfortunate accident?'

Devlin looked at Jamie as if he'd just grown another head and the Englishman was almost as bemused, because he'd swear his lips never moved. The words had the metallic flatness of a recording and came from the door behind Keith Devlin. As the tycoon turned in astonishment they were repeated again.

Andy and Joe moved fast for the door, hands going for the guns at their belts.

'I wouldn't do that.' Two white men in T-shirts and jeans appeared from the balcony like ghosts. One ghost carried a machine pistol and the other a pump-action shotgun. Andy sensibly froze, but his partner turned with the gun rising to bear on the intruders. It was very brave, but also very foolish because the blast of the shotgun shook the whole room and Jamie thought he'd gone deaf as the bodyguard was smashed against the rear wall and bounced to land face down on the wooden floor. The door behind Devlin burst open and Michael appeared like an avenging angel holding a pistol in one hand and a badge in the other. Magda Ross followed him, her eyes wide with concern and only relaxed when she saw Jamie was safe. It had all happened so quickly that the sound of the shotgun still reverberated in the room as Michael pushed Keith

Devlin back into his chair and placed the badge on the desk in front of him.

'You've no right . . .' the businessman spluttered.

'Take a look at the badge, Mr Devlin. Will he live, Steve?' This to the man leaning over the prone body of the bodyguard. The other covered Andy with the machine pistol, which was largely unnecessary because the security man seemed to have decided the whole affair had nothing to do with him.

'A baton round,' Steve shrugged. Baton rounds were designed for riot control to shock and debilitate the target, but at close range they'd been known to kill. 'He still has a pulse.'

'Get him to the doctor and get him,' Michael pointed to Andy, 'out of here.'

A shout brought four other white men into the room and they picked up the wounded guard and carried him out. The man with the shotgun escorted Andy after them.

Magda came to stand beside Jamie and placed her hand on his shoulder. 'Looks like I was wrong about heroes.' She whispered the words so only he could hear and he grinned at the praise.

Meanwhile, Michael turned back to Devlin. 'As an officer of the Australian Security Intelligence Organization I am detaining you under the special investigative powers delegated to me by the Attorney General, on suspicion of suborning members of the national legislature in the Australian Capital Territory, interference in the internal governance of an Australian ally, namely Papua New Guinea, and the instigation of fraudulent conduct in another ally, namely the Autonomous Region of Bougainville.'

'That's all very clever, Mr . . .' he picked up the badge and his lips twisted into a sneer, 'Taruko. But I think you'll find that the powers that be on Bougainville won't recognize that warrant of yours.'

Michael ignored the insult and picked up his badge, replacing it with an oblong of black plastic. He pushed a button and there was a long squeak in which could just be heard the sound of voices being played backward at speed. He pushed a second button and a distinctive voice echoed from the digital recorder.

'The funny thing about worker ants, son, is that as long as you give them a roof over their head and food in their belly, they don't even know they're worker ants.'

Devlin shrugged. 'Things like that can be faked. I deny ever saying it.'

Michael nodded. 'That's your right, Mr Devlin, and I'm sure you'll enjoy explaining it to the special committee of the Bougainville House of Representatives who listened to it in real time by satellite link. I'm told they included a few of your friends, who are no longer quite so well disposed towards you.'

Jamie saw Devlin go pale as the full implications of Michael's carefully constructed sting operation dawned.

'You can't—'

'We will also have the testimony of Mr Douglas Stewart, former security director of Devlin Metal Resources, who is currently cooperating from a hospital bed in Buka.'

'Doug's not dead? Well, I'll be—'

'Yes, Keith, old chum,' Jamie said, 'I think you probably will. I'd suggest you go along with Michael here, before the Bougainville Revolutionary Army hears about your real plans for their island paradise.'

The tycoon's shoulders slumped and Jamie had never seen anyone look more defeated, but the mood only lasted for seconds. He saw the broad back straighten and the big farmer's head come up. Keith Devlin's eyes narrowed. 'I'll come along with you, son, but don't think I'm beaten yet.' He rose from his chair and marched to the door followed by the final member of Michael's team. 'It'll take more than a few black backstabbers and pansy politicians in Canberra to take Keith Devlin down.'

The door closed behind him and Jamie exchanged a wry glance with Michael. 'I wish you luck.'

'In a way,' the black man shrugged, 'it doesn't matter much if he ends up in the slammer or not. His great plan for the island is finished and he'll have his hands full staying out of jail and keeping Devlin Metal Resources afloat.'

'Then you've won,' Magda said.

Michael gave them a long look. 'You still don't understand us, do you? On Bougainville there are no easy answers. No winners and losers. We move on and face the next crisis and the next, holding on to what we can of our culture and our values, but deprived of a little more every time. There'll be another Devlin, or another BCL, or that Chinese gentleman Jamie spoke to earlier . . . But one thing I can say is that my people are

468

in debt to you both. You returned my ancestor's head to its rightful place and you helped bring Devlin down. You've given us hope. My people and my government will always be grateful.'

They shook hands and Michael went out to join the special team of Australian undercover cops he'd called up to help out with the arrest. Magda watched Jamie cross to Devlin's desk where Admiral Yamamoto's leather briefcase still sat with the surviving document at its side. He picked up the sheet and ran his eyes over the columns of figures.

'All that for this insignificant piece of paper and the other great secret didn't matter a damn.' He picked up Keith Devlin's lighter and met Magda's gaze. She nodded and he flicked the mechanism allowing the flame to touch the corner of the geological survey. The paper disintegrated with a flash and he dropped the blackened cinders to the floor, distributing it across the boards with his foot. 'If it *is* out there, let the Bougain-villeans find it in their own time.'

Magda took his arm and they left the room side by side. 'I'm going to miss working with you, Jamie Saintclair.'

EPILOGUE

'And this is where you'll be staying until the end of the school holidays,' Jamie explained to Lizzie when they emerged from the lift at the Kensington High Street flat. 'The park is just along the road and there's a pond with ducks.'

'And shops?' the little girl cried.

'Oh, enough shops to keep even your mummy happy.' He grinned at Fiona. She returned it with a look of appraisal. They still had a few things to work out. She wasn't too happy he hadn't warned her how foolish she'd been to be seduced by Keith Devlin's grand scheme, or how he'd risked his neck while she and Lizzie had flown off to Port Moresby and safety. In addition, when he'd mentioned Magda Ross she'd read something in his voice that shouldn't have been there and he'd found himself saying less than he intended. An unanswered question of trust acted as a barrier to a complete renewal of their previous relationship. The damage Devlin had done went more than skin deep.

Jamie had no idea how he'd feel having Lizzie living

in the flat with them, but he was willing to give it a try. Michael's bosses in Canberra had advised safety in numbers for their potential witnesses while they were making certain they had the lid on Devlin and his cronies. Jamie also had a feeling Madam Nishimura might cast a shadow long enough to reach London. Overall it had seemed too good an opportunity to pass up.

He laid down their suitcases and was about to put the key in the lock when a creak alerted him to the door opening on the far side of the hall.

'Mrs Laurence.' Jamie turned to greet his elderly neighbour. A wizened face was just visible in the gap, suspicious eyes taking in the newcomers. He decided a preemptive strike was in order. 'This is my partner Fiona and her daughter, Lizzie.' He smiled. 'They're going to be staying for a while.'

The eyes narrowed and he winced at the prospect of the lecture on morals and how things had never been like that in her day, but she surprised him. 'I hope you don't mind that I let them in with the spare key, Mr Saintclair. They brought it on Tuesday and I didn't want it lying about the flat. I watched them every second they were in the house,' she assured him. 'And they left this with me.' She handed him a white envelope that proved to have something solid inside.

'Brought what, Mrs Laurence?' He frowned.

'Your package.'

'I wasn't expecting a package.' Jamie went very still.

'It was about this size.' She indicated an object about three feet high and two feet wide and Jamie relaxed. In his experience lethal surprises tended to be on a smaller scale. 'I didn't have room for it. I'm not a storehouse, you know.'

'I appreciate you dealing with it for me, Iris.' He thanked her and she sniffed and disappeared back indoors.

Jamie turned to Fiona. 'Maybe you'd better stay out here while I check it out?'

'No way, Jamie Saintclair.' She shook her head. 'I thought I'd made it clear on the plane home. Either we're all in this together or we're not in it at all.'

'Okay, have it your way, but keep Lizzie with you.' He nodded thoughtfully. 'It's probably just something I ordered and forgot about.' The big oak door opened smoothly to release the familiar welcoming scent of Victoriana that always greeted him after an extended absence; a sort of museum smell of age and dust and slow, glacial decay, caused by the years taking their toll on wood and brick and plaster. The 'package' lay against the side of his green leather Chesterfield, a sturdy cardboard box of slightly larger dimensions than Mrs Laurence had indicated and about ten inches deep. He approached it warily. A label with his name and address on it, but – he turned it over – no return address or sender's name. No suggestion of who the carriers were.

'Why don't you show Lizzie her bedroom?' Fiona opened her mouth to protest, but he put a finger to her lips. 'I don't think it's anything dangerous, but I'd like to be sure. No point all three of us being here. In any case, I'm more intrigued than concerned. Anyone sending me a painting – if that's what this is – would normally send it to the office.'

'All right,' she said warily, 'you're the boss.'

He grinned. 'I'm not so sure about that.'

When he was alone he used the blade of a paper knife to pry open the staples that held the cardboard closed. It took him about five minutes to slide the contents free, and if anything he was left even more puzzled. An aluminium container almost like a small suitcase. It was padlocked. He opened the envelope to find a silver key.

He took a deep breath and snapped back the lid to reveal a bubble-wrapped package. The bubble wrap was fixed with sticky tape and it took another search for a pair of scissors before he could begin to unwind it.

'Christ,' he swore in exasperation.

It was now clear what object he was dealing with, but the true identity still lay hidden beneath a layer of brown paper. Slowly, he peeled it back.

For a moment he would swear his heart stopped. If people did die on the operating table and came back this must be what it was like, this floating above the scene looking down at yourself and the explosion of gold that had burst from the wrapping to temporarily end your life.

'It can't be.'

But as he floated back down to rejoin the earthly remains of Jamie Saintclair it became clear that it could. A simple painting. Still life, in the post-Impressionist style. Three blooms, in a stubby, green-glazed vase against an aquamarine background. A Post-it note was fixed to the bottom left hand corner of the frame: *It's all yours, AB.*

I want you to track down the person who took my friend's painting and negotiate its recovery.

'You look as if you need this.' Jamie looked up as Fiona emerged from the kitchen carrying a tray with teapot and cups, followed by her daughter. 'What was it anyway?' She looked over his shoulder and her eyes widened. 'Not a bomb then?'

Jamie Saintclair, art dealer and temporary owner of one of the most valuable paintings on the planet, regarded his partner with a dazed smile as Lizzie came to join them in the glow of Vincent Van Gogh's golden sunflowers.

'Not the kind you can defuse.'

ACKNOWLEDGEMENTS

Enormous thanks to my friend Corfiot Magda Rapsomaniki for providing the inspiration for the next Jamie Saintclair outing and unwittingly supplying my new heroine's first name. To Martina Stammler at the Staatsbibliothek Zu Berlin for her help in tracking down 1936 bound copies of the *Berliner Morgenpost* for me. And to Doug Stewart in Australia for his background knowledge on military matters. To Simon my editor and all at Transworld for their input and encouragement and last, but not least, to my agent Stan, for keeping the faith.

James Douglas is the pseudonym of a writer of popular historical adventure novels. This is the fourth novel to feature art recovery expert, Jamie Saintclair – the first three being *The Doomsday Testament*, *The Isis Covenant* and *The Excalibur Codex*. James Douglas lives in Scotland.

THE DOOMSDAY TESTAMENT
James Douglas

1937, Hitler sent an expedition to Tibet in search of the lost land of Thule.

1941, Heinrich Himmler spent a huge fortune, and sacrificed the lives of hundreds of concentration camp prisoners, to turn Wewelsburg Castle in Germany into a shrine to the SS.

Art recovery expert Jamie Saintclair thought he knew his grandfather, but when he stumbles upon the old man's lost diary he's astonished to find that the gentle Anglican clergyman was a decorated hero who had served in the Special Air Service in World War Two. And his grandfather has one more surprise for him. Sewn in to the endpaper of the journal is a strange piece of Nazi symbolism.

This simple discovery will launch him on a breathless chase across Europe and deep into Germany's dark past. There are some who will kill to find that which is lost, and although he doesn't know it, Saintclair holds the key to its hiding place.

THE ISIS COVENANT
James Douglas

The Crown of Isis, once part of the treasure of Queen Dido of Carthage, was reputed to grant its wearer immortality. In AD 64 it was stolen from the Temple of Isis. It was believed lost forever. Until now.

Art recovery expert Jamie Saintclair receives an unexpected phone call from Brooklyn detective Danny Fisher. Two families have been brutally murdered, one in New York, the other in London. The only link is a shared name, that of a German art thief who disappeared at the end of the war.

Jamie's investigation will take them into the dark past of Nazi Germany, to a hidden world of the occult – where a carefully guarded secret reveals a legacy of bloodshed. As Jamie and Danny will discover, for the promise of eternal life there are those who would kill, and kill again.

THE EXCALIBUR CODEX
James Douglas

It had been kept hidden for centuries, in readiness for a time of need. But not hidden well enough, it seems. One night in July in 1937, it vanished – its disappearance swallowed up in the storm clouds of the war that was about to engulf the world . . .

In 1941, twelve of Himmler's most trusted generals gather at a grim castle in East Prussia, chosen to re-enact an ancient rite steeped in blood. At its heart is a pentagram formed by five swords. One of them is King Arthur's mystical Excalibur . . .

Seventy years later, and art recovery expert Jamie Saintclair laughs in disbelief as he reads the codex to a German war veteran's will, the strange ritual it describes and the mention of a sword named Excalibur. But obsessive collector Adam Steele is convinced – and if Saintclair can trace the legendary blade, he will pay a small fortune for it . . .

The search leads Saintclair into a dangerous hinterland where the loyalties and hatreds of the past live on, and the line between fanaticism and madness is gossamer thin. As the last piece of the puzzle falls into place, it becomes clear that some mysteries should be left unsolved . . .